Barreled Over

JENNA SUTTON

BARRELED OVER/published by Jenna Sutton
Copyright © 2017 by Jenna Sutton

eBook ISBN: 978-0-9974032-5-1
Print ISBN: 978-0-9974032-6-8

Publishing history: Jenna Sutton eBook edition/December 2017; Jenna Sutton print edition/December 2017

Published in the United States of America

Cover photos: Stacked barrels in warehouse ©Rob Stokes/Shutterstock; Couple image © Vasyl/Adobe Stock; Bottle © Farr Studios/Shutterstock; Standing barrel © Kelly vanDellen/Shutterstock

Cover design by Asha Hossain Design
Formatting by Polgarus Studio

Books by Jenna Sutton

Full-Length Titles

All the Right Places
Coming Apart at the Seams
Hanging by a Thread

Novellas

A Kick in the Pants
The Perfect Fit
Will Never Fade

Novella Collection

Forever in Blue Jeans

CHAPTER ONE

As Ava Grace Landy followed the maître d, the noisy buzz of conversation filling the upscale steakhouse gradually dwindled to murmurs before fading to complete silence. She could feel hundreds of curious eyes on her, wondering if she was the real deal or a look-alike.

She was used to the attention ... used to being watched and whispered about. Ever since she'd won the TV singing competition, *American Star*, more than six years ago, she'd been in the spotlight.

Usually, she handled the glare just fine, but sometimes—like this moment—it made her uncomfortable. Strangely, she felt more at ease standing on a stage in front of thirty thousand fans than she did walking through a crowded restaurant in downtown Nashville.

Conversation sparked again, and as she passed tables and booths swathed in snowy white linens, she caught snippets of the chatter. As she expected, the patrons were talking about her.

"She lives here."

"... love her voice."

"She won a Grammy last year for Best Country Album."

"... even hotter than Carrie Underwood."

Tuning them out, she focused on the reason she was here: dinner with Lexington Ross, the new head of her record label. According to his bio, he'd worked for River Pearl's parent company for nearly twenty years before being promoted to his current position. He'd joined the company right out of law school, working in the contracts group.

She was excited to meet him. And just a tiny bit nervous, too. The music business was brutal. Every year, more record labels went under than started, and more and more artists fought to be signed.

She wanted this dinner to go well. She'd always been happy at River Pearl, and she wanted to stay with the label. She wasn't sure how quickly or easily she could sign with another one if something went wrong. It was a lot like finding a job—it was always easier to nab a position when you were gainfully employed.

If River Pearl kicked her to the curb, she'd be branded like Hester Prynne in *The Scarlet Letter*. Ava Grace would be tainted, and other labels would wonder why River Pearl had severed their relationship. They'd assume she was the problem, even if she wasn't.

Her manager, Wallace Whit, had assured her she had no reason to worry. After all, she was River Pearl Records' number one selling artist.

Wally had planned to eat dinner with her and Lexington Ross. Unfortunately, his return flight to Nashville from Los Angeles was delayed. A computer glitch grounded all the flights out of LAX, so she was on her own tonight.

She breathed deeply, catching whiffs of freshly-baked bread and sizzling beef. Despite her nerves, her stomach growled, eager to sample the chef's specialties.

As she moved deeper into the restaurant, she let her gaze wander. Unlike many steakhouses, this one wasn't dark and formal. It was a mix of modern and rustic with tall, leather-backed booths, walls made of reclaimed railroad ties, and clear pendant lights hanging from the lofty ceiling.

Through the windows, she could see the twinkle of the city's skyline. She easily spotted the AT&T building, colloquially known as the "Batman Building" because of its resemblance to the superhero's mask.

The maître d stopped in front of an L-shaped booth. She smiled at the man occupying it, recognizing him from the photo on River Pearl's website.

"Mr. Ross, I hope you haven't been waiting long."

He didn't return her smile or respond to her comment. Instead, his dark blue eyes skimmed over her, from her loose blond bun to her raspberry-colored toenails revealed by strappy sandals.

She was accustomed to men staring at her—leering, even. But Lexington Ross's gaze wasn't admiring; it was judging. And she sensed he found her lacking.

She'd put a lot of thought into her outfit for this evening, finally deciding on a royal blue mini dress with a sheer poncho-like overlay. It was sexy without being revealing or unprofessional, stylish and edgy without being trashy. She'd paired the dress with silver metallic heels that showed off her bare legs, a hammered silver cuff bracelet, and chunky silver earrings.

Lexington Ross stood, and she struggled to keep her surprise from showing. She towered over him. In her bare feet, she was five-ten, and her three-inch heels made the height difference even worse.

Reba gestured toward a guy a couple of tables away. "That's my husband, Kevin. We're here for our anniversary." She clasped both hands over her belly. "We picked 'Empty Places' for our first dance as husband and wife. Every time I hear it, I think of our wedding. It's my favorite song."

"It's one of my favorites too." She beckoned the other woman closer. "I'll tell you a little secret … I wrote that song for my best friend, and I sang it at her wedding."

Lex sighed. Hearing the unmistakable annoyance in the sound, Ava Grace said, "Thank you for naming your daughter after me, Reba. Good luck with everything."

Reba stood awkwardly for a moment before blurting out, "Can I have your autograph?"

"Of course."

Realizing Reba had nothing for her to sign, Ava Grace found a pen in her matte silver clutch and wrote a short note to Reba on the restaurant's menu. After scrawling her name, she handed the heavy cardstock to the woman.

"I'm going to frame this and put it in the baby's room," Reba vowed, not even bothering to read what Ava Grace had written.

Ava Grace stood and hugged her. "Congratulations on the anniversary *and* the baby."

As Reba hurried back to her husband, Ava Grace sat down and met Lex's gaze. She'd felt his eyes on her during the whole exchange with the expectant mother.

"I'm sorry our conversation was interrupted," she told him, smiling apologetically. "I can't really go anywhere without people asking for autographs or wanting to take a picture with me."

"Your fans are very devoted," Lex noted.

"Yes, they are."

Before she could say anything else, the server returned to take their order. Once they'd made their selections, Lex leaned back in the booth. He idly swirled his drink while he stared at her.

"I've taken a look at the demographics of your fan base. It skews toward younger women. Did you know that?"

"Yes. Most female singers have more female fans than male fans."

He nodded. "That's true. But your fan base is overwhelmingly female compared to other female singers. Close to ninety percent."

She'd seen research documenting an equal split between male and female fans for the country music segment. But that percentage shifted depending on the singer or band. She was disappointed she had so few male fans.

"Do you know why the board fired Jim Healy and asked me to take over River Pearl Records?" Lex asked.

She blinked at his unexpected question. "I assume it was because the board was unhappy with him."

"No," Lex replied flatly. "It was unhappy with the artists on his label."

"Which ones?"

"*All* of them."

CHAPTER TWO

Lex's emphasis on the word "all" made Ava Grace's throat tighten. Wally had been wrong. This wasn't just a casual "get-to-know-you" dinner meeting. It was a performance review.

"I don't..." Her voice was even huskier than usual, and she paused to clear her throat. "I don't understand why the board is unhappy with *me*. My last album debuted at number one. It sold three million copies in a single calendar year, and every stop on my recent tour sold out in less than an hour."

Lex arched his eyebrows. "All six of Carrie Underwood's albums debuted at number one. Adele's last album sold five million copies. And Beyoncé's concerts sold out in one minute."

Unable to dispute his facts, she just sat there. She wanted to point out that Adele and Beyoncé weren't her direct competition, but she didn't bother. Obviously, that didn't matter to Lex.

The server's arrival interrupted their conversation. He delivered Lex's wedge salad with bacon and blue cheese and her kale salad topped with currants, almonds, and parmesan.

The conversation had wrecked her appetite, but Lex didn't seem to suffer the same problem. While she pushed her greens around on the plate, he shoveled salad into his mouth as if he were dining in a prison cafeteria.

When Lex finished, he set down his fork and pushed the plate away. "I'm not dropping you from the River Pearl label."

That assurance should have made her feel better. It should have unraveled the tension knotting her neck and shoulders. It should have loosened the invisible bands squeezing her chest.

But it didn't. All she could think about was the one word he hadn't said: *yet.*

"You need to diversity your fan base, Ava Grace. That's the bottom line. If you gain male fans, you'll also expand your total fan base."

She nodded slowly. "Right."

Just then, the server reappeared with their entrées. She'd ordered the bone-in ribeye with truffle butter, while Lex had picked the wagyu strip. At sixty-five dollars, his steak was the most expensive item on the menu.

It hadn't been that long ago when Ava Grace worked a ten-hour shift at a mom-and-pop dry cleaners and earned less than sixty dollars after taxes. Never in her wildest dreams had she imagined she'd be eating in a restaurant like this.

As Lex spooned potato gratin onto her plate, he said, "You need to think about the kind of music men listen to, and for your next album, you need to record songs that appeal to both sexes. Right now, your songs appeal to women only."

Lex made a lot of sense. She didn't disagree about the need to appeal to a broader audience, and he wasn't asking her to do anything unreasonable. She wanted new people to discover her music, and if she had to make a few changes for that to happen, she was willing to do so.

The tension gripping her body slowly diminished, and her

appetite made a reappearance. Retrieving her fork and knife, she sliced a piece of steak and ate it. The meat was so tender it almost melted on her tongue.

"I talked with Wally," Lex said, "and I suggested he get in touch with the NFL and pitch you to cover the theme song for the upcoming season of Sunday Night Football."

"That would be awesome! I'd love that!"

Ava Grace had been born and raised in Texas, where people glorified our God in Heaven on Sunday mornings and glorified the Gods of the Gridiron later in the day. As a result, she loved football.

She spooned a dollop of potato gratin into her mouth. Made with gruyère cheese, the side dish was so creamy and rich, she expected butter to seep out of her pores later on.

"Are you seeing anyone?"

Taken aback by Lex's question, she just stared at him. Why did he want to know if she was seeing anyone? Was he hitting on her? She'd heard stories from other singers who'd experienced sexual harassment, but she'd been fortunate enough to work with people who respected her.

After swallowing her bite of potatoes, she asked, "Is that relevant to our conversation?"

"Is that relevant to our conversation?" Lex mimicked. "Yes, it's relevant, or I wouldn't have asked."

"Why does it matter?"

"If you're single and unattached, we can use it to our advantage. What would you think about a contest? Something along the lines of 'Win a Date with Ava Grace Landy'."

She couldn't prevent the grimace that twisted her face. Wasn't there a movie with a similar premise?

"Going on dates with strangers doesn't sound like much

fun," she noted, ignoring the sad fact that going out with men she knew hadn't been much fun, either. "Nor does it sound very safe."

Lex continued, as if she hadn't spoken. "Or maybe we could do a reality TV show."

Although she'd gotten her big break because of a TV singing competition, she didn't watch reality TV shows. She definitely didn't want to star in one. Leave that to the Kardashians. They seemed to be good at it.

Lex snapped his fingers. "I know! You could go on a date with a different guy for every episode." His eyes lit up. "Or you could go on dates in all fifty states and do something unique to that state, like snorkeling in Hawaii."

Snorkeling in Hawaii sounded fun—she'd never done that before. But she had no desire to frolic in the ocean with a stranger while a film crew recorded their every move. Undoubtedly, she'd get a bikini wedgie and sand would stick to her butt cheeks. Her ass would look like a sugar-sprinkled donut.

"I don't think guys would watch a show like that, Lex. Plus, everyone looks bad on those shows, and I'm not talking about their physical appearance."

Lex's eyes narrowed. "I know some producers. I'll talk to them about it."

He could talk to all the producers he wanted, but she wasn't going to participate in a reality TV show. Ava Grace wanted to focus on making music.

She popped another bite of steak into her mouth. *Mmm.* Maybe it *was* worth the exorbitant price.

"You've been on the cover of nearly every women's magazine," Lex noted.

She nodded as she chewed. She'd lost count of the number

of times she'd been interviewed and photographed. Unlike a lot of high-profile people who avoided the media, she took a different approach and made herself available. Her visibility made her less of a target for the paparazzi, who were after shots of secretive celebrities.

Last month, she'd been on the cover of *Mesmerize*. The pub airbrushed the gigantic pimple on her chin, which she appreciated. It also airbrushed her upper arms until they looked like matchsticks, which she did *not* appreciate.

Lex continued, "I want you in men's magazines too. I'd love to see you on the cover of *Rule*. I'm making that a priority for our publicity team."

Rule. The magazine that featured famous women in a variety of provocative poses and in various states of nakedness.

The thought of being spread out on the cover of *Rule* in her underwear made Ava Grace choke on the piece of steak she'd been in the process of swallowing. Covering her mouth, she sputtered and coughed until it dislodged. Lex barely registered her distress. He just continued to chew his wagyu.

Dabbing her watering eyes with her napkin, she asked, "Are you serious?"

Lex nodded. "Katy Perry was on the cover of *Rule*. So was Christina Aguilera."

If Katy and Christina wanted to bare their bodies for *Rule*, Ava Grace fully supported their decision. More power to them.

But she wasn't interested in stripping down for millions of people. Her list of life goals did not include being the picture teenage boys used to jack off into their socks.

"I saw their covers," she said. "They both looked beautiful. But I don't want to be on the cover of *Rule*."

Lex exhaled loudly, obviously annoyed. "Except for the

Sunday Night Football theme song, you've shot down all my ideas."

Because your ideas suck.

"You have two weeks to come up with something else," he warned. "If you don't, we're moving forward with mine."

"Okay," she agreed, confident she could come up with something better than what he proposed.

Lex tossed back the remainder of his drink and set the empty glass down with a thump. "You're lucky your looks match your voice. If you were ugly, you wouldn't have won *American Star,* and River Pearl wouldn't have signed you."

He didn't notice the look she gave him—the one her best friend referred to as the "death stare." His heart should have immediately stopped beating. Too bad it still was.

After carefully folding her napkin and placing it on the table beside her plate, she fished a hundred-dollar bill from her clutch. She put the money in the middle of the table, right next to the flickering votive candle.

She slid out of the booth and looked down at Lexington Ross. Aware other people might be watching, she smiled widely. Only someone who knew her well would be able to tell she was struggling against the urge to dump her sweet tea over his head.

"I won a Grammy for my songwriting. I performed in front of forty thousand people when I was sick with the flu and had a fever over one-hundred-and-two. I finished every album ahead of schedule. And *none* of that had anything to do with the way I look." She tilted her head toward the Benjamin on the table. "That should cover my dinner. If it doesn't, take it out of my next royalty check."

She left him sitting in the booth and strolled out of the steakhouse as if she hadn't a care in the world. At least Wally hadn't accompanied her to dinner. Her manager was intensely protective, more surrogate father than employee, and he probably would have gotten in Lexington Ross's face and made a huge scene.

She'd had a great relationship with Jim Healy, the previous head of River Pearl Records, and had been upset when she heard he'd been fired. Now that she'd met his replacement, she was even more upset.

As she waited for the valet to retrieve her Camaro, she huddled next to a planter overflowing with vibrant purple crocus. Although the calendar said spring was only a month away, the chilly evening air made goose bumps pebble up and down her arms.

Her hands were shaking, but not from cold. Anger made them shake. Only one person could calm her down right now: her best friend, Amelia O'Brien.

Ava Grace checked the time on her phone. Amelia lived with her husband, Quinn, in San Francisco, which was on Pacific Time. It was nine o'clock in Nashville, so it was seven o'clock on the West Coast. Amelia should be home from work by now.

Once Ava Grace was in her car and heading out of downtown on Interstate 65, she used her Bluetooth to call Amelia. Her BFF picked up on the first ring.

"Hey, chickadee."

Amelia didn't sound as upbeat as she usually did, and Ava Grace immediately pushed her own problems to the back burner. "Everything okay, Millie?"

"Yes. I'm just tired."

"Did Quinn keep you up all night again?"

"No." Amelia snickered. "But he woke me up early."

Quinn couldn't keep his hands off his petite, redheaded wife.

Ava Grace was glad her best friend had married a solid guy who adored her. No one deserved love more than Amelia.

"Is your dinner already over?" Amelia asked.

"Yes. I just left the restaurant."

"How'd it go?"

"Not great. Lexington Ross is an asshole."

Ava Grace spent a few minutes filling Amelia in, explaining what Lex said about her fan base and his suggestions to attract male fans. She also repeated his insult, the taste of the words bitter on her tongue.

When she finished, Amelia said, "William Howard Taft."

Despite her lingering anger, Ava Grace smiled. Her best friend didn't curse like most people. Instead, she used the names of U.S. presidents as imprecations.

Ava Grace heard Quinn's voice in the background, but she couldn't make out his words. "What did he say?"

"He wants to know how your dinner went. Alright if I tell him?"

"Go ahead."

While Amelia shared the details, Ava Grace moved into the left lane to pass an eighteen wheeler. She lived about an hour outside the city, in a town called Hendersonville. Before Amelia had moved to San Francisco, she and Ava Grace shared an old farmhouse.

"Quinn wants me to put you on speaker," Amelia said.

Suddenly, Quinn's baritone filled the car. "Hey, AG."

Before Ava Grace had met Quinn, no one had ever called her anything other than Ava Grace or Miss Landy. But Quinn had a habit of giving people nicknames they didn't ask for—he called his wife *Juice*, for God's sake—and he'd shortened Ava Grace's name to AG.

"I think I have a solution to your problem," Quinn said. "You should partner with Trinity."

This wasn't the first time Quinn had mentioned partnering with Trinity Distillery, a small company in San Francisco that produced bourbon. Quinn and Trinity's CEO, Jonah Beck, had been in the same MBA program at Stanford.

When Beck had launched Trinity with his buddies, Gabriel Bristow and Renner Holt, Quinn provided the start-up capital. Supposedly, he was a silent partner, but Ava Grace couldn't imagine him being silent about anything.

Quinn continued, "I can get in touch with Beck and set up a meeting."

Beck.

She clearly remembered the first time she'd set eyes on Jonah Beck, more than two years ago at Quinn and Amelia's wedding. Beck had been a guest too.

His deep laugh caught her attention from across the room … that and the way his broad shoulders filled out his light blue dress shirt and the way his butt looked in his charcoal suit pants.

With his wavy, chocolate-colored hair, Beck was one of the most handsome men she'd ever seen. And that said a lot, since she was acquainted with famous musicians, movie stars, and pro athletes.

Beck was more than just handsome, though. He was one of those guys who had *it*—that special something that made women fluff their hair and swing their hips.

They hadn't spoken at the wedding, but when they were officially introduced several months later, she realized he was even better-looking up close. His eyes were the same color as a triple shot espresso, and just like that highly caffeinated drink, they gave her a jolt.

When he looked at her, she felt it *everywhere*. She'd never experienced anything like it.

"Are you there, AG?" Quinn's voice dragged her back into the phone conversation.

"I'm here."

"Do you want to come to San Francisco and meet with Beck or not?"

CHAPTER THREE

The heavy steel door banged shut behind Beck as he entered the warehouse that held Trinity Distillery's grain boilers and fermentation tanks. Gabe insisted they needed to name all the buildings to avoid confusion, but so far, no one had come up with anything more creative for this one than *Warehouse Number Two.*

Located in the trendy South of Market neighborhood in downtown San Francisco, the warehouse was part of a four-building complex. It had been vacant for more than thirty years before they'd moved in.

The warm, moist air from the boilers filled the cavernous building with the smell of baking bread. The aroma always reminded Beck of his childhood in Kentucky, of visiting his dad at the family distillery after school, watching the yeast work its magic in the fermentation tanks and running through the maze of stacked oak barrels.

His memories were bittersweet. He hadn't stepped foot in the Jonah Beck Distillery in more than fifteen years, not since he was a senior in high school and his world fell apart.

Beck's ancestor, Jonah Martin Beck, built the distillery in the early 1800s in rural Nelson County, near Lexington. It had operated continuously, even during Prohibition, thanks to some very powerful men who refused to give up Beck bourbon.

Today, the distillery was the largest producer of bourbon whiskey in the world. But the Beck family didn't own the Jonah Beck Distillery any longer. A British company had bought it when Beck was a sophomore at the University of Kentucky.

After passing the massive grain boilers, Beck reached the industrial stairs that led to the suspended catwalk. His boots thumped on the grate treads as he climbed the stairs, and once he arrived at the top, he took a moment to survey the six round fermentation tanks.

Measuring fourteen feet in diameter and ten feet tall, the tanks were constructed of cypress wood. Each one was filled with Trinity's mash bill, a proprietary blend of boiled corn, barley, and rye. Once yeast joined the party, the fermentation process began. It took several days and created enough heat to make sweat bead on Beck's forehead.

The catwalk shuddered under his feet, and he glanced over his shoulder to see what caused the movement. He grinned when he saw his master distiller heading toward him wearing tan canvas work pants and a black T-shirt with *You had me at bourbon* in white block letters.

Ellis Oglesby reached Beck's side and slapped him on the back in greeting. "How's it going, boy?"

Beck shook his head in amused exasperation. Ellis never called him anything but *boy*. He doubted the wiry old man ever would, regardless of the fact Beck was nearly a foot taller and outweighed him by at least eighty pounds. He didn't know if Ellis called him boy because every male in Beck's family was named Jonah or because Ellis had known Beck since he was in diapers.

"Afternoon, Ellis."

"Whatcha doin' up here?"

"Checking the mash."

"You pay people to do that." Ellis raised a bushy gray eyebrow. "Don't you have better things to do?"

Beck shrugged. "I like doing it."

Bourbon was in Beck's blood. Hell, his last name was synonymous with the spirit. When people walked into bars, they asked for Beck and Coke or Beck on the rocks.

He'd learned to distill bourbon before he had been able to drink it … legally, that is. He enjoyed his first sip of bourbon when he was ten years old, and he'd eaten food flavored with bourbon for as long as he could remember—French toast with bourbon syrup, bourbon beef tenderloin, bourbon-roasted vegetables. He wouldn't be surprised to find out his baby food had been laced with bourbon.

Sighing loudly, Ellis leaned against the side of the nearest fermentation tank. "You only come up here when somethin's botherin' you."

He studied Beck, his pale blue eyes clear and astute despite the wrinkles around them. Beck looked away from the older man's penetrating gaze and focused on the little yeast bubbles covering the surface of the mash.

"Aren't you meetin' with that singer this afternoon?" Ellis asked.

"Yeah. At two o'clock."

When Quinn had called to let him know Ava Grace Landy and her manager wanted to have a conversation about a possible partnership, Beck was floored. He never imagined she'd be interested in working with Trinity, but he was thrilled she was willing to consider it.

Trinity had reached the point where it needed a spokesperson, and Ava Grace Landy would be perfect. Although Beck was the founder and CEO, he had no desire to be the face of the company. He wanted to stay in the background as much as he could. He wanted to focus on making great bourbon while someone else—preferably Ava Grace—told the world about it.

"You've met her before, right?" Ellis asked.

Beck nodded. He and Ava Grace hadn't exactly gotten off on the right foot when they were introduced. She told him she didn't like Trinity "all that much." Her dismissive attitude stung, more than he liked to admit.

If someone else had disrespected his bourbon, he would've ignored them. But when Ava Grace did it, he retaliated by tossing her words in her face, saying he didn't like her music "all that much."

The moment the words had shot out of his mouth, he was ashamed of himself. He was still embarrassed by what he'd said to her.

"What do you think of her?" the older man prodded.

I think she's hot enough to melt the polar ice caps.

And Beck wasn't made of ice. He was just a flesh-and-blood man ... a man who was attracted to her, even though he didn't want to be.

The first time Beck saw Ave Grace in person, he was at Quinn and Amelia's wedding. She was the maid of honor, and she outshined every woman there, even the bride.

They hadn't officially met until Amelia introduced them several months later during a group outing at a bowling alley. When he'd looked into Ava Grace's face and clasped her hand, her beauty slammed into him so hard, he felt as if a heavyweight boxer punched him in the gut. He hadn't been able to form a single word so he just nodded like a mime.

"I saw her on TV the other day," Ellis said. "A woman like that improves blood flow to a man's most important organ."

Although Beck knew exactly which organ Ellis meant, he replied, "You could use some extra blood flow to the brain."

Ellis chuckled, his voice raspy from decades of pipe smoking. "That's not a man's most important organ, boy. I'm talkin' about the power sprayer, the hot rod, the jackhammer, the broadsword—"

"*Ellis*," Beck groaned, "shut up."

Ellis's booming laugh bounced off the high ceiling. "Did I tell you I went out with that sweet thang I met at the farmers' market?"

Everywhere Ellis went, he attracted women. He picked them up at gas stations, grocery stores, in the park, standing in line at the bank … just about anywhere. Despite his puny stature, sun-weathered countenance, and sparse gray hair, women of all ages seemed to find him irresistible. It baffled the hell out of Beck since Ellis reminded him of a scrawny rooster.

"No, you didn't tell me," Beck answered before rushing to add, "and I really don't want you to. *Please* don't."

Ellis ignored his plea. "*Mmm, mmm, mmm.*" He smacked his lips. "Her tits were so—"

"*Jesus Christ.*" Beck shook his head, both awed and disgusted by Ellis's active sex life. "You're such a poonhound." He pointed his forefinger at the horny old goat. "Are you aware there's been a spike in syphilis, chlamydia, and HIV among seniors? I hope to hell you're using a rubber when you screw these women."

"You don't need to worry about me. I've been pumpin' for nearly sixty years, and I haven't caught anything yet." Ellis patted the front pocket of his worn pants. "I always carry protection. Don't you?"

Beck barked out an incredulous laugh. "No, Ellis, I don't carry condoms, hoping to get laid. I haven't done that since I was a teenager."

And back then, Beck had sex with only one person: Callie Boone, the most beautiful girl in Nelson County. She'd been his first *everything*.

The first girl he'd ever loved. The first girl he'd had sex with. The first girl who'd broken his heart. The first (and only) girl who'd tried to ruin his life.

"I worry about you, boy. I really do." Ellis shook his head sorrowfully. "When's the last time you got some?"

"I don't kiss and tell," Beck quipped. "You shouldn't either."

"I hope to hell you're doin' more than kissin'," Ellis shot back.

Beck wasn't about to admit Ellis got more action than he did. He hadn't been on a date in … *Shit*, he couldn't remember the last time he'd been on a date. Maybe last fall?

Unfortunately, he had no trouble remembering the last time he'd gotten laid. It had been more than a year ago, shortly before he and Olivia broke up.

"I know you've been workin' hard … tryin' to get Trinity off the ground," Ellis said, "but there's more to life than makin' bourbon."

"I'm surprised to hear you say that since you've dedicated your life to it," Beck replied dryly.

Without question, Ellis was the best master distiller in the nation, maybe the best in the world. He'd spent more than thirty years as the master distiller for Jonah Beck Distillery, and while he had worked there, he won Master Distiller of the Year five times.

Beck lured Ellis out of retirement six years ago to take over the master distiller job at Trinity. He had no doubt the old man was the reason Trinity found success when other craft distilleries failed.

"You know, women are like bourbon," Ellis said.

Beck laughed. "I think the saying is, 'Women are like fine wine. They only get better with age.'"

Ellis shook his head. "No, they're like bourbon," he insisted.

"How so?"

"A good one is warm and smooth and just a little sweet. But she's got some kick to her … a bite that makes you flinch. She makes your throat burn and your chest tight, and then she settles in your belly and glows like an ember." Ellis eyed Beck for a moment, a smile playing around his lips. "You ever met a woman like that?"

"Not yet."

"Or maybe you just weren't payin' attention." Ellis tilted his head toward the door. "You better hightail it. You don't wanna be late for your meetin'."

Beck checked his watch, a vintage Tag Heuer his dad had given him. Realizing the meeting started in five minutes, he patted Ellis on the back. "See you later, old man."

As he jogged toward the stairs, he heard Ellis yell, "Damn it, boy, be careful! You're gonna break somethin'!"

Once Beck was outside he took a moment to smooth his hair and check his clothes for stains. Today, he wore a beige vintage-style T-shirt with brown-and-orange cursive lettering on the front that said, *Hello, bourbon, my old friend. I've come to talk with you again.*

His faded jeans had worn spots on both knees. The bottoms were frayed, and one of the side seams was split over his brown leather work boot.

He'd thought about dressing up for today's meeting, but

decided against it. He didn't sit behind a desk all day. He got his hands dirty.

And now he was going to get his hands dirty with Ava Grace Landy.

CHAPTER FOUR

When Beck walked inside the cavernous warehouse that housed Trinity's office Ava Grace and her manager were already there. They stood in a small cluster with Gabe and Ren.

"Beck is checking the mash," Gabe said. "He'll be here soon."

"I'm here," he called out.

Everyone turned toward him. As he hurried over to the little group, he zeroed in on Ava Grace. Sunshine filtered through the wide windows and slanted across her face. Her skin looked like silk, not a single blemish to mar its smooth surface.

As he came to a stop next to his partners, he met Ava Grace's hazel gaze. Her eyes glimmered with flecks of green and gold.

"Hello. It's good to see you again."

"Hello, Beck."

The husky rasp of her voice skipped down Beck's spine. It sounded even better in person than it did on the radio or TV.

Ava Grace's unique voice, along with her Texas twang, stunning good looks, and tall, willowy body, enthralled the entire nation when she competed on *American Star* several years ago. Not a week went by that she didn't show up on TV or the cover of a magazine.

The media, both legit and paparazzi, had a huge hard-on for Ava Grace. And in that respect, Beck and the media had a lot in common.

Beck couldn't imagine living his life under a microscope the way she did. It'd make him crazy.

He'd had enough of that when his dad was accused of embezzling twenty-five million dollars. Reporters descended on his hometown like a plague of locusts. Even though Jonah Beck Distillery was a private, family-held company, the news its president and CEO had stolen millions of dollars garnered national attention.

TV vans clogged the road leading to his house, and reporters camped out on the expansive lawn. They'd even shown up at his high school, following him from his Jeep to the entrance, shouting questions and shoving microphones in his face.

The memory made his chest tighten. He forced himself to think about the present instead of the past.

"How have you been?" he asked Ava Grace, genuinely interested in her answer.

"Finer than frog hair."

Her answer made him chuckle. Ellis said "finer than frog hair" all the time. It was an old southern idiom, and Beck hadn't expected it to come out of Ava Grace's luscious mouth.

She smiled. Like most celebrities, her teeth were blindingly white. But they weren't perfect. She had a slight overbite, and one of her front teeth edged over the other. And in Beck's opinion, those tiny imperfections elevated her from beautiful to breathtaking.

Somehow, he managed to drag his gaze from Ava Grace's gorgeous smile and focus on her manager. Everything about Wallace Whit was thick except his hair. Paint him green, and he could be The Incredible Hulk's balding older brother.

Beck and Wallace Whit exchanged brief, perfunctory handshakes. "Thanks for inviting us out," Wally said, glancing around the rundown warehouse.

Noting Wally's review of the building, Ren grimaced. "Sorry about the mess."

"I'm sure it will be great once you've finished with the renovations." A tendril of platinum-blond hair had escaped from Ava Grace's braid, and she brushed it away from her face. "I'm excited to see what you guys do with it."

"We weren't going to move in until the new space was finished," Gabe chimed in, "but we'd already transferred all the operations here—the fermentation tanks, the distillers, the bottling line—so it made sense to go ahead and move the office."

Ava Grace laughed softly. "You're going to regret that decision. I renovated my house a couple of years ago, and I lived there during the construction. It was *not* pleasant. Every morning at seven o'clock, a crew showed up at my door, and I had no peace for the next twelve hours."

She wrinkled her nose. "It's not just the hammering and the drilling, either. It's the constant questions. The crew couldn't leave me alone for more than ten minutes without asking for direction."

Beck barely suppressed a rude snort. Her contractors hadn't needed direction. They just wanted to listen to her sexy voice and ogle her fine ass. He couldn't blame them, though, since he wanted to do the same thing.

"Renovations always take longer and cost more than you expect," Ava Grace added. "And the dust gets everywhere."

Wally cleared his throat. "Maybe we should start discussing the details of a potential marketing partnership between Ava

Grace and Trinity," he suggested. "We have a lot to talk about."

Ava Grace flashed a smile at her manager. The relationship between them seemed more than professional. Not sexual, but definitely affectionate.

"Wally is eager to get back to Nashville because he has tickets for the Predators game," Ava Grace said, nudging her shoulder against the man's beefy arm. "Hockey is far more important than I am."

Wally chuckled. "Come on, Ava Grace. It's game seven of the conference finals. If they win, they'll play for the Stanley Cup."

"It's all about priorities," she replied, a teasing note in her raspy voice.

Beck gestured to the conference table and chairs in the far corner. "Let's sit down."

He led the way to the frosted glass table and waited patiently for everyone to get settled in the black leather chairs. He tried not to stare as Ava Grace took a seat and crossed her long legs, but he couldn't help himself.

Her denim dress, which hit well above her knees, had metal buttons down the front and on the pockets. She'd left the three bottom buttons undone to show her lean thighs and the two top buttons open to reveal some cleavage. A wide brown belt and brown leather cowboy boots completed her look.

Ava Grace flipped her long braid over her shoulder, and he jerked his eyes away just as she looked up. He dropped into the chair at the head of the table. Gabe and Ren were on his right, next to each other, while Wally and Ava Grace sat directly across from them.

Beck leaned back in his chair, trying to relax. When he was around Ava Grace, his muscles stiffened as if preparing for a brutal attack. To his disgust, they weren't the only things that stiffened.

He caught Gabe's eye and gave him a non-verbal go ahead to kick off the pitch they'd prepared. But before Gabe could begin, Wally said, "I'm going to be honest with you guys ... I'm not convinced Ava Grace should partner with Trinity."

"You haven't even heard our pitch," Gabe pointed out, his voice hard. "How do you—"

Beck held up his hand. "Hold on, Gabe. Let's give Wally a chance to talk." He met the older man's eyes. "What's your biggest concern?"

"Your product." Wally linked his hands together on top of the table. "Alcohol is *very* controversial. Underage drinking. Binge drinking. Alcoholism." He shook his head emphatically. "We don't want anyone to think Ava Grace is encouraging those things. She has millions of fans still in high school."

Beck and his partners considered Wally's words. He wasn't wrong. It was something the industry struggled with daily.

"We understand where you're coming from," Ren said. "But we advocate responsible drinking, and we'd work with Ava Grace to make sure she can promote Trinity without encouraging irresponsible drinking."

"Alcohol isn't all bad," Gabe chimed in. "Research proves teetotalers are more likely to be depressed than those who drink moderately."

"Is that true?" Wally asked.

"Yes, it's true," Beck confirmed. "Spirits are good for the spirit."

Ava Grace smiled at his quip. "I agree. When I have a bad day, I always feel better after I have a mango margarita."

"Mango margarita?" Beck grimaced. "You and I have a

different idea about what constitutes an alcoholic beverage."

She laughed. "They're good. You should try one."

She leaned sideways and whispered something to Wally. His forehead furrowed in a frown before he sighed.

"Ava Grace says I need to have an open mind." Wally inclined his head. "Start talking. I'll listen."

Without delay, Gabe began his spiel. "It's a really exciting time for Trinity. Two years ago, we decanted our first barrels of bourbon. Beck's vision, which Ren and I shared, was to produce ultra-premium bourbon, and that's exactly what we did. We've been honored by the American Distilling Institute as one of the best craft distilleries in the nation, and we've signed agreements with several distributors to put our product in liquor stores, hotels, and restaurants across the U.S. Since then, our sales have exceeded our forecasts."

"I thought bourbon had to be made in Kentucky," Wally said.

"That's a common misperception," Beck replied. "Bourbon can be produced anywhere in the U.S. People get confused because Kentucky is the ancestral home of bourbon, and the state produces more than ninety-five percent of the world's bourbon. Trinity is the only company in California that distills bourbon."

Wally nodded. "Yeah, California isn't exactly known for bourbon."

"We've managed to build a very loyal following for Trinity in a remarkably short time," Gabe said. "The market for spirits, especially brown spirits, is growing."

"My grandfather drank bourbon," Wally said. "I've always thought of it as a drink for old men."

"Old men still drink bourbon," Beck noted. "But the popularity of mixology has made bourbon trendy."

Ava Grace's gaze swung to him, and he forgot what he was saying. She stared unblinkingly, her bright eyes framed by absurdly long eyelashes. He wished she wouldn't look at him because it made his skin feel raw and hot—like when he'd worn a cheap tux to his high school prom.

"What the hell is mixology?" Wally asked.

"The art of making craft cocktails," Ren explained. "Bourbon is one of the fastest-growing categories in the alcohol category, thanks to a rise in interest from Millennials, as well as women."

"It's a very competitive category, though," Beck added. "Attracting new customers is a challenge. We're not only competing against other bourbon and whiskey producers, we're also competing against other spirits—gin, tequila, rum, vodka. The stringent regulations for advertising alcoholic beverages make it even more difficult."

Beck glanced at Ren, who picked up the conversation. "In the past, the big bourbon distilleries have largely ignored women. They've marketed their bourbon almost exclusively to men."

Ren looked back and forth between Ava Grace and Wally. His mouth usually reminded Beck of a hyphen—straight and serious—but now it was stretched in a smile. Beck had no doubt Ava Grace was the reason. Men turned into grinning, drooling idiots around her.

"That's not very smart," Wally noted, absently scratching his bald head. "With the exception of automobiles, women account for the overwhelming majority of discretionary spending."

"Right," Ren agreed. "And other spirits categories have done a much better job of marketing to women. Vodka, in particular. Women represent a very large and very lucrative market for bourbon distillers. We think a lot of women would like bourbon if they tried it."

Leaning forward, Beck braced his elbows on the table and spoke directly to Ava Grace. "That's where you come in. We need someone who connects with women. Someone women identify with. Someone they admire. That's you."

He paused to drive home the next point. "We want *you* to tell women how great Trinity is. We want *your* female fans to become fans of Trinity. We think you and Trinity could be a great pairing—like mint and bourbon."

She arched her eyebrows. "Even though you don't like my music 'all that much'?"

And there it was. Beck had wondered if she remembered his insult. In some way, he was glad she hadn't forgotten their exchange because it meant he'd cut her as much she'd cut him.

He stared at Ava Grace for a moment, debating how to handle the situation. Making his decision, he rose from his seat. Gabe and Ren followed his lead and stood.

"How 'bout a tour?" Beck asked.

Ava Grace and Wally looked at each other. Their faces clearly expressed surprise and confusion.

Wally slowly stood. "I'm not sure we have time for—"

"Don't you want to see how bourbon is made?" Beck prodded.

After a moment, Ava Grace grabbed her hobo bag from the floor and came to her feet. With an internal sigh of relief, Beck walked toward the front of the building. The rest of the group trailed behind him.

When he reached the door, he stepped aside. He gestured for his partners to exit and casually moved in front of Ava Grace so Wally went out the door first. As soon as the older man cleared the threshold, Beck stopped. Ava Grace bumped into him from behind, letting out a little *oof.*

"Gabe. Ren. Why don't you take Wally to see the continuous still and the doubler? Miz Landy and I need to have a little chat. We'll catch up later."

Before Wally could protest, Beck pulled the door shut and turned to face Ava Grace. He was close enough to catch her scent. She smelled like brown sugar, and he wondered if her skin would taste like it too. He shook off the thought.

"Can I get you something to drink?" he asked. "Something other than Trinity since you don't like my bourbon 'all that much'."

Her eyes narrowed. "That really bothered you, huh?"

"It bothered me as much as it bothered you when I said I didn't like your music 'all that much'."

"That didn't bother me."

She denied it so quickly Beck knew she was lying. "Then why bring it up?"

The crests of her cheeks flushed, and he felt an insane urge to run his thumb across the pinkness. Instead of giving in to it, he crossed his arms over his chest.

"I was going to apologize for what I said that night." Beck shrugged with sham nonchalance. "But if it didn't bother you, I guess there's no reason to say I'm sorry."

Her mouth fell open. "What?"

"Did it bother you when I said I didn't like your music 'all that much'?" He tilted his head to the side. "Tell the truth now."

After a long moment, she nodded. "Yes, it bothered me."

"I'm sorry for insulting you. I acted like an immature jerk."

She stared into his eyes, as if trying to assess his sincerity. The rigid line of her shoulders gradually softened, and the flush left her face.

"I'm sorry too. I swear I wasn't trying to be rude when I said that about Trinity." She sighed. "I was just being honest. I don't drink a lot of hard liquor. I'm more of a Dr Pepper kind of girl."

Mollified by her apology, Beck added, "You're a very talented singer. I actually like your music a lot."

She huffed out a laugh. "Then you're one of the few."

Now he was the one who laughed. "What are you talking about? You have millions of fans."

"Ninety percent of my fans are women. You're one of the few *men* who likes my music." She shifted her bag from her shoulder to the crook of her elbow. "The new head of my record label wants me to expand my fan base. He has all these ideas to increase my visibility among males."

"What kind of ideas?"

Her eyes darted away from him, and her cheeks pinked again. "Crazy, stupid ideas."

Now he really was intrigued. "Like what?"

"A contest. A reality TV show. A magazine cover."

"*Hmm.* Those ideas don't sound crazy or stupid."

In fact, they sounded like good ideas to Beck. Maybe she wasn't the right person to represent Trinity if she was unwilling to consider them.

"They *are* crazy and stupid," she insisted, her voice rising. "The contest is 'Win a Date with Ava Grace' and the reality TV show would follow me around while I went out on blind dates."

Her expression clearly conveyed her disgust. She looked as if she'd just smelled a skunk.

"That'd definitely increase your visibility among males."

He'd said it tongue in cheek. He understood why she was upset. He'd be upset too if he were in her position.

Ava Grace obviously didn't hear the facetiousness underlying his statement because she exclaimed, "He wants to pimp me out!"

Beck burst out laughing. He couldn't help it.

She glowered. "He wants me to pose for the cover of *Rule*."

Beck's laughter died in his throat. *Holy shit.* He'd love to see her all tousled and rosy and wearing next to nothing. But he hated the thought of the whole damn world seeing her like that.

"You're…" Arousal made his voice husky, and he cleared his throat roughly. "You're right. Those are not good ideas." She transferred her bag to her other arm, and he held out his hand. "Give me that. I'll hold it for you."

She hesitated for a moment before passing the leather bag to him. "Thanks."

Tucking her bag under his arm, he said, "Partnering with Trinity would give you access to a new audience. The overwhelming majority of our customers are men. Most bourbon drinkers—most whiskey drinkers, for that matter—are men, age twenty-five to fifty-five."

He gave her a moment to digest that information. "I honestly believe a partnership between you and Trinity would be mutually beneficial. I promise we won't try to pimp you out." He smiled when her lips twitched. "So what do you think, Miz Landy? Should we grab a couple of cans of Dr Pepper and drink to our new partnership?"

CHAPTER FIVE

Ava Grace stroked a hand over her guitar's cocobolo body. The handmade instrument had very little in common with her first guitar, a cheap, factory-made model with enough scratches to prove she hadn't been the first person to own it.

Her dad had given it to her during one of his infrequent visits. It was an "I'm sorry" present to make up for missing her ninth and tenth birthdays and the Christmas in between. She'd been too angry and hurt to take any pleasure from the gift, and the beaten-up guitar languished in her closet for months before she picked it up and strummed her fingers over the strings.

"I need a break, Ava Grace."

Ava Grace glanced at her favorite songwriter, Mercedes Guthrie. They were hanging out on the back porch of Ava Grace's old farmhouse, working on her next album. She'd written some of her best songs while sitting on the porch swing.

"We've only been out here a couple of hours, Mercy."

"I'm hungry. And you know I can't concentrate when I'm hungry."

A lot of great songwriters lived in Nashville, and Mercy was one of the best. She'd won a Grammy a couple of years ago for

Best Country Song, at the ripe old age of twenty-five, and most of big names in the industry wanted to work with her. Despite her success, she remained the same funny, down-to-earth woman Ava Grace had met at the famed Bluebird Café on Hillsboro Pike.

After Amelia had moved to San Francisco, Ava Grace's friendship with Mercy deepened. They spent a lot of time together, usually at the farmhouse so they wouldn't be hounded by the media or aggressive fans.

Mercy tossed her notepad and pencil on the cocktail table where Ava Grace's feet rested. Using both hands, she tugged loose the elastic band holding her long hair in a ponytail. Shiny curls the color of licorice fell past her shoulders.

As Mercy massaged her head, she said, "I need something to eat. Do you have anything to snack on?"

"I made red velvet cupcakes with cream cheese icing last night."

Ava Grace was a decent cook, but she could whip up cakes, muffins, scones, cookies, and other assorted sweets with an expert hand. And when she had the time, she made bread too. Baking relaxed her, and it also made the people around her happy because they got to enjoy some tasty treats.

Mercy rose from the wooden patio chair. She was on the short side, around five-three. Some people would call her chubby, but Ava Grace thought curvaceous a more accurate description since most of Mercy's weight was concentrated in her boobs, hips, and butt.

"No cupcakes." Mercy adjusted her fuchsia T-shirt to cover the waistband of her cut-off denim shorts. The bright top outlined her DDs and complemented her dark bronze skin. "Brian wants me to lose some weight before the wedding."

Ava Grace had to bite her tongue to keep her thoughts to herself. Mercy's fiancé was an arrogant, self-aggrandizing asshole. Somehow he'd convinced her that she was lucky to have him. Ava Grace hoped Mercy would realize the truth—Brian wasn't worthy of her—before they walked down the aisle.

Hearing the squeak of the screen door, she and Mercy looked toward the noise. Kyle Hood's tall frame filled the doorway. He'd worked for Ava Grace for about five years, starting out as her driver-slash-bodyguard after leaving the Marine Corps. More often than not, she drove herself, but when she needed protection, Kyle was there.

Several months ago, the former Marine moved into the farmhouse to help with Ava Grace's father, Chuck. He suffered from early onset Alzheimer's, and it was advanced enough he needed round-the-clock care.

Usually, Chuck was mild-mannered, almost docile. But when he wasn't ... well, it was good Kyle was around. Chuck wasn't overly tall, but he was thickly muscled from years of hard labor on oil rigs.

"How's it going out here?" Kyle asked.

He stepped onto the porch, using his body to keep the screen door open. He still cut his dark hair in a military high-and-tight, with a short mohawk quiff on top that faded into shaved sides.

His regular daily uniform consisted of jeans or cargo pants and T-shirts that either promoted the Marine Corps or his favorite bands. He wasn't a fan of Ava Grace's music, as evidenced by the T-shirt he wore today—a black Avenged Sevenfold tee printed with white skulls and bat wings.

The short sleeves revealed tattoos that illustrated Kyle's past as a military sniper. Army green cargo pants and scuffed hiking boots concealed his lower body.

"You need anything?" he added.

As usual, Kyle's timing was perfect. Ava Grace didn't know how he did it.

"We could use a snack," Ava Grace replied. "Something healthy. We're being good girls today."

Kyle's bottle-green eyes moved from her to Mercy. "You're *always* good girls. That's the problem." He flashed a teasing smile. "Hang tight. I'll get your snack." He disappeared back inside the house, catching the old-fashioned wooden screen door behind him so it didn't bang against the jamb.

"I still don't understand why you haven't stripped that man naked and had your way with him," Mercy whispered, her midnight gaze staring after Kyle.

There was no question Kyle was a good-looking guy, but he didn't do it for her, unlike Jonah Beck. When Beck looked at her, her skin tingled and her belly warmed with desire. She wished she could strip him naked and have her way with *him*.

Ava Grace tucked her guitar into its case and fastened the latches. "I've told you a million times," she said, nudging the guitar case to the side with her foot, "there's no spark between me and Kyle."

In truth, she suspected he had a "spark" for Mercy. But he was too honorable to make a move on her when she belonged to another man.

Mercy shook her head, visibly mystified by Ava Grace's lack of romantic feelings for Kyle. As his employer and his friend, she cared for him in a purely platonic sense and trusted him implicitly. She'd do anything for him, and she knew he felt the same way about her.

"I'm going to run to the bathroom," Mercy announced. "Back in a minute."

Alone on the porch, Ava Grace placed the tip of her red ballet flat on the whitewashed planks and set the swing in motion. As it glided back and forth, she let her gaze wander. The farmhouse was situated on several acres filled with tall trees, lush grass, and colorful wildflowers.

It was nothing like the landscape where she'd grown up. There were a lot of beautiful places in Texas, but the town of Electra was not one of them. Located in the Texas Panhandle, the town was flat and dry, and the vegetation was limited to the occasional tumbleweed.

It was scorching hot in the summer and bitterly cold in the winter. That probably was why fewer than three thousand people lived there, and the population decreased every year.

She had wondered if she'd ever get out of her hometown. But then she'd auditioned for *American Star*.

She and Amelia had been so excited to shake the Texas dust from their boots. When Ava Grace had first seen the old farmhouse nearly six years ago, she'd known it was perfect for them. With its bright white paint and dark green shutters, the farmhouse always gave her a sense of peace.

Her phone chimed, and she scooped it from the coffee table. The text came from Wally: "It's a go. Lex loves the idea. He's a big fan of Trinity."

Now that she had Lex's blessing to partner with Trinity, nothing stood in her way. And she wasn't sure how she felt about that.

Mercy returned from the bathroom and stopped next to the porch swing. "Is that Amelia?" she asked, tilting her head toward Ava Grace's phone.

Mercy's question was nosy, but Ava Grace didn't mind. She was just as nosy. Oh, alright, she would admit it … she was nosier than almost everyone.

"It's Wally," Ava Grace replied. "He says Lex gave the green light to partner with Trinity."

"That's good news." Mercy arched her eyebrows. "Right?"

After a moment, Ava Grace said, "I guess so."

Trinity wasn't the first company to ask Ava Grace to promote its products or services. In fact, Wally fielded requests every week, from birth control pills and bicycles to shampoo and skis. Companies tried to lure her with millions of dollars. Occasionally she said yes, but usually she said no.

Ava Grace Landy, country singer, was a brand, and the integrity of that brand had to be protected. She never signed on with a company if it could damage her brand or if she didn't use its products or services.

Of course, the situation with Trinity was different. A partnership with a bourbon distillery would be a better alternative than any of the ideas Lex had proposed.

"You don't seem very excited," Mercy noted. "Are you worried Beck is a crook like his father? Or that his family history might reflect badly on you?"

Ava Grace shook her head emphatically. "No. Not at all."

At her request, Wally had researched Beck's background and shared the highlights with her. She, in turn, shared them with Mercy.

According to Wally's research, Beck had ties to some of the wealthiest and most prominent families in Kentucky. His father's family, the Becks, made a fortune from bourbon, while his mother's family tree was heavy with senators, congressmen, and even a governor.

Beck grew up in the heart of Kentucky's bourbon country in a place called Bardstown, the only child of Sibley and Jonah Lawson Beck, known by family and friends as Law.

When twenty-five million dollars went missing from the family distillery, Law was the prime suspect. But his younger brother was the real culprit.

"Beck's dad was *not* a crook. He was cleared of any wrongdoing. And Quinn trusted Beck enough to invest millions in his company. Quinn is a good judge of character."

"So what's the problem?" Mercy asked.

"There is no problem."

Except I keep imagining how Beck's hands would feel on my skin ... on my nipples ... between my legs ...

Mercy studied her for a moment before plucking her tablet out of her satchel. She flipped open the cover and tapped the screen a few times.

"*Damn,*" she breathed. "Those Trinity guys are hot with a capital H."

Mercy stuck the tablet in front of Ava Grace's face, so close she had to lean back to get her eyes to focus. A picture of the Trinity guys covered the screen. Beck stood in the middle with Gabe and Ren flanking him. All three wore burnt orange T-shirts with the Trinity logo and dark-washed jeans.

Beck was a big guy, close to six-four she'd guess, and his partners were about the same height. They weren't as gorgeous as Beck, but they still were extremely good-looking. All three had similar builds: broad shoulders, lean waists, and long legs.

"Is Beck the one in the middle?" Mercy asked, scrutinizing the photo.

"Yes."

"Does he look that good in person?"

"Better."

Mercy gave her a sideways glance. Whatever she saw on Ava Grace's face made her mouth kick up in a smile.

"You like him."

"No, I don't," Ava Grace protested.

Liar, liar, pants on fire.

She could feel her face turning red. Mercy laughed.

Flipping the tablet shut, she said, "Yes, you do. You like Beck."

"I barely know him."

"Well, now you have the opportunity to get to know him better." Mercy waggled her dark eyebrows. "Like *really* get to know him."

Mercy shoved the tablet back into her satchel and plopped down on one of the chairs around the café table. "You're always complaining how it's impossible to meet a guy who you can trust." She pursed her lips. "Or is it whom you can trust? I never get that right." She lazily waved her hand. "It's not like country songs are grammatically correct."

Ava Grace joined her friend at the table. "It's hard to know if a guy wants *me* or Ava Grace Landy, country singer."

She'd always been selective with her sexual partners, but now she was selective *and* suspicious. She didn't want to let down her guard and trust the wrong guy. That was a sure way to end up with the details of her sex life splashed across the tabloids and the money drained from her bank accounts.

"You just said Beck is trustworthy, and you already know he wants Ava Grace Landy, country singer, to promote his bourbon." Mercy crossed her legs and let her leather flip-flop dangle from her toes. "He might want *you* too. You just need to feel him out." She snickered. "Or should I say, feel him up."

Kyle's arrival interrupted their conversation. He carried a tray with two tall glasses of sweet tea, plates, a platter of colorful veggies, and a big bowl of guacamole. Carefully balancing the tray on the table, he unloaded the contents.

"You haven't been on a date in forever. Do you even remember the last time you had sex?" Mercy asked before taking a sip of her sweet tea.

"It's been a while," Kyle said as he placed a turquoise Fiesta plate in front of her. "Almost six years."

Mercy choked on her tea. "What?" she gasped, wiping droplets from her mouth and chin with the back of her hand. "You haven't had sex in six years?"

"That's an extremely personal question. Why do you care?" His lips twitched when Mercy's face turned as pink as her T-shirt. "I was talking about Ava Grace. I don't think she's had sex this decade."

"Your hymen is going to regenerate," Mercy warned Ava Grace. "Like a lizard growing a new tail."

Kyle guffawed, and Mercy's lighter laughter joined his. Ava Grace shot them her legendary death stare. Kyle responded by winking and spooning a dollop of guacamole onto her plate. He added a handful of baby carrots, red and yellow peppers, and black olives before serving Mercy.

"You're going to turn into an organism that reproduces asexually—like a copperhead," Mercy said, laughter threading her voice.

"Copperheads reproduce asexually?" Kyle asked, clearly astonished. "I didn't know that."

"Shut up," Ava Grace ordered sourly. "Both of you. This conversation about my sex life—"

"Or lack thereof..." Mercy inserted before popping a black olive into her mouth.

"—is over," Ava Grace finished.

Kyle loaded guacamole onto a carrot and bit into the veggie

with a loud crunch. After he swallowed, he said, "Chuck should be up from his nap soon. I'm going to sit with him so he won't be alone when he wakes up."

Kyle and Ava Grace agreed it was best to call her father by his first name at all times and to never refer to her as his daughter. His Alzheimer's was advanced enough he didn't recognize her any longer, and it upset him when someone mentioned Chuck had a daughter.

Ava Grace took a drink of cool, sweet tea. "I don't know what's worse. When he doesn't take a nap, he gets overtired and belligerent, just like a toddler. But when he takes a nap, he wakes up scared and disoriented."

"And violent," Kyle chimed in.

"He's deteriorating faster than Dr. Hanna expected," Ava Grace lamented. "He told me it would be *years* before the disease progressed to this point. But it's only been months."

Mercy nodded. "I know."

"I'll bring Chuck out when he wakes up," Kyle promised before heading back inside the house.

"You've done more for your father than most children would," Mercy said. "You renovated your whole house so he'd be comfortable, and you're paying for round-the-clock care."

"It's not a hardship. I have the money."

"You're a good daughter." Mercy patted Ava Grace's hand. "I'm sorry, sweetie. I know this is hard for you."

"It is hard. But it's hard for everyone who has a parent with Alzheimer's. I had no idea how horrible this disease is."

Just before Ava Grace had won *American Star*, Chuck was diagnosed with early onset Alzheimer's. She didn't know he was sick because he didn't bother to contact her until his doctor in Texas forced the issue. That was two years ago, and he moved in with her three months later.

Some people might assume Chuck hadn't told Ava Grace about his disease because he didn't want her to worry. But those people would be wrong. He hadn't told his only child about his dire diagnosis because it never crossed his mind ... just like she never crossed his mind.

When Ava Grace had been two years old, her mother died in a car accident. Chuck took a week off from his job as a roughneck on an offshore oil rig to bury his wife, pack up their home, and dump his daughter on his mother, June.

Chuck had promised he'd support Ava Grace financially. He also promised to visit every chance he got.

He'd lied.

Payments from Chuck had been infrequent, and his visits had been even more infrequent. Before he moved in with Ava Grace, she could've counted on both hands the number of times she'd seen her father.

She'd tried to understand his choice to leave her. She'd told herself a million times his job had taken him away from Electra for months at a stretch, and he'd needed to make a living.

But she really *didn't* understand. Even though jobs hadn't been plentiful in their small town, he could have found something there if he'd wanted to.

And that was the whole point—he hadn't wanted to.

"At least you don't need to worry or feel guilty when you're not here," Mercy said. "Chuck doesn't notice you're gone. He doesn't miss you."

Mercy wasn't being cruel. She was just telling the truth. Nonetheless, a spear of pain pierced Ava Grace because it was a reminder that her father had never missed her. Not even when she'd missed him.

Ava Grace and Mercy nibbled on their snack for a while before the screen door squeaked again. Chuck emerged with Kyle close behind him. To Ava Grace's relief, her father looked calm and refreshed, his silver hair combed neatly.

For most of his life, Chuck had worn oil-stained jeans, faded button-down shirts, and boots. But now his wardrobe consisted of shirts and trousers in soft, stretchy fabrics and slip-on shoes.

Both Ava Grace and Mercy stood, and Chuck looked back and forth between them. He zeroed in on Ava Grace, his eyes filling with recognition. Hope sparked inside her.

"I know you," Chuck stated. "You won that singing competition."

Despite the despair choking her, she smiled. "You're right, I did. My name is Ava Grace."

"That's a pretty name. I'm Chuck." He paused, confusion filling his face as he looked toward Kyle. "That big fella ... What's your name again?"

"Kyle," the former Marine answered.

It was a question Kyle answered several times a day. He had an endless supply of patience and not just with Chuck. He'd told Ava Grace it was because he was a sniper, and snipers had to "lie on their bellies for hours, sometimes days, to take out the target."

Chuck nodded. "Kyle says I live here."

"Yes," Ava Grace confirmed. "You live here with me. This is my house."

His light blue eyes darted around the porch and landed on her guitar case. "Is that your guitar?" he asked, a hint of excitement in his voice.

"Yes." She walked over to the case, unlatched it, and pulled out her baby. Cradling it carefully, she scooted onto the porch swing. "Would you like to hear a song?"

Chuck nodded. Kyle guided him to a patio chair before taking the seat she'd vacated at the café table.

"Do you have a favorite?" she asked, even though she knew the answer. This was a scene repeated too many times to count.

"I like Johnny Cash," Chuck replied.

As she played the first notes of "I Walk the Line," a smile blossomed on his lips. He began to sway in his seat, like the thousands of people who attended her concerts.

But this was a private concert just for her dad. The dad who'd never attended any of her high school choir performances. The dad who hadn't been in the audience when she won *American Star*, even though she asked him to come.

The dad who didn't even know who she was.

CHAPTER SIX

Leaning over the pool table, Beck lined up his cue stick and took his shot. The cue ball shot across the green wool, ricocheted off the side rail, and slammed into the blue two ball, propelling it forward. The ball teetered on the edge of the pocket before falling in.

"Nice shot," Gabe praised. "But you're still going to lose."

Beck flipped him off, and Gabe chuckled before taking a swig of his beer. He pointed to Beck with the bottle. "Fifty bucks says you lose this rack."

"Forget it. I'm not taking your bet."

"A hundred bucks," Gabe offered.

"No."

Gabe shrugged and threw a handful of nuts into his mouth. The man was always hungry, and he ate constantly, kind of like a cow grazing in a grassy pasture. It was a miracle he didn't weigh eight hundred pounds.

Beck took advantage of the silence and scoped out his next shot. Maybe the orange five ball.

Beck and his two best friends always spent Thursday nights at The Tweed Trilby, an old-fashioned bar near Trinity's headquarters in SoMa. Sometimes they played pool, sometimes they took in a game, and sometimes they just talked.

Tonight they were celebrating the partnership with Ava Grace Landy. They'd planned to meet at seven, but Ren was running late, something that rarely happened.

Beck had been shocked yesterday when Wally notified him that she was willing to work with Trinity. When Beck told Gabe the good news, the man nearly hurdled his desk to give him a high five. And Ren, the most stoic of all, let out a high-pitched noise that sounded remarkably like a preteen girl's excited squeal.

Lining up his stick, Beck took the shot. The cue ball slid into the yellow-striped nine ball, which pushed the orange five ball into the pocket.

Gabe whistled. "Well done."

As Beck walked around the table to get an alternate view, Gabe said, "Fifty bucks says you miss your next shot."

"How 'bout I give you fifty bucks just to shut up?" Beck asked, keeping his eyes on the pool table.

Gabe laughed. "A hundred bucks says you miss it."

Beck shook his head. "You're such a hustler."

"In this particular instance, I'm not hustling. I'm sharking. By definition, hustling is disguising one's skill with the intent of luring someone of lesser skill into gambling. We've played together before, and you're well aware of my skill. Therefore, I cannot hustle you. Sharking, on the other hand, is the process of distracting, disheartening, and enraging opponents so they'll play poorly, lose the game, and thus lose the bet."

"Thanks for the clarification," Beck replied.

"Happy to help, brother." Gabe grinned. "You can always count on me to explain complex subjects in a way your underdeveloped brain can understand."

Beck knew he could count on Gabe for more than that. He was one of the few people in the world who hadn't let Beck down. From the day they'd met as freshmen in high school, Gabe was there for him. He'd proven his loyalty time and again. Ren and Gabe were more than just his best friends. He wasn't ashamed to admit he loved them like brothers. They'd had each other's backs since high school.

Gabe and Ren stood beside Beck like sentinels when his dad was accused of embezzlement. Their friendship never wavered even as the whole world turned against Beck and his mother, seemingly overnight.

Beck's girlfriend, Callie, broke up with him the day after the Feds arrived to investigate. Her beautiful exterior hid a malicious spirit, but he was too enthralled by her sultry good looks to notice, at least until she ended things in the cafeteria in full view of the entire school.

"Everyone is talking about what your dad did," she'd said loudly, her voice carrying to every corner of the room. "I don't want to be with the son of a criminal."

She'd sniffed, as if his smell offended her. Yet she'd been on her knees in front of him the day before, his hands fisted in her inky-black hair and his dick in her mouth.

And she swallowed, thank you very much.

"You're poor now," she'd added, referring to the government freezing all of Law Beck's bank accounts and investments. "You don't even have a place to live because Jonah Beck Distillery owns your house. My mom told me the board of directors hired movers to throw out all your stuff."

He'd been young and stupid enough to love Callie, and she'd broken his heart. She mocked his personal tragedy and humiliated him, but even then, he hadn't realized how hateful she truly was.

Unfortunately, he found out several months later when she accused him of assaulting her. That was the first and only time he'd been arrested. He spent a night in jail before making bail the next day.

"Are you going to take your next shot or just stand there playing with your stick?"

Gabe's jeer startled Beck so much he dropped his cue stick. He'd totally forgotten where he was. Instead of playing pool and drinking beer with Gabe at the Trilby, he'd been back in Kentucky, scared shitless his life was over before it'd even begun.

Bending down, he grabbed his cue stick from the floor. He gave the pool table a brief glance before he took his shot. His aim was off, and the cue ball missed the target by a good nine inches.

"*Shit.*"

Gabe laughed. "Good thing you didn't take my bet."

Gabe's phone buzzed, and he snatched it up. He stared at the screen for a moment before returning it to the table.

"Was that Ren?" Beck asked.

Gabe shook his head, his shaggy brown hair falling over his forehead. "No."

Their eyes met, and Beck could read the worry in Gabe's gaze. He was worried too. Neither of them had seen Ren since he'd left the office three hours ago, and they hadn't been able to reach him via phone or text.

Beck wouldn't be so worried if Ren was unreliable. But the man was like a military precision watch. He was *never* late.

"Do you think we should go to his apartment?" Gabe asked, concern shading his voice.

"Maybe."

Beck didn't want to be an alarmist, but the thought of

something happening to Gabe or Ren sent a stab of fear through him. "I'll take care of the check while you get your truck."

As Gabe gathered his jacket and phone, Beck returned their sticks to the wall-mounted storage rack. Behind him, he heard Gabe say, "Ren's here."

The knots in Beck's gut immediately unraveled. But when he got a good look at Ren's face, they pulled tight again. Even from several feet away, Ren's face was waxy, his eyes glazed.

Gabe noticed the same thing. "Oh, shit. Something must've happened to his dad."

The moment Ren reached them, he blurted out, "I have to go to Atlanta."

"Atlanta?" Gabe echoed. "Your dad lives in Louisville."

Ren frowned. "I know."

"Then why do you have to go to Atlanta?"

"Because..." Ren swallowed noisily. "Because I have a nine-year-old daughter, and she's in Atlanta."

It took a moment for Beck to digest Ren's words. He glanced at Gabe to see if maybe he'd misunderstood, but Gabe's eyes were wide with shock.

"What the hell?" Beck exclaimed. "You have a daughter, and you never told us about her?"

"I didn't even know she existed," Ren snapped. "I just found out about her."

"*Jesus Christ*," Gabe swore.

Beck tilted his head toward an empty booth near the back of the bar. "Let's sit down. It looks like you could use a drink."

Gabe disappeared, presumably to find some liquor, and Ren dropped down into the black leather booth. Beck slid into the seat opposite him.

Ren pushed a hand through his tawny hair, and Beck noticed

it was shaking. His hands probably would be shaking too, if he'd just discovered he was a daddy. He couldn't imagine how awful it would be to realize you'd missed out on nine years of your kid's life.

Beck and Ren sat silently until Gabe returned to the booth, a bottle of premium vodka in one hand and three shot glasses in the other.

Frowning, Ren asked, "Why didn't you get Trinity?"

"They're out," Gabe explained as he placed the liquor bottle on the scarred table. "I didn't want to support our competition, so it was either vodka or tequila."

Gabe slid into the booth beside Beck before deftly pouring the shots. They swallowed them in a nearly synchronized movement, and then Gabe filled Ren's glass again before setting aside the bottle.

"Start at the beginning," Gabe ordered.

Ren threw back his second shot. "God, I hate vodka almost as much as I hate tequila," he groused, his face contorting.

"What's her name?" Beck asked.

Ren laughed mirthlessly. "Gatsby. Her name is Gatsby. As in *The Great Gatsby*." He shook his head in disgust. "What a ridiculous name for a little girl."

Beck agreed wholeheartedly with Ren, but chose not to voice his opinion. "And her mother?" he prompted.

"Corinne Nolan."

"Corinne Nolan," Gabe repeated slowly. "That doesn't sound familiar."

Ren pressed his thumb into his eyebrow as if pain had settled there. "I didn't recognize it either."

"Did we go to school with her?" Gabe asked.

Although they'd planned to attend college far from home, all three of them ended up at the University of Kentucky in Lexington. They lived in dorms during freshman year and then moved into a shabby apartment near campus.

"Yeah. She went by Corie in college."

Gabe shook his head. "I don't remember any girl named Corie."

Ren dug around in his jacket and pulled out two pictures. He stared at one before turning it facedown on the table. He held up the other one, and both Beck and Gabe leaned forward to get a better look.

It was a graduation photo, and the young woman wore the royal blue cap and gown of UK. She was neither pretty nor ugly. Her dark brown hair wasn't particularly thick or shiny, and her brown eyes were nothing special. She had a nice smile though.

Beck lifted his gaze from the picture to meet Ren's eyes. "Never seen her."

"Me neither," Gabe chimed in.

Ren rolled his lips inward. "Remember that party we went to a couple of days before graduation … the one in that old, rundown mansion on the western edge of campus?"

"Vaguely," Beck answered. "That was ten years ago."

Ren rubbed the back of his neck. "She was there. Supposedly we had sex in the pantry. I was drunk. I don't remember."

Beck frowned. "What do you mean *supposedly*?"

"The PI told me."

"PI?" Gabe asked.

"Yeah. He was waiting for me when I got home."

"Corinne Nolan hired a PI to find you?" Beck asked. "Why now, after all these years? Why didn't she bother to track you down when she found out she was pregnant? And why did she hire a PI? It's not like you're hard to find. She could've just done a web search."

"She's dead," Ren muttered . "She died in a car accident three months ago. Gatsby has been living with Corinne's aunt, but she's old and sick. Really sick. Corinne didn't have any other family, and the aunt didn't want Gatsby to become a ward of the state. She's the one who hired the PI. Corinne didn't name a father on Gatsby's birth certificate, and she never told her aunt who Gatsby's father was."

Gabe grabbed the vodka and filled their glasses to the rim. They threw them back, gasping at the burn.

When Beck got his breath back, he asked, "How did the PI find you?"

"The aunt had a box of Corinne's old journals in the attic, and he read them for clues. He said she wrote about everything. Every guy she'd been with. When, where, how."

"Did the bitch also write about why she didn't bother to tell you that you had a daughter?" Beck asked sarcastically.

Gabe kicked him in the shin. "Not now," he hissed under his breath before saying in a louder voice, "Just because Corinne wrote about you doesn't mean you're Gatsby's father. You need to take a DNA test."

"She's mine," Ren stated flatly. "I have no doubt."

"How do you know?" Beck asked.

Ren flipped over the facedown picture and pushed it across the table with his forefinger. Beck and Gabe peered down at the image of a little girl. She had bright blond hair, big silvery eyes, and a cute bow at the top of her pink mouth.

"Damn," Gabe breathed, "she looks just like you, Ren. Except for the long hair and the dolphin earrings."

"I know." Ren brought Gatsby's picture back to his side of the table and traced her little face with his fingertip. "I have a daughter," he whispered, "and I want her with me."

Beck nodded. If he had a daughter, he'd want her with him too. But he'd be scared shitless in Ren's position.

Ren looked up. "I couldn't get a flight to Atlanta until tomorrow morning. I don't know how long I'll be gone. I can't force Gatsby to come back to San Francisco when she doesn't even know me."

"Don't worry about it," Beck said. "We can handle things here. Take as long as you need."

"What are we going to do about Ava Grace?" Ren asked.

Earlier, Beck asked Ren to be Ava Grace's main point of contact within Trinity. It made sense for him to work with her since he was in charge of marketing.

"She can wait until you get back," Beck answered.

Gabe shook his head. "I disagree. We're damn lucky she agreed to work with us in the first place, and we need to make the most of our time."

"She can wait," Beck repeated. "Ren has more important things to think about."

"She's on a plane right now, flying here," Ren announced. "When I talked to her yesterday, she said she was eager to get started. We were going to meet tomorrow afternoon. She doesn't know much about bourbon, so I was going to give her a lesson on bourbon basics, and then we were going to brainstorm ideas for our marketing campaign."

"Don't worry," Beck assured him. "Gabe and I can handle that."

Gabe frowned. "I'm flying home tomorrow morning. Remember? I promised my mom I'd go antiquing with her this weekend. I canceled my last trip, and I really don't want to disappoint her again."

Gabe's mother, Annabelle, was one of the nicest women

Beck had ever known. When his dad had died, and he needed a place to live so he could finish his senior year of high school, Annabelle welcomed him into her home. And when Callie tried to ruin his life, Annabelle was one of the few people who hadn't believed his ex-girlfriend's lies.

"I don't want you to disappoint her, either." Beck rubbed the top of his head. "Don't cancel your trip."

Ren grimaced. "Why would you waste your time antiquing? There are so many better things to do."

"Because it makes my mom happy, and I want to spend time with her."

Beck could understand why Gabe wanted to make Annabelle happy and spend time with her. In fact, if she were Beck's mother, he might be one of those sons who went antiquing too. But his mother wasn't anything like Annabelle, and he couldn't care less about making Sibley Beck happy or spending time with her.

He hadn't seen or spoken to his mother since she'd packed up her belongings and blown out of town shortly after the Feds knocked on their door. Beck hadn't been surprised when Sibley decided not to stand by her man, but he hadn't expected her to forget she had a son.

Gabe nudged Beck's forearm with his elbow. "Since Ren and I are going to be unavailable, it looks like Ava Grace is all yours."

CHAPTER SEVEN

Deep cracks snaked across the sidewalk leading to Trinity's office, and Ava Grace gingerly picked her way around them. She didn't want the five-inch heels of her strappy black stilettos to get stuck. At best, she'd be embarrassed. At worst, she'd break her ankle.

She usually wore cowboy boots or ballet flats, but she'd decided today's meeting with Beck required do-me heels and a short, sexy dress. Admittedly, it was an outfit better suited to a night out. But she had a very good reason for wearing it. She wanted Beck's attention. She wanted to see lust burning in his dark eyes.

Ever since she and Mercy had talked at the farmhouse, Ava Grace couldn't stop thinking about the sad state of her sex life. It really was pathetic.

Mercy was right—working with Trinity offered Ava Grace the perfect opportunity to get to know Beck better. She needed to take advantage of it. Take advantage of *him*.

As she reached the door, she gripped the handle. Nerves made her hands sweaty, and the steel slipped through her fingers.

Beck was the first man she'd ever chased, and she wasn't

entirely comfortable being the pursuer. She didn't want to come across as desperate, but she didn't want to be too subtle either.

Irritated with herself, she shook her head and wiped her hand on the stretchy material of her red dress. *There's no reason to be so nervous!*

She'd sung live in front of millions of people when she competed on *American Star*. She'd toured the nation with some of the hottest acts in country music. She'd been a guest on every major morning and late-night TV show.

If she could handle all that, she could handle a one-on-one meeting with Beck.

Suddenly, lurid images of being *one-on-one* with him flooded her mind—his hard body on top of hers, his chest cushioned against her breasts, and her legs wrapped around his waist.

Her stomach fluttered and warmed, and she pressed her palm against it. Maybe she couldn't handle a one-on-one meeting with Beck after all ... not without making a fool of herself.

Why was it easier to flirt with guys she wasn't attracted to rather than a guy she really was interested in?

She took a deep breath and slowly exhaled before pulling open the door. It was cool and quiet inside the warehouse, but she heard the faint sound of male voices. She ventured deeper into the building, her heels clicking against the concrete floor.

"Hello," she called out, wincing when her voice echoed.

Beck's voice boomed from the back of the warehouse. "Be right there."

She turned toward his voice, and he emerged from an open doorway. He wore jeans topped with a faded maroon T-shirt inscribed with: *Keep Your Friends Close and Your Bourbon Closer.* She wondered how many of those bourbon shirts he owned.

He made his way to her in a long-legged stride, his boots

making a hollow thump with every step. As he stopped in front of her, one side of his mouth lifted in a smile.

"Good afternoon, Miz Landy."

She held out her right hand, and he stepped closer. With her sky-high heels, they were almost the same height. "Total strangers stop me on the street and call me Ava Grace. You can too."

Staring into her eyes, he took her hand. "Good afternoon, Ava Grace."

It was the first time she'd heard him say her name. His deep drawl, along with his warm, callused hand, made her mind go blank. It took her a moment to respond.

"Good afternoon, Beck," she replied, her voice huskier than normal.

Her extreme response to him sent unease slithering through her. She couldn't think of any other man who impacted her like Beck.

"Thanks for coming by today," he said.

"I'm…" Her lips were dry, and when she licked them, his gaze dropped to her mouth. The warmth in her belly started to simmer. "Excited," she finished breathlessly.

His fingers tightened on hers before he abruptly dropped her hand and stepped backward, putting more space between them. "Ren was upset he couldn't be here, but he had a family emergency."

"What happened?" she asked, knowing the question was nosy, nosy, nosy.

Beck gave her a censuring look. "It's a *family* emergency."

She smiled, neither embarrassed nor repentant. Her *curiosity* was one of her worst and best traits.

"I'm horribly nosy," she confessed, pushing her loose hair over her shoulder. "I don't even try to control it anymore. It takes too much effort. And I eavesdrop too."

Beck stared at her, clearly stunned by her admissions. Then he threw back his head and laughed. The rumbling sound ricocheted off the high ceilings.

"Amelia says I could've had a great career in law enforcement if I hadn't won *American Star.*"

"Landy, Texas Ranger." Beck's grin showed off his straight, white teeth. "It has a nice ring to it."

She laughed. "Well, I'd rather use handcuffs than wear them, that's for sure."

His eyes widened, a swath of red settling high on his cheekbones. He cleared his throat roughly. "Umm…"

She hadn't intended any sexual innuendo, but he certainly had heard one. And now that he obviously had sex on his mind, she decided it was the perfect time to call attention to her outfit.

"If I were a Texas Ranger, I couldn't wear a dress like this." She skimmed her hands over the red fabric covering her hips. "Where would I put my gun?"

She tapped a finger against her bottom lip, and his gaze fell to her mouth. "I'd probably have to strap it to my leg," she said, pivoting her knee outward and patting her bare thigh.

His glance slid down to her leg, and she watched him as she stroked her hand a little higher, just under the hem of her dress. He breathed deeply, the movement of his broad chest noticeable.

"And I'd have to put my badge here," she added, trailing her hand from her thigh to her chest.

His eyes followed her hand. She stopped when she reached the low-cut square neckline.

Dipping her forefinger into her cleavage, she murmured, "I'd put it right here."

She moved her finger up and down. His nostrils flared, and the color on his cheekbones spread to the rest of his face.

"Where would you put it, Beck?" she asked softly.

His head snapped up, and when their eyes met, she saw exactly what she'd hoped: lust. A volcano of desire erupted inside her, flooding like lava through her veins and pooling between her legs.

They stared at each other, still and silent. All too soon, the fiery lust in his eyes cooled.

"This is a working distillery," he growled. "Next time you visit, wear something more appropriate."

His chastising words made embarrassment creep through her. But she hid it behind a sarcastic question, "And what would be more appropriate?"

She knew the answer, of course. But overalls and steel-toed boots wouldn't have caught his attention.

"Clothes," he snapped.

"I *am* wearing clothes," she replied in a dulcet tone.

He snorted. "Just barely." Looking down at her feet, he snorted again. "And your shoes ... are you training to be a dominatrix?"

"No." She smiled sweetly. "I already graduated."

He barked out a harsh laugh. "With straight As, no doubt." He studied her for a moment before tilting his head toward the doorway. "Ready to learn about bourbon?"

He didn't wait for her to respond. He led the way, and she followed, taking care not to trip. He'd probably laugh if she did, or say *I told you so*. She growled under her breath, overwhelmed with a new desire—the desire to kick his tight butt with the pointy tip of her dominatrix shoe.

"This is my office, at least until we renovate the warehouse," he announced as she crossed the threshold.

The cardboard boxes were the first thing she noticed. They covered every inch of the concrete floor. She wasn't an organization freak, but her fingers itched to unpack them.

The back wall was exposed red brick and featured several large windows. A rectangular whiteboard hung on the side wall, also red brick. The walls, coupled with the sleek glass-and-metal desk and black leather chairs, created an industrial-meets-high-tech vibe. A large computer monitor and keyboard sat on the desk, along with several bottles of bourbon and a number of crystal tumblers engraved with the Trinity logo.

"Have a seat," he invited, gesturing to the chairs.

While he stood next to his desk, watching her with those coffee-colored eyes, she tossed her purse in one of the chairs and sat in the other. She crossed her legs, slowly, deliberately, and enjoyed a whisper of satisfaction when his gaze flicked to them.

His jaw tightened before he moved toward the whiteboard. After picking up the dry erase marker, he began to write. His shirt pulled tight across his shoulders, emphasizing the lean muscles of his back.

Clenching the armrests, she scooted the chair until it faced the whiteboard. He'd written *Bourbon 101* at the top in large block letters, but his body hid the rest of the board. After a couple of minutes, he shoved the cap back on the marker and turned.

"You might want to take notes," he suggested curtly.

"I think I'll be okay. I have a good memory." She gave him a teasing, flirtatious smile. "And if I have to, Professor Beck, I'll stay after class for special tutoring. Maybe you can suggest a couple of ways I can earn some extra credit."

*****

Beck kept his gaze on Ava Grace's face, trying not to think about her earning "extra credit" on her knees with her hot mouth wrapped around his cock. Her plump lips were slick with red gloss the same color as her miniscule dress.

Jesus, that dress. And those shoes. Just kill me now.

She tilted her head, and long hair spilled over her shoulders in a waterfall of pale amber and champagne. It was beautiful—thick and shiny—and he wondered if she was a natural blonde. An evil voice inside him whispered, *Why don't you find out?*

Taking a deep breath, he forced his mind to focus on bourbon instead of blow jobs and blond bushes. He spun to face the whiteboard again and shifted to the side so she could see.

"Okay, the first thing you need to know: bourbon is an alcoholic distillate from a fermented mash of grain. That definition applies to all whiskey, and it's important to understand all bourbon is whiskey, but not all whiskey is bourbon."

"What's the difference?"

"There are several differences." He pointed to the first bullet point on the whiteboard. "First, bourbon is an American spirit. Federal regulations require whiskey to be made in the U.S. to qualify as bourbon."

"So other countries can make bourbon, but they just can't call it that?"

He glanced over his shoulder and found Ava Grace's gaze locked on his ass. He wasn't sure any woman had ever ogled him quite so blatantly. Her obvious appreciation made his cock throb.

He swallowed hard before turning back to the whiteboard. "If other countries make bourbon, they have to label it whiskey," he confirmed. "The second thing that differentiates whiskey from bourbon is the grain, both the types of grain and the percentage of each grain. Bourbon is made from corn, malted barley, and either rye or wheat."

He moved to his desk and picked up one of the glass containers used to bottle Trinity. Instead of liquid, however, the triangular-shaped vessel was filled with layers of grain.

Holding the bottle in one hand, he pointed to the grain with the other. "This is Trinity's grain recipe. It represents the percentages of each grain we use."

He extended the bottle to Ava Grace, and she grasped it with her slender hands. Raising it in front of her face, she studied the contents.

"Most bourbons on the market today are made with rye," he continued. "Trinity is a rye bourbon."

She looked up, her eyes more green than gold in the late-afternoon sunshine. "How many bourbons are on the market?"

"If you include all the craft distilleries like Trinity, there are hundreds of bourbons. But only fifteen or so use wheat instead of rye."

Her dark blond brows rose. "You *do* have a lot of competition. Maybe you should make Trinity with wheat instead of rye so you'd have less."

"The overwhelming majority of bourbon drinkers prefer rye bourbon. Plus, I'm not afraid of a little competition." He smiled at her. "And I know you're not either. You not only beat out thousands of people to be on *American Star*, you won the whole damn contest."

Beck wasn't a fan of reality TV. Nonetheless, he knew winning a national singing competition like *American Star* required more than just talent. It required a hell of a lot of guts and determination.

He propped his ass on the edge of his desk, stretched out his legs, and crossed his ankles. He was curious about her experience with *American Star*. Hell, he was curious about *her*. He had been since he heard her sing at Quinn and Amelia's wedding.

"How many people try out for *American Star*?"

"Something like fifty thousand."

"*Holy shit!* That would fill an entire football stadium."

She laughed softly. "And now I sing for entire stadiums." She rested the grain-filled Trinity bottle in her lap and leaned forward, her luscious breasts just inches from his thigh. "Can I tell you a secret?"

Tell me all your secrets.

"Go for it," he invited.

"You have to promise not to tell anyone."

"Yeah, okay, I promise."

"I just heard from Wally that the NFL wants me to record the Sunday Night Football theme song—the one that kicks off all the games." She gave him one of her breathtaking, imperfect smiles. "Sunday Night Football is the most-watched prime-time show. More than twenty million viewers. It's a really big deal for me."

He whistled. "That is a big deal. Congratulations."

The NFL deal was further proof Ava Grace had some serious star power. He was damn lucky she was willing to work with Trinity, and he silently vowed to be polite and professional, regardless of how short and tight her dress was.

"Thank you." She leaned back in her chair. "Please, Professor Beck, continue with your lesson."

"Where were we?"

"Grain percentages."

"Okay. For a whiskey to be considered bourbon, it must be

made from *at least* fifty-one percent corn and *no more* than seventy-nine percent corn."

He stood and rounded his desk. He pulled open the bottom drawer, and as he rummaged around in it, he said, "That brings me to the next difference between whiskey and bourbon: the barrel and aging." He looked up. "Do you know what aging is, or do I need to explain it?"

"Isn't it just the process of putting bourbon in a barrel and letting it *age*?"

"Yeah, basically," he answered, resuming his search for the four-inch piece of wood he'd cut from one of Trinity's used barrels. "By law, bourbon must age for at least two years in a *new* oak barrel. Distillers can't use barrels more than once."

He finally spotted the wood and nabbed it from the drawer. Straightening, he nudged the drawer shut with his knee before holding up the wood.

"This is a piece of oak from a Trinity barrel." He passed it to Ava Grace. "See how it's black on one side? The inside of the barrels are burned at very high temperatures. They're *charred*. The charring gives the bourbon its color and adds to its flavor."

She rubbed her fingers over the burned wood before raising it to her nose. "I can smell the bourbon."

He nodded. "The oak is porous enough that some of the bourbon soaks into it. When that happens, the char flakes off. A lot of distilleries sell dried char pieces to barbeque joints."

She held out the wood, and he took it from her, making sure not to touch her. He didn't need to be reminded how soft and smooth her fingers were.

"Bourbon must be distilled at no more than 160 proof, which is eighty percent alcohol by volume," he explained. "Do you know how proof is determined?"

She looked at him blankly, and he chuckled. "That's okay. We can discuss proof another day."

After depositing the wood on his desk, he picked up a bottle of bourbon. "The final difference is nothing can be added to the bourbon to enhance it. The color and the flavor must come solely from the mash, the water, and the barrel."

He worked the cork out of the bottle and poured a finger of bourbon into a tumbler. "This is from Jonah Beck Distillery in Nelson County, Kentucky." He passed the glass to her. "It's won several awards. By the way, if you drink your bourbon without water or ice, you drink it *neat*."

"There's not a lot of creativity in your family, is there?" she asked.

Her question, her *criticism*, was so out-of-the-blue it took him a moment to reply. "What makes you say that?"

"You're all named Jonah. That's just pure laziness."

He laughed. "We have different middle names. My dad was Jonah Lawson Beck. Everybody called him Law. And his father, my grandfather, was Jonah Sanger Beck. He went by Joe."

"And everybody calls you Beck."

"Yeah."

"Always? No one calls you by your first name?"

"No. I've been Beck since birth."

"I like Jonah."

Hearing her husky voice say his name—the name no one used—sent a weird thrill through him. He didn't think he'd mind if she called him Jonah.

"What's your middle name?" she asked.

That was something he didn't want to share, so he ignored her question. "What's your middle name?"

"Grace," she answered with a smirk. He slapped his palm

70

against his forehead, and she snickered. "Now that you know my middle name, are you going to tell me yours?"

"No."

She sighed gustily. "It must be really embarrassing ... like Percival or Mortimer."

He ignored her jibes. "Do you know how to drink bourbon?"

She stared down into the tumbler before looking back at him. "With my mouth," she answered, her voice as dry as a creek during a drought.

Her quip made him laugh, but it died in his throat when he realized he couldn't remember the last time he'd been amused and aroused at the same time. She was even more dangerous than he'd thought.

"Bourbon is a sipping whiskey, not a slam-it-back whiskey," he explained. "You have to take your time with it." He gestured to the tumbler. "Hold your glass in both hands for a few seconds to warm the bourbon."

She immediately wrapped her fingers around the tumbler, her nails shimmering with sparkly beige polish. He wondered what those fingers would feel like wrapped around his cock, and he barely bit back a groan.

"What next?" she asked. "Should I swirl it around?"

"Bourbon isn't watered-down grape juice. You shouldn't swirl it or stick your nose into your glass."

"Watered-down grape juice?"

"Also known as wine."

"I don't like wine," she said as if she were confessing a terrible crime. "I like beer better."

"Me too." He picked up an empty tumbler. "Place your nose just above the rim of the glass." He showed her what he meant. "Open your mouth a bit and breathe through your mouth and nose at the same time."

She followed his lead, and he said, "You should be able to smell vanilla and caramel."

Nodding, she said, "I smell it."

"Now sip just enough bourbon to cover your tongue. Part your lips slightly and draw in some air over the liquid. Hold it in your mouth for a few seconds and let it wash over your tongue."

She followed his instructions, and he noticed a droplet of liquid glistening on her lower lip. Her pink tongue darted out to catch it, and in that moment, he couldn't think of anything he wanted more than to sip bourbon from her mouth.

An image flashed across his mind—Ava Grace's smooth skin drenched in Trinity, the liquor dribbling over her breasts and pooling in her belly button before trickling into the fluff on her pussy. He'd suck every last droplet off her body, starting with her nipples and ending with her clit.

"What next?" Ava Grace asked, forcing his mind back to their bourbon lesson.

Trying to ignore his thickened cock, he said, "Now take a swallow."

She raised her glass and took a drink. He gave her a moment before asking, "Did you feel it on the way down?"

She placed her hand on her throat, just above the smooth skin of her chest. "Feels like fire," she gasped.

He plucked the glass from her hand. "Yeah, it could be smoother."

Leaning over, he grabbed a bottle of Trinity and removed the cork. After splashing some into an empty tumbler, he held it up.

"This was five years in the making. It won the bronze medal in the International Spirits Competition last year."

Passing the tumbler to her, he said, "Same process."

He crossed his arms over his chest while she drank his pride and joy. His blood, sweat, and tears.

His future.

CHAPTER EIGHT

Learning the proper way to drink bourbon really changed the way it tasted. Even so, the spirit would never be Ava Grace's beverage of choice, unless it was mixed with Dr Pepper.

"You should've let me try Trinity first instead of the other one," she told Beck. "Always start with the best. That's what I do at my concerts."

"What about saving the best for last?" he countered.

"I'm kind of impatient," she admitted. "Another one of my stellar personality traits."

"So you're a nosy, impatient eavesdropper." He shot her a teasing look. "Do you have any good qualities, Miz Landy?"

"You're going to have to figure that out on your own."

He dropped his arms to his sides, his short sleeves revealing muscular forearms dusted with dark hair. A stainless-steel watch encircled his left wrist, along with a thin brown leather bracelet. Something was engraved on the clasp, but she wasn't close enough to read it.

"How do you think Trinity compares to the bourbon from Jonah Beck Distillery?" he asked.

"I definitely like Trinity more."

He smiled. "I'm glad to hear that."

What she didn't say was both bourbons had set fire to her throat and scorched her lungs. She was afraid she'd never sing again, which would be extremely unfortunate because, one, she was good at it, and two, she made a lot of money doing it.

"You should be proud of your bourbon, Beck. You should be proud of what you've accomplished."

He stared at her for several heartbeats. "Are you proud of what you've accomplished?"

It was an intensely personal question, one that surprised her. "Sometimes."

"Sometimes?" His eyebrows arched. "Your last album went platinum in less than three weeks, and you have five number one songs. I'd say that's something to be proud of."

She shrugged. "The music business is cutthroat, and I'm not just talking about record label executives and other artists. I'm talking about the fans too. You're only as good as your next song, your next concert, your next public appearance. It's hard to stay on top. Everything could be gone this quick," she said, snapping her fingers.

A loud *ding-dong* filled the room, and she jumped. It sounded like the noise had come from his computer.

He glanced at his watch. "Sorry, that's my reminder." He uncrossed his ankles and straightened from his perch on the desk. "I didn't realize it was already six."

Her curiosity must have been evident because he explained, "I lose track of time when I'm working in the office, and if I don't set a reminder, I'm here until eight or nine o'clock. And by then, my dog has chewed through the door." He grimaced. "I know we were supposed to brainstorm ideas, and I hate to do this but—"

"Maybe your dog can help us brainstorm."

He frowned. "What?"

"We can brainstorm at your place. I don't mind. You can take me back to Quinn and Amelia's when we're finished."

His eyes widened, and she swallowed a giggle. She knew it was rude to invite herself into his home. She wasn't completely lacking in manners—her grandmother had seen to that. But she wanted to spend more time with Beck.

Leaning forward, she placed the tumbler of bourbon and the grain-filled bottle on his desk and then rose from the terribly uncomfortable chair. She made a mental note to tell him that he needed to replace these chairs and repair the cracks in the sidewalk leading to the front door.

She grabbed her bag and headed for the door. Once she reached it, she looked over her shoulder. Beck stood frozen next to his desk, a bewildered frown on his face.

"Why are you just standing there? Your dog is waiting. Let's go."

Twenty minutes later, Ava Grace followed Beck down a narrow sidewalk beside his apartment building. "What is this neighborhood called?" she asked.

"Dogpatch."

"That's an ugly name for such a cute neighborhood."

"It's been gentrified over the past fifteen years or so." Beck stopped in front of a bright yellow door with a decorative metal 4 on the front. "It's one of the oldest neighborhoods in the city. It used to be mostly blue-collar."

After unlocking the door, he placed his hand on the knob and glanced over his shoulder. "A word of warning: my dog is very friendly. And my loft is very…"

She waited, but he didn't finish his sentence. "Well-decorated?" she teased. "Well-kept? Well-organized?"

He chuckled. "Not exactly."

He opened the door, and a wiggling mass of curly orange fur slammed into him, whining loudly. Beck stepped backward and grabbed the doorjamb with one hand to steady himself.

"Hey, boy," he crooned, dropping his hand to rub the dog's head. "Did you have a good day?"

The pooch closed his eyes in bliss, and she couldn't help laughing. She'd probably do the same thing if Beck rubbed her with those big hands. She shifted, and the dog's eyes popped open and turned toward her.

"Sit," Beck commanded, making a grab for the dog's collar. He missed, and the dog darted around him.

"Brace yourself," he warned at the same time the large animal lunged for her, his head ramming into her crotch. She stumbled in her stilettos, and Beck caught her arm before she windmilled backward. Placing her free hand on top of the dog's head, she gently pushed him back.

"Sit," she ordered softly.

The dog immediately obeyed, his black eyes worshipping her and his pink tongue lolling out of his mouth. Beck released her arm, and she looked back and forth between him and his pet.

"Is he a Labradoodle?" she asked, having seen one in pictures but never in person.

Beck nodded. "Part Labrador retriever, part poodle." He glanced down at his dog and pointed toward the interior of the apartment. "Inside."

The dog jumped to his feet and dashed inside. Beck caught her eye and tilted his head toward the door. "You too. Inside."

"Careful now," she warned lightly. "You're not my master."

He muttered something under his breath … something that

sounded a lot like *thank God*.

She entered the apartment with him close behind her. Slipping past her, he hurried to the French doors at the back of the room and jerked a retractable leash off a hook.

"This won't take long," he promised as he snapped the leash onto the dog's collar. "Make yourself comfortable."

After Beck and his dog disappeared into the courtyard, she checked out his digs. Designed as a true loft, it was completely open with no partitions except for the bathroom. Exposed metal ductwork spanned the high ceiling. Windows stretched across two walls, which were painted a soothing bluish-gray.

A gray leather sectional and big-screen TV filled the majority of the living space. His sleeping area was tucked into a corner, a long espresso-stained wood dresser and matching armoire against the exterior wall. Two matching nightstands flanked his low-platform bed.

She let her eyes linger on the king-size bed. It was unmade, the cream-colored sheets rumpled and the comforter pushed to the footboard. She couldn't stand an unmade bed and had to suppress the urge to straighten the bed linens and fluff the pillows. If she got her way, someday soon she'd be naked in that bed with Beck, and then she wouldn't care if it was made or not.

She spotted a horizontal cabinet under the TV dotted with several picture frames. Curious about the photos, she made her way over to them. One caught her attention immediately, and she picked it up. A man and a little boy stood in front of a massive stainless-steel pot. It was an old picture, but the man looked just like Beck.

Was this a young Beck and his father, the man everyone called Law?

She knew bits and pieces about Beck's life before he'd moved to San Francisco, but she wanted to know more. She wanted to hear it from the man himself, preferably over dinner.

The French doors opened, and Beck's dog bounded inside. He immediately ran to her, panting with doggy joy. Too bad Beck didn't act the same way when he saw her.

"What's your name, sweet boy?"

"Chicken," Beck said.

She bent down and scratched behind one of the dog's floppy ears. Beck made a muffled noise, kind of a strangled moan, and she glanced up. He was staring at her boobs, his eyes slightly glazed.

Good. That was why she'd worn the dress.

"Chicken?" she repeated. "Why would you name him that? He looks like a stuffed animal."

Beck jerked his eyes from her chest. When he realized she'd caught him checking her out, a wave of red washed over his face.

He cleared his throat roughly. "What?"

"Why did you name your dog Chicken?"

He smiled slowly, the skin around his eyes crinkling. "Because he looks just like fried chicken. Extra crispy." His smile widened. "Don't you think so?"

She eyed Chicken. His burnished orange fur was groomed close to his body, the curls springy and tight.

"Well, now that you mention it, he *does* look like extra-crispy fried chicken." She ran her fingernails through Chicken's soft fur. "You should've named him Colonel Sanders."

Beck laughed softly. "I guess you were right when you said my family isn't very creative with names."

She crossed to the sectional and sat down on one end before patting the cushion next to her. "Here, boy."

Chicken jumped up beside her, stretched out his long body,

and put his head in her lap. As she stroked his warm belly, she caught Beck's eyes.

"Speaking of chicken, I'm hungry," she said casually. "Why don't you order some takeout, and we can brainstorm over dinner."

"Takeout?" he echoed.

"I'm fine with whatever you want. Pizza. Chinese. Indian. Greek."

"Umm ... okay," he replied, looking dazed and confused.

And that's just the way I want him.

*****

The drive from Beck's loft in Dogpatch to Quinn and Amelia's house in Laurel Heights took about twenty minutes. Beck and Ava Grace made the trip in silence. It wasn't an awkward silence; instead, it felt strangely comfortable to Beck.

As he drove up in front of the house, Ava Grace glanced out the window. The porch light illuminated the black front door and the flower-bordered steps leading up to it.

"I always worry the paparazzi will show up here, but so far that hasn't happened." She held up her hand and crossed her fingers. "Fingers crossed."

"Fingers crossed," he echoed, a hollow feeling in his chest.

Her comment was a reminder their lives couldn't be more different. She was so famous paparazzi stalked her, hoping to get a photograph of her without makeup. He, meanwhile, could take Chicken out for a walk in his pajamas, and no one noticed or cared.

She shifted in her seat to look at him. He got a waft of her perfume, a sweet cream-soda smell that made his mouth water.

"Thanks for driving me home," she said.

"You're welcome." Unable to ignore the manners Miss

Hazel's School of Etiquette had drilled into him, he switched off his Jeep. "I'll walk you up."

She waited for him to open the car door, and he had the bizarre feeling they were on a date. As she stepped out of the vehicle, he stared off into the distance, making sure not to look at her.

When she'd gotten into the Jeep earlier, he'd been stupid enough to check out her legs. Now he couldn't stop thinking about them wrapped around his waist, or better yet, hooked over his shoulders while he ate her pussy.

He followed Ava Grace up the steps to the front door, keeping his distance so his face wasn't anywhere near her ass— that tight, round ass that just begged him to squeeze it. When they reached the porch, she turned to him. The porch light created a halo around her head, glinting off her bright hair.

"Thank you for the bourbon lesson and dinner, Beck. I had a really good time."

Her words sounded a lot like something a woman would say at the end of a date, just before the guy moved in for a good-night kiss. Beck reminded himself this wasn't a date, so therefore he wasn't going to pull her close and taste those luscious lips.

He waited, expecting her to unlock the door, but she just stood there in front of him, a tiny smile curving her lips. As he stared into her face, his muscles tightened and the fine hair on his body lifted.

"Would you like to come in?" she asked, her voice barely above a whisper.

Yeah, I'd like to come in. And then I'd like to come in you.

"No," he answered curtly.

Ava Grace was critical to Trinity's future, and Beck had no intention of jeopardizing the company he'd built from nothing.

Trinity's success was far more important than his personal happiness.

Besides, he and Ava Grace were all wrong for each other. She stood in the spotlight, on a stage in front of thousands of fans. He stood in the shadows of the rickhouse, surrounded by hundreds of bourbon barrels.

Ava Grace lightly touched his bicep, and he jerked involuntarily. "Come in," she coaxed, "and have some pie."

Pie?

"I made it myself," she added.

He started to shake his head, but then she said, "Bourbon pecan pie with maple whipped cream."

And those were the magic words. "Okay," he agreed, because a smart man never turned down bourbon pecan pie, especially when it was topped with whipped cream.

A huge smile lit up her face, and he couldn't help smiling back. She unlocked the door, and they entered the big Victorian. It was the kind of home he'd like to own eventually, but Trinity was his priority right now.

He couldn't count the number of times he'd been in Quinn and Amelia's house. When they entertained as a couple, Beck was usually on the guest list, and he was a regular at Quinn's monthly poker night.

"I'm back, and I invited Beck in for some dessert," Ava Grace announced loudly as she walked toward the living area. She'd obviously made the mistake of not announcing herself in the past. She must've learned her lesson.

In the living room, Quinn and Amelia were relaxing on the brown leather sofa. She sat on one end, while he was stretched out with his head in her lap.

As usual, Quinn was wearing jeans. Beck knew without

looking Quinn's last name was stamped on the back pocket of his jeans. His great-great-grandfather, Riley O'Brien, had founded the nation's first denim company in the mid-1800s.

The company's signature jeans, known as Rileys, were as American as baseball and apple pie. Quinn served as the president and CEO of Riley O'Brien & Co., and Amelia was in charge of the women's division.

Quinn grabbed the TV remote and muted the sound. "Good to see you, chief."

"Did you kids have a good time?" Amelia joked.

"Yes," Ava Grace replied. "A very good time."

To Beck's surprise, he agreed with Ava Grace. He'd enjoyed spending time with her. She was surprisingly witty, and her self-deprecating sense of humor made him laugh.

Quinn sat up. "Did I hear you say something about dessert, AG?"

Ava Grace nodded. "Bourbon pecan pie with maple whipped cream. Want to join us?"

Quinn practically leapt from the sofa. "Hell, yes."

Minutes later, the four of them were in the kitchen nook, grouped around a dining room table that looked like a white picket fence. Beck stared down at his plate, trying not to drool over the huge slice of bourbon pecan pie. A giant dollop of whipped cream covered it, a sprig of mint crowning the fluffy peak.

He loaded some pie onto his fork and took a bite. Flavor exploded in his mouth, and his eyes nearly rolled back in his head.

"*Oh, Jesus*," he moaned, feeling like he was having an out-of-body experience.

Quinn laughed. "I guess we should have warned you."

Beck shoveled another bite into his mouth. The rich taste of caramel blended with the crunch of toasted pecans and the mellow vanilla undertones of bourbon. The buttery crust was so light and flakey it melted in his mouth, and the whipped cream was sweet and cool.

As he swallowed, he looked at Ava Grace. She was staring at him, a hint of a smile on her lips.

"There are no words to describe this pie, only noises," he told her.

"I can't take all the credit. You had something to do with it."

He frowned in confusion. "What did I do?"

She laughed softly. "You made the bourbon, handsome."

Her casual endearment sent shockwaves down his spine, and he struggled to gather his thoughts. "You made this with Trinity?"

"Of course," she answered, as if no other bourbons existed.

"This is the best bourbon pecan pie I've ever had, and I've had a lot," he said.

Ava Grace's cheeks turned pink. "Thank you. I've been thinking about writing a cookbook."

Although Ava Grace had referred to herself as an artist, Beck thought businesswoman was a more accurate description. During their brainstorming session at his loft, he'd discovered she understood sales and marketing better than ninety-nine percent of the people who had attended Stanford with him.

"Other country singers have written cookbooks, and they've been very successful," Amelia noted. "Trisha Yearwood's cookbooks were *New York Times* best sellers."

Quinn chimed in, "Cookbooks have given her another way to connect with fans and make new ones."

"What if I wrote a cookbook of bourbon recipes?" Ava Grace suggested. "It would build brand awareness for Trinity, kind of like the Pillsbury cookbooks."

Taking another bite of pie, Beck considered her idea. Like wine, bourbon added flavor to almost any food, even fish.

"You said you wanted to attract more women consumers," Ava Grace reminded him, clearly trying to sell him on the idea. "Most women cook, and even if they don't drink bourbon, they might be willing to cook with it."

"I think it's a great idea," he said.

Quinn and Amelia spoke simultaneously. "Me too."

"How difficult is it to get a cookbook published?" Beck asked, directing his question to no one in particular.

"I don't know about cookbooks specifically, but several publishers have contacted me about writing an autobiography." Ava Grace snorted. "I wouldn't pay to read that book."

I would.

Ava Grace intrigued him, even though he didn't want to be intrigued. When he saw her on the cover of a magazine, he read. When he saw her online, he clicked. When he saw her on TV, he watched.

And when he saw her in person, he wanted.

"I'll have Wally contact some of those publishers and see if they might be interested in a cookbook," Ava Grace said. "I think it could be a really effective way to market Trinity. Several cooking shows have asked me to be a special guest, and a cookbook would be the perfect tie-in. And every major morning show has a cooking segment."

Beck nodded. "It would be awesome to see Trinity on TV."

"Then let's make it happen," she said before taking a big bite of pie.

Whipped cream clung to her upper lip, and she removed it with a delicate flick of her tongue. His cock hardened with alarming speed, and he jerked his eyes from her mouth and looked down at his pie. Shifting in his seat, he tried to make room in his jeans for his hard-on.

"Beyond the cookbook, did y'all come up with any good ideas for Ava Grace to promote Trinity?" Amelia asked.

"I think so," Ava Grace responded. "Beck had the best idea though."

"What is it?" Amelia asked him.

"I think we should take advantage of Ava Grace's talent, not just her name," Beck answered. "I want her to write a song for Trinity—one that can be downloaded for free only on our website."

Amelia's eyes widened. "That would send millions of people to your site."

"Yeah. That's the whole idea. And fans would have to connect with us on social media to get access to it. Social media is the most effective way distilleries connect with customers nowadays."

"That's not a great idea, that's genius!" Quinn exclaimed.

"Don't get too excited," Ava Grace cautioned. "I have to clear it with my label. I don't know if it will be a problem. I'm going to talk with Wally about it tomorrow."

"I also want Ava Grace to do an invitation-only concert at Trinity's warehouse campus. People would have to enter a drawing on our website or social media pages. I'm not sure what kind of permits we'd need for that kind of thing or how large it could be, but we were thinking fewer than a hundred people."

"That sounds good too," Quinn said before looking toward Ava Grace. "Are you okay with all this, AG? It seems like a lot of work."

Ava Grace tilted her head, obviously considering Quinn's

question. "Yes, I'm okay with it," she finally answered. "For a concert, the hard work is the planning and promotion leading up to it, and that's not my job. That's all Wally and the Trinity guys." She wrinkled her nose. "The song is a different matter. When I *have* to write a song, I get writer's block."

"You just need to be inspired by something," Amelia said.

Ava Grace's hazel gaze locked on Beck. "Or someone."

CHAPTER NINE

The reporter from *San Francisco Living* was much younger than Beck had expected. With his shaggy hipster hairstyle, wispy goatee, and spotty acne, he looked like a recent college grad. His clothes—a wrinkled blue cotton oxford shirt, rumpled khakis, and an ill-fitting sports coat—reinforced the idea.

Beck reminded himself youth and wrinkled clothing did not necessarily indicate incompetence, but he was worried nonetheless. He didn't want the article on Trinity to turn out badly, especially since Ren worked for months to get the lifestyle magazine to do a story.

Beck, Gabe, and Ren had planned to do the interview together, but Ren was still in Atlanta. Beck had wanted to postpone the interview until Ren returned since he was better with the media than his business partners.

But Ren had almost burst a blood vessel at the thought of postponing. He insisted the interview occur as scheduled, suggesting Ava Grace take his place since she was still in San Francisco.

"She knows how to deal with the media," he'd pointed out when Beck protested. "And she's enthusiastic about partnering with Trinity. She'll be a good interview."

Since they were talking with Ethan Maynes instead of a more experienced journalist, Beck could only assume the Trinity article was a low priority for the publication.

"This is the first big story I've been assigned," Ethan said, confirming Beck's suspicions. "Jeanette Lin was supposed to work on it, but she's in the hospital with appendicitis."

"That's bad luck for Jeanette." Ava Grace shifted on the dark green leather sofa next to Beck. "But we're happy to have you working on the story, Ethan. I'm sure you'll do a great job."

Ethan's face turned bright red. Looking down, he fiddled with his phone and accidentally dropped his spiral-bound notepad on the floor. As he lurched from his chair to retrieve it, Beck sent up a silent prayer the guy was just nervous rather than inept.

Since the Trinity offices were still in disarray, they'd decided to meet at the Hudson San Francisco, one of the city's oldest and most luxurious hotels. Several spots in the lobby and bar were ideal for a business meeting.

Beck and Gabe had arrived well before the appointed time to scope out the best place for the interview. Ethan had shown up a few minutes later.

Ava Grace strolled through the hotel's sliding glass doors with five minutes to spare, dressed in a sleeveless white dress with a thin black patent leather belt cinched around her slender waist. She'd smoothed her long blond hair into a low bun, and subtle makeup emphasized her big eyes, smooth skin, and plump lips.

Every person in the lobby had turned to stare at her, entranced by her beauty, and poor Ethan almost swallowed his tongue when Gabe introduced them. She, meanwhile, had waited patiently for the reporter to stutter out a greeting.

"I didn't have time to do a lot of research," Ethan admitted.

"That's okay," Ava Grace replied, her voice soothing. "We'll tell you everything you need to know."

Beck shot her a surreptitious glance, wondering if she really was as calm as she sounded. With her sitting so close to him, he was having a hard time concentrating. Even though her dress had a high neck and a knee-length hem, all he could think about was the kind of underwear she wore underneath it. A silky slip or a lacy camisole? Or maybe nothing at all?

She crossed her long legs, her foot angled toward him, and he studied her black patent leather shoe. It had a narrow heel at least four inches tall and showed her toes. He couldn't help smiling when he noticed her toenails were painted bright white with little black polka dots.

"Isn't that right, Beck?" she said, nudging his knee with her foot.

Jerking his eyes away from her sexy shoes and cute toenails, he met her gaze. "What?"

She frowned at him before flashing a bright smile at the reporter. "I was just telling Ethan that we were really looking forward to this interview."

"That's right," Beck agreed enthusiastically.

He was glad he wasn't hooked up to a polygraph machine because it would've flagged his answer as a big, fat lie. From the moment Ren had told Beck about this interview, he'd dreaded it. Although he understood spreading the word about Trinity was important, he hated dealing with the media.

The memory of the circus surrounding his dad's embezzlement scandal made his chest tight. As he inhaled deeply, Ava Grace's sweet scent filled his nostrils. To his surprise, the reminder that she was nearby comforted him and made it easier to breathe.

"I'd like to start off the interview by confirming some details," Ethan began. "Is that okay with you?"

"Sure," Beck answered.

Ethan clicked on the recorder app on his phone and placed it on the glass cocktail table. "You started Trinity Distillery after you graduated from Stanford."

"That's right."

"And there are four equity partners in Trinity: you, Gabe, Renner Holt, and Quinn O'Brien. Are you equal partners in the company?"

"We haven't disclosed that information publicly," Gabe said, always a lawyer.

"How much did Quinn O'Brien invest in Trinity?"

"A lot," Beck answered succinctly. "If not for Quinn, Trinity wouldn't exist." Ethan opened his mouth, but Beck pre-empted him by saying, "I'm not going to give you an exact figure."

The reporter scribbled something in his notebook. "When did you come up with the idea to start a craft distillery?"

"I started thinking about it when I worked for Boire," Beck replied.

Ethan's brow furrowed. "Boire?"

"Boire is the world's largest alcohol distributor," Gabe explained. "It's headquartered in Paris. Beck worked for the company's North American subsidiary for two years in between undergrad and grad school."

"Got it," Ethan said. "I read somewhere that you did the business plan for Trinity for one of your MBA classes at Stanford."

"Yeah, that's right. Dr. Huang said any business that required more than five years to create a marketable product wasn't worth starting. He said the business was doomed to fail and gave me a

D on the assignment. I barely passed the class." The memory made him chuckle. "After we decanted our first barrel, I drove down to Stanford and handed him a bottle of Trinity."

Gabe laughed. "He shouldn't have doubted you."

"Why were you so sure Trinity would work?" Ethan asked.

Beck considered the reporter's question. "I wasn't sure," he admitted. "There's no way of knowing whether something is going to work or not. But I wanted it badly enough to take the risk."

Ethan shifted in his seat to look at Gabe. "You must've had a lot of faith in Beck to give up a partnership at one of the most prominent law firms in Washington, D.C., and move across the country to work with him."

Gabe nodded. "I had no doubt Trinity would be a success."

"Did you follow your business plan from Dr. Huang's class when you launched Trinity?" Ethan asked, directing his question to Beck.

"Mostly. But my revenue projections were off."

Ethan nodded. "New businesses always make less money than projected."

"Not always," Beck countered with a smile. "Trinity has made more money than I thought it would."

Ethan's eyebrows arched. "Do you think your last name has contributed to Trinity's success? Or do you think it's a drawback?"

Beck studied the young reporter. Maybe he hadn't given him enough credit.

"A little bit of both," he hedged.

"How do you think it's helped?"

"The Beck name is synonymous with bourbon. It gives Trinity credibility in the industry, with other distillers and distributors."

"I'm sure that's true." Ethan's eyes narrowed. "But the Beck name is a little … tarnished, wouldn't you say? Your father was accused of embezzling twenty-five million dollars from Jonah Beck Distillery."

Beck felt Ava Grace's gaze on him, but he didn't break eye contact with Ethan. "My dad didn't embezzle a single penny," he replied, doing his best to keep his voice even.

Ethan cocked his head. "Are you in contact with anyone in your family?"

"No," Beck answered curtly.

"Not even your cousin Emmaline Beck?"

"No."

Beck hadn't spoken to Em in fifteen years. She was one who exonerated his dad. She'd heard her parents talking about their plan to frame him and played Nancy Drew. After she found the evidence she needed, she'd gone to the Feds. Then she left Kentucky in her rearview mirror.

Ethan flipped a page in his notebook. "You did your part to tarnish the Beck name too. Your high school girlfriend, Calliope Boone, accused you of assault just a couple of months before you graduated."

Ava Grace's knee knocked into Beck's, drawing his attention from the reporter. Her eyes were wide with shock when they met his. He shook his head, a reflexive movement spurred by the instinctive impulse to defend himself.

He didn't want Ava Grace to think he was the kind of guy who hurt women. He wasn't. He never had been, and he never would be.

How the fuck had Ethan Maynes dug up that information anyway? All that shit happened fifteen years ago. Beck thought it was buried deep in his past, so deep no one could find it.

Beck's arrest had generated a couple of articles in the local newspaper, but he doubted those articles were available digitally. Back then, social media was in its infancy. Smart phones didn't exist, and most people used dial-up modems to connect to the web.

When it came to news or fake news, the world had changed a lot. Beck was grateful his arrest occurred when the word "viral" applied only to infections.

Gabe waded into the awkward silence. "Ethan, my man, are you a bourbon drinker?" he asked with false cheer, obviously trying to change the subject. "Or do you prefer another type of liquor?"

"I talked with your high school principal," Ethan continued, ignoring Gabe.

Beck laughed mirthlessly. *What a little fucker.*

"I thought you didn't have time to do a lot of research."

"I did enough," Ethan replied. "According to Mr. Lamont, you were accepted to Duke University, but the school rescinded its offer when you were arrested."

If Mr. Lamont had been within touching distance, Beck would have drilled his fist right into the high school principal's flappy mouth. Ethan glanced at him expectantly, tapping his pen on his notepad in an annoying, steady rhythm.

"Was there a question there?" Beck asked sarcastically. "I didn't hear one."

Ethan's smile held a sharper edge than before. "Do you have anything to say about Calliope Boone?"

"No," Beck snapped.

"And what about Duke University?"

"What about it? It's a great school, but its basketball team isn't as good as UK's. Go Wildcats."

Ethan's mouth flattened. "And what about your father?"

"What about him?" Beck asked, his muscles tightening with dread.

"Do you think his death was really an accident? Or do you think he committed suicide?"

CHAPTER TEN

Suicide. Assault. Arrest. Beck had some skeletons rattling around in his closet.

Why hadn't Wally's research into Trinity uncovered those old bones? If Ava Grace had known, she could have controlled the interview more effectively and prevented this mess. She'd dealt with overzealous and inexperienced reporters like Ethan Maynes before.

"Maybe you didn't hear a question that time either," Ethan said snidely, directing his comment to Beck. "I'll repeat it: Do you think your father's death was really an accident, or do you think he committed suicide?"

Beck rose from the sofa like an old man, stiff and slow. His dark eyes met hers, and the misery she saw there made her stomach clench. Overwhelmed with the need to comfort him, she caught his hand in hers. Their fingers tangled, and he looked down at them before bringing his gaze back to her.

He was pale under his tan, and he was clenching his jaw so hard the tiny muscles around his mouth created deep grooves. Without a word, he gently shook off her hand and walked away. She watched him as he made his way out of the hotel, his broad shoulders rigid under his navy plaid sports coat.

She glanced at Gabe. Beck's best friend had turned toward Ethan, obviously ready to give him a serious beat down. The reporter, meanwhile, still stared after Beck, a mix of speculation and malice on his pimply face. She had no doubt he planned to write a salacious article about Beck instead of a positive piece on Trinity.

She couldn't allow that to happen. She and Trinity were linked now, for better or for worse. A negative article about the company would damage her brand. It would hurt Beck too.

Although she didn't know the details of Beck's assault accusation or his arrest, she wanted to believe he was a good guy. She hadn't seen any evidence he wasn't, and she wasn't going to jump to conclusions and assume he was guilty.

Stopping Ethan Maynes from doing a hatchet job on Beck and Trinity might be impossible, but she was going to do everything she could to prevent it. She had no choice but to use every weapon in her arsenal.

"Ethan," she said, just loud enough to get the reporter's attention.

His muddy brown gaze locked on hers, and she gave him an enticing smile. She patted the seat next to her—the seat Beck had just vacated. "Why don't you come and sit next to me?" she invited.

He vaulted to his feet and almost tripped over the cocktail table in his haste to get to her. He plopped down next to her, and she shifted on the cushions so her body leaned into his.

"I've always been in awe of people who can write," she gushed, stroking his forearm. "It's such an amazing talent. You know, I'm in the process of writing a cookbook, and it's so dang hard."

"Hard?" Ethan swallowed noisily. "Cookbook?" he repeated dumbly.

She nodded. "A cookbook of bourbon recipes. Trinity is good for more than drinking, you know. A lot of people cook with bourbon." She lightly squeezed his arm. "Have you ever had bourbon pecan pie?" She licked her lips, and his glance dropped to her mouth. "*Mmm.* It's the closest thing to heaven on earth."

He gulped, and she moved a little closer. "Did you know Trinity has won awards for its bourbon?"

He shook his head, and she smiled. "It's true. Trinity is one of the best bourbons on the market." She laughed lightly and trailed her fingers down his arm to touch his hand. "Are you a bourbon drinker, Ethan?"

He shook his head again, and she pouted. "Oh, you have to try it." She leaned closer and whispered in his ear, "There's a special way to drink it. You have to hold it in your mouth so your tongue can enjoy the different flavors."

She drew back. "Can I tell you about all the things Trinity is doing right now? They're so interesting, and I'm really *excited* about them."

Ethan's eyes widened. "Tell me," he breathed.

As she dropped her hand to his knee and squeezed, she said, "You might want to take notes."

*****

Two hours later, Ethan left the hotel. Ava Grace waved good-bye as he walked through the sliding glass doors.

Once the reporter was out of sight, she stalked back to the green leather sofa and grabbed her bag. She glanced at Gabe as she slipped the straps over her shoulder. His face was solemn, worry shadowing his blue eyes.

"Impressive," he said. "I've never seen anyone manipulate

someone so skillfully, and that's saying something, since I used to be a lawyer."

She didn't reply. She wasn't proud of what she'd just done, but it had been necessary.

Gabe shoved his hands in the front pockets of his black dress pants. "Do you think it worked?"

"I don't know. I hope so."

He shook his head. "I can't believe you gave him your phone number. What if he calls?"

"Voice mail." She tilted her head toward the hotel bar. "I need a margarita." She pointed at him with her forefinger. "You're buying. And while I'm drinking, you're going to talk."

He eyed her, a hint of trepidation on his handsome face. "Why do I feel like I'm about to be interrogated?"

She smiled sweetly. "Because you are."

Minutes later, she and Gabe were ensconced in a circular booth upholstered in wine-colored velvet. A tall hurricane glass was on the table in front of her, filled with frozen mango margarita. She took a long sip out of the red straw, moaning as the cool, fruity drink hit her taste buds.

"I'm definitely going to have more than one of these."

"Have as many as you like," Gabe offered. "It's the least I can do since you just saved our bacon."

"We won't know for sure until the article comes out."

Their conversation stalled, and they sipped their drinks in silence for several minutes until Gabe abruptly asked, "Are you hungry?" He didn't wait for her to answer before saying, "I'm hungry. Let's order some food."

Raising his arm, he waved the cocktail waitress over and requested a couple of menus. "If you were going to suggest we share something, forget it," Gabe said. "I don't share. And if you're one of those women who orders a salad and then tries to eat off my plate, I'm warning you now, I'll stab your hand with my fork."

After the server came by and they placed their order, she took a deep breath and asked the question knocking around in her head. "Did Beck really assault his high school girlfriend? What was her name? Calista?"

"Calliope. Like the musical instrument. Everybody called her Callie."

"Did he assault her?"

Gabe sighed softly. "You should talk to Beck about this."

Shaking her head, she said, "He's not here. You are. I want answers. *Now.*"

A laugh rustled in Gabe's throat. "You are a real ballbuster."

"I'm going to take that as a compliment instead of an insult."

His lips twitched. "Please do."

"Start talking," she ordered before taking a sip of her margarita. It had melted a little, and it was even more delicious than before.

"Beck didn't assault Callie," Gabe said flatly.

"Okay. What *did* happen?"

Gabe sighed and rubbed his hands over his face before dropping them to the table. "Callie was the most popular girl in our high school. All the girls wanted to be her friend, and all the guys wanted to be her boyfriend."

"Did you?"

"No," he answered promptly.

"Why not?"

"Because I like blondes." He gave her an exaggerated wink. "Callie was a brunette. She was gorgeous, and she knew it. She had money too. Her dad owned a bunch of car dealerships, and she thought she was better than everyone else ... everyone except Beck. He was the only one she considered worthy of her."

"She doesn't sound very nice."

"Nice?" He huffed out a derisive laugh. "She was a bitch through and through."

"What did Beck see in her?"

Gabe shrugged. "She was nice when he was around. Ren and I used to joke she had an evil twin because she only acted like a bitch when Beck wasn't there to see it."

"I've known a few girls like that." She licked some sugar sprinkles off the rim of her margarita glass. "Stop dragging out the story, Gabe."

He chuckled ruefully. "Can't play a player."

"Tell me about the assault. There was no mention of it in the report Wally put together on Trinity and its owners."

"Probably because Beck was never convicted of a crime. The prosecutor dropped the charges before his case went to trial. Arrests stay on your record for seven years max. When someone runs a background check on Beck, his rap sheet is clean."

Gabe picked at the edge of the paper napkin under his beer bottle. "Callie broke up with Beck after his dad was accused of embezzlement, but when the truth came out, she and her best friend, Melissa, went to the cooperage where he worked after school—"

"What's a cooperage?"

Giving her a censuring look, Gabe said, "You should know what a cooperage is. It's the place where bourbon and wine barrels are built and charred."

"Right." She nodded. "Go on."

"Beck was rolling barrels into a truck behind the warehouse when Callie showed up. I wasn't there, but Beck told me that she started crying and begging him to forgive her ... saying she wanted him back."

Gabe picked up his beer and took a swallow. "She tried to kiss him. When he jerked away from her, she stumbled, hit her face on the dolly he'd been using to roll barrels, and then fell to the ground. Beck was trying to help her up when the driver came out of the warehouse and asked what was going on. Callie told him that Beck had hit her and Melissa had witnessed everything."

"Oh, no."

"Oh, yes." A grimace twisted Gabe's face. "Melissa backed up Callie's story. Then the sheriff's department showed up and arrested Beck. My mom and dad had to post his bail because he didn't have anyone else to do it."

"Then what happened?"

"When Melissa realized Beck was in serious trouble—that he could actually go to prison—she admitted she'd lied by corroborating Callie's story. By then, Duke had rescinded its offer."

Beck and Ava Grace were worlds apart when it came to education. He had degrees in chemical engineering and biochemistry from the University of Kentucky. And if that wasn't impressive enough, the guy had gone to one of the best business schools in the nation to get his MBA.

She, meanwhile, had a diploma from Electra High School. She'd graduated at the bottom of her class with a C average because she worked nights to support herself.

While other teenagers were busy with extracurricular activities and homework, Ava Grace worked ten-hour shifts at the local dry cleaners pressing clothes. While other teenagers slept in on Saturday mornings, she was up at five to help the owners prepare for their busiest pick-up and drop-off day.

Gabe shifted restlessly in the booth, his knee brushing hers. "I still can't believe how vindictive Callie was."

"Vindictive?" Ava Grace could feel her mouth curling in disgust. "It's women like Callie who make it difficult for real victims to get the help they need. I hope she got in trouble for making a false claim."

The server arrived with their food, and they halted their discussion while she arranged the plates in front of them. As soon as she moved out of the way, Gabe grabbed his fork and attacked his chicken pasta as if he hadn't eaten in weeks.

"Did you miss lunch?" Ava Grace asked.

He shook his head before shoveling another forkful of pasta into his mouth. At this rate, he'd be finished in less than three minutes, so she didn't pressure him to talk.

She dipped the tines of her fork into her cilantro lime dressing and tasted it before pouring a dab on her southwestern grilled shrimp salad. She'd taken only a few bites when Gabe pushed his bowl away and wiped his mouth.

"Tell me about Beck's dad," she requested.

"Law was a good guy. A more approachable version of Beck. More easygoing. More trusting, I guess you could say. Beck was really close to him."

"And his mom?"

He grimaced. "She always made me think of a venomous snake. You know the ones I'm talking about ... beautiful to look at, but if you get too close, they strike, and the bite is *deadly*."

"That's horrible," Ava Grace whispered, hoping no one would *ever* describe her that way.

"Yeah, she was horrible." He pointed to her salad. "Are you going to eat the rest?"

"I'll give it to you after you tell me how Beck's dad died."

"Law crashed his Lexus into a tree."

"On purpose?"

Gabe shrugged. "Who can say for sure? It was a gravel road, so there was no way of knowing if he braked or not. The road had a lot of sharp curves, but he'd driven it a million times. He was sober, but it was late. He might have fallen asleep. No one knows, and that's why his death was ruled an accident. But people wonder. Beck wonders. Law was depressed ... with good reason. He was under investigation by the Feds, and Beck's mom served him with divorce papers the day before he died. She didn't even come back for his funeral. Only a few people bothered to show up because everyone believed he was an embezzler."

Ava Grace pushed her salad toward Gabe. As he speared a shrimp with his fork, he said, "All the stuff that happened ... it's still with Beck ... still weighing him down."

CHAPTER ELEVEN

"You told Quinn, didn't you?" Ava Grace accused.

Confusion filled Amelia's face. "Told him what?"

"You know what." Ava Grace leaned against the soapstone island in her best friend's kitchen. "It's obvious he's trying to play matchmaker with me and Beck." She shook her head in disgust. "He's not very subtle."

Amelia's chocolaty gaze gleamed with amusement. "His lack of subtlety is one of the things I like best about him."

Ava Grace rolled her eyes. "Seriously, Millie. Everyone here is a couple except for me and Beck."

Amelia and Quinn had decided to host a s'mores party at their house, and they'd invited eight people to sit around the fire pit. In addition to Ava Grace and Beck, both of Quinn's siblings were there with their spouses, along with some friends from work.

"Everyone here is a family member or close friend," Amelia corrected gently. "It's just a coincidence you and Beck are the only single people."

Ava Grace shot the petite redhead a doubtful glance. "Really?"

Amelia's lips twitched. "Well, maybe not a *total* coincidence."

With an annoyed growl, Ava Grace grabbed a chocolate bar from the kitchen counter. She ripped off the paper wrapping and the foil underneath, wishing it were Quinn's dark hair.

"Why are you so mad, chickadee?" Amelia asked. "This gives you an opportunity to"—she waggled her russet eyebrows—"*get a little closer* to Beck."

Ava Grace snapped the chocolate bar into little pieces, imagining it was Quinn's arm. "Beck doesn't want me closer," she muttered glumly. "He's gone out of his way to avoid me."

Ava Grace hadn't seen or talked to Beck since the *San Francisco Living* interview three days ago.

"I'm sorry." Amelia held up one of the long metal skewers she'd bought for her guests to roast marshmallows over the fire pit. "You can use this to stab him."

"Quinn or Beck?" she asked as she dumped the chocolate pieces into a shiny red bowl.

"We have enough skewers for both of them."

Tearing open a bar of orange-infused dark chocolate, Ava Grace said, "I'd like to turn both of them into human voodoo dolls."

"Just make sure to avoid the important parts." Amelia snickered. "Your first stab should be in the head."

While Amelia arranged graham crackers on a tray, Ava Grace broke the chocolate into smaller pieces and tossed them into an orange bowl. She reached for another chocolate bar, this one infused with red chili, and removed the wrapper.

"I decided to take a couple of days off so we can hang out before you head back home," Amelia announced.

Joking, Ava Grace asked, "Was your boss okay with that?"

"He's pretty flexible." Amelia's lips quirked. "And for some reason, he gives me special treatment."

JENNA SUTTON

Just then, Quinn appeared in the open doorway that led to the back deck. Strolling into the kitchen, he flashed a smile at Ava Grace.

"Yes, her *boss* is okay with her taking some time off to spend with her best friend." He turned his dark blue gaze to Amelia. "You're pretty flexible too."

He grinned roguishly, and Amelia's cheeks flushed at his sexual innuendo. Laughing softly, he grabbed her around the waist and lifted her up until their faces were even.

"You get special treatment because you *are* special," he murmured before pressing a kiss on her lips.

Ava Grace stared at the pile of chocolate pieces. Quinn rarely stopped with one kiss, and eavesdropping was her thing, not voyeurism.

She kept her eyes down until Quinn finally said, "Do you need help with anything, Juice?"

As Ava Grace lifted her head, Amelia pointed to an oval tray piled high with puffy marshmallows. "Can you take that outside and put it on the s'mores station?"

"Sure." Quinn evaluated the tray's contents. "These don't look like your average marshmallows."

"They're gourmet. Three different flavors: vanilla bean, caramel swirl, and peppermint."

Quinn's eyes widened with anticipation. "Now I wish I hadn't eaten so much lasagna at dinner."

He slid the tray off the counter and sauntered out of the kitchen. Ava Grace brought her attention back to Amelia, who was staring at the doorway where Quinn had disappeared, a love-struck expression on her face.

Ava Grace had never looked at any man the way her best friend looked at her husband. She'd never been in love or anything close to it.

In fact, she'd never experienced more than mild attraction for any man ... any man except Beck. There was nothing mild about the way she felt about him.

Beck was constantly on her mind. If she were fifteen, she'd characterize her feelings as a crush. But she wasn't a boy-crazy teenager. She'd celebrate the big three-o this year, so maybe obsession was a better word to describe her feelings.

"This is ready to go," Amelia announced as she picked up the graham-cracker-filled tray.

Ava Grace took the tray. "What else needs to be done?"

"Nothing." Amelia tucked a coppery ringlet behind her ear. "I'm going to load up the skewers and chocolate, and I'll be right behind you."

Ava Grace headed toward the deck, and as she stepped onto the wide redwood planks, Amelia called out, "AG!"

Still moving forward, Ava Grace glanced behind her. "What?"

"Can you make sure the little chalkboard food signs are in the right places?" Amelia requested.

Ava Grace nodded. Before she could bring her head front and center, she slammed into something hard and unyielding. She gasped as the tray was whisked from her hands and a strong male arm wrapped around her waist.

Instinctively extending her arms, she pushed against the broad chest with her palms until she realized it was Beck who held her. She let her arms relax, and as she looked up into his dark eyes, her stomach somersaulted.

"You should watch where you're going, sugar," he advised in his rich southern drawl, his face only a couple of inches from hers.

He was so close she could see the inky striations in his coffee-colored eyes. He was so close she could see the grain of his sooty stubble and the faint laugh lines around his eyes. He was so close she could see the smooth texture of his lips.

He was so close...

But not close enough.

She sucked in a deep breath, and his scent enveloped her. Thanks to the knowledge she'd gained while working with a perfumer to create her own fragrance, she could identify the crisp, intoxicating notes of amber and cedarwood along with something just Beck.

They stood there, their gazes locked together. Time seemed to slow, the seconds stretching like saltwater taffy.

Finally, she said the only thing she could think of that didn't involve his body or hers. "Thanks for saving my crackers."

Amusement sparked in his eyes, and the corner of his mouth kicked up in a sexy smile. "It would've been a crushing disappointment if you'd dropped them."

"A crushing disappointment?" She tipped her forehead to his chest with a heartfelt groan. "That was *so* lame," she grumbled into his soft wine-colored sweater.

He laughed quietly, his warm breath stirring her hair. His arm tightened around her waist, and he drew her closer. Leaning down, he placed his mouth against her ear. "It's impossible to make s'mores without crackers. Wouldn't you have felt *crumb-y* if you'd ruined everyone's night?"

She groaned again, both from the feel of his body against hers and his terrible pun. She turned her head, oh so slowly, letting his mouth skim over her cheek. She wanted his kiss so badly, but to her disappointment, he drew back before their lips touched.

She lifted her head until she could see his face. "Beck—"

"It's time for s'mores," Amelia called out.

108

Beck jerked in surprise and dropped his arm from her waist. He stepped back, the tray of crackers in his big hand, and stared down at her for a heartbeat before he turned and headed toward the s'mores station on the far side of the deck.

She watched Beck as he walked away, his tight backside covered by faded Rileys. If Amelia hadn't interrupted her, she would've begged Beck to kiss her. The thought was appalling. She'd never begged *any* man for anything, and she wasn't going to start now.

Amelia stopped beside Ava Grace, holding a wooden serving tray. A dozen or so skewers rested on top, along with several colorful bowls overflowing with chocolate pieces.

"Would you take this to the s'mores station while I explain how all this is going to work?" Amelia asked.

Just as Ava Grace reached for the tray, Beck nudged her out of the way. "I got it."

Amelia flashed a smile at Beck. "Thank you."

"My pleasure," he replied before turning on his heel.

Amelia elbowed Ava Grace in the ribs. "He likes you."

"Why? Because he carried a tray for me?" She scoffed. "We're not in high school, Millie."

Amelia glanced at Ava Grace, her eyes round with surprise. "Your panties sure are in a bunch tonight." She smiled ruefully. "I never *ever* thought I would say this, to you or anyone else, but you need to get laid."

"Obviously," Ava Grace replied, sarcasm dripping from her voice.

Even before *American Star,* Ava Grace found it difficult to trust a guy enough to let him into her life, her bed, and her body. A good therapist would say she had abandonment issues, first from her mom dying and then from her dad dumping her on her grandmother.

Yes, Ava Grace was a country star, but that didn't mean she didn't have insecurities. She wasn't like a lot of women who lacked confidence in their looks. She didn't believe in false modesty, and she knew exactly what she looked like.

Mother Nature had blessed her with a face and form that embodied today's standard of beauty. They were a gift, and she appreciated them, just as she appreciated her musical gifts.

Ava Grace's insecurities were rooted in the need to feel worthy—worthy of esteem, worthy of friendship, and most of all, worthy of love. She'd wondered if she'd ever overcome her past, but Amelia's relationship with Quinn gave Ava Grace hope.

Amelia had just as many scars from her childhood, maybe more. Yet she'd found the strength to trust a man enough to fall in love and marry him.

Of course, Quinn O'Brien wasn't just a regular guy. He was *solid*.

A solid guy did what he said he was going to do. He took care of the people he loved. And most important, he had staying power. He stuck around, even when things got ugly.

Ava Grace wanted a solid guy like Quinn. Unfortunately, solid guys were a rare breed, kind of like snow leopards.

Right now, Amelia's solid guy stood next to Beck, eyeing the s'mores station like a jewel thief at Cartier. Ava Grace laughed under her breath as Quinn snatched a caramel swirl marshmallow from the tray and surreptitiously shoved it in his mouth. A second one quickly followed.

"Quinn O'Brien!" Amelia shrieked. "Get away from those marshmallows!" She clapped her hands together. "Okay, everyone, gather 'round."

The little group converged on Amelia, and she explained the s'mores-making process. When she finished, she pointed to the s'mores station. "Everything you need is over there. Let the s'mores begin."

Ava Grace waited patiently for her turn at the s'mores station. By the time she'd filled her plate, most of the Adirondack chairs surrounding the fire pit were taken. Only two were available, one on each side of Quinn.

"I saved this seat for you, AG," Quinn announced loudly, pointing to the chair on his left—the one right next to Beck.

CHAPTER TWELVE

Beck's marshmallow had turned a nice golden brown, so he pulled it from the fire pit and carefully removed it from the skewer. Hot to the touch, the melted marshmallow oozed over his fingers as he placed it on the chocolate and graham cracker stack.

"What kind of s'more are you making?" Ava Grace asked.

As he pressed a graham cracker on top of the marshmallow, he thought about ignoring her question. He didn't want to be drawn into conversation with her. It was bad enough he had to sit next to her and pretend not to notice the lacy waistband of her pastel pink panties when she leaned forward to toast her marshmallow.

Good manners eventually prevailed. "I'm a traditionalist. Plain graham crackers, milk chocolate, and vanilla marshmallow." He sucked the marshmallow from his fingers before asking, "What about you?"

"I'm a non-traditionalist," she answered with a smile, rotating her skewer over the fire pit. "Chocolate graham crackers, dark chocolate, and peppermint marshmallow."

"That's adventurous," he gibed.

She glanced at him, the flames of the fire bringing out the gold in her eyes. "Under the right circumstances, I can be *very* adventurous."

"Hmm," he replied noncommittally while his cock demanded to know two things: what were the right circumstances, and how adventurous was *very* adventurous?

He looked toward the fire pit, and when he noticed her marshmallow was getting a little too done, he tapped her forearm. "Your marshmallow's burning."

She immediately pulled it from the flames and began to ease it from the skewer. She hissed when gooey marshmallow got all over her hand.

"Dang, that's hot," she murmured, raising her fingers to her mouth.

As she licked the pink stickiness from them, blood rushed to his groin, his cock throbbing with every beat of his heart. He mentally reminded himself to avoid situations that involved Ava Grace and sticky or creamy foods.

In fact, he needed to avoid all situations that involved Ava Grace. *Period.*

He couldn't think straight with her around. Earlier this evening, he'd almost kissed her, and a crazy, stupid part of him—his dick—wished he hadn't pulled back. His dick wanted to know if she tasted as good as she smelled ... if her petal-pink lips were as soft as they looked.

Trying not to think about her mouth and all the *adventurous* things she could do with it, he took a big bite of his s'more. As he chewed, he tried to recall the last time he'd eaten one. Probably back in high school, before everything turned to shit.

"You seem to be an expert marshmallow toaster," Ava Grace noted, a teasing lilt in her husky voice. "How'd you gain that experience?"

"I went camping a lot when I was little, and we always toasted marshmallows over the fire."

The memory made him a little sad. Even after all these years, he still missed his dad. Nothing could fill that void.

"So you learned by example," she said as she built her s'more.

"I guess you could say that." He leaned back in the Adirondack chair and propped his ankle on his knee. "Did you go camping when you were a kid?"

"No. I've never been camping. But I'd like to go someday. Sleeping under the stars sounds so romantic." She flashed a teasing smile at him. "Maybe you can take me."

Strangely, the thought of taking Ava Grace camping sounded like fun. He had no doubt she'd have plenty to say about the outing, and she'd deliver those observations in that sexy, wry tone that both amused and aroused him.

And after the sun went down, he'd build a blazing fire and stretch out under the stars. He'd pull her on top of him and watch her as she rode him, her head thrown back, her eyes shut, and her thick hair streaming behind her.

Fuck.

"Sleeping under the stars is not as romantic as it sounds," he growled, trying to convince himself. "The ground is hard, and the bugs are vicious."

Her smile widened. "How else am I going to achieve your level of marshmallow-toasting expertise?"

He lowered his voice. "I'll let you in on a little secret that might help..."

"What?" she asked eagerly.

"Toasted marshmallows are even better when you douse them in bourbon before you put them on the fire."

Her eyes widened. "Isn't that dangerous? Don't they catch on fire?"

He chuckled. "Sometimes. But usually the fire just caramelizes the sugar in the bourbon and the marshmallow. Kind of like using a kitchen torch on crème brûlée."

"Oh," she breathed. "I get it. That does sound yummy." She pursed her lips. "You know, there are all kinds of marshmallow flavors now. Lemon meringue, cinnamon, coffee. I wonder how a bourbon marshmallow would taste?"

"I'm going to go out on a limb and say it would taste pretty damn good."

"I think I'll play mad scientist and come up with a bourbon marshmallow recipe to include in our cookbook."

Our. He liked the way that sounded. Like they were a team.

They finished their s'mores in silence, the fire crackling in front of them. Conversation buzzed, and music drifted through the night air.

Ava Grace rose from her chair. "I'll be right back."

He watched her as she walked away, letting his gaze wander from her platinum blond ponytail to her navy-blue suede flats. She wore skinny jeans the color of pistachio ice cream and a form-fitting striped sweater in coral, navy blue, white, and pistachio green.

Earlier, Quinn had mentioned Amelia had designed Ava Grace's outfit. It was part of Riley O'Brien & Co.'s line of women's clothing.

Over the past couple of years, Ava Grace had been involved in several ad campaigns to market the company's apparel. According to Quinn, she'd been willing to do it for free, simply because it benefited Amelia. When he insisted she receive compensation, Ava Grace donated the money to charity.

Ava Grace's willingness to help her best friend hadn't surprised Beck. It was obvious how much she adored Amelia. But Ava Grace's philanthropy had surprised him. Now that he knew her better, he wasn't surprised at all. She was generous, not only with her time and her money, but also herself. Her generosity was just one of the things he admired about her.

Moments later, Ava Grace returned with a couple of bottled waters. She held one out to him, and he took it from her, murmuring his thanks.

Ava Grace sat down with one long leg tucked under her. "Wesley."

"What?"

"Your middle name is Wesley."

Laughing, he shook his head. "Nope."

"So who did you go camping with?"

"My dad and Grandpa Joe."

As she twisted the plastic cap on the water bottle, she asked, "What about your mom? Did she go camping with y'all too?"

He laughed mirthlessly. "No."

"She didn't like spending time outdoors?"

His mouth opened, and words spilled out before he could swallow them. "She didn't like spending time with us. She had better things to do."

Beck had no idea why he'd shared such private information with Ava Grace. He didn't like to talk about his mother, yet here he was, spilling his guts over s'mores.

Ava Grace melted his brain just like fire melted his marshmallows. If he didn't watch out, he was going to turn into a puddle of goo.

"Do you ever see your mom?"

He shook his head. "I haven't seen or talked to her since I

was eighteen. I don't even know where she is."

Or if she's alive.

"That's sad." She sighed softly. "I feel sorry for her."

He snapped his head toward her. "Why the hell would you feel sorry for *her*?"

Ava Grace met his eyes. "Because her son grew into an amazing man, and she missed out. I pity her because she doesn't know you."

A shiver chased over him, and he broke out in goose bumps. *You think I'm amazing?*

"Yes."

He winced when he realized he'd asked the question out loud.

"If I had a son like you, I'd probably call him every day." She gave a self-deprecating laugh. "I'd be one of *those* mothers."

He was suddenly curious about her parents. None of the articles he'd read about Ava Grace had mentioned her mother or father.

"What was your mom like?" he asked.

She shrugged. "I don't know. She died in a car accident when I was two."

Her answer surprised him. He'd had no idea she had grown up motherless.

"So it was just you and your dad?" he asked, studying her face.

Her lips turned down at the corners. "My grandmother raised me."

Again, her answer surprised him. "What about your dad? Where was he?"

She didn't reply for a long moment. Finally, she said, "I guess you could say he was in and out of my life. His job took him away from home for months at a time, and when my mom died, he left me with Grandma June."

"What did he do?"

"He was a roughneck on offshore oil rigs. I only saw him every couple of years."

"You only saw your dad *every couple of years*?"

She nodded.

"Why didn't you see him more often? Those jobs don't last two years, do they?"

"No, they're usually three- to six-month gigs." She smiled sadly. "He just didn't bother to visit."

White-hot rage rushed through him, the intensity of the emotion catching him off guard. Her fucking father had washed his hands of the responsibility of his daughter, leaving Ava Grace to fend for herself. If Beck had a daughter, only one thing would keep him from her: death.

"I guess he didn't think it was important to see me," she added softly.

Beck could hear the pain in her voice … the kind of pain that came from knowing the person who was supposed to love you the most didn't care about you at all. He understood her pain because he'd experienced the same thing when his mother left.

"When was the last time you saw your dad?"

She took a drink of water and screwed the cap back on the bottle. "A few days ago. He lives with me in Nashville."

"He does?" Beck asked, not bothering to hide his shock.

"Yes. He moved in with me a couple of years ago. He has early onset Alzheimer's." She stared into the fire. "His disease has progressed much faster than anyone expected. He doesn't recognize anyone or anything. He requires round-the-clock care."

Incredulous, Beck asked, "And you foot the bill for it?"

"Um-hum."

He shook his head. "I can't believe you're willing to take care of him after he abandoned you. He should reap what he sowed."

"He's my dad," she said, as if it were that simple.

"I wouldn't lift a finger to help my mother."

He wasn't that softhearted or forgiving. Apparently, Ava Grace was.

She stared at him for several seconds, her eyes locked with his. "I think you would, Beck. You'd help her, not because she deserved it, but because you couldn't live with yourself if you didn't."

Uncomfortable with the turn of the conversation, he placed the water next to his chair and rose. "Excuse me."

As he approached the sliding door, Quinn called out to him. "Hey, Beck, can you grab some graham crackers from the pantry?"

Beck waved his hand in acknowledgement of Quinn's request. Once he was inside the house, he made his way to the walk-in pantry hidden under the staircase. After flipping on the overhead light, he shut the door and leaned back against it.

Closing his eyes, he heard Ava Grace's words echo in his head. *You'd help her, not because she deserved it, but because you couldn't live with yourself if you didn't.*

Ava Grace was right. If his mother came to him for help, and he turned her away, the guilt would crush him. He'd never be able to forgive himself.

But he hadn't realized that truth until Ava Grace pointed it out. How did she understand him better than he understood himself?

He and Ava Grace had a lot more in common than he'd ever imagined. They'd both been abandoned in one way or another, and they both carried scars from it.

Suddenly, the door opened behind him. Grabbing hold of one of the wooden shelves, he managed to avoid falling backward.

"Oh!" Ava Grace's raspy voice was an octave higher than usual. "I didn't know you were in there!" She joined him in the pantry. "Did you find the graham crackers, handsome?"

He should have snapped, *Don't call me handsome*. But the truth was, he liked it.

She stepped closer, and his eyes found a tiny smudge of chocolate at the corner of her mouth. He couldn't seem to tear his gaze from it.

Her lips moved, and he heard her voice. His brain had stopped working, though, so he couldn't comprehend her words. Suddenly, their bodies were touching, and their mouths were pressed together.

Had he kissed her? Or had she kissed him?

He froze, his eyes open and his hands clenched by his sides. Now he knew—her lips were even softer than they looked. They also were a little sticky from the marshmallow.

Her eyelids fluttered shut, her long lashes feathering over her cheeks. Her chest moved in a long, deep inhalation, and then she opened her mouth over his.

All the blood drained from his head, rushing straight toward his cock, and his vision blurred. Closing his eyes, he dug his fingers into her hips to steady himself. As her lips moved over his in a soft, slow caress, he opened his mouth too.

Underneath the dark chocolate and peppermint marshmallow from her s'more, he got his first taste of her. And now he knew— she tasted even better than she smelled. She was so fucking delicious every other woman he'd kissed was flavorless in comparison.

Tilting his head, he aligned their mouths so he could kiss her even deeper. With a breathy moan, she looped her arms around his neck and plastered herself against him. Her tongue swiped across his lower lip, and he eagerly sucked it into his mouth. She twirled her tongue around his, sending his heartbeat thundering in his ears like a stampede of wild horses.

As he sipped from her lips and stroked the interior of her mouth, he savored the wet slide of his tongue against hers. He fed her several kisses, and she devoured them, her mouth hungry and demanding.

Somewhere in the back of his mind, he knew he had to stop. He had to stop kissing her. Kissing Ava Grace was bad.

Bad. Bad. Bad.

But it feels so good.

Tugging her closer, he pressed his erection into her lower stomach. When that wasn't enough, he hooked his arm under her round ass and lifted her those crucial inches so his cock nestled in the apex of her thighs.

He maneuvered her back against the shelves, and she did a little shimmy that rubbed his hard-on against the seam of her jeans. Stars burst behind his eyelids. As he rocked into her softness, tingles radiated from the base of his spine and spread throughout his body.

His lungs burned from lack of oxygen, but he couldn't— *wouldn't*—let go of her mouth. Finally, she pulled away with a gasp, panting heavily. While she struggled to catch her breath, he rested his forehead against hers and gulped in several lungfuls of air.

When his breathing evened out, he drew back so he could see her face. Her eyes gleamed with desire, her cheeks were rosy, and her luscious mouth was red and swollen. An alarm bell clanged in his head, and he jerked her arms from around his neck.

"We shouldn't have done that," he growled.

"Why not? I enjoyed it." She gave his hard-on a pointed look before bringing her eyes back to his. "Looks like you did too."

Nabbing the box of graham crackers from the shelf above her head, he vowed, "This is *never* going to happen again."

As he walked away, he heard her murmur from behind him, "We'll see."

CHAPTER THIRTEEN

"Are you busy?" Gabe asked, hovering just inside Beck's office.

"Of course not," Beck answered without glancing away from the spreadsheet on his monitor. "You know I don't do anything all day except look at porn and shop for shoes online."

A husky giggle floated to his ears, and he jerked his head toward the sound, recognizing Ava Grace's sexy laughter. She peeked out from behind Gabe, her glossy mouth stretched in a grin.

"Sounds like you've got your hands full," she noted, her hazel eyes glinting with amusement.

He scowled, embarrassed by what he'd said and annoyed by the delight that rushed through him when he realized she was there. He *wasn't* happy to see her, damn it. Just like he *hadn't* been thinking about her almost non-stop since the s'mores party three nights ago.

Yeah, right.

"Do you know where Ellis is?" Gabe asked. "I can't find him."

"He's supervising the corn delivery. Why?"

Gabe grimaced. "I need him to finish Ava Grace's tour."

"Why can't you do it?"

"American Spirits Distribution rescheduled our call, and it starts in ten minutes."

Beck knew Gabe couldn't blow off that call. American Spirits Distribution was the largest alcohol distributor in the Southeast, and if Gabe could negotiate a deal, Trinity would be sold in thousands of stores across Florida, Georgia, and the Carolinas.

Beck sighed. He didn't want to spend time alone with Ava Grace, especially not after that kiss. But he couldn't hand her off to Ellis. God only knew what the old goat would say or do if he got her alone.

And Beck couldn't ask one of the other employees either. They were good at their jobs, but they didn't know enough about Trinity to give Ava Grace a proper tour.

"I can come back later," Ava Grace offered.

Knowing he had no other choice, he rose from his office chair. "No. I'll finish your tour."

Gabe patted Ava Grace on the shoulder. "I'll see you later," he said before sprinting off.

When Beck reached her side, he evaluated her outfit. She wore a cherry-red button-down shirt, a denim skirt, and red cowboy boots. The shirt was tied at her waist, exposing a sliver of her stomach above the waistband of her skirt, which stopped mid-thigh.

She was so fucking gorgeous he wanted to throw back his head and howl. Instead, he said, "Jeans and a T-shirt."

She tilted her head, and her braid swung over her shoulder. "What is the majority of your wardrobe?" she quipped, phrasing her response in *Jeopardy!* form.

He shook his head in exasperation. "The next time I see you in this building, you better be wearing jeans and a T-shirt."

"At least I'm wearing boots instead of heels."

"At least," he echoed dryly.

He led the way out of the building, and she followed. "Thanks for taking time to show me around."

"No need to thank me. I'm just glad you want to learn more about the distilling process."

As they walked down the cracked sidewalk, she said, "Quinn told me that you named your company Trinity because of the river that flows through Northern California."

He nodded. "The Trinity River is where miners found gold in 1845. But that's not the only reason we named it Trinity. Trinity means three, and since there are three of us, it seemed appropriate."

"I like the Trinity bottle … the little gold flecks in the glass."

"That was Ren's idea."

As they passed warehouse number two, he asked, "How far did Gabe get in the tour?"

"He showed me the grain boilers, the fermentation tanks, and the copper-pot stills. Those are so cool, by the way. I can't believe you shipped them all the way from Scotland."

Her enthusiasm made him smile. "Our biggest still is fifteen feet tall. The one at Jonah Beck Distillery is thirty-five feet tall."

"That's huge!"

"Before we move on from the distilling process, I'm going to give you a quiz to see how well you understand it."

She tossed him a big smile. "Ask me anything, Professor Beck. I might surprise you."

She'd already surprised him. And he wasn't sure he could survive any more surprises, especially if they were anything like the hot kiss she'd laid on him.

"What is alcohol proof and alcohol by volume?" he asked.

"Alcohol proof is a measure of how much alcohol is in an alcoholic beverage. Alcohol by volume is the percentage of alcohol based on total volume."

"By law, bourbon cannot be distilled to more than 180 proof. How much is that alcohol by volume?"

"Ninety percent," she answered promptly. "Alcohol by volume is always half of proof."

"Here's a hard one: what is the legal limit for bourbon when it goes into the barrel?"

She worried her lower lip between her teeth. "I know this. Just give me a second." She snapped her fingers. "Got it: one hundred twenty-five proof or 62.5 percent alcohol."

He nodded. "And what is that alcohol called?"

"High wine."

"Good job. I give you an A+ on your quiz."

Placing his hand on her lower back, he ushered her toward warehouse number three. His fingers touched silky skin instead of fabric, and he jerked his hand away before he was tempted to slip it under her shirt.

Once they were inside the warehouse, he led her past the stills and stopped when they reached a manual conveyor system with a couple of high-backed metal stools in front of it. Empty barrels rested on their sides on the steel grates, and several long hoses hung from the ceiling, the ends fitted with nozzles.

"This is the area I call the filling station. This is where we fill the barrels with high wine. We—"

"What's goin' on back here?"

Recognizing Ellis's cantankerous voice, Beck groaned under his breath. This was going to be interesting.

"It's just me, Ellis," he called out.

Ellis stomped around the still. When he saw them, he came

to an abrupt halt, his eyes widening. He gave Ava Grace the once-over, trailing his lascivious gaze from the top of her head to her feet and back up again.

Beck glared at Ellis, hoping he'd behave, but the older man didn't even acknowledge his presence. He took off his baseball cap and smoothed the wild tufts of his gray hair as he walked toward her.

Gesturing toward Ellis, Beck said, "Ava Grace, I'd like you to meet Ellis Oglesby. He's the most important guy in this entire place: the master distiller. Ellis, this is Ava Grace Landy."

Ava Grace smiled and held out her right hand. "It's a pleasure to meet you, Ellis."

Ellis took her hand and raised it to his mouth. "The pleasure is all mine, Miz Landy," he said before kissing the top of her hand.

She giggled, and Beck rolled his eyes. Old Ellis had made another conquest.

"What are y'all doin' in here?" Ellis asked.

"Beck's giving me a tour. He was showing me the filling station."

"Did he tell you about the head, heart, and tail?" Ellis asked.

She shook her head. "No."

"We put the heart of the spirit into these here barrels."

"What's the heart of the spirit?" she asked, looking back and forth between Beck and Ellis.

"The liquid that comes off the stills first is called the head, and it's too strong," Ellis explained. "The liquid that comes off last is called the tail, and it's too weak. It's the liquid that comes off in between—the heart of the spirit—that's the right potency."

"Head, heart, and tail," Ava Grace repeated. "I'll remember that. Thanks for telling me, Ellis."

Ellis gave Beck a sideways glance. "Miz Landy, will you excuse us for a moment? I need to talk to this fella."

Ellis scurried several feet away from Ava Grace, and Beck followed. The noise from the stills provided some privacy for their conversation, but she could still see them.

"What's up?" Beck asked.

Ellis poked his gnarled finger into Beck's chest. "Boy, you gotta get yourself some of that."

Beck frowned in confusion. "Some of what?"

Ellis huffed. "Are you a goddamn fool?" He cocked his head toward Ava Grace. "Some of *that*."

Beck laughed incredulously. "That's what you wanted to talk to me about?" Ellis nodded emphatically, and Beck shook his head in disgust. "*Jesus*. I can't believe you. I have a million fucking things to do, but I'm giving a tour instead. And now you're wasting my time with *bullshit*. I should fire your scrawny ass and kick it all the way back to Kentucky."

Beck took a step away from Ellis, but the old man's hand shot out and grabbed his forearm in a claw-like grip. "Listen to me, Beck."

Ellis had called him *Beck*. His mouth fell open in shock. Had hell frozen over? Were pigs flying?

"A ripe, juicy peach just fell from the tree and landed in your lap," Ellis said urgently. "You're hungry. Go ahead and take a bite."

"Stop it," Beck hissed, worried Ava Grace might overhear them. "She's not a piece of fruit."

But she probably is juicy, the devil inside him whispered.

Ellis reached into the pocket of his workpants and pressed something into Beck's palm. "Here, take this."

Beck looked down, and it took his brain a second to process

the fact that Ellis had given him a condom. Praying Ava Grace wasn't watching them, he grabbed Ellis's hand and tried to return the little foil square.

"I don't need it," he growled, darting a glance toward her. Her gaze was locked on the two of them, her eyes wide and curious.

"Yes, you do." Ellis closed his hand into a fist to prevent Beck from giving back the condom. "This is a rare *opporpoonity*."

Beck squeezed the old man's hand until it opened. Shoving the condom into Ellis's palm, he said, "Get out of here before I douse you with high wine and light a match."

Ellis jerked away from him. "I'm just trying to do you a favor, boy."

Before Beck could respond, Ellis lunged forward and slipped the condom into Beck's shirt pocket. He slapped his hand over it, fumbling to find the opening so he could pull out the foil packet.

Ellis dashed toward the stills, and as he passed Ava Grace, he gave her an exaggerated wink. Rounding the copper pots, he called out, "Enjoy your tour." Then he hightailed it out of sight.

Ava Grace looked at Beck. "What was that about?"

Her eyes zeroed in on his hand, which was still pressed over his pocket. He hastily dropped it to his side. "Nothing. He just wanted to discuss..."

Peaches. Ripe, juicy peaches.

"Corn," he finished. "He wanted to discuss corn."

She smiled slowly. "Ellis is quite a character."

"You have no idea," he muttered.

Ava Grace slid into one of the chairs, and her tiny skirt hiked up. Saliva pooled in his mouth as he thought about the moist, pink flesh barely covered by that scrap of denim.

Ripe and juicy…

She crossed her legs, and suddenly, all he could think about was how it would feel to have those red cowboy boots dig into his ass as he thrust into her. His cock thickened, and he started to sweat.

The condom Ellis had given him burned a hole in his pocket, branding his chest, and he cursed under his breath. He needed to finish this tour and get as far away from Ava Grace as he could before he totally lost it.

"The rickhouse is the next stop. It's just a few steps away."

"What's the rickhouse?"

"It's where we store the barrels while the bourbon ages."

Less than two minutes later, they stood inside the four-story rickhouse. Her gaze wandered around the dimly lit space.

"This is amazing," she breathed. "How many barrels are in here?"

"About twelve thousand. Each barrel holds fifty-three gallons of bourbon."

"It's so quiet."

"Unless we're rolling barrels, no one is allowed in here."

She wandered down one of the long rows, her ass swaying under her skirt. He followed, trying to keep his eyes above her waist. When she reached the end of the row, she turned to face him.

"It's cold in here," she murmured, chafing her palms up and down her arms. The motion lifted her shirt and revealed a smooth expanse of stomach. He imagined kneeling over her, working his cock in his fist, and then shooting cum all over that pale gold flesh.

Groaning under his breath, he closed his eyes. He tried to envision the chemical equation for yeast fermentation in his mind, but the only thing he could see was Ava Grace spread out on his bed, those long legs open wide, just for him.

Ava Grace spoke again, but he couldn't hear her above the frantic beat of his pulse. She moved closer, and even the musty odor of the rickhouse couldn't disguise her sweet scent.

Placing her palms on his chest, she lifted her head until their lips almost touched. She murmured something, her mouth brushing against his, and he dropped his hands to her waist. The feel of her warm skin made his cock even harder, and the muscles along his spine tightened with arousal.

"Jonah," she whispered, and the use of his first name—the name no one ever used—finally got his attention.

He opened his eyes. "What?" he asked hoarsely.

"What's in your pocket?"

Before he could stop her, she delved into his shirt pocket and pulled out the condom.

CHAPTER FOURTEEN

Ava Grace stared at the bright orange square in her hand. Its white lettering was barely visible in the dimly lit rickhouse, but she didn't need to see to know what she held: a condom.

Questions buzzed through her head. Why did Beck have a condom in his shirt pocket? Why had Ellis given one to him? With whom was Beck going to use it?

It was the last question that made her chest tight. She didn't want Beck to have sex with anyone but her.

She took a deep breath, trying to gather her thoughts. She and Beck were completely alone in a huge warehouse filled with wooden racks. They stretched high overhead, filled with barrels of bourbon, narrow rows in between. The air was moist and cool, kind of like a cave, and so quiet she could hear Beck's harsh breaths.

Clenching the condom, she looked up at him. The lack of lighting made it difficult for her to read his expression, but she sensed he was as turned on as she was. He'd barely touched her, just his hands on her waist, yet her nipples were tight and pebbled under the stretchy lace of her bra, and the flesh between her legs was damp and throbbing.

As they stood there, still and silent, a long-ago conversation she'd had with a NASCAR champion flickered in her memory. He told her rookie drivers made the mistake of letting up on the gas when they were ahead. Experienced drivers did the opposite. They didn't back off. They pushed the gas pedal to the floor.

She wasn't going to make a rookie mistake by backing off. She was going to *push*.

She held up the condom in front of Beck, and his eyes almost crossed as he looked at it. "Do you have plans for this?" she asked.

His eyes shot to her face, wide with surprise. He swallowed visibly, his Adam's apple bouncing with the movement.

"No?" she guessed when he didn't answer. "That's good. 'Cause I do."

His mouth fell open. "*What?*"

She tucked the condom into her bra, slid her hand between their bodies, and cupped it over his fly. He was long and hard under her fingers, and she stroked his erection through the denim of his jeans.

He moaned and pressed his hand over hers, holding it immobile. She wove the fingers of her other hand into his thick hair and brought his mouth to hers. She licked his lower lip and gave it a gentle nip before sucking lightly.

She'd never been so bold, so aggressive. She barely recognized herself. She was shocked by her behavior. But she wanted this. She wanted *him*.

She'd *never* wanted anything or anyone the way she wanted Jonah Beck.

"Jonah," she murmured against his lips. "I want you."

He shuddered against her, his breathing ragged, and she slipped her hand from beneath his. "I want to feel your hands on me."

Grasping his big hand, she guided it under her skirt to the

apex of her thighs. She pressed it against her, feeling the heat of his palm through her panties. He spread his hand, covering her mound more fully.

"Touch me," she urged, widening her legs.

He traced the edge of her panties, his fingers rubbing over the lace trim. She held her breath, waiting for the moment when they'd slip inside and touch her sensitive flesh, but it never came.

"I'm wet," she whispered.

"Oh, Jesus," he groaned.

"Don't you want to feel how wet you make me?"

He eased his fingers under the lace. He smoothed the springy hair inside before finding her slit and dipping a finger into it.

"Ah, *fuck*. You *are* juicy." He delved deeper, swirling his fingers through her arousal. "Ripe and juicy."

The tip of his finger grazed her clit, and little shocks radiated down her legs. Her knees shook, and he steadied her with his other hand, bracing it against her lower back.

He trailed his fingers from her clit to her opening, circling with light strokes, over and over until she squirmed against his hand. "You're so soft," he rasped. "So soft ... just like a peach."

Abruptly, he pulled his hand from her panties. She moaned in protest, but the sound died in her throat when he brought his fingers to his mouth and licked them. It was the hottest thing she'd ever seen, and arousal gushed out of her.

"Delicious," he growled.

He worked his hand back into her panties and thrust two fingers inside her. She gasped as her flesh stretched around them. Shifting his hand, he pushed deeper, and she cried out when her internal muscles clenched.

She was aching ... empty ... and she wanted him to fill her.

She reached for his belt, fumbling to unbuckle it. Once she

got it loose, she popped open the stud on his jeans. As she slid down his zipper, he pressed the tip of his finger against the front wall of her vagina. The pleasure rippled from that one spot like a stone thrown into a pond, and she had to lean against him to stay upright.

Suddenly, he hooked his arm under her butt and lifted her. With his other hand still wedged deep inside her, he walked them backward until they bumped into something. Glancing behind her, she glimpsed an upright barrel just before he set her down on top of it.

The barrel's rough edges dug into her thighs, but she forgot the discomfort when she saw Beck's face. The industrial cage light hanging on the wall above their heads revealed every nuance of his expression.

His features were rigid with desire, the skin stretched tightly over his cheekbones and flushed with hectic color. His eyes were so dark they were almost black.

Spreading her legs, she hooked a finger in his belt loop to pull him closer. When she had him where she wanted him, she shoved down his jeans and underwear just enough to release his erection.

She nearly whimpered when she saw it, but she wasn't sure it if was from anticipation or anxiety. Probably both.

She'd been with two other guys, and Beck's erection seemed enormous in comparison, long and thick and topped with a wide, fleshy head. Fluid glistened on the tip, and she swirled her thumb through it before wrapping her hand around the shaft. It was hot, covered in velvety smooth skin, and ridged with veins. She squeezed firmly, and he groaned deep in his throat.

Unwilling to wait any longer to feel him inside her, she plucked the foil packet from her shirt and opened it. She'd never put a condom on a guy—her previous partners always took care of that—but she was driving this racecar, so it was up to her.

Grasping his shaft, she carefully rolled on the latex. When the condom was in place, she hooked her legs around his and brought him closer. She reached between them, tugged her panties to the side, and placed the plump head of his erection at her opening.

She met his eyes. "I want you," she said, slowly and deliberately. "I want you inside me. I want you to be so deep—"

Gripping her hips, he thrust hard into her, forcing the breath from her lungs. Even as her flesh struggled to accommodate the huge, scorching intrusion of his penis, her internal muscles contracted, and she started to come.

"Tight." His word was nothing more than a guttural groan. "*So fucking tight.*"

She clutched his broad shoulders, and he rooted deeper. Dark spots danced in her vision as her orgasm claimed her, her body clenching rhythmically around his. Tingles sparked through her, and she couldn't hold back the gasps and moans that spilled out of her mouth.

He didn't give her a chance to catch her breath. Instead, he hooked his arms under her legs, her knees resting in the crook of his elbows, and slid his hands under her butt.

Gripping the rim of the barrel for balance, she locked her arms and leaned back on them. The new position opened her fully, and he grunted as he slid farther inside.

He looked down, staring at the place where they were connected, and blew out a harsh breath before lifting his gaze to hers. It was so hot it smoldered.

She wanted to tell him how good he felt. She wanted to tell him that she'd never felt so full ... so complete. But the pleasure—the relief—of finally having him inside her had stolen her voice.

Holding her gaze, he palmed her butt cheeks and pulled out completely. He surged back inside her, bumping against her cervix, and her eyes almost rolled back in her head.

"*Oh, God,*" she moaned, raising her hips. "*Jonah.*"

He rocked into her, his penis caressing her clit with every deep stroke. She was so wet she could hear it as he thrust in and out, and the sound turned her on even more.

She felt another orgasm building, the ache in her lower pelvis intensifying with each smooth slide. She tightened her vaginal muscles to ease the ache, and he grunted again, his rhythm faltering.

He paused with just the tip of his erection inside her, his chest moving like bellows. When he plunged forward, she came again. She cried out as it crashed over, a tsunami of sensation that made her vision blur and her ears ring.

His fingers dug into her as he increased his pace. He pounded into her, his hips like pistons. She moved with him, wanting to give him the same pleasure he'd given her.

Suddenly, he stiffened. He came with a hoarse shout, and she watched it happen. As his penis jerked inside her, he closed his eyes, and his head dropped back, the tendons in his neck cording.

The sight of him losing himself inside her body sent satisfaction spiraling though her. When he gave one final, shallow thrust, another orgasm blindsided her. It blasted through her like a bomb, the pleasure so sharp it actually hurt. Her internal muscles clamped down on his erection, and he gave a strangled moan. The pulses seemed to go on and on, and she whimpered softly.

She closed her eyes, and as the tingles dissipated, she became aware of her uncomfortable position. Bourbon barrels were *not* an ideal place for sex. But she wasn't going to complain, not when she'd just come three times.

Beck had given her *three* orgasms. Three amazing, wonderful, incredible orgasms. She'd hoped it would be good between them. But she never could've imagined it would be *that* good.

She opened her eyes as he slid his hands from beneath her and let her legs drop against the side of the barrel. She tried to sit up, but he was still inside her—still hard. He slowly withdrew from her body, holding the condom in place, and she caught her breath as his penis rubbed against her sensitive flesh.

His dark eyes locked on her face. The haze of lust had disappeared, leaving them clear and cold. A knot of dread formed in her stomach, and she swallowed to ease her dry throat.

He glanced away from her and turned his back. After tugging her panties back in place, she hopped down from the barrel. Her legs weren't steady, and she had to lean against the rough wood for support. Once she could stand on her own, she straightened and wrenched down her skirt.

Seconds later, Beck turned to face her. He'd disposed of the condom, she had no idea where, and had fastened his jeans and belt.

He rubbed his hand over his face before suddenly jerking it away. She flushed when she realized it was the same hand he'd put between her legs. He must have smelled her on his fingers.

"Beck, this was—"

"*A huge fuckin' mistake.*"

His voice was so harsh she flinched involuntarily, her head jerking back as if he'd slapped her. A physical blow couldn't have hurt worse than his words.

She cringed at the disgust she heard in his voice. The knot in her stomach pulled tighter, and nausea crawled up her throat.

He turned in a circle, his head tilted toward the ceiling. "*Fuck me.*" He glanced at her, his face contorted with loathing. "I knew somethin' like this would happen. I *knew* you'd fuck up my life somehow."

She was so hurt, so humiliated, she couldn't even formulate a response to his verbal attack. Finally, her mouth caught up to her brain.

"You're an asshole," she hissed.

His eyes narrowed. "I'm an asshole?"

"That's a rhetorical question, right?"

Before he could reply, she took a step forward, eager to get away from him and his hurtful words. His eyes widened, and he took a hasty step backward, as if she carried an incurable and fatal disease.

She took another step forward, and he took another hasty step backward. His bootheel got caught on one of the wooden planks, and he teetered for a second before crashing into the tall wooden racks. Although he tried to catch himself, he tumbled to the floor.

As Ava Grace left the warehouse, she reveled in the satisfying sight of Jonah Beck knocked on his ass.

CHAPTER FIFTEEN

With shaking hands, Beck gripped the edge of the cast iron sink in the men's bathroom in Trinity's office. He braced his arms against it and looked at himself in the chipped mirror hanging above the rust-stained sink.

"You just fucked Ava Grace in the rickhouse," he said to his reflection. "What the hell is *wrong* with you?"

Give yourself a break, chief. How many single guys would walk away from Ava Grace Landy when she told them how wet she was?

He laughed mirthlessly. He couldn't think of one. Not a single goddamn one.

Millions of men—single, married, young, old—had fallen under her spell. Her sexy voice and hot body fueled their fantasies. She certainly starred in his, and now that he'd had her, it would be even worse.

Closing his eyes, he let his head drop forward. He had to forget. He had to pretend it'd never happened. He wished to Christ it never *had* happened. If he could go back in time and change things, he would ... even if it disrupted the space-time continuum and sent the earth spinning into another Ice Age.

Knowing he couldn't hide in the bathroom any longer, he

opened his eyes and turned on the faucet. He vigorously scrubbed his hands, determined to rid them of any trace of Ava Grace's delicious scent. When he was done, he splashed cold water on his face.

After drying his face and hands, he looked in the mirror again. "You have to apologize," he told himself.

No matter how upset he was, he never should've talked to Ava Grace like that. Even though he'd meant every word, he shouldn't have said them out loud.

He needed to find her and apologize for his colossal meltdown. And then he needed to ask her, very politely, to stay the fuck away from him.

He opened the steel door and headed down the hall toward the executive offices. As he passed the breakroom, he heard his name. Backtracking, he glanced inside. Gabe stood in front of the white refrigerator, a chocolate-covered ice cream bar in his hand.

"Where have you been?" Gabe asked, his mouth full of ice cream. "I've been looking for you."

"Were you looking for me in the freezer?"

Gabe swallowed before saying, "I needed sustenance." He smiled broadly. "I have good news: American Spirits agreed to distribute Trinity."

"Holy shit!" Beck gave him a high five. "That's awesome, Gabe! You're a fucking rock star!"

"You're just now noticing that?" Gabe quipped before taking a big bite of ice cream. "I'm guessing the tour with Ava Grace didn't go as well as my negotiations with American Spirits."

Just the sound of her name made Beck's muscles tight. "Where is she?"

Gabe shrugged. "I have no idea. She came stomping into my

office while I was still on the phone, grabbed her purse, and left without a word." He took another bite. "So what happened?"

Beck looked down at the scarred linoleum floor. "Nothing happened."

Nothing except the hottest sex he'd ever had. Fast and rough and so goddamn incredible he was sure he'd remember it until the day he died.

"You're lying," Gabe replied, his voice mild. "I've known you for more than half your life, and I can tell when you're lying. What did you do?"

I did Ava Grace.

He'd never been with a woman who was so ... *primed.* He'd barely gotten inside her before she came.

He groaned under his breath. He had to stop thinking about how tight and wet she was. The sexy sounds she made when she came. The sweet taste of her pussy on his fingers.

Beck reached around his best friend and grabbed a can of soda from the refrigerator. After popping the top, he took a big swig, hoping it would wash the taste of Ava Grace from his mouth.

"What did you do?" Gabe repeated before sucking the last bit of ice cream off the stick.

"Nothing."

"Bullshit." Gabe tossed the little wooden stick into the garbage can. "She looked like she wanted to kill someone, and I have no doubt that someone was you."

Beck chose not to acknowledge Gabe's comment. Instead, he said, "Until Ren gets back, you're responsible for everything related to Ava Grace."

Gabe's eyebrows rose. "Why?"

"Because I said so," Beck snapped. "I'm the CEO of this

company, and I don't have to explain myself."

"Did you just pull rank on me?" Gabe asked softly, his eyes narrowed. "What the fuck is going on with you?"

"I just don't want to be around her, okay?"

Gabe shook his head. "No, it's not okay. What's your problem with Ava Grace? She genuinely wants to help us ... to help Trinity." He studied Beck, his gaze assessing. "Why don't you want to be around her?"

Beck thought about lying but decided he needed to be honest with Gabe. More than likely, Ava Grace would want out of her agreement with Trinity now, and that would affect all of them.

"I had sex with Ava Grace," he announced baldly.

Gabe stared at him unblinkingly for several seconds before jerking open the freezer door and grabbing another ice cream bar. He made his way to the small circular table in the corner and dropped into one of the red plastic chairs. Leaning back, he set the cold treat on the tabletop and propped his ankle on his knee.

"So how was it?"

Gabe's question was so unexpected Beck barked out a surprised laugh. "That's what you want to know?"

The corner of Gabe's mouth lifted in a rueful smile. "I have a few questions, but that's the first one that popped into my head."

Beck rolled his eyes in exasperation. "What was the second question?"

"When?"

"During the tour."

Gabe's eyebrows crawled up his forehead. "Where?"

"Are you working your way through the five *W*s of basic information gathering: who, what, when, where, and why?"

"I'm more interested in the *how* ... as in *How the hell did this happen?*"

"I am too," Beck muttered as he sat down across from Gabe. He was a normal guy with a normal sex drive, but he'd never slept around. His mother's propensity to fuck strangers steered him away from meaningless sex. He'd never been into one-night stands or hookups, and he'd never had sex with a woman he wasn't in a serious relationship with. This was a first.

Today, he'd wanted Ava Grace so badly he'd done her on top of a bourbon barrel. Another first.

Gabe's lips twitched. "You don't seem too happy about it."

"I'm not happy about it. I'm not interested in getting tangled up with her."

"A small part of you must have been interested," Gabe noted with a smirk. "A very small part."

Beck sighed, knowing Gabe was right. No matter how much he wanted to, he couldn't blame Ava Grace for what had happened. He was equally responsible.

Yes, she'd come on to him. But he could've turned her down. He could've laughed it off. But he hadn't. Instead, he'd fucked her as hard and as deep as he could.

He had no excuse for his behavior—nothing except mind-numbing lust. He couldn't think of another occasion when he'd been so turned on. Every bit of sense he possessed had disappeared the moment she'd put her hands on him. She made him forget all the reasons he needed to stay away from her.

"If you gave Ava Grace what she wanted, why was she so mad?" Gabe didn't wait for Beck to respond. "The sex must've been bad."

"It wasn't bad," Beck replied flatly.

And that's the biggest understatement of the century.

"She didn't look like a satisfied woman when she left," Gabe noted dryly.

"I said some things afterward I shouldn't have."

"What did you say?"

He repeated what he'd said to Ava Grace, or as much as he could remember. When he finished, Gabe shook his head in disgust. "Shit, Beck. Couldn't you have just said, 'Thanks, babe. That was great, but let's not do it again'?"

"I wasn't thinking," Beck admitted. "The words just spewed out ... like projectile vomit."

Gabe grimaced. "That's vivid." He settled his hands over his flat stomach, linking his fingers together. "You really fucked up."

"I know," he acknowledged, meeting Gabe's eyes. "I'm sorry. I fucked it up for all of us."

"Yeah, you did." Gabe sighed. "The agreement between Ava Grace and Trinity allows either party to terminate within the first ninety days for any reason without any financial consequences. We'll probably get a call from her manager tomorrow morning."

"I'm going to apologize. Maybe that will—"

Gabe shook his head. "It won't do any good. You'll probably just piss her off more. Or you'll end up having sex with her again."

"That's not something I want to repeat."

Gabe smiled knowingly. "If you say so, brother."

*****

Something was stuck under Ava Grace's skin—something other than a tall, dark, and handsome *asshole*. She thought it was a splinter from the bourbon barrel, but she couldn't tell for sure since she couldn't see the back of her thigh.

Gripping the handheld mirror, she bent over in front of the full-length mirror on the back of her bedroom door and tried to get a better look. All she could see was raw, abraded skin in the shape of the barrel's rim.

Beck's version of a rim job, a naughty voice inside her whispered.

"Ugh," she muttered, disgusted with herself and the entire world.

Just then, a soft knock sounded on the door. "Ava Grace? Are you in there?"

Ava Grace straightened and opened it. Amelia stood on the other side, a big smile on her freckled face. Since she'd married Quinn, it seemed as if she had lost the ability to frown.

"Hey," Amelia chirped. "How was your day?"

"Hey," she replied flatly.

Amelia glanced at Ava Grace alertly, taking in her wet hair, oversized T-shirt, and bare legs. Catching sight of the mirror dangling from her left hand, her best friend asked, "What are you doing?"

"I think I have a splinter in my leg, and I was trying to look at it."

Amelia's eyebrows drew together. "Where is it?"

"On the back of my thigh."

The shorter woman tilted her curly red head toward the queen-size bed. "Lie down, and I'll take a look."

Ava Grace did as Amelia instructed, stretching out on her stomach on the black-and-white floral duvet. Turning her head sideways, she rested it on her crossed arms.

"Dwight David Eisenhower!" Amelia burst out. "What happened to your legs?"

Despite Ava Grace's bad mood, Amelia's "curse" made her smile. "Do you see the splinter?"

Amelia's hands were gentle as she inspected Ava Grace's leg. "I see it."

Ava Grace sighed, relieved the source of her irritation had been identified. Who knew such a tiny piece of wood could be so painful and annoying?

"Will you fix me up?" she requested, her voice muffled by her arms. "Tweezers and supplies are on the dresser. I already disinfected the tweezers."

Ava Grace heard Amelia gather the supplies. Seconds later, she was back, depositing alcohol, cotton balls, antibiotic ointment, and bandages on the bed next to her.

Amelia swabbed the back of Ava Grace's leg with an alcohol-soaked cotton ball. The antiseptic stung her raw skin, and she flinched.

"How did this happen?" Amelia asked, blowing lightly on the stinging flesh.

Ava Grace knew she couldn't continue to ignore her best friend's questions. "I sat on a bourbon barrel during my tour this afternoon."

"Ouch. Guess you should have worn pants. Or picked another place to sit." Amelia pressed a hand on Ava Grace's thigh. "Okay, I'm going to get the splinter now. Don't move."

Ava Grace did her best to remain motionless while Amelia played surgeon. After several minutes of excavation, she crowed, "Got you, you stubborn splinter!"

Amelia leaned over and held the tweezers near Ava Grace's face. The shiny metal tips gripped a sliver of wood about a half inch long.

"I didn't think it would be so big," Amelia said.

An image of Beck's erection popped into Ava Grace's head, and she groaned under her breath. She didn't want to think about that … or how good he'd felt inside her.

She didn't want to think about *him*.

Ava Grace jerked in surprise when Amelia dabbed more alcohol onto her wound. "Sorry, chickadee. Almost done." After smearing antibiotic ointment on Ava Grace's leg, Amelia applied the bandage and patted it. "There you go."

Ava Grace rolled over and sat up. She scooted backward until she could recline against the puffy pillows and crossed her ankles. Amelia crawled up onto the mattress and sat cross-legged facing her.

"Does it hurt?" Amelia asked, her chocolaty gaze loving and sympathetic.

Yes, it hurts.

Suddenly, tears welled in Ava Grace's eyes and spilled down her cheeks. Her throat ached, and when she tried to swallow, a sob escaped from her mouth.

Amelia's eyes widened in horror. "Ava Grace!" She lunged across the bed and grabbed her shoulders. "What is it?" she demanded, her voice panicked.

Ava Grace understood Amelia's alarm. She was rather alarmed herself because she didn't cry ... not when she was sad and not when she was happy.

In fact, she couldn't remember ever crying, not even when she was a little girl. She hadn't cried when she broke her arm when she was seven, or when she burned it on the commercial press at the dry cleaners. She hadn't cried when her dad missed her birthdays and Christmases, and she hadn't cried when she won *American Star.*

But she was crying now, huge gulping sobs that almost choked her. Her eyes were so blurry she could barely see Amelia kneeling in front of her, and her chest ached so badly she wondered if maybe she was having a heart attack.

Amelia shook her a little bit. "Tell me where you're hurt."

Ava Grace buried her face in her hands, and her best friend wrapped her arms around her. "You're scaring me, Ava Grace," she whispered.

And that was enough to stop her tears. "I'm fine," she croaked. "I'm fine."

Amelia sat back on her heels, and Ava Grace swiped the tears from her face. "I'm sorry I scared you."

"I've never seen you cry like that ... not once in twenty-six years." Amelia searched her eyes. "This must be really bad. What happened?"

"I had sex with Beck."

Amelia's eyes narrowed. "Consensual sex?"

Her voice held a note Ava Grace had never heard before—one that made the fine hairs stand up on her arms. "Of course. I would have said rape otherwise."

"Thank God." Amelia blew out a relieved breath. "I didn't want to have to ask Quinn to help me hide a dead body."

Ava Grace laughed soggily. "I love you, Millie."

"I love you too." Amelia's freckled nose wrinkled. "It must have been really bad sex if it made you cry like that."

Ava Grace looked down and picked at the hem of her T-shirt, an old ragged one from her first tour. "That's not why I was crying."

"So the sex was good?"

Ava Grace brought her gaze to Amelia's. "I'm not going to discuss it."

"Why not?"

"Because when I asked you the same thing, back when you and Quinn first got together, you refused to tell me."

Amelia's lips quirked. "I'll tell you now."

"I don't need you to tell me. Your bedroom is right above this one."

Amelia's cheeks turned red, and she smacked Ava Grace's leg. "Just tell me what happened with Beck."

She recounted the events in the rickhouse, making no effort to censor. She told her best friend everything, from discovering the condom in Beck's pocket to knocking him on his ass.

Amelia sighed softly. "What a disaster."

Anger simmered inside Ava Grace, right alongside the hurt and humiliation. "He could have said no. It's not like I forced him into it. He was there with me. I didn't give myself three orgasms."

"Three?" Amelia's head snapped back. "How is that possible? Wasn't it kind of ... quick and dirty? And weren't you uncomfortable, sitting on that barrel? You got a huge splinter."

Ava Grace could feel the blood rushing into her face. "I was really into it. I haven't had sex in six years," she added defensively. "I was overdue for a few orgasms."

Amelia giggled. "You'll get no argument from me."

Just then, the doorbell chimed. As Amelia scooted off the bed, she said, "I'll be right back. It's probably just the mailman."

Ava Grace's damp hair was making her neck clammy, so she grabbed a ponytail holder from the nightstand and twisted her hair into a messy bun. She wished she could terminate the arrangement with Trinity, but she knew Lex would throw a fit if she did.

He'd demand to know why, and she couldn't admit she'd had sex with Trinity's founder and CEO. She'd just have to cowgirl up and try to limit her interactions with Beck.

Amelia rushed through the open door and shut it behind her. She leaned against it, her eyes huge.

"He's here," she said in a loud whisper.

"Who?"

"Beck!"

"Oh, my God!" Ava Grace leapt from the bed, her inner

thigh muscles twinging in protest. "Tell me you're joking!"

Amelia vigorously shook her head. "He wants to talk to you."

With her heart pounding, she begged, "Please, please, please tell me that you said I wasn't here."

A grimace flashed over her best friend's face. "I told him I would see if you were available. He's waiting in the living room."

"Oh, my God, Millie!"

"I'm sorry! I didn't know what you wanted me to do!"

Pressing her palms against her hot face, she asked, "Why is he here?"

"Probably because he knows he acted like a jerk and wants to apologize."

A distressed whimper escaped from Ava Grace's mouth. "Look at me!" She gestured to her bare legs. "I can't see him like this! I'm half-naked!"

Amelia made a funny noise, a mix between a snort and a laugh. "Seriously? You had sex with him on a *bourbon barrel.*"

Closing her eyes, Ava Grace focused on her breathing and willed herself to calm down. She did the same thing before she performed, but talking to Beck was far more nerve-wracking than singing in front of fifty thousand fans. She hadn't had sex with any of them.

"What do you want me to do?" Amelia asked.

Ava Grace opened her eyes. "Can you tell I've been crying?"

She didn't want Beck to know how badly he'd hurt her. That would only give him more power over her, and he already had too much.

Amelia's gaze skipped over Ava Grace's face before she huffed out an incredulous laugh. "You are the only woman on the planet who actually looks better *after* you cry your eyes out." She arched her eyebrows. "Are you going to talk to him?"

"Do you think I should?"

"Yes, but if the first words from his mouth aren't 'I'm sorry,' you need to drop-kick him out the door."

"Right."

Ava Grace straightened her spine. She was strong. She could handle Beck.

She stomped toward the door and stopped in front of Amelia. "I can't talk to him if you don't move."

"You might want to put on a bra and some pants first." Amelia's lips twitched. "Unless you want more than an apology from him." She turned and opened the door. "I'll be upstairs if you need me."

Ava Grace took Amelia's advice, donning a bra and relaxed black running pants before walking barefoot down the hall. She stopped just inside the living room, her gaze immediately landing on Beck.

He sat on one end of the brown leather sofa, his hands clasped between his knees and his chin dropped to his chest. His right leg bounced up and down, the movement betraying his nerves.

"Amelia said you wanted to talk to me."

His head jerked up, and he vaulted to his feet. His dark eyes found hers, and she remembered staring into them as he moved inside her. The room seemed to pulse with sexual tension. She crossed her arms over her chest, waiting for him to speak.

"You were right," he blurted out.

"I'm usually right."

He nodded. "I *am* an asshole."

"I know," she replied, unwilling to make this any easier on him.

A laugh rustled in his throat. "I guess forgiveness isn't one of your finer qualities."

"I haven't heard an apology."

"I'm sorry, Ava Grace. I shouldn't have said those things after we … after we … finished."

Leaning her shoulder against the bright white trim framing the wide doorway, she said, "I knew you'd fuck up my life."

"What?"

"That's what you said: *I knew you'd fuck up my life.*"

His face flushed. "Yeah. That's what I said." He sighed loudly. "I wish I could get a do-over."

"If you got one, what would you say instead?"

A frown contorted his face. "I'm not sure I'd ever say the right thing, no matter how many do-overs I got."

"You never know 'til you try."

He slowly made his way across the room and came to a stop in front of her. Looking down into her eyes, he said, "That was the best sex I've ever had."

All the breath in her lungs rushed out. That was the absolute *last* thing she'd expected him to say.

"But it never should've happened," he continued.

It took her a moment to find her voice. "Why? Because we have a professional relationship?"

"That's a big part of it, yes. But it's more than that."

To her shock, he brought his thumb to her lower lip and brushed the pad back and forth in a ticklish caress. His touch made her aware of her tight nipples and the swollen, slick flesh between her legs.

"I like you, Ava Grace. More than I should." He dropped his hand to his side. "But our lives are like bourbon and olive juice."

His comparison stumped her. "What does that mean?" she asked.

"Do you know what makes a dirty martini *dirty*?"

"Umm ... no," she replied, wondering where he was going with the question.

"Olive juice. To make a dirty martini, you mix olive juice with a little vermouth and either vodka or gin. But you never use bourbon." He shook his head. "Bourbon and olive juice are a bad combination. They just don't mix."

"And you think we're bourbon and olive juice?"

"Yeah. We're wrong for each other, in every way."

"Not in *every* way," she pointed out.

He swallowed audibly. "We need to stay away from each other. This can't happen again." He stepped back. "That's what I should've said in the rickhouse." Shoving his fingers into the front pocket of his Rileys, he fished out his keys. "I have to go. If I don't, I'll end up saying or doing something I'll regret. *Again.*"

When he reached the front door, he turned to look at her. "I know I don't deserve your forgiveness, but I hope you'll accept my apology. Someday."

He was gone before she could tell him that she accepted his apology ... but not his explanation.

CHAPTER SIXTEEN

Beck adjusted the baseball cap to shade his eyes from the midday sun and scoped out the park. Since it was Thursday afternoon, the park wasn't too crowded.

His gaze settled on Ren's daughter, who was playing fetch with Chicken. The two of them had fallen in love at first sight.

Ren and Gatsby had returned from Atlanta last week. Since school was out for summer, and he hadn't found childcare yet, he brought his daughter to the Trinity office to hang out while he worked. Today, they'd decided to go to the park so Gatsby could play while the adults talked business.

So far, Ren was still in the dark about Beck and Ava Grace rocking the rickhouse three weeks ago. He knew he should tell his friend and business partner about it, but he hated to admit how weak and stupid he'd been.

And really, there was no reason Ren *had* to know. Ava Grace was still working with Trinity, much to Beck's relief. He wasn't delusional enough to think she'd forgiven him, though.

He hadn't seen or talked to her since he'd apologized. She had flown back to Nashville the next day.

Gatsby waved a tennis ball in front of Chicken's face and

then tossed it at least forty feet across the park. The dog darted forward, running as fast as he could to chase it down for his new favorite person.

"Gatsby has a good arm," Beck noted, leaning back on his hands and stretching his legs out in front of him. "Maybe you should sign her up for a summer softball league."

Ren nodded. "That's a good idea. I don't know if she likes softball, but I'll ask if she wants to do something like that."

Beck glanced toward Ren. He was watching Gatsby, a little smile playing around his lips.

"I know you haven't been home for long, but how do you think she's adjusting?" Beck asked.

"I don't know." Ren's mouth turned down in a frown. "She doesn't say much. And she doesn't smile or laugh unless she's with Chicken."

"Maybe she takes after you. You're not exactly talkative."

"Maybe. Maybe not." He looked toward Beck, his eyes shadowed. "I don't know anything about little girls. I don't know what's normal and what's not."

"I don't either. My knowledge is limited to big girls," Beck quipped.

Ren sighed. "I don't know how to be a dad, Beck."

"I'm sure every guy feels that way, but you'll learn. You've only been a dad for a few weeks. Give yourself some time to get up to speed."

"If I mess this up—if I mess *her* up—she'll end up dating losers, hooked on drugs, and wearing an orange jumpsuit in a state prison."

Beck couldn't help laughing at the other man's dire predictions. "Jesus, Ren. Do you always have to think worst-case scenario? You're not going to mess her up."

"There's a high probability I will, especially since I have to raise her by myself."

Beck nudged Ren's foot with his own. "You don't have to raise Gatsby by yourself. You've got me and Gabe. Between the three of us, we'll figure it out. I promise. We'll make sure she dates good guys, stays clean, and abides by the law."

"Three men and a little lady … plus a distillery and a dog?" Ren asked wryly.

Beck laughed. "Something like that."

Ren glanced away from Beck, his eyes scanning the park until he found his daughter. "Come a little closer, Gatsby," he called out.

She waved and obediently trotted toward them. Ren returned her wave before bringing his attention to Beck.

"Before I found out about Gatsby, I wasn't even sure I wanted kids," he confessed. "I just never felt the desire to…" He paused, obviously struggling to find the right word.

"Procreate?" Beck suggested.

Ren huffed out a laugh. "Yeah. Procreate." He eyed Beck. "Do you?"

"Yeah, I want kids."

When he'd been younger—when his dad was still alive and his family owned Jonah Beck Distillery—he'd wanted to continue the family tradition. He'd assumed he'd teach his children the bourbon business just as his dad taught him and then pass the reins of the company to the next generation of Becks.

Now that he was older, he felt differently about having children. He still wanted them, but not because they would carry on the Beck tradition of distilling bourbon. He wanted them for himself.

He wanted a family. He hadn't been part of one for nearly

fifteen years, and even then, it lacked the closeness he'd craved. Yes, he had Gabe and Ren, but he wanted a wife who stood by him and a houseful of kids proud to call him Dad.

He didn't want to make the same mistake his father made and end up with a beautiful, but unfaithful and unloving wife. He wanted his children to have a better mother than he had, and to make that happen, he needed a better wife than Sibley Beck. He needed a woman who was loyal and loving.

Suddenly, an image of Ava Grace roasting marshmallows popped into his head. Wow. He'd managed to *not* think about her for a whopping two minutes. That was a new record.

Even though he tried not to, he thought about Ava Grace constantly. Every time he talked with Quinn, the conversation worked its way around to her, usually because of Beck.

He'd been curious about her before the rickhouse sex. Now he wanted to know everything about her.

Mostly, he wanted to know if he was just one name on a long list of guys she had sex with. He wanted to be special to her, which didn't make a damn lick of sense.

"I feel like Gatsby has changed everything about my life," Ren added, bringing Beck back to the current topic of conversation, which was not Ava Grace Landy.

Beck eyed his best friend. "What's everything?"

"Everything," Ren repeated. "Yesterday we went to the grocery store, and while I was in the beer aisle, I started talking to this woman. She was wearing these tight workout clothes, and *goddamn*, her ass was amazing."

"So far, I'm not hearing any difference, chief," Beck replied, swallowing back a laugh.

"Before Gatsby, I probably would've asked her out just to get my hands on it. I was about to get her number, and it suddenly crossed my mind she might not be a good role model. So I said good-bye to her and her amazing ass."

"Yeah," Beck agreed, "you have to think about Gatsby now. You can't just hook up with a woman because you like her ass."

"You see what I mean ... *everything* is different." Ren sighed gustily. "I'm going to have to find a new place to live too. My apartment doesn't have enough space, and it has zero privacy. Gatsby needs her own room where she can do girly stuff." He flashed a rare smile. "And I need my own room where I can do guy stuff."

"*Guy stuff?*" Beck laughed. "Like scratching your balls and trimming your nose hair?"

Ren's laughter joined his. "Exactly." When it trailed off, he said, "Thank you, Beck."

"For what?"

Ren stared at him for a moment. "For being someone I can trust with my daughter. For having my back. For trying to make this situation a little less fucked up."

Beck shrugged off his friend's gratitude, uncomfortable with the shift in conversation. He was just doing his best to be a decent human being, and he didn't want or need any thanks for it.

Ren cleared his throat. "I also wanted to apologize for not being here for the interview with *San Francisco Living*. Gabe told me what happened. I know how much you hate it when reporters bring up that shit."

Beck glanced away from Ren's sympathetic gaze. Unfortunately, Ethan Maynes hadn't been the first reporter to ask Beck about his dad's death, and it was doubtful he'd be the last. After all this time you'd think Beck would be used to those kinds of questions, but they always hit him with the force of a Mack truck.

Although Beck had managed to push the awful interview out of his mind, he couldn't shake the memory of Ava Grace clasping his hand before he'd walked out. When he'd looked down into her wide hazel eyes, he could've sworn they were filled with concern for him.

As Beck's gaze wandered around the park, he caught sight of Gabe making his way toward them, carrying a brown paper sack and cardboard drink caddy. Beck raised his hand in a wave, and Gabe held up the bag in acknowledgement.

"What a shock," Ren said dryly. "He stopped for a snack."

"What do you think? Hot dogs?"

Seconds later, Gabe stopped beside them. "*Hola.*"

Beck and Ren looked at each other and simultaneously said, "Tacos."

Gabe passed the drink holder to Ren before dropping down beside Beck. He crisscrossed his jeans-clad legs and placed the bag on top of them. "Brisket tacos from I Heart Tacos. I got enough for everyone." His gaze found Gatsby, and he shouted, "Gats, tacos!"

Ren grimaced. "Please don't call my daughter by a nickname that rhymes with rats. Her real name is bad enough."

Chicken sprinted toward them, and Gatsby followed in hot pursuit, her golden hair streaming out behind her. The dog skidded to a halt like a cartoon animal, his front paws digging up grass and his rear paws leaving the ground. He flopped down next to Gabe, and when Gatsby reached them, she collapsed next to Chicken.

"Hi, Gabe," she said softly.

"Hey there, pretty girl." He tilted his head toward the drink caddy. "I got you raspberry iced tea."

She gave him a shy smile. "Thanks."

Gabe had three younger sisters, so it was no surprise he'd bonded with Gatsby. He knew how to expertly handle both little girls *and* big girls.

"I talked with the hotel," Gabe announced as he passed out tacos. "Even though they're completely booked because of the International Wine and Spirits Show, I was able to finagle one more room for Ava Grace." He glanced toward Ren. "I also switched your room to a suite so you can bring"—he tapped Gatsby on the nose with an aluminum foil-wrapped taco—"our favorite girl."

"Good." Ren unwrapped his taco. "Now no one has to double up."

Gabe slanted a mocking glance toward Beck as he peeled the aluminum foil from his snack. "Yeah, it would've been a real shame if Beck had been forced to *double up* with Ava Grace."

Beck glowered at Gabe. *Shut up,* he mouthed, even as images of sharing a bed with Ava Grace filled his head. Gabe grinned before taking a huge bite of his taco, his eyes glinting with amusement.

"I'm really excited Ava Grace will be at the show with us," Ren said around a mouthful of taco.

The International Wine and Spirits Show was the biggest event in the spirits industry, attracting tens of thousands of people, from distillers and distributors to restaurateurs and hoteliers. It was a great opportunity for Trinity to get in front of new and existing customers, as well as connect with new distributors.

Each year, the show was held in a different city. Last year, it had been in San Francisco, which had been very convenient. This year it would take place in Seattle, which wasn't as inconvenient as New York City or Miami, but they still had to ship crates of Trinity along with the tradeshow booth.

The show started Monday morning, but exhibitors arrived a couple of days early to set up. Beck and his partners (and Gatsby) were flying into Sea-Tac Airport the day after tomorrow to get an early start Sunday morning. Ava Grace's flight arrived later that day, and the five of them were supposed to eat dinner together.

"I think Ava Grace is going to bring a lot of foot traffic to our booth," Ren added.

"I still think it's a mistake to bring her," Beck countered with a frown. "No one is going to pay any attention to Trinity if she's there. She's a distraction."

Gabe laughed softly. "Only for some people."

CHAPTER SEVENTEEN

The black newsboy cap and oversized sunglasses had done the trick, allowing Ava Grace to slip into the medical office building without anyone noticing her. The media had never followed her to Dr. Hanna's practice before, but she never knew when a *pap* or a reporter would pop up.

Plucking her phone from her purse, she checked the time. She'd been waiting in the neurologist's book-lined office for thirty minutes while he assessed Chuck's physical and mental condition.

Naturally, her father was more comfortable when she wasn't in the exam room, so Kyle stayed with him instead. Dr. Hanna would join her in his office when he finished with Chuck, and they'd discuss his findings and options for dealing with her father's disease. Dr. Hanna was one of the nation's top Alzheimer's experts.

Her phone vibrated in her hand, and a text from Ren floated across the screen. "HOTEL RESERVATIONS CONFIRMED FOR IWSS!"

She couldn't help smiling when she saw the exclamation point. In person and on the phone, Ren Holt was reserved. In writing, however, the man used exclamation points as if they were the only way to end a sentence.

Another text from Ren popped up. "WE'RE SO EXCITED TO SEE YOU ON SUNDAY!"

She snorted under her breath. Gabe and Ren might be excited to see her, but she doubted Beck was. Instead of being appreciative she had agreed to help promote Trinity at the International Wine & Spirits Show, he probably was annoyed.

More than likely, he was thinking of ways to avoid her. That was fine with her. She didn't want anything to do with him either.

How many lies can you tell yourself, Ava Grace?

Irritated by her honest conscience, she turned her phone to silent and tossed it back into her purse. She wished she could just forget Beck. The glint in his dark eyes. The sound of his voice. The way he'd felt inside her.

But she couldn't forget him. He was under her skin, like a splinter, and she couldn't seem to dig him out.

She shifted in her seat, struggling to find a position that would alleviate her numb butt. Why were the chairs in doctors' offices always so uncomfortable? Was that part of the Hippocratic Oath?

Trying to distract herself, she dug through her purse and found a notepad and a pen. She needed to finish the song she'd promised to write and record for Trinity.

Ellis had provided the inspiration when he told her about the head, heart, and tail of bourbon distilling. The song's chorus and melody had come easily, but she was struggling with the rest of the lyrics. She hoped to get them down soon so she could run the song by the Trinity guys at the spirits show.

The lyrics compared the process of distilling bourbon to a romantic relationship that burned out fast. In the beginning, the feelings were too strong, and in the end, the feelings were too weak. But the feelings in between—those were the ones you wanted to savor.

As she sang the last verse into the empty room (which had *terrible* acoustics), the door opened behind her. She shoved the notepad and pen into her purse before standing to greet Dr. Hanna.

A Vanderbilt University Medical Center badge hung on the breast pocket of his white coat. Underneath it, she caught a glimpse of his blue plaid button-down shirt and khaki pants.

Ava Grace wasn't sure of Dr. Hanna's exact age. His daughters were in college, so she estimated he was in his early to mid-fifties. He wore his silver hair in a short Caesar cut, and a white horseshoe mustache framed his mouth. It always distracted her when he spoke.

"I heard you singing down the hall. Is that a new song?"

"Yes."

Stopping beside her, he gave her a brief hug. She was wearing flats today, so they were about the same height.

"It's good to see you, Ava Grace."

"You too, Dr. Hanna. Thank you for fitting us into your schedule."

Chuck's appointment had been scheduled for next Tuesday, when she was supposed to be in Seattle at the tradeshow. Fortunately, Dr. Hanna's receptionist worked them in early.

Kyle had assured Ava Grace he could handle the appointment without her, but she wasn't okay with that. She already felt like she relied on him too much.

Chuck was her father. He was her responsibility, not Kyle's.

"Kyle wanted me to let you know he's taking Chuck for a walk," Dr. Hanna said.

That information gave Ava Grace a measure of relief. She'd

worried Chuck would become agitated if he had to sit in the waiting room or the SUV.

Dr. Hanna gestured to the chair. "Please, have a seat."

She reclaimed the uncomfortable chair while he settled his thin frame behind his walnut-stained desk. It was completely bare except for a computer monitor, keyboard, and a mesh cup filled with markers, pens, and pencils.

"So…" Dr. Hanna's pale blue eyes studied her from behind his rimless glasses. "Tell me how things have been at home."

"It seems like Chuck is getting worse every day. This time last year, he still recognized me and Kyle. He still recognized his surroundings. He was able to dress himself and go to the bathroom on his own. But not now."

Dr. Hanna cupped his hands together on the desk. "I'll be honest with you. I thought your father's disease would plateau. But it has continued to progress." He twisted his thick platinum wedding band around his finger. "I'm sorry to tell you this, Ava Grace, but Chuck is showing signs he's in the sixth stage of Alzheimer's."

She nodded slowly. "I thought that might be the case."

She'd spent hundreds of hours reading about Alzheimer's, everything from first-person accounts to scientific research studies. The Alzheimer's Association broke the disease into seven stages.

The sixth stage was severe decline, and it was characterized by loss of recognition of people and places, personality changes, inability to remember personal details, and wandering. Verbal outbursts and violent behavior were common as well.

"There's no way to predict how long this stage will last," Dr. Hanna said, "but studies indicate it usually lasts two years."

Two years.

She closed her eyes for a long blink. Sometimes she felt as if she couldn't get through the next two hours without losing it.

"During the examination, Kyle mentioned Chuck has experienced a few outbursts, both verbal and physical."

"Yes. It usually happens when he's confused or afraid." She glanced at the framed diplomas hanging on the beige wall before bringing her attention back to Dr. Hanna, a graduate of Harvard Medical School's Class of 1988. "He seems more agitated when I'm around. Every time he's had an outburst, I've been nearby. He's okay when it's just Kyle."

Dr. Hanna leaned forward and braced his elbows on his desk. "I know your father wasn't part of your life growing up, and you're probably thinking his current behavior is related to his past behavior."

She looked down at her lap. "He didn't want to be around me then, and he doesn't want to be around me now."

"Chuck's outbursts aren't personal, Ava Grace. Alzheimer's isn't a truth serum. It doesn't reveal people's true selves or their true feelings. It erases them. Alzheimer's makes people do and say things they never would've done otherwise. That's one of the most painful things about watching a loved one succumb to this disease."

Shrugging, she said, "It doesn't matter if it's personal. The point is, he's more agitated when I'm around and more likely to have an outburst. I don't know what to do."

"There's a simple not-so-simple solution."

She shook her head in confusion. "I'm sorry ... what?"

"The simple solution is limiting your interactions with Chuck." Dr. Hanna sighed. "But that's not so simple because he lives with you."

She stared at Dr. Hanna, trying to process his words. "Are

you telling me that I should stay away from my father?"

"Yes, that's what I'm telling you," he replied, a solemn expression on his face. "And you also need to think about how you're going to keep him safe. At this stage, he's a danger to himself and the people around him."

"I've already hired one of Kyle's Marine Corps buddies to help out."

"Chuck needs to be monitored every minute of the day, Ava Grace. I've had patients who've woken up in the middle of the night, while everyone was asleep, and accidentally set fire to the house by trying to make a cup of tea. I've had patients who've wandered away, fallen into ditches, and broken their necks. That's why most people choose to put their loved one in a memory care facility. It's safer for everyone."

He rolled his lips inward before saying, "I know I've thrown a lot at you today, but you need to know emotional and behavioral issues typically occur toward the end of the sixth stage."

It took her a moment to digest his statement. "You're saying Chuck is already at the *end* of the sixth stage?"

"Possibly."

"Is there anything that can be done to slow the progression of the disease?"

"We're already doing everything we can."

"Are you sure?" she asked, her voice tinted with desperation.

He gave her a sympathetic smile. "I'm sure."

After a long silence, Ava Grace rose from the torture chair. "Thank you, Dr. Hanna."

"I'm sorry. I know this is hard." He rounded his desk. "Have you thought about joining a local support group?"

"I can't do that."

Tilting his head, he asked, "Why not?"

She laughed, but the sound held no amusement. "If I go to a support group, it would be all over social media and TV and in every magazine and tabloid in the world."

As a public figure, she had very little privacy. People thought they had a right to know everything about her life, and she accepted that reality.

Unfortunately, the people around her—the people she cared about—were targets too. She did her best to protect them, mostly by being available to reporters and paparazzi so they didn't feel compelled to go after anyone else.

So far, she'd managed to keep Chuck's illness a secret. Only a handful of people knew he lived with her, and an even fewer number knew he had Alzheimer's. She wanted to keep it that way. Her father deserved his privacy, especially when it came to his health.

"There are some online support groups you could join anonymously," Dr. Hanna said.

She nodded. "That's a good suggestion. I'll look into it."

He walked her to the check-out station. "You know how to reach me if you need me." He hugged her. "See you in three months."

After scheduling another appointment for her father, she slipped on her newsboy cap and concealing sunglasses and took the elevator to the first floor. As she exited the cab, she remembered her phone was on silent.

Worried Kyle might have texted her, she rummaged around in her purse for her phone. The automatic doors slid open, and she walked into the bright sunshine … and a throng of media.

At least twenty reporters and photographers clogged the sidewalk in front of the medical office building, and she was trapped in the middle. They squeezed closer, jostling her between them, and shoved microphones in her face.

"Ava Grace! Ava Grace! Over here!"

"When are you due?" a female reporter shouted.

Another voice yelled, "Who's the daddy?"

She abruptly remembered an obstetrics/gynecology practice also was a tenant in this building. Of course, the media would assume she was pregnant, as opposed to having problems with her nervous system or her ears, nose, and throat.

A horn blared, and the knot of reporters and photographers loosened enough for her to break free. The horn blared again, closer this time, and she saw the hood of a black SUV. *Her* SUV, if she wasn't mistaken. She couldn't tell for sure, though, because the windows were tinted.

She pushed and shoved her way to the passenger door. Just as she reached for the handle, the door flew open. She clambered in and pulled it shut, breathing hard.

"Didn't you get my texts?" Kyle asked, slapping his palm against the automatic door lock.

"I was just about to check my phone when I walked out." She exhaled harshly. "I wasn't paying attention. They've never tracked me here."

As Kyle inched through the crowd, she twisted to look in the backseat. She was worried about her father—worried the crowds of reporters might have frightened him.

Chuck sat behind her, earphones snug over his head. His eyes were glued to the small TV screen that dropped down from the SUV's ceiling.

"He's fine," Kyle muttered. "He's watching *Dukes of Hazzard.*"

She couldn't help laughing. "No wonder his eyes are glazed."

The SUV finally cleared the horde of reporters. As Kyle steered the big vehicle toward the exit, she clicked her seatbelt into place. She waited until they were on the interstate to give him an abbreviated version of her conversation with Dr. Hanna.

When she finished, she asked, "Have you noticed Chuck gets more agitated when I'm around, or is it just my imagination?"

Kyle glanced sideways, his eyes shaded by sunglasses with mirrored lens. "It's not your imagination."

"I can't believe Dr. Hanna suggested I limit my interactions with Chuck." She shook her head. "Can you?"

Kyle's silence spoke louder than words.

"You think he's right?" Her voice betrayed her shock.

Flipping on the blinker, Kyle moved into the fast lane. "I think it's something you should consider."

She stared out the window. Buildings and trees flashed by in a blur of colors.

"Even if he no longer recognizes me, I want to spend as much time with him as I can … while I still have the chance."

"I get it," Kyle replied. "But that's what you want. It's not what he needs."

CHAPTER EIGHTEEN

Hundreds of people crammed Trinity Distillery's booth at the International Wine and Spirits Show. To be specific, hundreds of *men* crammed the booth. It had been that way since the show had opened yesterday morning.

The visitors weren't there because they were interested in bourbon. As Beck had expected, they were there to see Ava Grace. But he hadn't expected to be so impressed with the way she handled the crowd.

They all wanted something from her—a smile, an autograph, a picture—and she gave them what they wanted. She greeted each and every one with a smile, graciously signed whatever was put in front of her, from pictures to magazine articles to CDs, and patiently posed for pictures.

Bracing his shoulder against one of the tall displays that illustrated Trinity's distilling process, Beck crossed his arms. From his slightly elevated position, he could see Ava Grace clearly, and he let his gaze wander over her as she posed between two vice presidents from American Spirits Distribution.

She smiled widely for the picture. Her shiny platinum hair was pulled into a low ponytail just below her right ear. It draped over her shoulder and curled under her breast.

His gaze dropped to her chest and lingered there. Her Trinity Distillery T-shirt was slightly different than the one he wore. Hers was a dusky purple hue and clung to her curves. *Real Women Drink Bourbon* was printed across the front in a sparkly, feminine font. The Trinity Distillery logo was on the back.

His eyes continued their path, trailing down her tight Rileys. They showed off her long legs, and even though she faced him, he knew the jeans shaped her ass perfectly because he could barely keep his eyes off it.

She shifted from one brown leather boot to the other, and he glanced up just in time to see her wince slightly. When she quickly hid her discomfort behind a bright smile, he frowned.

She'd pitched in as they rushed to get the booth ready this morning, and like him, she'd been standing for hours without a break. Her feet were probably aching like a bitch, but she hadn't whined or complained.

Pushing away from the display, he stepped down and weaved his way through the throngs of people. All the chairs in the Trinity booth were occupied, so he headed to the booth next door. It was nearly empty, only a few people milling around.

After snagging an unused stool, he shouldered his way over to Ava Grace. When he reached her side, he placed the stool behind her. He waited until she had finished talking to a guy in an expensive suit before clasping her elbow and tugging her toward the high-backed chair. She glanced up, surprise etched on her beautiful face.

"I got you a stool." He cocked his head toward it. "I figured your feet must be barking."

Her eyes widened before she glanced over her shoulder. She slowly brought her gaze back to his. "Thank you," she replied, a grateful smile on her lips. "That was really thoughtful."

The skin of her inner elbow was soft and smooth against his fingers, and he couldn't stop himself from stroking his thumb over it. "No problem, sugar."

Her smile widened, and he grimaced, annoyed with himself for calling her *sugar*. He was worse than the starstruck fools who flocked to the Trinity booth. He dropped her elbow, and she slid gracefully onto the stool.

Tilting her head, she said, "I finally figured it out: your middle name is Crispin."

"No."

"Am I close?"

Not close enough.

As he turned to leave, she stopped him with a hand on his shoulder. "Stay," she requested softly. "Keep me company."

He glanced at the line of men waiting to meet her. "You have plenty of company," he pointed out dryly, pushing down the urge to do exactly as she'd asked.

She beckoned him closer with a crook of her finger. He leaned toward her, and she placed her mouth near his ear.

"I don't want them, Jonah," she whispered. "I want *you*. I want *your* company."

His cock twitched, and he drew back to stare into her eyes, wondering why he couldn't stay away from her … why he couldn't stop wanting her.

Suddenly, an accented male voice called out, "Ava Grace, my darling!"

My darling?

She jerked her head toward the voice, her eyes scanning the crowd. "Shy!" she squealed, jumping from the stool and plunging into the crowd.

All the guys in line turned to watch her, giving Beck an unimpeded view of her and the tall son of a bitch who wrapped his arms around her waist and picked her up until she dangled above him.

She laughed joyously. "Shy, it's so good to see you!"

Shy? What kind of name is Shy?

The auburn-haired man let her slide down his body—*fucking lucky bastard*—and dropped a loud, smacking kiss on her plump lips. "When I heard you were here, I had to come and see you," he said.

"I'm so glad you did," she replied, her eyes shining brightly under the harsh fluorescent lights of the exhibition hall.

She patted Shy's chest, and Beck eyed the other man, desperately searching for flaws. Unfortunately, he didn't find any. Shy's coppery mustache and goatee were neatly trimmed, and he looked fit enough. His light gray button-down shirt, charcoal gray trousers, and black leather shoes were obviously expensive.

A couple of men waiting in line muttered irritably, visibly unhappy Ava Grace's attention had been diverted. She gave them an apologetic glance.

"Gentlemen, this is a good friend of mine," she explained, smiling sweetly. "Can you give me a few minutes to catch up with him? I'll be back soon."

She hooked her arm through Shy's and pulled him toward the back of the booth. Beck watched as she visited with the other man, wondering who he was and what she'd meant by *good friend*.

Were they friends with benefits? Had she fucked him?

Shy caressed Ava Grace's cheek with the back of his fingers, and Beck had a sudden, overwhelming urge to snap the bastard's wrist. A fire ignited in his gut and spread to his chest, and he abruptly realized he was jealous.

He didn't want any man to touch Ava Grace ... any man except himself.

With his insides smoldering like a foundry, Beck stalked to the other side of the booth, where they'd set up the tasting area. He was tempted to throw back a shot of bourbon. He needed something strong to wash away the sour taste in his mouth—the sour taste of jealousy.

Gabe stopped beside him, and Beck spared him a brief glance before returning his attention to Ava Grace and Shy.

"Why do you look like you want to kill someone?" Gabe asked.

Beck didn't bother to answer, and Gabe followed the direction of Beck's gaze.

"*Oh*," Gabe said, amusement coloring his tone.

"Do you know who that guy is?"

"Yeah."

Beck jerked his gaze from Ava Grace to spear Gabe with an intent look. "Well?"

"I'm surprised you don't recognize him. That's Andre Shiroc," Gabe answered, pronouncing the man's last name as *Shy-rock*.

Beck's eyebrows arched. He certainly hadn't expected Ava Grace's *good friend* to be a celebrity chef. Andre Shiroc had his own TV show on The Food Network, and he owned several restaurants in Seattle, San Francisco, and Los Angeles.

"I didn't recognize him without that checked bandana he always wears on his head and his chef jacket," Beck said. "And he's usually clean-shaven."

He glanced at Shiroc again, clenching his teeth when the chef dropped his hand to Ava Grace's slender waist. *Fucker.*

"How does she know him?" he asked, his voice little more than a growl.

"Why don't you ask her?" Gabe suggested with an arch smile.

"I'm not going to ask her anything," Beck muttered. "I don't care."

Gabe chuckled. "I can see how much you *don't care*." He tapped Beck on the forearm with his surface tablet. "You need to read this."

"What is it?"

Gabe handed the tablet to Beck. "The *San Francisco Living* article. It came out this morning."

"*Shit.* I don't want to read it. Just tell me how bad it is."

Gabe pointed to the article. "Read it."

Beck dropped down into one of the chairs behind the tasting station. He *really* didn't want to deal with this right now.

Gabe sat down beside him. "Read it, Beck," he urged quietly.

Beck took a deep breath and began to read. Although the article didn't start off negatively, he had no doubt it would go that way eventually. It took him several minutes to read through it, and when he finished, he placed the tablet on his knee.

"Well?" Gabe asked. "What do you think?"

"I can't believe it," he answered, shaking his head in disbelief.

He double-checked the byline. There in black and white: *Ethan Maynes.*

"How did *that* article come out of the interview we did?"

The article wasn't positive; it was damn near glowing. Beck sounded like a trailblazer, and Trinity sounded like the best bourbon in the world.

It didn't mention Beck's dad. Nor did it mention Beck's arrest for assault.

"This is the best media coverage we've *ever* received," Beck added, incredulity making his voice higher than normal. "How the hell did this happen?"

"Ava Grace."

"What?"

"Ava Grace made it happen. After you walked out, she spent two hours with Ethan. She saved our bacon."

Beck nodded emphatically. "She sure as hell did."

"You should fall to your knees and thank her." Gabe's mouth curled into a smirk. "I'm sure she'd enjoy that."

When Beck finally realized what Gabe was suggesting, he didn't know whether to laugh or groan. Now he wouldn't be able to stop thinking about "thanking" Ava Grace with his mouth between her legs.

Gabe nabbed the tablet. "There's something else I think you should see."

He tapped the screen a couple of times before handing the tablet back to Beck. The first thing he saw was a headline: *Who's the Daddy?*

Frowning, Beck scrolled down. A picture of Ava Grace appeared. A black cap covered her bright blond hair, and huge sunglasses hid half her face.

He read the caption: *Ava Grace Landy was spotted leaving her doctor's office in Nashville last week. Sources close to the country star say she's expecting her first child early next year. The question on everybody's mind: Who's the daddy?*

Chills prickled Beck's scalp. With his heartbeat thundering in his ears, he looked up and met his best friend's gaze.

Gabe arched his eyebrows. "Are *you* the daddy?"

CHAPTER NINETEEN

"My daughter is a big fan of yours, Miss Landy."

Even though Ava Grace's cheeks ached, she summoned a smile for the short, middle-aged man in front of her. "How old is your daughter?"

"Eighteen. She's going to the University of Texas this fall."

"That's a good school. You should be proud of her."

Ava Grace had always been good at making small talk with strangers. All she had to do was ask a question, and the conversation flowed from there. It was a skill that came in handy when she interacted with fans.

She plucked a rolled-up poster from the tall cardboard box beside her. "Do you think she'd like an autographed poster for her dorm room?"

The man nodded. "She'd love it."

"What's her name?" she asked as she unrolled the poster.

"Ashley."

Grabbing a metallic marker, she wrote a short note: *To Ashley, Study hard. Dream big. Best wishes, Ava Grace.*

After capping the marker, she handed the poster to Ashley's dad.

"Thank you," he said with a wide smile.

"You're welcome." She patted his shoulder. "Try not to worry too much when she goes away."

He shook his head. "I'm a dad." He rolled the poster into a long tube. "It's my job to worry about her."

"She's lucky," she replied sincerely. "Not every girl has a dad who takes his job so seriously."

My dad didn't.

After Ashley's father left, Ava Grace glanced around. The show closed a few minutes ago, and except for her, Beck, and Gabe, the booth was empty. The guys were stacking dirty shot glasses in a plastic dish tub, and she slowly made her way over to them. Although shows like this one could be fun, they also were exhausting.

Her hand was cramped from the hundreds of autographs she'd signed, and even though she'd worn her most comfortable boots, her feet were killing her. She wished she had a man in her life to massage her hands and her feet … among other things.

Noticing a couple of dirty shot glasses on a display, she detoured to grab them. Beck looked up when she approached him and Gabe. She held out the glasses, and as he took them from her, she said, "I'm going to head back to my room."

Beck glanced toward Gabe. "Can you finish up here, chief?"

"Yep. There's not much left to do."

Beck stepped out from behind the blue tub. "I'll walk you to your room."

He ushered her forward with a hand on her lower back. As they left the booth, they passed the easel display with a barrel lid that informed everyone of Trinity's gold medal award in the whiskey category.

Trinity beat all the big distilleries, including Jonah Beck

Distillery. The winner had been announced last night at the show's awards dinner.

"I'm so proud of you, Beck."

His head snapped sideways. "For what?"

"For winning the gold medal. Gabe told me what a big deal it is—like an athlete winning a gold medal at the Olympics or a singer winning a Grammy." She nudged her shoulder against his. "I'm impressed."

His entire face turned as red as a fire truck. Even his ears reddened.

"Thanks," he muttered, looking down at his feet.

Beck's response made her think very few people had praised him or acknowledged his hard work. Despite all his accomplishments, he remained humble and worked hard. She liked to think that was something they had in common.

As they approached the hotel lobby, Beck gently grasped her elbow. His fingers were warm and slightly rough, a reminder of how good they'd felt between her legs. Her stomach turned warm and liquid, and she fervently wished she'd packed her vibrator.

Show attendees clogged the spacious lobby, and a couple of guys bumped into her as they hurried toward the revolving doors. Beck draped his arm around her shoulders and brought her close to his side. Although the protective move surprised her, it also sent a thrill through her.

A large group of people were waiting for the elevator. As she and Beck joined them, several men recognized her and murmured her name to their companions. When they pulled out their phones and snapped pictures of her, Beck's arm tightened around her shoulders, tucking her into his body.

One of the younger guys called out, "Ava Grace, can I have an autograph?"

Before she could reply, Beck drilled the guy with an icy glare. "She's signed autographs all day," he growled. "She's done for now. You can come by the Trinity booth tomorrow and get one."

The elevator doors opened, and Beck didn't wait for the people in front of them to enter first. He pushed his way through the crowd, holding her tight against him. Once they were in the cab, he stood in the opening and prevented anyone else from getting on.

She gasped. "That was rude."

Jabbing the button for their floor, he replied, "*They* were rude."

"No, they weren't," she countered, shaking her head. "I know you think you were helping me, but you can't be rude to my fans, especially when they're polite and respectful."

He leaned against the back wall of the elevator and crossed his arms over his chest. His olive-colored T-shirt stretched over his biceps, and her eyes locked on those well-defined muscles. She wondered what he did to make them so *lickable*.

"Maybe you didn't notice, but you were about to be swarmed by a group of men who've been drinking all day." The Sahara couldn't have been any drier than his tone. "I'm not going to stand by and let someone hurt you."

She stared at him, stunned by his words. Goose bumps broke out all over her body, and her knees wobbled like Jell-O.

"Thank you," she said huskily.

The elevator dinged, and Beck pushed away from the wall. Placing a hand on the edge of the door, he held it open for her. She exited the cab on shaky legs, and he followed.

Their rooms were located at the end of the hall, across from each other, and they made their way down the carpeted corridor side-by-side. Stopping in front of her door, she turned to face him.

"What did you want to talk about?"

He studied her intently. "Are you pregnant?"

His question flustered her so much, she couldn't do anything but stare at him for a moment. "Why would you ask me that?"

"I saw a bunch of articles and pictures online."

She shook her head. "It's just gossip."

"So you're not pregnant?"

"No."

He stared into her eyes as if trying to assess her honesty. "The articles said you were spotted leaving your doctor's office last week."

Suddenly, his question made a lot more sense. "*Oh.*"

His eyebrows jumped up his forehead. "*Oh?* What does that mean?"

"My dad had an appointment with his neurologist. That's why I was there. I've kept his condition a secret, and there's an OB/GYN in the building, and everybody immediately jumped to the conclusion I was pregnant. If I were pregnant every time a gossip rag or website said I was, I would have fifty children."

The stiff line of his shoulders softened, and he exhaled softly. "Doesn't it bother you?"

"What?"

"Doesn't it bother you when people spread lies about you?"

"Not really. I'm used to it." She waved her hand. "It's just harmless gossip."

"It's not harmless when other people believe the lies."

She considered his words before nodding. "That's true. It hurts when people believe the worst of you."

A tight smile creased his mouth. "Speaking of people

believing the worst … Did you see the *San Francisco Living* article on Trinity?"

"Yes, Gabe showed it to me."

"He told me what you did."

"What did I do?"

"To quote Gabe, you saved our bacon. That was the most positive coverage we've ever received."

He moved closer, and she leaned back against her door. The steel was cold through her thin T-shirt, and she shivered.

"Thank you," he murmured.

"You're welcome."

He propped his palm on the door over her head, and she clasped her hands behind her, worried she might do something stupid like throw her arms around his neck and tug his mouth down to hers. The last time she'd done that, he hadn't responded very well.

His eyes darkened until they looked almost black in the corridor's muted lighting. "Can I take you to dinner tonight?"

Her heart stuttered. After all this time, Beck had finally asked her out on a date.

"To thank you for making the article a success," he added.

All her excitement drained away. He wasn't asking her out on a date. He was inviting her to a business dinner.

"I can't have dinner with you tonight. I have plans."

His eyes narrowed. "What kind of plans?"

"Dinner plans."

"With whom?"

"Shy."

She planned to pick Shy's brain about her cookbook. She knew he'd have a lot of great ideas for fresh, fun recipes.

"Your good friend Shy."

She frowned, confused by the strange note in Beck's deep voice. "Yes. Shy and I are good friends."

Quinn's brother had introduced her to Shy a few months ago. They'd bonded over baked goods, and she'd been a guest on his cooking show a couple of times.

"Are we *good friends?*"

As she stared into Beck's eyes, she abruptly realized what he was asking: he wanted to know if she'd had sex with Shy.

Debating whether to tell him what he really wanted to know, she turned toward the door and fumbled in her pocket for her key card. Before she could fish it out, Beck crowded closer, gripping her hips in both hands and pressing his front against her back.

"You didn't answer my question, sugar."

"If you're asking if I've had sex with Shy—"

Before she could finish her sentence, he spun her and covered her mouth with his. His lips were warm and firm yet soft too.

Perfect for kissing.

As he licked the underside of her upper lip, her eyelids slid closed, and she fisted his T-shirt in her hands to pull him closer. He turned his attention to her lower lip, sucking it into his mouth before giving it a gentle nip.

She opened to him, and he plunged his tongue inside her mouth. She welcomed his aggressive strokes by twining her tongue around his and sucking lightly. He tasted even better than she remembered, like rich, buttery caramel.

She sucked on his tongue, just a little harder, and he moaned. His fingers flexed on her hips before one hand slipped under her T-shirt. He stroked upward over her side until he reached the edge of her bra.

She licked into his mouth, and he cupped his hand over her breast. His palm was so hot she felt the imprint on her skin. He found her nipple, his thumb brushing rhythmically over the tight peak as he thrust his tongue into her mouth.

He tugged down the lacy cup of her bra, and her nipple popped over the top. As he rolled it between his thumb and forefinger, he squeezed gently. When he scraped his nail over the tender bud, ribbons of pleasure unraveled inside her.

Moaning against his lips, she dropped her hand to his erection and pressed her palm against it. With a gasp, he pulled his mouth from hers. He reared back, and she opened her eyes to meet his. They stared at each other, trying to catch their breath.

"*Damn*," he cursed hoarsely.

She licked her lips, wanting one last taste of him, and his erection twitched against her palm. She jerked her hand away and tucked it into the front pocket of her jeans.

As she took a deep breath, his thumb accidentally grazed her nipple. Tingles radiated down her spine, and she gasped softly. His fingers flexed around her breast, and her flesh seemed to swell in his hand.

"*Damn,*" he cursed again before slowly pulling his hand from her shirt.

Looking down, he rubbed the top of his head in agitation. His wavy hair stuck up in the front, and she smoothed the dark strands, savoring the feel of the silky tendrils against her fingers. His head lifted, and she got lost in his intense gaze.

"Why did you kiss me?" she asked.

She hoped he'd admit that he wanted to be with her … that he had feelings for her. He stared at her for a charged moment, but didn't answer.

"Why did you kiss me, Jonah?"

"*Shit*." He rubbed his hands over his face. "I don't know."

"Wrong answer," she shot back, poking him in the chest with her forefinger. "Don't kiss me again—"

To her surprise, he caught her hand in his, turned it over, and kissed her palm. Little shocks traveled up her arm, and she yanked it away.

This man confused her more than a logic puzzle. He threw her off-balance and made her unsure of herself. She didn't like it one bit. And his waffling pissed her off. She knew what she wanted, and he needed to get with the program.

"Don't kiss me again unless you plan to take me to bed," she snapped.

She heard a deep chuckle, and she and Beck jerked their heads toward the noise. Gabe stood a few feet away, a key card in his hand. He looked back and forth, a wicked glint in his blue eyes.

"Excuse me," Gabe said, his voice threaded with laughter. "Did I interrupt your *discussion*?"

CHAPTER TWENTY

Beck tossed the suitcase on his bed, unzipped it, and threw back the top. He'd returned from the International Wine & Spirits Show only five days ago, and now he had to leave again.

Chicken jumped up beside the suitcase and stretched out. Beck looked toward his canine best friend.

"Can you believe this bullshit?" he asked Chicken. "I have to go to Los Angeles. Gabe has food poisoning and can't make the trip. And Ren can't leave Gatsby on such short notice. The plane takes off in less than two hours."

Tucking his paws under his body, Chicken laid his head on the bed and gazed unblinkingly at Beck. His tail thumped a steady rhythm against the down comforter.

"I have to go. Gabe says we can't cancel the meeting with West Coast Wine & Spirits."

West Coast Wine & Spirits was Trinity's largest distribution partner. The relationship with the Los Angeles-based company was critical.

"That's not the only reason I have to go. Ava Grace is the guest star on *Roarke* tonight. She's going to be talking about Trinity, and Gabe says someone from the company should be there for moral support." He shook his head. "I know … Gabe says. What does Gabe know? Nothing. He's obviously not very smart if he ate sushi from a food truck."

He glanced at Chicken. "Don't worry. You're not going to the kennel. You're going to stay with Gabe and watch over him while he's puking his guts out."

Beck jerked open his sock drawer. "Black socks, black socks, where are you?" he muttered.

Finally, he spotted the elusive socks and tossed a pair toward his suitcase. He missed, and they landed on Chicken, who shot him a baleful glance.

"Sorry, buddy." He closed his sock drawer. "Underwear, undershirts, socks. What else?"

After adding a T-shirt and Rileys to his suitcase, he made his way to his closet. He looked over his shoulder. "What do you think, Chicken? Do I need to wear a suit to the meeting with West Coast Wine & Spirits?"

Chicken yawned, and Beck nodded. "I agree. A sports coat and tie should be fine. Now what about the *Roarke* show?"

Thirty minutes later, Beck was in his Jeep heading to Gabe's apartment. Chicken sat in the passenger seat, his head hanging out the window.

Realizing his hands were clenched on the steering wheel so tightly his knuckles were white, Beck took a deep breath and loosened his fingers. "Calm down, chief," he told himself. "You can handle an overnight trip with her."

But deep down, he worried he *couldn't* handle an overnight trip with Ava Grace, not without handling *her*. He had zero confidence in his intellect and self-control, the two things that made him a reasonable man instead of a wild animal.

He knew Ava Grace wasn't right for him. He knew he needed

to stay away from her. Yet that knowledge hadn't stopped him from putting his hands and mouth on her when they'd been in Seattle.

He'd replayed everything that happened during the show, over and over until it was a continuous loop in his head. He'd had a tenuous grip on his emotions from the moment he saw her on Sunday night.

His jealously over Andre Shiroc. His anxiety in the hotel lobby when he realized Ava Grace was about to be mobbed by a bunch of drunk guys. His fierce need to protect her ... to make sure she was safe.

But it was his reaction to her possible pregnancy that confused and confounded him the most. The realization that he could be the father of Ava Grace's child made him light-headed with panic.

Then the realization that *another* man could be the father of her child almost sent him to his knees. Even though he didn't want to be Ava Grace's baby daddy, he didn't want any other man to be either.

He hadn't planned to ask her to dinner. He hadn't planned to ask her whether she'd had sex with her good friend Shy. He hadn't planned to shove his tongue in her mouth and his hand up her shirt.

But he'd done all those things. And he probably would've done more if Gabe hadn't interrupted their kiss.

Beck thought about that kiss too much. The softness of her lips, the taste of her mouth, the texture of her tongue. And when he wasn't thinking about that, he fantasized about her breasts. He knew what they felt like in his hands—smooth and plump and firm—but he didn't know how they looked or how her nipples tasted.

And he was desperate to know.

A loud honk jerked him from his thoughts. Once again, he was fantasizing about Ava Grace's breasts while sitting in traffic. It was a miracle he hadn't rammed his Jeep into the car in front of him.

Before he'd met her, he'd been able to drive around the city without endangering himself and others. He'd been able to sleep through the night without having dreams so X-rated they'd make veteran porn stars blush.

Before he'd met her, he was able to concentrate on Trinity. But now he ignored it. He'd spent nearly every moment of the International Wine and Spirits Show with her when he should have been mixing and mingling with customers.

He'd wanted to hear her sexy laugh and smell her cream soda scent. He'd wanted to talk to her more than anyone else.

Before he'd met Ava Grace, he had been *fine*. And now he wasn't.

He groaned, and Chicken pulled his head from the window and turned to look at him. Beck was sure he saw curiosity in the canine's face.

"I don't want to go to LA with Ava Grace." Chicken gave a little bark, and Beck sighed. "I know you like her. But that's only because she scratches your belly."

The truth was, Beck liked Ava Grace too. There were just so many things to like about her, from her intelligence and inquisitiveness to her sense of humor and smart mouth. If you excluded her fame and tendency to eavesdrop, there weren't many things to *not* like about her.

Beck turned his attention back to the road. Traffic wasn't too bad, and he and Chicken made it to Gabe's building faster than expected.

Gabe lived in a high-rise just south of downtown, and Beck parked in the garage under the building. After fastening the leash to Chicken's collar, he helped his dog from the Jeep and took the elevator to Gabe's floor.

When Gabe opened the door, Chicken lunged toward him.

"Hey, guy," Gabe said, patting the dog's side.

Gabe unhooked Chicken's leash, and he sprinted into the apartment. Beck followed, and once he and Gabe reached the living room, Beck gave his best friend a thorough evaluation. He'd expected Gabe to look like death, but he looked perfectly fine.

He wore tan cargo shorts, a black T-shirt, and flip-flops. The shirt was printed with a modified food pyramid that included a bottle of bourbon. *Bourbon: Part of Every Balanced Meal* was written in white block letters below it.

"I thought you were sick."

Gabe covered his mouth and coughed loudly. Beck's eyes narrowed at the fake sound.

"You said you had food poisoning."

Gabe's hand fell to his abdomen, and he moaned pathetically. Chicken shot to Gabe's side and sat near his feet.

"*You bastard*," Beck snarled, tossing the leash on the antique trunk that served as Gabe's cocktail table. "You're not sick at all."

Gabe's eyes widened innocently. "Why else would I have called you at six o'clock this morning and told you that you had to go to LA with Ava Grace?"

Beck crossed his arms over his chest. "I don't know. Why would you?"

Gabe's lips twitched. "You're not being very sympathetic. I wouldn't expect you to go on a business trip if you were sick. I wouldn't expect you to fly on a luxurious private jet for an hour and a half with only a gorgeous woman for company. And I certainly wouldn't expect you to stay in the same suite with her."

"*What the fuck?*" Beck burst out.

Gabe guffawed. "You should see your face," he gasped around his laughter.

"I'm supposed to share a room with her?" Beck asked, both aroused and appalled by the thought.

"No, you're not sharing a room with her. I wanted to see how you'd react."

"You're such a jackass."

Gabe dropped down onto the brown leather sofa and propped his feet on the trunk. Chicken immediately jumped up beside him and settled near Gabe's hip.

"So you're ready to go?" Gabe asked.

Beck pushed his thumb into his chest. "I'm not going." He pointed to Gabe. "You're going."

"I can't go. I don't have time to pack."

"I'll help."

Gabe shook his head. "Sorry. All my dress shirts are at the dry cleaners." He slowly shook his head. "And I'm sick. Really sick. I hope I don't have to go to the ER. That'd be a bummer."

Beck eyed Gabe rancorously. "You're not sick."

The amusement in Gabe's eyes faded. "Yes, I am. I'm sick of watching you pretend you don't want Ava Grace."

Beck opened his mouth, and Gabe held up his hand. "Don't bother to deny it. I saw you with her outside our hotel rooms, remember?"

"I remember you being a goddamn voyeur."

Gabe snorted. "If you didn't want to be *watched*, then you

193

shouldn't have made out with her where you could be *seen* by anyone who walked by."

Closing his eyes, Beck rubbed his hand over his forehead. "You're right." After a long silence, he dropped his hand and met Gabe's eyes. "I just wasn't thinking."

Gabe studied him intently. "You're so on edge, you're almost vibrating."

Beck didn't respond because he knew the other man was right. He'd never been this worked up over a woman. He felt like nitrogen triiodide. He'd done experiments in college with the highly unstable chemical compound, and it had exploded at the lightest, briefest contact, leaving behind a stinky, purple cloud.

"What's going on in your head?" Gabe asked. "Why aren't you taking what she's offering, free and clear?"

Beck sat on the arm of a leather club chair. "Nothing is ever free and clear, Gabe. There's always a price."

If he got involved with Ava Grace, he'd pay a hefty price. Maybe not now, but later.

"I know you don't want to feel anything for Ava Grace. I know you've tried to stay away from her."

"If you *know* those things, then why are you so determined I go to LA with her?"

"Because you need to accept the reality of the situation."

"The reality of the situation?" Beck repeated. "What reality is that?"

Gabe speared him with his blue gaze. "The reality in which you have sex with her in the rickhouse and grope her in a hotel hallway."

"I shouldn't have done those things."

"I think it's time for you to wave the white flag of surrender to Ava Grace." Gabe shrugged. "And if you can't find a flag, just use your underwear. It'll send the same message."

Beck scowled. "You may think it's time for me to wave the white flag of surrender, but I don't."

Are you sure about that?

"What's the worst that could happen?"

"The possibilities are endless. Nuclear war. Zombie apocalypse. Epic flooding."

Gabe chuckled. "Possible but unlikely."

"You saw all those articles and pictures of her—the ones that said she was pregnant."

"Yeah." A frown creased Gabe's forehead. "You're worried about getting her pregnant?" His lips twitched. "You know, there are ways to prevent pregnancy. Have you ever heard of a condom? It's a useful contraceptive device that shrink wraps your dick. It also helps prevent disease."

Beck barely refrained from rolling his eyes. "She has no privacy. Everything in her life is fodder for public consumption. I don't want to be part of that. I don't want the whole world knowing my business."

Gabe balanced his elbows on his thighs. "I don't know what to tell you, chief. She is who she is."

"When I get back from LA, I'm going to force-feed you rotten sushi for faking food poisoning and putting me in this position."

"I doubt it." Gabe rose and faced him. "When you get back from LA, the only position you're going to remember is Ava Grace's favorite one."

CHAPTER TWENTY-ONE

"Five minutes, Miss Landy."

Beck glanced toward the stage manager for the *Roarke* show. The forty-something woman wore a bulky headset over her hair and carried a tablet computer. She adjusted the small black mic hooked to Ava Grace's dress before moving a few feet away and speaking softly into her headset.

Next to him, Ava Grace closed her eyes and took several deep breaths. His gaze touched on her long, feathery lashes and the glittery gold eye shadow before trailing to her glossy mouth. It was the same shade of grapefruit pink as her dress.

"Are you nervous?" he asked, making sure to keep his voice down.

She snapped her head toward him, their faces only inches apart. They were so close he could see the dark gold starbursts around her pupils.

"Of course I'm nervous," she replied, a hint of laughter in her voice. "Why does everyone think I don't get nervous?"

Feeling compelled to ease her nerves, he said, "You're going to be great. You always are."

Every time he saw Ava Grace perform, he was impressed.

She blew him away with her talent and her stage presence.

She wasn't just a songstress or a musician. She was a *performer*.

If he'd been born to distill bourbon, she'd been born to perform. He couldn't imagine her doing anything else. She was too extraordinary to do something mundane.

"Are you trying to calm my nerves by flattering me?" Ava Grace asked, her lush lips tipped up in a small smile.

"It's not flattery. It's the truth." He arched his eyebrows. "Is it working?"

She laughed softly. "No. But I appreciate the effort." She bit her lip. "I know something you can do that would calm my nerves."

"What?"

"Tell me your middle name."

Her persistence made him chuckle. "Guess."

"Abernathy."

"No."

She licked her lips, and his stomach muscles tightened with arousal. Blood pooled in his groin, making his cock throb, and he glanced away and stared up at a thick cable hanging from the rafters.

"How do I look?" she asked.

Reluctantly, he brought his gaze back to her. She smoothed a hand over her shiny hair, the hammered gold bangle on her wrist glinting as she fiddled with the sleek bun near her neck. Little crystals sparkled in the pale blond strands, and delicate gold earrings dangled from her earlobes.

"Beautiful."

So beautiful you make my throat tight and my chest ache. So beautiful I can barely breathe.

The stage manager stepped closer. "Two minutes, Miss Landy. We need to move you to the center stage."

Ava Grace nodded before her gaze swung back to him. She leaned forward and brushed her lips against his in a soft, fleeting kiss. "For luck," she whispered.

He froze, his mouth tingling from the warm imprint of her lips, and watched her walk away. Her heels were outrageously tall, yet her gait was smooth and graceful, her hips swaying under her short dress and the lean muscles of her long legs flexing with each step.

A brightly colored gift bag swung from her left hand. A bottle of bourbon nestled inside the bag—a present for Roarke and a shameless product placement for Trinity.

"Mr. Beck."

He jerked his eyes away from Ava Grace and focused on the young stagehand next to him. "Yes?"

"You can sit in the audience or watch the show from the wings," the guy explained. "Which do you prefer?"

"The wings," he answered, knowing he was too antsy to sit still.

The stagehand led him to an alcove that held a large stationary camera. An older man stood behind the camera, a dingy baseball cap covering his hair along with a black headset. He gave Beck a thumbs-up.

"Try not to make any noise," the stagehand told Beck before pointing to a steel door with an illuminated exit sign. "If you need to leave for any reason, there's the exit."

Nodding, Beck tucked his hands in the front pockets of his black dress pants and focused on the stage. The *Roarke* show taped in front of a live audience and would air later tonight. Although people watching at home would have commercial breaks, no breaks occurred during the live taping.

The tall talk show host rose from his chair and made his way to a large curtained stage. "Our next guest is one of my favorite people. Ladies and gentlemen, please welcome the lovely, the talented, the incomparable … *Ava Grace Landy!*"

The blue curtains opened to reveal Ava Grace, and the audience went wild. A cacophony of loud cheers, earsplitting whistles, and deep catcalls filled the studio.

Ava Grace gave Roarke and the audience a blinding smile as she met him in the middle of the stage. He grabbed her in a bear hug, picked her up, and spun her around. She laughed and clutched his shoulders, the gift bag bouncing against his suited back.

"Put me down," she demanded with mock outrage.

Roarke complied, and Ava Grace turned to the audience and waved. "Thank y'all for such an amazing welcome."

Ava Grace settled in a blue chair next to Roarke's desk. After placing the gift bag on the floor, she crossed her legs, exposing a smooth, tan thigh.

"I'm so happy to be here."

From behind his desk, Roarke looked out over the audience. "I'm the one who's happy." He waggled his coppery eyebrows. "Every time I see you, you look better than the last time."

Amen, brother.

The talk show host curled his hand into a claw and made the signature growling noise he reserved for attractive female guests. And then he did it again for emphasis.

Ava Grace giggled. "Thank you, Roarke."

"What've you been up to since your last visit? You just got back from the International Wine and Spirits Show in Seattle, right? How was it?"

"It was a lot of fun. I'd never been to a show like that before. Hundreds of wineries and distilleries attend." She flashed a smile toward the audience. "And they give out free samples."

The audience cheered wildly, and she laughed. "It doesn't sound like there are many teetotalers in the audience." She looked directly into the camera. "Did you know teetotalers are more likely to be depressed than people who drink moderately?"

Beck laughed under his breath. He could never accuse her of not paying attention.

"Really?" Roarke asked.

She nodded. "It's true. Research shows moderate drinking makes people happier, probably because of the social aspect." She paused meaningfully. "Moderate drinking, people. *Moderate drinking.*"

"Why were you at the show?" Roarke asked.

"I was there with this fabulous craft distillery called Trinity. They make the best bourbon in the world. They won the gold medal in the whiskey category at the show."

Beck smiled. Who would've guessed Ava Grace Landy would become Trinity's most vocal supporter?

"Tell us about Trinity," Roarke requested. "What is a craft distillery, exactly?"

Beck frowned. He and Ava Grace hadn't talked about the differences between larger distillers and small distilleries like Trinity.

"The short answer is craft distilleries make bourbon in smaller batches than the big guys, and they produce fewer barrels." She smiled. "And I'd argue craft distilleries make better bourbon. But that's just my opinion ... and the opinion of the experienced judges at the International Wine and Spirits Show."

Her subtle put-down of the larger distilleries made Beck smile. He'd been saying the same thing for years.

Roarke picked up his notecard again. "It says here the guy

who started Trinity is a descendant of Jonah Beck, the founder of the oldest distillery in the U.S."

"That's right," Ava Grace replied with a nod. "His name is Jonah Beck too, and he's a bourbon genius."

Bourbon genius?

Beck realized Ava Grace was still talking. "Nowadays, Trinity is the only distillery in the world still owned by a descendant of Jonah Beck," she explained with a smile. "Jonah Beck Distillery, which makes Beck bourbon, is owned by some big conglomerate in Britain."

Beck shook his head, awed by how deftly she handled Roarke's questions. Her answers were truthful, yet they painted Trinity in a more positive light than its competitors.

Ava Grace bent down and scooped the gift bag from the floor. She placed it on Roarke's desk. "I brought you a little present."

Roarke rubbed his hands together, his expression gleeful. "I *love* presents."

As the talk show host pulled the tissue paper from the bag and tossed it over his shoulder, Ava Grace cautioned, "Careful, Roarke. It's fragile."

Roarke gingerly removed the bottle of Trinity from the bag and held it up like a trophy. The audience applauded, and Ava Grace laughed. "Bourbon is so much better than a bouquet of flowers or a bottle of wine," she said.

Roarke studied the bottle, turning it over in his hands. "Should we open this right now?"

"Sure," Ava Grace agreed. "I'd love to have a drink with you. There are some glasses in the bag."

She pulled out a couple of shot glasses and handed them to Roarke. "Bourbon is a sipping whiskey. But you can also cook with it. I'm working on a cookbook of recipes that use bourbon. It should be out early next year. I haven't decided what to call it yet, so if anyone in the audience has an idea, please share them on Trinity's website or social media."

After Roarke tore off the paper seal around the cork, he worked the cork out of the bottle and poured a splash of bourbon into the shot glasses. He held his glass up in front of his face and looked at it.

"That's the heart," Ava Grace said.

"The heart?" Roarke echoed.

She nodded. "There's this old saying that describes the distilling process for bourbon." She repeated Ellis's head, heart, and tail lesson almost verbatim. "That's where I got the inspiration for my new song. I'm going to sing it for y'all later."

Roarke took a sip of Trinity. "I've always liked tequila more than bourbon."

Ava Grace jerked her head toward him. "Tequila?" she repeated, her lip curling in disgust. "Why do you like tequila more than bourbon?"

Roarke smiled devilishly. "Because you can do body shots with tequila."

She blinked, her eyes round and wide. "Body shots?"

Roarke looked at the audience. "You guys know what body shots are, right?" he asked, and the audience answered with a cheer.

"You can do body shots with bourbon too," Ava Grace assured Roarke.

Beck frowned. Trinity was supposed to be sipped, not sucked down.

Roarke narrowed his eyes doubtfully. "Are you sure you can do body shots with bourbon?"

"Absolutely," she answered, nodding her head emphatically.

"Maybe we should test it."

To Beck's surprise, Ava Grace said, "That's a *great* idea, Roarke. We can do body shots off you."

Roarke looked at the audience. "Should we do body shots off me or someone else?" he asked, shaking his head toward Ava Grace.

The audience went wild, chanting Ava Grace's name. She shook her head and gestured to her torso.

"I'm not dressed for body shots," she protested.

"That's the whole point of body shots," Roarke quipped.

The chanting grew louder, and Ava Grace grimaced. "Okay. *Okay.* Calm down." She pointed to the crook of her elbow. "I can hold the shot glass right here." The audience booed loudly, and she threw up her hands. "I can't hold it anywhere else!"

Roarke turned to the audience and waggled his eyebrows. "Do you have any suggestions?"

A male voice shouted, "Between her legs."

The audience began to chant *legs*, and Beck's heart rate picked up until it thudded in a hard, fast rhythm. This was turning into a fucking circus with Ava Grace as the main attraction.

Ava Grace smiled widely. "What a fantastic idea!" She rose from her chair and picked up the full shot glasses. "Roarke, clear off your desk."

Roarke grabbed the bottle of Trinity in one hand and swiped his other arm across his desk in a dramatic move. After handing the shot glasses to Roarke, she sat down on top of the desk.

Beck's eyes shot to the TV monitors hanging from the ceiling. Somehow Ava Grace managed to swivel and swing her legs up without flashing the whole goddamn world. She reclined on the desk, and it was just long enough only her ankles and feet hung off.

She looked just like a virgin sacrifice, her arms straight by her side and her legs closed tightly together. She turned her head to look at the audience.

"Is this what you wanted?" she called out.

The audience roared its approval, and she laughed. She beckoned Roarke, and when he leaned down, she whispered into his ear. The mic picked up only one huskily spoken word: *thighs*.

Roarke placed a shot glass between Ava Grace's toned thighs, several inches above her knees. As he rose and looked into the camera, he pointed to his head. "Head." He pointed to his chest. "Heart." He pointed to Ava Grace's crotch. "And this is the tail."

Bending down, Roarke wrapped his mouth around the shot glass. He slowly straightened with the glass clasped in his mouth, and when he reached his full height, he threw back his head and gulped the bourbon.

The talk show host jerked the shot glass from his mouth with a gasp and smacked his lips. "Bourbon is definitely better than tequila, especially when you get to drink it off a beautiful woman."

The audience cheered, and Roarke held up the shot glass. "Who wants to go next?"

CHAPTER TWENTY-TWO

As the makeup artist swept the eye shadow brush over Ava Grace's lids, she impatiently tapped her foot against the metal rung of her chair. She hated to keep Beck waiting, but stage makeup was too heavy for normal everyday wear, and she'd needed a quick touch-up before she left the studio.

After the show had wrapped, she made sure to introduce Beck to Roarke. As always, the talk show host was gracious and affable. Beck, meanwhile, was friendly but more reserved than usual, and he'd been silent on the walk back to the green room.

Beck's mood had been drastically different before the show. Earlier he'd said some really sweet things, and no matter how much she told herself not to ascribe too much importance to them, she hoped he'd meant them.

Unfortunately, she had a feeling he wasn't too happy about the show. Although it hadn't turned out exactly as she'd expected, she still thought it went well. It certainly could've turned out a lot worse. She hoped Beck realized that.

"Time for mascara," the makeup artist said.

Ava Grace obligingly opened her eyes wide and blinked against the mascara brush several times. As she repeated the process on her other eye, she decided to casually strike up a conversation with Beck in the limo to suss out his feelings about the show. His answers would determine her strategy for dinner.

After a slick of tinted lip gloss and a dusting of face powder, Ava Grace was ready to go. She thanked the makeup artist, grabbed her bag, and exited the dressing room. Beck was waiting for her, propped against the wall with his muscular arms crossed over his chest.

The sight of him made her heart rise like a hot air balloon. She was always happy to see him.

Earlier today, she'd been shocked when she entered the Riley O'Brien & Co. jet and found Beck sitting in the cabin. She'd hoped he had wanted to come with her, but he doused her with cold water when he told her that Gabe had food poisoning.

The flight to Los Angeles had been tense, silent, and uncomfortable despite the plush leather seats. She tried to engage him in conversation, but he shut her down.

His mood had been as dark as his eyes, and she hadn't been able to charm or tease him out of it. By the end of the flight, she was irritated with him and even more irritated with herself for putting up with his rudeness.

Beck pushed away from the wall, and she allowed herself a moment to enjoy the sight of him in his button-down shirt and flat-front trousers. With thin stripes of light blue and black, his long-sleeved shirt made his chest look even broader, and the expensive cotton emphasized the dense muscles of his shoulders and arms.

He'd paired the stylish shirt with black pants that looked just as good from the back as they did from the front. They highlighted his lean waist, made him look even taller, and showed off his tight butt. A black leather belt with a matte silver buckle and black leather dress shoes with a tapered toe finished his dressy look.

"Ready?" she asked.

He responded with a curt nod, and she headed down the hall. With him following, she put an extra sway in her hips, hoping he was watching.

As they reached the door, he moved in front of her and opened it. To her surprise, he didn't hold it for her but stepped through and blocked the opening. A second later, he moved to the side so she could exit, and she realized he'd checked to make sure it was safe for her to leave the building.

A heavyset, uniformed driver stood in front of a long, black limo. He immediately opened the door for them, and she slid into the car as gracefully as possible given her short dress and ridiculously high heels. Beck climbed in behind her, but instead of sitting next to her, he settled in the seat along the side and stared out the window.

The driver shut the door behind them, and when he got in the car, he looked over his shoulder and asked, "Back to the hotel, Miss Landy?"

She darted a glance toward Beck, noting his tight mouth, the stiff set of his shoulders, and the clenched fists resting on top of his thighs. Anger emanated from him like a sonar signal from a submarine.

"Back to the hotel," she confirmed before pressing the button to raise the privacy glass.

As the car glided forward, she angled her body toward Beck. "That went really well," she chirped, knowing she was antagonizing him.

His head snapped toward her, his brows lowered and his eyes narrowed. Dark color flushed his face, and he rolled his lips inward, obviously struggling to control his temper.

She smiled brightly. "Roarke was funnier than usual, and the audience had a ton of energy. I've been on the show a few times, and it's never been like tonight." She waited for him to respond, and when he didn't, she prompted him. "Did you enjoy the show?"

His eyes narrowed into slits. His nostrils flared, and he looked away from her, his dark eyes drilling a hole in the privacy screen.

"I think 'Head, Heart, and Tail' is going to be a hit," she added. "I can always tell when people connect with a song because they tap their toes without meaning to."

He didn't respond, and her bravado ... her defiance ... drained away. Her throat closed up, and she had to swallow a couple of times to relax it.

"I know you're upset," she began, a placating note in her voice. When he gave no outward sign he'd heard her, she said, "Please look at me, Jonah."

He slowly turned his head to meet her eyes. "I know you're upset," she repeated quietly. "But please believe me when I say nothing like that has ever happened before."

She gave him an apologetic smile. "You've worked so hard to build Trinity ... to create bourbon you can be proud of. I know you think the show damaged your brand. I know you think *I* damaged it." She grimaced. "Body shots and premium bourbon don't really go together."

Leaning closer, she put her hand on his knee. "I understand you don't want people to associate Trinity with drinking games, but I couldn't let Roarke imply tequila was better than bourbon. I didn't want anyone who watched the show to have a bad impression of Trinity. I was trying to protect Trinity's brand, not hurt it."

He moved his knee out from under her hand. She stared at him, her guilt and regret morphing into anger. She'd done the best she could under the circumstances, and he should be thanking her.

"What was I supposed to do?" She threw herself back into the seat and crossed her arms over her chest. "You don't know what it's like to be in front of a live audience. It can get really ugly, really fast, if you don't give them what they want. Do you think I wanted complete strangers to do body shots just inches from my..."

Crossing her legs, she shifted away from Beck and looked out the window. Tears clogged her throat, and she cleared it roughly. She wasn't going to cry over this man ever again.

As the lights of Hollywood slid past the car window, she said, "I should have spent my time on *Roarke* talking about myself. But I didn't. I talked about Trinity the whole time, and I performed a song I'm not making a penny on."

The limo slid to a stop. She grabbed her bag and jumped out before the driver could open the door. Beck had already exited by the time she rounded the back of the limo, and he grasped her elbow. She shook off his hand and gave him the "death stare" before stalking through the revolving doors.

She hurried to the elevators as fast as her shoes would allow and stabbed the up button. She felt Beck's solid presence behind her, and she was tempted to ram her elbow into his gut. She'd never considered herself a *physical* person before, but she turned into one whenever he was around.

The moment the elevator arrived, she rushed inside. Unfortunately, Beck was right on her heels.

Roarke's people had booked the hotel for her, so she had a suite on one of the higher floors. Beck's room was a few floors below hers, and she hoped it was the size of a shoe box and infested with bedbugs.

He pressed the button for her floor, obviously planning to see her safely to her room. Even when he was being a jerk, he retained some gentlemanly qualities.

The elevator dinged, and as she pushed past him, she said, "I don't want you to walk me to my room. The last time you did, you stuck your tongue in my mouth and your hand up my shirt."

When he closed his eyes and dropped his head back, she just knew he was counting to ten ... or maybe twenty. She spun and stomped down the carpeted corridor. He caught up with her halfway to her suite.

After unlocking the door, she paused with her hand on the handle and sought his dark gaze. "Everything I did tonight, I did for you. I didn't do it for myself or for Trinity. I did it for *you*."

He stared unblinkingly before turning on his heel and striding away. With tears burning her eyes, she entered her room and slowly closed the door.

Maybe it's time to give up on Beck.

Even as the thought skipped through her mind, her heart whispered, *Not yet. Please, not yet.*

After tossing her bag on the purple velvet sofa, she went into the bedroom. As she unbuckled her sparkly shoes, she decided to take a long shower, put on her snuggliest pajamas, gorge on room service, and fall asleep on the sofa after watching a movie with hot superheroes.

Half an hour later, she stepped out of the shower and smoothed brown-sugar-scented lotion into her skin. After taking her hair down and brushing it out, she donned her favorite pajamas and padded barefoot into the living area. She'd just picked up the room service menu when she heard a knock on the door.

With some trepidation, she crossed the cold, gray marble tile.

Only a few people knew she was in town, and she wasn't interested in any company.

She looked through the peephole, and surprise made her head snap back. Beck stood outside her door, obviously impatient because he knocked again, this time a little longer and a little louder.

She opened the door just a crack and peeked around the edge. "What do you want?"

"May I come in?" he asked, his tone more polite than she'd ever heard it.

"No. I don't want to talk to you. And I'm in my pajamas."

He stared at her for a long moment. "May I come in?" he repeated.

She hesitated, and he added quietly, "Please, Ava Grace."

"Fine," she muttered, pulling open the door and standing to the side so he could enter.

Once he was inside, she slammed the door and stomped into the living area. She turned to face him, her hands on her hips. "What do you want, Beck?"

He looked her up and down, his gaze lingering on her bare feet, her breasts, and her face. His lips twitched.

"Those are some interesting pajamas," he said.

She crossed her arms over her chest. "Amelia bought them for me." She stroked her fingers over the soft, aqua-colored cotton printed with small red crabs. "They're my favorite."

"Why do you have crabs on your pajamas?" he asked, his eyes gleaming with amusement.

"Because I'm crabby in the morning," she replied crabbily.

His answering laugh was barely a breath of sound. "Is that right?"

"Yes. *Very* crabby."

"Maybe I can help with that."

"Oh, yeah?" she asked sarcastically. "How do you plan to succeed when cinnamon rolls and French press coffee have failed?"

He walked toward her until only a few inches separated them. Looking down into her face, he smiled slowly. It was a smile she'd never seen before—one that made her stomach quiver and her knees turn to jelly.

"I have a few ideas, sugar."

CHAPTER TWENTY-THREE

Beck was waving the white flag of surrender. Metaphorically, at least.

He didn't have a white flag on his person, but he had six condoms in his pocket. He'd cleaned out the hotel gift shop after walking Ava Grace to her room.

He was so damn tired of fighting his overwhelming, unrelenting desire for her. So damn tired of going to bed every night thinking about her and waking up aching for her.

He wasn't going to fight anymore. He was giving up.

Sliding his hands into her thick hair, he gently tilted her head and stared down into her face. Completely bare of makeup and dewy from the shower, it was almost more beautiful than he could stand. Her long eyelashes were darker than her hair and looked like they'd been dipped in liquid gold. A few freckles dotted her nose, and her lush lips were petal-pink even without gloss or lipstick.

He dropped his head and settled his mouth over hers. Her lips fell open, and he lightly stroked his tongue across her bottom lip before nibbling on the luscious curve. She sighed softly, and he angled his head, licking deeply into her mouth. Her tongue

213

slid against his, twirling in an erotic dance.

Every time he kissed her, she tasted better than before. Sweet and light like cotton candy but also spicy and hot like cinnamon. As he sucked on her tongue, he thought about doing the same thing to her nipples and her clit. His erection lengthened and throbbed against his zipper, and he shifted a hand to the waistband of her pajama pants. He slid it under the soft material and found nothing but smooth, warm skin.

Fuck, yeah. No panties.

Palming her bare ass, he tugged her closer until his cock pressed into her lower stomach. She clutched his biceps, jerking her lips from his. She stared up at him with wide eyes, her mouth rosy and swollen.

She swallowed noisily, her throat rippling with the movement. "I told you not to kiss me again."

"You told me not to kiss you again *unless* I planned to take you to bed." He lightly squeezed her ass cheek. "And that's exactly what I'm going to do."

"I don't understand you," she whispered. "I thought you were angry."

"I was angry, but I'm not anymore." He rubbed his thumb against the silky skin of her neck. "What you said in the limo … you were right about everything. I understand why you went along with Roarke and the audience."

"I didn't know what else to do."

"You did just fine." He stroked his fingers over the crest of her cheek. "The show probably will create some positive buzz for Trinity. The segment with Roarke doing body shots off you is going to go viral, and we'll probably see a huge spike on social media. Hopefully, we'll see an increase in sales too."

As he began to unbutton her pajama top, he said, "I'm sorry

about the way I acted in the limo. I was just…"

He didn't know how to describe how he'd felt. He'd barely been able to keep it together at the studio. He'd wanted to choke-slam every guy within ten feet of her including Roarke.

The plain truth was he didn't want other men to touch Ava Grace. Hell, he didn't want other men to even *look* at her.

If Roarke had done Trinity body shots with anyone other than Ava Grace, Beck probably would've seen the humor in the situation. He wouldn't have been all that thrilled his award-winning bourbon was associated with a trashy drinking game, but he wouldn't have been enraged either.

When he moved on to the next button, she placed her hand over his, stilling his fingers. "Are you sure you want to do this?"

"Yes." He took her hand and pressed it against his erection. "Here's the proof."

Her fingers flexed under his before she pulled her hand free. "The last time we had sex, it was—"

"So fucking hot I'm surprised the rickhouse didn't explode."

Her lips twitched. "I'm surprised too. There's a lot of flammable liquid in there."

"Yeah, about six hundred thousand gallons." Bending down, he nuzzled his nose behind her ear. "You smell good."

"It's my body lotion."

He licked a circle on her smooth neck. "You smell like a blondie."

"Do all blondes smell the same to you?" she asked breathlessly.

It took him a second to comprehend her question, and when he finally did, he laughed so hard he almost choked. When he could speak, he explained, "A blondie is a kind of dessert. Like a brownie."

"Oh. Right." Her face pinked. "I knew that."

He sucked lightly on her fragrant skin. "You taste good too."

She tilted her head to give him better access, and he trailed his mouth down to the place where her neck and shoulder met. He nibbled at the delicate flesh, and she gasped softly.

"Jonah, I don't want…"

"What?" Lifting his head, he met her eyes. "I thought you wanted this."

He waited for her to respond, his breath trapped in his chest. He honestly didn't know what he'd do if she turned him down. He liked to think he'd accept her rejection with dignity, but it was quite possible he'd howl at the moon and turn into a werewolf.

"I *do* want to be with you, but not if…" Her eyes searched his, and he wondered what she hoped to see there. "Are you going to regret this tomorrow?"

Not tomorrow. And maybe not the day after. Eventually, though, I will regret it.

Being with Ava Grace wasn't smart. It couldn't—*wouldn't*—end well for him. But he just didn't care anymore.

On the ride back to the hotel, he'd realized his feelings for her were similar to a common cold—there was no cure. You just had to let the virus do its worst. You had to suffer through it and then give yourself some time to recover once it left your body.

"No, sugar," he answered quietly. "I'm not going to regret this tomorrow."

She stared at him for a long moment before grasping his hand. Weaving her slender fingers through his, she led the way toward a set of double doors on the far side of the room.

As they entered the bedroom, she flipped a switch near the door. A metal lamp with a black-and-gray-striped shade flared to life, creating a pool of golden light near the king-size platform bed.

A silvery-gray duvet covered the mattress, the material gathered into swirls to look like huge flowers. Puffy pillows in a variety of fabrics nestled against the black tufted headboard.

Stopping next to the bed, she turned to face him. With her eyes locked on his, she deftly unbuttoned the remaining buttons on her pajama top and shrugged it off her shoulders.

As he eyed her chest, a moan built in his throat. Her breasts were beautiful, firm and full. Rosy areolas and tight little nipples tipped the creamy mounds.

"After that day in the rickhouse, I thought about your breasts all the time. I knew how wet and tight your pussy was, but I didn't know how your breasts felt in my hands or the color of your nipples. And not knowing made me crazy."

She sucked in a harsh breath, and her breasts lifted. Before he could touch them, she untied the drawstring of her pajama pants. The waistband loosened, and the pants slipped over her hips. She gave a little shake, and the soft cotton fell to the floor.

As she stepped out of the pants, he let his gaze wander over her. With clothes, she looked willowy, maybe even a tad too thin. But without clothes, she was a fucking goddess. Her stomach was flat and toned, yet her hips were curvy. Her legs were long and lean but retained their womanly shape.

His eyes zeroed in on the place between her legs. He'd wondered if she was a natural blonde, and the neatly trimmed pale gold fluff at the juncture of her thighs proved she was. His mouth watered, and he swallowed thickly.

He couldn't wait to taste her juice again. And this time he wasn't going to lick it from his fingers. He was going to shove his face between her legs and gorge himself on her plump pink flesh and her sweet cream.

Like a zombie, he moved toward her, his arms outstretched.

He didn't bother to hide his hunger for her, and she backed away from him, probably frightened by the look in his eyes.

The back of her legs hit the bed, and she dropped heavily onto the edge. Before she could move, he fell to his knees between her legs and clamped his hands around her thighs.

"I've been thinking about this too. Your juice is the sweetest I've ever tasted."

She gasped, and he slid his hands up her legs before cupping them around her hips. He gently pulled her forward until her ass rested on the edge of the bed.

"I told myself it couldn't have been that good." He looked up into her face. "Lie back. I want to know if you taste as sweet as I remember."

Bracing herself on her hands, she slowly leaned back, and he immediately bent down until his face hovered over her pussy. He breathed deeply, the earthy musk of her arousal filling his nostrils and making his cock throb.

"Hook your legs over my shoulders, sugar, and widen your knees," he cajoled.

As soon as she did what he'd asked, he used his thumbs to spread the lips of her pussy. Her delicate tissue glistened with juice, her clitoris plump and engorged.

Leaning forward, he wrapped his lips over the little knot of nerves and sucked gently. She jerked against him, her thighs quivering around his head. He sucked a little harder, and she moaned low in her throat.

He released her clit and slowly swirled his tongue around it before licking toward her opening. Her juice trickled over his tongue, and he filled his mouth with the sweet tanginess.

"I am so fucked," he groaned. "Your juice tastes even better than I remember."

He was never going to be able to go down on another woman without comparing her to Ava Grace's delicious pussy. In fact, the thought of doing this to another woman made him sick to his soul.

He circled her opening with slow, light strokes of his tongue. As she lifted her hips against his mouth, he increased the pressure and the pace. He darted the tip of his tongue inside her, and she clutched his head in both hands, panting loudly.

Licking his way up, he found her clit again. It was hard against his tongue, and he pressed against it. She moaned, and he rolled his tongue over her sweet nub until she rocked against his mouth.

When he sucked on it, she whimpered. "Jonah," she gasped. "Help me."

He knew exactly what she needed. As he increased the suction on her clit, he slipped two fingers inside her and pressed them into the smooth wall of her vagina.

Her beautiful body bowed, and she cried out, coming against his mouth. He felt the ripples of her pussy against his fingers, and his balls twinged.

He stayed with her as she came down, his fingers wedged deep inside her and his tongue firm against her clit. After several minutes, her legs slipped from his shoulders, and her hands fell from his head. As he pulled his fingers from her body, he sat back on his heels and wiped his forearm across his mouth.

She rose up on her elbows. "Thank you," she said, her voice low and raspy. As she sat up, she asked, "Ready for your turn?"

"Maybe later," he replied, shaking his head. "Right now, I just want to be inside you."

She stood abruptly and did a one-eighty. Her perfect ass was just inches away from his face, and as she leaned over the bed to pull back the duvet, he got a flash of her pussy.

Unbelievably, his cock hardened even more. When she placed a knee on the bed to climb in, he vaulted to his feet. Settling a hand on her lower back, he asked, "Do you like it from behind?"

She looked over her shoulder. "I like it any way you want to give it to me."

"This way," he said, his voice gravelly.

As she crawled onto the bed on her hands and knees, he jerked his shirt from his pants. He unbuttoned his cuffs, but was too impatient to deal with the ones on the front. Instead, he just pulled the dress shirt over his head.

She shook her ass. "Hurry."

He clumsily unbuckled his belt and tore the fastening on his pants in his haste to get them open. He didn't bother to kick off his shoes. He could do that later, after he'd fucked Ava Grace so hard he couldn't remember his own name. He'd remember hers though.

After yanking down his zipper, he hooked his thumbs into his boxer briefs and shoved down his underwear and pants. His cock was so hard it pointed toward his stomach, and he prayed he'd last long enough to get her off.

Sliding his forearm under her stomach, he pulled her backward until her knees reached the edge of the bed. He stepped behind her, his stomach flush against her ass. Fisting his cock, he placed it against her opening.

She looked over her shoulder. He saw her mouth move, but he couldn't hear anything over the pounding of his heart. He focused on her lips and finally realized what she was saying: condom.

Holy shit!

He'd almost forgotten a rubber. He'd never been so worked up he'd neglected to think about protection.

He grabbed a condom from his pants, ripped it open, and sheathed his cock with trembling hands. Once again, he positioned himself against her opening and took a deep breath.

Gripping her hips in both hands, he plunged into her in one deep stroke. Just like last time, she came the moment he filled her. She cried out, arching her back, and he worked his cock deeper. Her pussy clenched around his length, and his vision blurred.

He dug his fingers into her hips, trying not to come. When he thought he could handle it, he slowly pulled out until just the tip of his cock remained inside her. Before he could move, she pushed back against him, taking him to the hilt.

She moaned, and he grunted as his balls drew up. He leaned down and placed his mouth against her ear. "Let's take our time."

He eased out of her, letting his erection rub against her folds, before pumping back inside in shallow thrusts. He found a smooth, steady rhythm, nothing like the fast, furious fuck in the rickhouse.

He rode her, plunging deep, and she moved with him, her hips rocking back against him. The supple muscles of her pussy sucked him in with each thrust.

"Goddamn," he gasped, "you've got the tightest, wettest pussy I've ever felt."

To his amazement, her pussy tightened again, milking his cock in powerful squeezes. A shock zinged down his spine to his balls. He tried to hold back his orgasm, but the burn spread. His release burst through him, and he shouted hoarsely, his cock pulsing as cum jetted from the tip.

The pleasure pulled him down, and he drooped over her back. Although he tried to keep his full weight off her, her arms collapsed anyway. She flattened against the mattress, and he fell on top of her, his cock still wedged deep. She groaned, and he hastily pulled out, holding the condom to make sure it didn't slip off.

After rolling to his side, he brushed her hair away from her face. Her eyes were shut tightly, her long lashes curling upward.

"Are you okay?" he asked, worried he might've hurt her when he'd fallen on her.

Her eyelids fluttered before lifting. "Is that the only condom you have with you?" she asked, her eyes soft and hazy.

"No."

He'd been sure they couldn't go through six condoms in one night, but now he wondered if he was mistaken. He was still semi-erect, and it wouldn't take much to run the flag up the pole.

"How many condoms do you have?"

"Five."

Her lips tipped up in a satisfied smile. "You must've been a Boy Scout."

CHAPTER TWENTY-FOUR

Bright sunlight snuck beneath Ava Grace's tightly closed eyelids. With an annoyed growl, she threw her forearm over her eyes.

Ugh. Why didn't I close the curtains before I went to sleep?

The reason slammed into her, and she sat straight up in bed, completely naked. She looked around, noting the scrunched-up pillow beside her and the tangled sheets. Other than that, and the condom wrappers on the nightstand, there was no sign Beck had ever been there. His clothes and shoes were gone.

Tilting her head toward the closed double doors, she listened intently to see if anyone was moving around in the suite's living area. It was completely, oppressively silent.

He's not here.

She pulled her legs to her chest, wincing a little as her inner thigh muscles twinged. Resting her head on her knees, she tried to wrangle her runaway emotions.

She'd walked into this situation with her eyes and legs wide open. She'd asked Beck if he'd regret being with her, and he'd said no. But he'd never indicated this was anything more than a one-night stand. She should've clarified that point.

She'd never wanted a relationship with a man before, but she wanted one now. She wanted more than one night with Beck. She wanted *everything*.

Her stomach growled, and she glanced at the clock on the nightstand. It was after ten o'clock, and she decided to get up. With Beck gone, there was no reason to stay in bed.

In the bathroom, she took care of her morning business before brushing her teeth and pulling her hair into a messy bun. She stepped into the sumptuous walk-in shower and turned on the faucets. She hoped the hot water would ease her aches and pains. She wasn't used to this much sex, and she was sore inside and out.

As she waited for the water to heat, she evaluated her naked body in the full-length mirror. Beck had put his mark on her, from the faint fingertip bruises on her hips and inner thighs to the whisker burn on her neck, breasts, and belly. She even had a tiny hickey on her collarbone.

Beck wasn't a polite lover. He had no hang-ups in the bedroom, and he hadn't allowed her to have any either. She'd let him do things to her that she never imagined she'd allow anyone. His hands, mouth, or penis had touched every inch of her body. She'd experienced more orgasms in one night with Beck than her whole life.

Her stomach growled again, and she contemplated her need for food. She should probably order room service before her shower so she wouldn't have to wait for it when she got out.

After turning off the faucets, she shrugged into the fuzzy white robe provided by the hotel and padded barefoot to the bedroom's double doors. She pulled them open, crossed the marble floor to the living area, and came to an abrupt halt.

Her breath whooshed out, and she pressed her hand against her chest as her lungs worked to replenish the air. She blinked a couple of times, praying she wasn't imagining things.

He's still here.

Beck was lounging on the velvet sofa, his bare feet propped on the brushed metal cube that served as a cocktail table. He wore his black pants from the night before, but he was bare-chested, and his dark hair stuck up in the front.

He was reading the sports section of *USA Today*, and he must have sensed her presence because he glanced up. As he lowered the newspaper to his lap, his gaze lazily traveled up and down her body before settling on her face.

Their eyes met, and he smiled slowly, showing just the edge of his white teeth. That smile made her stomach feel wobbly. Or maybe it was just hunger pangs.

"Mornin', sugar."

His voice was morning husky, and she broke out in goose bumps as it seeped through her. She could hear the echo of his baritone in her ears, telling her how good she felt ... how tight ... how wet ... how much he wanted her.

She'd never liked pet names. She hated it when people called her *sweetheart* or *darling* or *honey*. But every time Beck called her *sugar* in his deep drawl, she melted like chocolate chips in a hot oven. She wouldn't mind if he never called her Ava Grace again.

"Are you crabby this morning, Miz Landy?" His smile widened. "Or did I take care of that?"

His deep voice held a teasing note she'd never heard before. Her heart rate picked up until it thumped in her ears like a bass drum, and she swallowed to ease her dry throat.

He folded the newspaper and placed it on the cushion next to him. As he rose from the sofa, she couldn't help staring. His pants were zipped but not buttoned, revealing his tight six-pack.

JENNA SUTTON

Dark hair arrowed toward his groin, and the same silky hair dusted his muscular torso.

He met her in the middle of the room. Snaking a hard arm around her waist, he bent down and dropped a soft kiss behind her earlobe.

"Maybe you need some more lovin'," he whispered, his breath hot against her ear.

Something sweet and warm filled her chest, and she let it radiate through her. Even though she'd never been in love before, she recognized it. And after last night, there was no doubt in her mind or heart.

She was in love with Beck. He was the solid guy she'd been searching for.

She'd watched him with Gabe and Ren, and she knew he was a good friend. Steadfast and loyal. He was attentive and patient with Gatsby, and she had no doubt he'd be the same way with his own children.

His relationship with Gabe and Ren, as well as Ellis, proved Beck stuck around. Even Trinity proved he knew how to commit. Distilling bourbon lacked immediate gratification, that was for sure.

She knew Beck wasn't in love with her ... not yet, anyway. But lust could turn into something more ... something deeper. It could turn into love.

Nothing in her life had come easily, and there was no reason to think Beck would be any different. She just needed to keep her heart—and her legs—open.

The thought made her laugh under her breath. Beck drew back and studied her thoughtfully. She winced, knowing she didn't look her best this morning. When she didn't get enough sleep, it really showed, and he'd kept her up almost all night.

226

"Are you sore?" he asked.

His eyes glinted with concern and something else. She hoped it was affection.

She nodded, knowing her cheeks were bright red. She'd never spent the night with a man before, and she was afraid her lack of experience showed.

"I'm sorry," he said. "I was greedy last night."

She finally found her voice. "It's okay." She smoothed a clump of dark hair that spiked over his forehead. "I wanted you just as much."

"You were pretty insatiable. You damn near sucked me dry."

"Oh, my God!" she whispered, covering her burning face with her hands.

He laughed softly. "Are you embarrassed?"

Her stomach chose that moment to growl loudly. It seemed to echo throughout the suite, and she cringed, wondering how much more embarrassment she'd have to endure this morning.

"Was that your stomach?" he asked.

She dropped her hands and gave him the "death stare." His lips twitched, and he looked toward the sofa. She followed his gaze, finally noticing the room service tray on one of the metal cubes in front of the sofa. Two covered plates were stacked on top of it, along with a silver coffee carafe.

"Did you already eat breakfast?" she asked. "Is there any left?"

He gave her a sheepish glance. "I was starving, so I ordered just enough to tide me over until you woke up. I thought we could have a late breakfast together."

His words sent a tingle of pleasure through her. He seemed perfectly content to be in her hotel suite after a long night of lovemaking, and now he wanted to share a meal with her.

"We probably should order more room service or eat downstairs in the hotel restaurant," she recommended. "If we go out of the hotel, the paparazzi will follow us."

"Room service. I sure as hell don't want to face a crowd of cameras this morning." He grimaced. "I couldn't live my life under a microscope the way you do. How can you stand it?"

"Whenever I run into them, I try to ignore them."

"I couldn't do it," he repeated, shaking his head emphatically.

Worry stabbed into her. Could Beck fall in love with her *and* her career? Could he accept her fame? Could he deal with people who thought they had a right to know everything about her life?

One step at a time, Ava Grace.

Desperate to change the subject, she said, "I was surprised you were still here when I got up this morning."

His eyes cooled, and he dropped his arm from her waist before taking several steps away from her. "Should I have left?" he asked quietly.

He crossed his arms over his chest, and she recognized the defensive posture for what it was. Her thoughtless statement had hurt him, and she wished she could press a rewind button and say something else.

Knowing she had to do some serious damage control, she closed the space separating them and wrapped her arms around his neck. She got as close as she could with his crossed arms between them and rose on her tiptoes to press her lips against his.

When he didn't respond, she drew back just enough to look into his eyes. "I want you here. When I woke up alone, I was…"

She hesitated, trying to find a word that would accurately convey how awful she'd felt. Heartbroken was the best adjective, but that might make him sprint out of the suite.

"Disappointed," she finally said.

His shoulders relaxed a little, but he didn't uncross his arms. She abruptly realized she'd have to be more open with her feelings if she wanted more than a sexual relationship with him.

"I'm lying," she announced flatly.

His eyes narrowed, and his shoulders tensed again. He reached for her hands, clearly intending to tug her arms from his neck, but she clung to him like a barnacle on a pirate ship.

As she stroked the fine hairs at his nape, she admitted, "I wasn't disappointed. I was upset. *Really upset.* I thought you'd left, and it made me crabby." His shoulders loosened, and she smiled at him. "When I saw you sitting on the sofa, my crabbiness disappeared."

He dropped his hands to her hips. "It disappeared?"

"Just like magic." She snapped her fingers. "Poof." She bumped her nose against his. "You must be a magician."

His mouth hitched up in a smile, and she was relieved to see it was real. The coolness had disappeared from his eyes, replaced by a look she recognized well after spending all night with him.

"Maybe I should make your robe disappear," he murmured.

She nodded eagerly. "And your pants."

CHAPTER TWENTY-FIVE

The dressing room door finally opened, drawing Ava Grace's attention to Mercy. The shorter woman held up the flowing skirt of the wedding dress with both hands and made her way to the platform in front of a wall of mirrors. The owner of the bridal boutique, a voluptuous black woman named Leticia, followed behind Mercy and fluffed the chapel-length train.

"What do you think?" Mercy asked. "Do you like it?"

Mercy hadn't been able to find a wedding dress in Nashville, so she and Ava Grace had driven to Atlanta to visit a boutique that specialized in curvy brides, size twelve and up. Mercy had told Ava Grace that she was tired of being unable to try on dresses because she was larger than the sample sizes in all the regular shops.

This was the first time they'd seen each other since Ava Grace returned from San Francisco almost two weeks ago. They planned to stay the night in Atlanta and head back to Nashville tomorrow.

Mercy had picked up Ava Grace at six o'clock this morning. They hadn't talked much during the four-hour drive because she was crabby in the morning … unless she woke up next to Jonah

Beck. Unfortunately, he and his good-morning kisses were on the opposite side of the country.

After their night together in Los Angeles, they'd flown back to Northern California and spent the weekend at his place in Dogpatch. They hadn't left the bed except to eat, shower, and walk Chicken around the block.

When the car service arrived Monday morning to take her to the airport, she'd been tempted to send it away. Instead, she kissed Beck good-bye and jokingly reminded him to change his sheets. He'd laughed so hard he almost choked.

"*Ugh*," Mercy groaned, drawing Ava Grace's attention. "I hate this dress."

"What don't you like about it?" Leticia asked.

"Everything." Mercy sought out Ava Grace's eyes in the mirror. "What do you think?"

This wasn't Ava Grace's first rodeo ... er, bridal excursion. She'd gone wedding dress shopping with Amelia, and she knew the rules.

"If you hate, I hate it," Ava Grace said. "I love the shoes though."

The platform sandals were made of matte gold leather. Sparkly crystals studded the heel and platform and a gold-beige chiffon flower adorned the ankle strap.

Mercy laughed. "You can take the girl out of the strip club, but you can't take the strip club out of the girl."

Ava Grace stuck out her tongue. "I have never stepped foot in a strip club in my life."

"That's what you claim, but your love of sparkly shoes says otherwise."

Mercy trudged back to the dressing room and shut the door with a soft click that communicated her disappointment more loudly than a slam.

Leticia glanced at Ava Grace, her eyebrows arched in question. "Did you really hate the dress?"

"No. I thought she looked beautiful. But it doesn't really matter what I think. What matters is the way she feels."

As the boutique owner disappeared into the dressing room, Ava Grace slipped her phone from her purse. It was almost noon in Atlanta, which meant it was almost nine a.m. in San Francisco.

She was surprised Beck hadn't texted her yet. He usually texted her when he got into the office. That thought had just crossed her mind when her phone vibrated in her hand and a text popped up from Beck.

"GOOD MORNING, SUGAR. OR SHOULD I SAY AFTERNOON?" Another text immediately followed. "DID YOU MAKE IT TO ATLANTA SAFE AND SOUND?"

Smiling, she typed a reply. "SITTING IN BOUTIQUE NOW. WAITING FOR MERCY TO MODEL ANOTHER DRESS. HOW'S YOUR MORNING?"

"GOOD." Another text came through. "ARE YOU SHARING A HOTEL ROOM WITH MERCY?"

She frowned a little, wondering why he wanted to know about her lodging accommodations. Why did he care?

"YES," she typed.

"TOO BAD. I WAS HOPING FOR A REPEAT OF OUR VIDEO CHAT FROM THE OTHER NIGHT."

Heat immediately suffused her, a mixture of arousal and embarrassment. A couple of nights ago while they had been video chatting, Beck had persuaded her to do a strip tease for him.

When he'd first suggested it, she'd said, "No way." But after he stripped down for her, she felt the need to reciprocate. She'd never imagined the strip tease would turn into an hour of self-pleasure for both of them.

If someone had told her three months ago she'd have sex on a bourbon barrel and masturbate on camera, she would've laughed herself silly. But she had a hard time saying no to Beck, especially when he was naked.

Another text from Beck floated across the screen. "MAYBE YOU CAN GO INTO THE DRESSING ROOM AND SEND ME A NAKED SELFIE."

She felt her eyes widen at his request. There was no way in hell she was going to send nude photos of herself to Beck or anyone else.

Shaking her head, she pecked out, "SORRY, HANDSOME. YOU'RE GOING TO HAVE TO USE YOUR IMAGINATION. OUR PHONES COULD BE HACKED, AND I DON'T WANT ANY NAKED PICTURES OF ME FLOATING AROUND. THEY'D BE ON THE HOMEPAGE OF EVERY GOSSIP WEBSITE IN THE WORLD."

Several seconds passed before he replied, "NO SELFIES."

She gnawed on her lip, knowing her text had reminded Beck how different their lives were. He believed their lives didn't mix, and she'd just reinforced his belief.

After he'd described their lives as bourbon and olive juice, she'd poured that combination into a tumbler and taken a sip. It had been worse than revolting. The awful taste had stayed with her for hours, even after she swished with mouthwash.

In Beck's little analogy, his life was bourbon, and her life was olive juice. Bourbon complemented almost anything, from sweet to salty to sour. But olive juice overpowered nearly everything.

Behind her, the door to the dressing room opened. When Mercy came into view, Ava Grace couldn't prevent the gasp that escaped her mouth. The bride-to-be looked stunning.

The strapless mermaid-style gown was a champagne shade that emphasized Mercy's bronze skin tone. The body of the dress, which featured a sweetheart neckline, was made of widely-ruched taffeta. It hugged every curve of her hourglass shape, while the chiffon tail of the dress flared out just above her knees.

Mercy stepped onto the platform and stared at herself in the mirror for a long time before turning to the side and then evaluating the back of the dress. Her long ponytail brushed over her bare shoulders like black feathers.

"What do you think?" Leticia's voice brimmed with excitement. "Is this the one?"

If Ava Grace were in Mercy's shoes, her answer would've been yes. The dress was perfect for Mercy. She would *never* find a better option, not even if she had one custom designed.

Shaking her head, Mercy said, "I don't like it."

The smile slid off Leticia's face. "You don't?"

"No," Mercy answered tersely. "I look awful."

She stomped down the stairs and rushed back to the fitting room. Leticia and Ava Grace shared a look of shocked dismay.

"That dress was *the one*," Leticia whispered.

Ava Grace nodded. "I'll go talk to her," she said before heading toward the dressing room. "Mercy?" She knocked lightly on the painted wood. "Can I come in?"

Hearing a muffled *yes*, she opened the door. Mercy sat on the gray velvet bench that stretched along the side of the dressing room, her torso slumped forward and her hands curled in her lap.

Ava Grace entered the small space and closed the door behind her. "Hey."

When Mercy didn't respond, Ava Grace nabbed a chair from the corner and dragged it in front of Mercy. She sat down and leaned forward to cover the other woman's hands with her own.

Meeting Mercy's black-as-midnight eyes, she asked, "What's going on, *chica*?"

Ava Grace suspected her friend was starting to get cold feet about her upcoming nuptials. Hopefully, she realized her fiancé wasn't the man for her.

Mercy's shoulders lifted in a shrug. "I can't find the right dress."

Because you're marrying the wrong man.

"So this is just about finding the right dress? Nothing else?"

The bride-to-be looked away from Ava Grace, turning her head to stare at a black-and-white photo of an old-fashioned church steeple. "I think Brian may be cheating on me."

Surprise made Ava Grace's head jerk back. "Why do you think that?"

"He works late almost every night. He goes into the office over the weekend and doesn't answer my calls or texts. He changed the passcode on his phone."

Mercy brought her gaze back to Ava Grace. "We haven't had sex in months. I offered to give him a blow job last night, and he said, 'Maybe later'." Her eyes widened. "What guy turns down a blow job?"

Even though Ava Grace detested Brian, she wasn't sure the things Mercy had mentioned were proof he was cheating. "I agree those things are suspicious, but maybe he's not interested in sex because he's overwhelmed with work."

Mercy shook her head. "I have a feeling it's more than that."

Suddenly, Ava Grace recalled the conversation she'd had with Beck about his ex-girlfriend Olivia. They'd been together for two years when he'd found out she'd cheated on him.

"Something similar happened to Beck," Ava Grace told Mercy. "He thought something was going on between his girlfriend and her boss, but when he asked her about it, she said their relationship was strictly professional. A couple of months later he walked in on them having sex in her office. He wishes he'd listened to his gut."

Now that Ava Grace thought about it, Beck hadn't had the best luck with women. His mother abandoned him. His high school girlfriend falsely accused him of assault. His live-in girlfriend/almost fiancée cheated on him.

Mercy exhaled loudly. "I don't know what to do. If I confront Brian and accuse him of cheating, he'll lie about it—just like Beck's ex-girlfriend."

"I don't know what to say. I've never been in a long-term relationship, and I have no experience with cheating." She squeezed Mercy's fingers. "Isn't this something you need to figure out *before* you buy a four-thousand-dollar wedding dress?"

Mercy looked down at her lap, where their hands were still linked. She abruptly jerked one of hers free and pushed back the cuff of Ava Grace's powder blue shirt to reveal the fingerprint-shaped bruises encircling her wrist.

Glancing up, Mercy said, "What the hell is this?"

Ava Grace tugged her arm free of Mercy's grasp and adjusted the cuff over the purplish bruises. She'd chosen this long-sleeved shirt specifically because it covered the unsightly marks.

"What happened?" Mercy demanded.

"Last night after dinner, Chuck got super agitated. I don't know what set him off. He started pacing, and then he started shouting and throwing things. Kyle couldn't get him to calm down, and I tried to help…"

Mercy's fierce expression softened into pity. "Your dad did that?" she asked, pointing to the hidden bruises.

"Yes."

For the first time in her life, Ava Grace had been afraid of her father. He'd been so out of control and so full of rage, it was as if he were possessed by a demon. He'd seized her wrist in such a tight grip, she worried he'd broken it.

Kyle—tall, muscular Kyle—struggled to contain Chuck without hurting him. Finally, the former Marine used his own body to trap her father against the wall, and he stayed in that position for an hour until Chuck finally calmed down.

Mercy wrinkled her nose. "This morning when I picked you up, I wondered why you were wearing a long-sleeved shirt. Hell is cooler than Atlanta in August." She wiggled forward on the bench. "Help me out of this dress, would you?"

Ava Grace stood and pulled her friend to her feet. After helping Mercy gather the train in her arms, she moved behind her and began to undo the hook-and-eye closures along Mercy's spine.

"What are you going to do about your dad?"

"I don't know." Ava Grace slipped a hook free. "I'm flying to San Francisco to perform at Trinity's invitation-only concert this weekend. I was planning to come back right away, but Kyle thinks I should stay a while because Chuck is more agitated when I'm around."

Chuck's outburst left Kyle emotionally ravaged, partly because he still struggled with post-traumatic stress disorder from his deployments overseas and partly because she'd been injured. He begged Ava Grace to either leave the farmhouse or immediately place her father in a memory care facility. She promised to think about it.

"How long is a while?" Mercy asked.

"Six weeks. Maybe seven. I have to be back in Nashville by early October for River Pearl's Artist Showcase."

"Do you need to be in Nashville for any reason?"

"Not really. I can write songs anywhere. And the same is true of the bourbon cookbook. It's due to my editor at the beginning of November."

Mercy stood patiently while Ava Grace worked on the hooks. Finally, Ava Grace reached the last hook.

"All done. Now how does this dress come off?"

"Over my head, I think."

Working together, they managed to liberate Mercy from the form-fitting wedding dress. If only she could be liberated from her fiancé so easily.

While Mercy donned her red-and-white polka dot sleeveless dress, Ava Grace hung up the wedding gown and shoved it into a clear plastic bag. As she zipped the bag, she said, "By the way, you didn't look awful in this dress. You looked gorgeous."

"Really?" Mercy's dark eyebrows lifted. "That's not what I saw when I looked in the mirror."

"What did you see?"

The petite brunette ignored the question and stepped into a pair of red open-toed flats. "So are you going to stay in San Francisco after the concert?"

"I haven't decided."

"I'm sure Beck would be happy to have you there for a while."

Ava Grace wasn't so sure about that. But there was only one way to find out.

CHAPTER TWENTY-SIX

Sweat dribbled into Beck's left eye, making it burn. Unfortunately, he couldn't do anything about it since his hands were occupied with a heavy cardboard box.

Thank God Ren and Gatsby's new apartment was on the first floor of the three-story Victorian. And thank God it was in Northern California.

Moving was never a pleasant experience, but it would've been even worse if they'd been in Kentucky. In late August, the temperature would've been in the low-nineties with ninety percent humidity. Here in San Francisco, it was cloudy and overcast, and the temperature hovered in the low fifties.

Beck entered the apartment and set the box on the floor. As he wiped his forearm over his sweaty forehead, his phone chimed with a text message.

He reviewed the images Ava Grace had sent. She and Amelia flanked Gatsby, their heads close together. Their huge smiles made Beck smile too.

Gatsby's first day of school was later this week, and Ava Grace had offered to take the little girl shopping for clothes. When Amelia found out, she begged to come along.

Ava Grace had been staying with Beck for two weeks now. Initially, she planned to stay in a hotel because she hadn't wanted to impose on Quinn and Amelia for such a long period. Even though the married couple hadn't minded, Ava Grace had balked at being a permanent guest.

When Ava Grace had mentioned her plans, the words *stay with me* formed deep inside Beck and clawed their way up his throat. He hadn't even known he wanted her with him until the words emerged from his mouth.

Once they were out there, floating on the air, he'd held his breath, hoping she'd accept his invitation. And she had.

Beck quickly adjusted to sharing his space with Ava Grace. Her expensive shampoo and brown sugar body scrub sat next to his cheap bar soap and value-size shampoo in the shower. Her short dresses and silky blouses hung next to his jeans and button-down shirts in the closet.

He found scraps of paper all over his apartment—receipts, envelopes, takeout menus—covered in her swirly handwriting with ideas for songs and music lyrics that just popped into her head. This morning, during the drive to Ren's old apartment, he discovered some in the console of his Jeep.

He never threw them away because one of those pieces of paper could be her next hit song. Instead, he shoved them into his pockets, and every night, he emptied them into a zippered pouch printed with big sunflowers. He'd bought it at an office supply superstore specifically for that purpose.

Seeing Ava Grace's stuff in his apartment gave Beck a weird feeling—a mix of pleasure and satisfaction and bewilderment. He didn't know how he'd ended up with one of the most famous women in the country—possibly the world—living in his apartment and sleeping in his bed.

Whenever she smiled at him ... whenever she said his name ... whenever she welcomed him into her body and cried out her pleasure, a voice inside him asked, *How the fuck did this happen?* He wished he knew the answer.

Beck's phone chimed again with another text from Ava Grace. In this picture, she, Amelia, and Gatsby were making silly faces. Ava Grace's eyes were crossed, Amelia's lips were pursed like a duck's, and Gatsby's tongue stuck out the side of her mouth.

Beck read the message that accompanied the photo: "Me & my girls! Best day ever!"

He huffed out a laugh. While he, Gabe, and Ren were busting their asses, lugging furniture and boxes around, Ava Grace and "her girls" were having the "best day ever."

He wasn't going to complain, though, not when his day started off with a bang—literally. This morning, he'd done Ava Grace against the wall in his walk-in shower, and he'd come so hard his ears rang.

Hopefully, he'd have enough energy to repeat the experience tonight. And if he didn't, maybe she'd do all the work and ride him hard and fast.

The thought made his cock twitch eagerly. Shaking his head, he silently ordered himself to stop thinking about how good she smelled and the sexy sounds she made when she came— something she did frequently when she was with him.

Every time they fucked, she came the moment he got inside her. He wanted to believe he was the only one who made her that hot, but he knew that was unlikely. It'd probably happened with her past lovers too. But that was something he didn't want to think about.

Beck heard footsteps outside the apartment. A moment later,

Gabe marched through the open door, his arms wrapped around a large cardboard box. Ren followed, carrying an identical box.

"This is it," Ren announced. "The last of the boxes."

Gabe moved deeper into the apartment and placed the box on the hardwood floor. Lifting his faded blue University of Kentucky T-shirt, he wiped his face and hair with the hem.

"I'm never doing this again," Gabe groused. "We're adults who own a small business, not poor college students. Adults hire movers."

Beck nodded vigorously. "My thoughts exactly."

As Ren deposited his box on top of the one Gabe had just set down, he said, "I'm sorry. I didn't think I had this much shit." He grimaced. "There's another dollar for the swear jar."

Shortly after Ren had returned to San Francisco with his daughter, he established a no-cursing mandate. Every time he, Beck, or Gabe said a dirty word, they had to pay a one dollar fine, even if Gatsby wasn't around.

Ren was determined to provide a wholesome environment for Gatsby. He'd enrolled her in one of the best private schools in the city and deliberately chosen an apartment in a family-friendly neighborhood.

The new apartment was a huge improvement over the old one. The contractor who'd renovated the Victorian had done an excellent job. He'd managed to create a somewhat open floor plan by widening the doorways between the kitchen and dining room and the dining room and living area.

By San Francisco standards, the apartment was huge. Ren and Gatsby had their own bathrooms, and he could use the small room off the living area as a home office.

A knock sounded on the open door, startling all three of them. Their heads swung toward the noise. A woman stood in the hallway, just over the threshold. The dim lighting made it difficult to see her clearly.

"Hello, I'm Sasha Ryan. I live upstairs." She lifted one hand, which held a cardboard carrier with six glass bottles. "I brought beer." She lifted her other hand, which held an aluminum-foil covered plate. "And brownies. I wasn't sure which you'd like better."

Gabe strode toward the door. "We like both." He removed the beer from her hand and pressed his back against the front door. "Come in. I'm Gabe." He pointed to Beck. "This is Jonah Beck. Everybody calls him Beck." He pointed to Ren. "And this is your new neighbor, Ren Holt."

Sasha hesitated. "I don't want to bother you. It looks like you're still moving boxes."

"We just finished," Gabe said. "Come in and have a beer with us. We're harmless, I promise. And we'll leave the door open, okay?"

Visibly relaxing, she said, "Okay."

Sasha took a few steps into the apartment. She was young, probably in her mid-twenties.

Gabe towered over her, so she couldn't be more than a couple of inches over five feet. If she were taller, she probably wouldn't look so plump.

She wore a loose black sweater that hung off one shoulder, revealing the strap of her black tank top and a colorful tattoo on her collarbone. If Beck wasn't mistaken, the body art was a dragonfly. Her bottom half was clad in skinny dark-washed jeans and black ankle boots.

Beck took the plate of brownies from her. "It's a pleasure to make your acquaintance, Sasha."

"Beck, right?"

He nodded, and she smiled widely, showing off straight, white teeth. Two tiny silver hoops pierced the corner of her bottom lip, and diamond studs highlighted the skin below her arched brow. Her eyes were a remarkable shade between blue and green, a little darker than the turquoise water surrounding The Maldives.

Her hair was styled in uneven chunks that ended above her shoulders. Blunt-cut bangs fell short of her eyebrows.

Her hair was so dark it looked black. Beck couldn't tell if it was her natural color or if it was a dye job, but the electric blue highlights shooting through the inky strands definitely came from a bottle.

Sasha's attention shifted to Ren. "Welcome to the neighborhood."

Beck slanted a sideways glance at Ren, who hadn't moved or replied to her greeting, before bringing his attention back to Sasha. Her smile faltered, and she licked her lip rings, obviously uncomfortable.

Beck darted another look toward Ren, whose gray gaze had locked on Sasha's mouth like a heat-seeking missile. Beck wondered why Ren was being rude to a woman he'd just met—a women thoughtful enough to bring a welcome gift to her new neighbor.

Sasha gave a tremulous smile. "You know what? I just remembered I'm late for ... something." She lifted her hand in a quick wave. "See you around."

She darted past Gabe and out the door. Her boots thumped as she ran up the stairs.

Gabe deposited the beer on the dining table. "What was that about, Ren?"

"What?" Ren asked, crossing his arms over his chest.

Gabe pulled a bottle out of the carrier. "Why were you so

rude? She brought us beer *and* brownies."

"I wasn't rude," Ren protested before glancing at Beck. "Tell him I wasn't rude."

"Sorry. Can't do that."

"Why not?"

"Because you *were* rude."

Gabe twisted the cap off the beer. "You didn't even thank her."

"I'll thank her the next time I see her, okay?" Ren tilted his head toward Beck's phone. "Have you heard from our girls?"

In response to the question, Beck held up his phone so Gabe and Ren could see the picture of Ava Grace, Amelia, and Gatsby. The guys moved closer to get a better view, and smiles flashed across their faces.

"Are there more?" Ren asked.

Nodding, Beck passed his phone to Ren. With Gabe looking over his shoulder, Ren swiped through the pictures.

"I'm glad they're having fun," Ren murmured.

Earlier, Ren had admitted he was relieved and disappointed he didn't have to go school shopping with Gatsby—relieved because he didn't know anything about little girl's clothing and disappointed because he'd been looking forward to the excursion with his daughter.

"I hope Ava Grace knows how much I appreciate her taking Gatsby shopping," Ren added.

After Beck and Ava Grace spent the weekend in bed together, following their trip to LA and her appearance on *Roarke*, Beck had bitten the bullet and told Ren everything. To Beck's surprise, Ren's first question had been: "How was it?"

Apparently, Ren and Gabe shared a brain, since that was the same question he'd asked when Beck came clean with him about fucking Ava Grace in the rickhouse.

Of course, Beck hadn't answered Ren's invasive question. His buddies didn't need to know sex with Ava Grace blew Beck's mind and shredded his soul.

When Ren asked if Beck planned to do it—and *her*—again, he'd answered honestly, confessing he was going to have sex with Ava Grace every chance he got. Until she no longer wanted him, that is.

As Beck had expected, Ren hadn't approved. He lectured Beck for an hour about the consequences of getting involved with Ava Grace, citing the negative impact on Trinity if things ended badly.

Beck listened without interrupting, knowing his friend and business partner was right. Once Ren finished his rant, Beck assured the other man there was no question things were going to end badly—it was a sure thing. Ren stared at Beck for a long time before responding with a simple *okay*.

Ren returned Beck's phone. "Your girlfriend is sweet for spending the day with Gatsby."

"She's not—"

"What?" Gabe challenged him. "Not your girlfriend? Or not sweet?"

Ren laughed softly. "Yeah, Beck, which is it?"

"She's not my girlfriend. And if you knew her better, you wouldn't describe her as sweet either."

Beck wasn't being entirely fair. Ava Grace *was* sweet. But she was tart too. She was a million different flavors, and all of them appealed to him.

Suddenly, Beck recalled when Ellis had compared women to bourbon. *A good one is warm and smooth and just a little sweet. But she's got some kick to her ... a bite that makes you flinch. She makes your throat burn and your chest tight, and then she settles in your belly and glows like an ember.*

Oh, yeah, Ava Grace was just like good bourbon. And Beck was going to savor every mouthful of her as long as he could.

"It doesn't matter what you call Ava Grace," Gabe said. "She's living with you, and you're sleeping together. Neither of you is seeing anyone else."

After Ava Grace's invitation-only concert for Trinity, Beck overheard her talking to the head of River Pearl Records. Unfortunately, Lexington Ross hadn't abandoned the whole Win-a-Date-with-Ava Grace idea.

When he'd brought it up, she shut him down by explaining she was seeing someone. Beck wondered if he was a convenient excuse or if she really had no interest in being with anyone but him.

The music exec had been angry to hear Ava Grace wasn't available for the contest and demanded to know whom she was dating. When she refused to tell him, he berated her and made snide comments about her looks and her talent.

Even though Beck knew Ava Grace could handle herself, he hadn't been able to stand there and let Lexington Ross disrespect her, especially after she'd just finished one of her best performances.

Beck casually interrupted the insulting exchange between Ava Grace and Lexington Ross and offered to give him a tour of the distillery. During the tour, Beck mentioned Ava Grace's work ethic, talent, and professionalism. His compliments were genuine, not just fake praise to get her boss off her back. She really was incredible.

"You and Ava Grace aren't friends with benefits," Gabe continued. "You're a couple."

Beck sighed. "It's just temporary ... until she goes back to Nashville. She doesn't want anything more."

Ren arched his dark blond brows. "Do you?"

CHAPTER TWENTY-SEVEN

The jams and jellies section of the neighborhood supermarket was well stocked with everything from blueberry and pineapple to jalapeño and red pepper. Apparently, Beck's preferred spread—plain ol' grape—was unsophisticated and unexciting.

"What are we looking for?" he asked Ava Grace.

"Peach preserves and orange marmalade," she answered without looking away from the shelves.

The grocery store was crowded this sunny Sunday afternoon. Tomorrow was Labor Day, and it seemed as if everyone in the city was out food shopping in preparation for a holiday get-together.

That was why he and Ava Grace were there. They'd been invited to a Labor Day gathering at Quinn's parents' home in the upscale neighborhood of St. Francis Wood.

Ava Grace was determined to try a couple of her cookbook bourbon recipes on the crowd. She'd decided to make meatballs with peach bourbon sauce as an appetizer and bacon-and-bourbon baked beans as a side dish.

She'd asked Shy to help her concoct new recipes, but she was determined to test every single one herself. Beck admired her commitment to the cookbook project, especially since she had so many other things to do. She worked hard, even harder than he did.

"Excuse me," a female voice said from behind him. "Can I squeeze in there? I need some strawberry jam."

Glancing over his shoulder, he spotted a dark-haired woman about his age with an overflowing grocery cart and two small children. "Sorry," he replied, stepping out of her way.

The brunette shopper plucked two jars of strawberry jam from the shelf, placed them in her cart, and hurried away. Her kids trailed along behind her, dragging their feet. They probably didn't want to be there anymore than Beck did.

Grocery shopping didn't rank high on his list of favorite things to do. Ava Grace did though, and he was willing to suffer the busy store for her.

This wasn't the first time they'd gone grocery shopping together. They ate most of their meals at home because it was easier than going out to a restaurant. Unless they went to one of Shy's establishments, her fans constantly interrupted their meals. It bothered Beck a lot, but she never seemed to mind.

Spotting the peach preserves on the top shelf, he asked, "How many?"

"Just one."

"Do you have a preference?"

She shook her head, and he nabbed a jar of peach preserves with a vintage-looking label. After placing it in the cart, he resumed the search for orange marmalade.

She found it before he did, and as she bent down to grab a jar, the waistband of her jeans gaped a little, revealing the top of her lacy black panties. A gentleman probably would've looked away, but he didn't feel like a gentleman with her. In fact, there had been a few times when he'd been so desperate to have her he'd been more animal than human.

After placing the jar of orange marmalade in the cart, she consulted her phone for the shopping list. She looked down, and the angle of her head drew his gaze to the nape of her neck.

Since she'd chopped off her hair, her nape had become his favorite part of her body. The baby-smooth skin just begged for his attention, and he had a hard time keeping his lips and tongue off it.

He'd been stunned when she strolled into the Trinity headquarters last week with her hair cut almost as short as his own. When he kissed her good-bye that morning before he left for work, her thick, glossy hair hung down the middle of her back.

Five hours later, she had a new hairstyle—one she described as a pixie cut. Side-swept bangs barely teased her forehead, and in the back, the soft blond tendrils had been razor cut above her nape.

He'd loved her long hair ... loved nuzzling his face in it while they were in bed ... loved sliding his fingers through it when he kissed her. And he'd really loved fisting his hands in it when she went down on him.

But she'd shorn it off for a good cause. The company that made the hair products she endorsed had a philanthropic program with the American Cancer Society to make wigs for women who were battling cancer, and Ava Grace gave her hair to the program to encourage more donations.

Beck had seen women with pixie haircuts before, and none of them had looked as good as Ava Grace. Somehow she looked even more beautiful without her long hair.

The short, almost masculine haircut made her look more

feminine. It highlighted her delicate bone structure, especially her high cheekbones, and made her eyes look larger and more luminous.

Her new haircut also made her less recognizable to her fans. And in Beck's opinion, that was a major bonus.

"Only a few more things on the list," she said.

"Where to next?"

"The meat department. I need ground beef and bacon."

She led the way down the aisle, and he followed with the cart. They had worked out their roles: she was the brains, and he was the brawn. She made the shopping list and kept them on task while he pushed the cart and carried the bags.

As they rolled toward the meat section, he noticed several other men pushing carts behind their women. Without exception, the guys either had a glazed look in their eyes or they were staring at their woman's ass with a lascivious gaze.

Beck fell into the second category. He never missed an opportunity to ogle Ava Grace's ass, and he never missed an opportunity to put his hands on it either.

He and Ava Grace looked like an average couple doing their weekly food shopping. But looks were deceiving. They weren't a couple, and she sure as hell wasn't average. She was a country star, and he was just the guy she had sex with whenever she was in town.

He had to remind himself of that several times an hour, especially on days like this. Today they'd woken up in the same bed, cocooned in the comforter and wrapped around each other. They'd enjoyed slow morning sex, shared a shower, eaten a late breakfast, and gone for a long walk with Chicken before jumping in his Jeep to head to the grocery store.

On days like this, Beck felt as if he and Ava Grace were a real couple—a real couple with real feelings and a real future together. They did more "couple" things than most of the couples he knew.

They definitely did more couple things than he and Olivia had done. He couldn't think of a single occasion when he and his ex-girlfriend went shopping together.

In fact, now that he thought about it, he and Olivia hadn't spent much time together. Work had been a priority for both of them. He'd been trying to get Trinity in the black, and she'd ... well, she'd been fucking her boss.

Even when they'd had the opportunity to spend time together, they found other things to do. Olivia had been into what he jokingly called "extreme self-improvement." She was obsessed with lessons and classes, from Chinese and tennis to wine appreciation and sushi making.

They could've done those things together, but she hadn't invited him, and he hadn't asked to come along. He preferred to hang out with Gabe and Ren instead of Olivia.

But he didn't feel that way about Ava Grace. He wanted to spend time with her, both in and out of bed. More than once, he'd turned down invitations from the guys in favor of being with her.

Now that he no longer had to fight his desire for her, he could just enjoy being with her. And he enjoyed it a lot more than he'd thought he would. That realization probably would've made him uneasy if she didn't seem to enjoy his company just as much.

Ava Grace stopped next to an end-cap display of peanut butter. Picking up a jar, she said, "My bourbon blondie bars didn't turn out, but maybe peanut butter bourbon bars would taste good."

Bracing his elbows on the plastic-covered handle, he propped his booted foot on the edge of the cart's lower storage area. "Peanut butter bourbon bars sound good." He laughed. "Try saying that a few times. Peanut butter bourbon bars. It's a tongue twister."

Her husky laughter floated to him. "Peanut butter bourbon bars," she echoed softly.

"Why don't you make a test batch and bring them to the cookout?"

She tilted her head. "I don't know if I have enough time to do the meatballs and beans and the bars too."

"I'll help."

Her lips twitched. "I appreciate the offer, handsome, but you're not very skilled in the kitchen."

"You seemed impressed with my skills last night."

She'd made chicken sausage lasagna with Alfredo sauce for dinner, and while it had baked, he'd picked her up and fucked her against the cold surface of the refrigerator. When the oven timer dinged, she was in the middle of her third orgasm.

Rosy pink color bloomed on her smooth cheeks, and he chuckled. "Are you sure you don't want my help?" he teased.

She smiled. "If *help* is another word for body, then yes, I want your help. Otherwise, I want you to stay out of the kitchen. You might set something on fire or cut off your finger."

"I have degrees in chemical engineering and biochemistry," he replied dryly. "I've worked with dangerous chemicals and a Bunsen burner. I think I can handle peanut butter bourbon bars."

"Good point. You can make everything while I just sit there and enjoy the view of your butt."

A surprised laugh escaped him. "You like my butt, huh?"

Her smile faded. "I like everything about you, Jonah."

Sincerity sweetened her voice, and her expression reinforced her words. As he stared into her face, warmth spread throughout his chest. *She likes everything about me.*

She smiled suddenly. "I like everything about you but your annoying habit of hanging your towel over mine. I always have to dry off with a damp towel."

He laughed. "Sorry, sugar. I'll make sure to hang my towel *next* to yours."

"What a creative solution to the problem," she mocked.

He only saw one problem at the moment: he wouldn't be able to get her naked for at least an hour.

She put the peanut butter into the cart, and they resumed their trek toward the meat department. Once they were there, it didn't take long to find the bacon and ground beef she wanted.

"Is that it?" he asked as she tossed two packages of bacon into the cart.

She nodded. "That's it."

They made their way to the front of the store, where they discovered every single checkout line was backed up with shoppers. Some of the lines extended into the aisles.

He caught Ava Grace's eyes. "Are all seven million residents of the Bay Area in this store?"

She wrinkled her nose. "Seems like it."

Maneuvering the cart into the nearest line, he settled in for a long wait. She shifted closer to him and wrapped her arm around his waist. As he draped his arm over her shoulder, she leaned against him, her head nestled on his shoulder.

"Your middle name is Oglesby, in honor of Ellis Oglesby. Am I right?"

"No."

The line slowly advanced. Finally, they were in sight of the checkout displays. Colorful magazines filled the metal racks, and he swept his gaze over them without noticing the covers.

Beside him, Ava Grace made a funny noise, kind of a choked snort. He looked down into her face. "What?"

She pointed, and he followed the direction of her finger to the magazines. He did a double-take when he realized her face was plastered on every cover. The pictures were obviously recent because her hair was short.

The headlines ranged from "Ava Grace's New Look" to "Get Ava Grace's Sexy Style" to "Ava Grace's Secret Heartbreak Spurs Makeover." That cover showed a photo collage of her with various men.

Dropping his arm from her shoulders, he lunged toward the display and jerked the gossip rag from the shelf. He studied the cover, shocked to see a small picture of himself and Ava Grace when they'd arrived at the hotel after the *Roarke* show.

One of the larger photos caught Beck's attention. In the image, a big, dark-haired man held Ava Grace protectively, their heads close together. Beck could only assume the man was Kyle Hood.

Dismay exploded inside his chest. Lifting his eyes from the cover, he met hers. She smiled ruefully.

"I guess my new haircut is big news," she said in a laughter-tinged voice.

Sensing the heavy weight of curious gazes, Beck glanced around at the other shoppers. They'd seen the magazines and spotted Ava Grace. Awareness raced through the crowd like a wildfire, and people began to point and murmur her name.

Several people pulled out their phones and edged closer to him and Ava Grace so they could snap pictures. Within seconds, a crowd surrounded them. She immediately went into what he thought of as her "star" mode, smiling and chatting and posing for photos.

The buzz of an entire colony of bees filled Beck's ears, obliterating the beeps from the electronic checkout scanners and the hum of conversation. He'd known Ava Grace was a celebrity ... known her life was fodder for the tabloids, but he'd always felt removed from her fame.

He'd envisioned himself as a piece of space debris floating around her planetary body, but he abruptly realized he was caught up in her force field. He was no longer on the periphery of her fame; he was right in the middle of it.

Nausea began to churn in his stomach. One of the reasons he'd supported the idea of Trinity partnering with Ava Grace had been to take the spotlight off him.

He didn't want to be the face of Trinity. He wanted his private life to stay private. And if he continued to spend time with Ava Grace, everything about his life would be scrutinized.

CHAPTER TWENTY-EIGHT

Ava Grace stood next to Beck, unloading groceries onto the kitchen island. After removing several items from the insulated tote bag, she brought them to the refrigerator and arranged them on the shelves.

As she closed the refrigerator, she checked the clock display on the microwave. Their shopping trip had taken much longer than she'd expected, and it was past three o'clock. The store had been busier than usual, and more than a dozen people had asked her to sign autographs and take pictures.

"It's way past lunchtime," she noted. "Are you hungry? I could make some sandwiches, or I could heat up the leftover lasagna."

When Beck didn't answer, she glanced sideways at him. "Did you hear me, handsome?"

"What?" he asked absently, removing several cans of pinto beans from a reusable grocery bag.

She studied him for a moment. He wasn't as talkative as Quinn and Gabe, but he wasn't as quiet as Ren either. Beck was somewhere in between, and he'd been quieter than usual on the way home from the grocery store. She couldn't tell if something was wrong or if he was just hungry.

"Sandwiches? Leftover lasagna?"

"Whatever you want," he answered flatly.

She bumped him with her hip. "I want you to tell me what you're thinking about."

"Nothing," he muttered, using his forearm to scoop several cans against his chest.

She hurried to the pantry and opened the door for him. He brushed by her as if she were invisible, and a stone settled in her stomach. She sensed him pulling away from her. Panic and worry collided inside her, but she instinctively knew he wouldn't respond to those emotions.

"If you're upset ... if I did something to upset you ... you should tell me instead of pouting like a little girl whose mommy refused to buy her a doll," she said, knowing she was picking a fight.

Beck stopped in his tracks. "Pouting like a little girl?" he repeated in a sharp, icy voice completely unlike his normal deep drawl.

"Yes. Pouting like a little girl."

His gorgeous eyes narrowed into slits, his long eyelashes tangling at the corners. "I'm not pouting."

She waited until he'd shelved the cans before asking, "Then what *are* you doing?"

"Thinking," he snapped.

"About what?" she asked, matching his tone.

He stomped back to the island. "About the fact you have to be the center of attention all the time."

Ah. He's upset about the impromptu meet-and-greet at the grocery store.

"I don't have to be the center of attention all the time," she countered calmly.

"And yet you always are," he replied, sarcasm dripping from his voice.

After gathering another armful of canned goods, he returned to the pantry. He put them on the shelves with jerky, uncoordinated movements that hinted at his emotional upheaval.

Slamming his palm against the pantry door, he forced it closed with a bang. She hadn't seen him this upset since the *Roarke* show, and she knew the situation could very easily escalate if she let it.

A cold feeling spread over her. She'd worried her high-profile career—her fame—would be a problem for Beck. He'd experienced the downside of being newsworthy when he was younger. And even if he'd started with a clean slate, her fame probably still would've created a strain in their relationship.

A lot of celebrities had no one in their lives except managers, assistants, and acquaintances. They hadn't found anyone who thought the benefit of being with someone famous outweighed the bullshit.

"Every time we go somewhere, even to the goddamn grocery store, there you are—chatting up strangers, signing autographs, posing for pictures," Beck said.

"I have to do that. It's my job."

"You don't *have* to do it," he countered, his brown eyes so dark they looked black. "You *want* to do it. You *like* to do it."

She shook her head, both confused and frustrated by his words. "Your job is distilling bourbon. You don't have to do it, but you do. You want to do it. You like to do it. What's the difference?"

He stared at her unblinkingly. "There's a difference."

"I don't see the difference. Explain it to me."

"When we go out, people fawn all over you. It happens when we go out to dinner, to the grocery store, walking in the park, standing in the line at the movies. *Every-fucking-where.*"

"I have fans. What do you think I should do? Just walk by and pretend they're not there? I can't do that. I can't ignore them."

He snorted rudely. "You love the attention. You eat up their compliments like a kid gorging on Halloween candy." Crossing his arms over his chest, he leaned back against the pantry door. "Ava Grace, you're even prettier in person. Ava Grace, you're my favorite singer. Ava Grace, I'm your number one fan." His eyes caught hers. "I almost forgot this one: Ava Grace, I love you."

She knew he was mimicking her fans. She knew he didn't mean those three little words. Yet hearing them in his baritone drawl made her stomach tremble.

Shoving his hands in his pockets, he rocked back on his heels. "Do you see the difference now?"

She wet her dry lips. "I understand why you're upset. I know my fame is inconvenient. I know it's hard to deal with ... that it's a huge pain in the ass for the people around me."

Beck wasn't the only person in Ava Grace's life who had to deal with her fame. Amelia had experienced both the positives and negatives of it. But she'd accepted the good, the bad, and the ugly because she loved Ava Grace.

"I know it's inconvenient for you, Jonah. It's inconvenient for me too. Don't you think I'd like to go out to eat without people staring at me ... without someone interrupting us? I'm there with *you*. I want to talk to *you*. I don't want to sign autographs on the back of receipts or stand up in the middle of the restaurant and take a picture."

Taking a deep breath, she continued, "I'd like to go grocery shopping with you without people recognizing me ... without people stopping me in the aisles and wanting to talk to me. I want to be just like every other couple there."

"Every other couple," he repeated, a weird note in his voice.

She frowned. "You know what I mean. I want you to be able to kiss me in the produce section without worrying it will show up on the front of *National Enquirer*."

Ava Grace moved to stand in front of Beck. She placed her palms on his broad chest, which was covered in a navy-blue T-shirt with white block lettering that said *Bourbon goggles work better than beer goggles*.

"I don't like being the center of attention wherever I go, but I am." She looked up into his face. "It's just the way things are. I can't change it."

He shook his head. "You love the attention. You light up when people tell you how much they love your music."

"I don't love the attention. But I won't deny it feels good when my fans compliment me." She gently poked him in the chest with her forefinger. "You need to think about your fans and how you feel when they compliment you."

"*My* fans? What are you talking about?"

"The people who drink Trinity. They're your fans. Don't forget I was at the International Wine and Spirits Show. I saw the smile on your face when they said Trinity was the best bourbon they'd ever tasted. It feels good when someone acknowledges your hard work."

She could tell she was getting through to him. His posture relaxed a little, and his face softened.

"You're right," he admitted quietly. "It does feel good."

"I still remember the first time one of my fans stopped me for an autograph. I was standing in line at a taco shop with Millie in LA, and this girl tapped me on the arm and held out a piece of paper. I thought she was passing out flyers until she said, 'You're my favorite singer on *American Star*. I vote for you every week. I hope you win. Can I have your autograph?'"

She smiled at the memory. "I was so amazed someone actually liked me enough to approach me. I could barely sign my name I was so nervous." She laughed softly. "I probably misspelled it."

The ghost of a smile emerged on Beck's mouth. "That's a good memory," he murmured.

She nodded. "Every time someone asks for my autograph, I'm still amazed." She smiled wryly. "Although sometimes I'm more irritated than amazed."

"You never seem irritated."

"I was irritated today. The whole time I was signing autographs and posing for pictures, I was thinking you'd probably never go grocery shopping with me again and the milk was going to sour if it sat in the cart much longer."

A laugh rustled in his throat. "The milk is fine, sugar."

He pulled his hands from his pockets and settled them on her hips. His fingers flexed lightly as he drew her to him.

"A lot of people want all the good things that come along with being famous but none of the bad," she said. "I swore I'd never turn into one of those diva singers—the ones who snub their fans and cover their faces when paparazzi take pictures. I want my fans to know I appreciate them, and the only way I can show them is signing autographs and posing for pictures and showing interest in their lives."

She looped her arms around his waist. "Amelia says I'm too accessible to my fans, and I think she may be right. When you and I are together, I'll do my best to avoid signing autographs and posing for pictures. I'll try to discourage conversation too.

I'll ask my fans to respect that I'm with you."

"You will?" he asked, his handsome face etched with disbelief.

"Yes." She laid her head on his chest. "I don't want you to think they're more important than you are. They're not."

CHAPTER TWENTY-NINE

The last notes of the ballad faded away, and Ava Grace pressed pause on her phone before the next demo came on. She tapped a pen against her bottom lip, debating whether she liked the song she'd just heard.

So far, she'd written seven songs for her next album. She needed at least fourteen, and she'd decided to consider songs written by someone other than herself. She knew it'd be almost impossible for her to compose seven more songs before she returned to Nashville in two weeks.

Next to her, Chicken shifted on the sofa. He propped his head on her thigh, and she absentmindedly scratched behind his ears.

She'd listened to more than sixty demos, dividing them into three categories: *maybe*, *no*, and *hell no*. She had twenty more demos to get through, and after that, she'd listen to all the *no* songs again to see if she was too harsh in her initial assessment.

She liked the ballad she'd just heard enough to put it in the *maybe* category. After cueing up the next demo, she leaned her head against the leather sofa cushion.

As the first notes filled her ears, she closed her eyes. Catching the melody, she began to hum. The chorus repeated, and she sang along, trying to get a feel for the words.

When the song ended, she lifted her head and opened her eyes. Then she squealed in surprise.

Beck sat on the cocktail table in front of the sofa, his knees just inches away from her crisscrossed legs. Chicken sat on the floor next to him, his tail wagging like a metronome. Beck pointed to her headphones, and she jerked them off.

"You scared me to death!" she burst out.

Holding his hands up like a criminal, he said, "I didn't mean to. I was trying *not* to."

She scowled. "You should've done something to get my attention."

"Like what?" He tweaked her big toe. "Should I have done this?" He tugged on a piece of hair behind her ear. "Or this?"

Before she could answer, he leaned forward until his lips almost touched hers. "Or maybe I should have done this?" he asked before covering her mouth with his.

He kissed her as if it had been years rather than hours since he'd seen her. His mouth was rough ... demanding ... *ravenous*. When he finally released her lips and drew back, she was breathless.

"Did that get your attention?" he murmured.

Nodding slowly, she pressed her fingers to her lips. How could a single kiss from this man make her feel so much? How could *he* make her feel so much?

So much love I'm drowning in it.

There were times she just wanted to grab him and say: "I love you. I want to spend my life with you. I want to be your wife. I want to have your babies, and I'd even be willing to name the boys Jonah as long as I got to pick the girl names."

Somehow she'd managed to push those words down deep

inside. But she was worried she wouldn't be able to do it much longer. Every time they made love, she was afraid the words would slip out. And she was even more afraid of what his response would be if they did.

Her gaze touched on his dark hair and handsome face. He hadn't shaved this morning because they'd stayed in bed longer than they should have, and dark scruff shaded his jaw. In her opinion, it made him even sexier. Plus, she liked the way it felt on her skin.

She dropped her gaze to his broad shoulders and muscular torso. He had an endless supply of bourbon T-shirts, and today he wore a sage-green one with *Let them drink bourbon* in chocolate-brown lettering.

He shifted on the table, and his tan cargo pants tightened over his thighs. "I thought you were going to stop by Trinity for lunch today?"

"I said I *might* stop by," she clarified. "I decided to have lunch with Amelia instead."

He braced his hands on the edge of the cocktail table, the muscles in his forearms flexing. "Just let me know next time, okay?"

His tone wasn't censuring, but she immediately felt guilty. "I'm sorry. That was inconsiderate of me." She nudged his knee with her foot. "If you wondered why I didn't show up, you could have texted or called."

"I did."

"You did? I didn't see any messages." She unhooked her headphones from her phone, checked the screen, and then showed it to him. "See? Nothing."

He frowned. "You need to get a new phone. Half of my texts don't come through. And my number never shows up in your call log. I swear your phone has some kind of grudge against mine."

She laughed. "I'll make sure to text you next time." She nudged him again. "I just figured you wouldn't miss me."

Her teasing tone masked the truth of her statement. She'd decided to go to lunch with Amelia because she assumed Beck wouldn't care either way, and her best friend wanted her company.

"I did," he said.

"You did what?"

He rolled his lips inward before saying, "I missed you."

"Really?" she asked, her heart tap-dancing in her chest.

"Yeah."

"I missed you too," she admitted softly. "I had a good time with Amelia, but I would've had a better time with you."

She wondered if he understood the significance of that statement. Before him, Amelia was the most important person in her life—her favorite person. But Beck had usurped her best friend's position.

Over the past five weeks, Ava Grace had casually and subtly insinuated herself into his life. She regularly dropped by the Trinity offices with lunch for the guys or just to hang out.

More than once, she and Beck escaped to the rickhouse for a quickie ... but never again on top of a barrel. She didn't want to risk bodily injury.

She'd told Beck about getting a splinter the first time they had sex, and he laughed so hard he almost passed out. Afterward, he made her show him where the "owie" had been, and he kissed it all better.

Unfortunately, he couldn't kiss her biggest "owie" away. A few nights ago, as she and Beck had driven home from dinner at

Quinn and Amelia's, she mustered the courage to ask how he'd describe their relationship.

He didn't say anything for a long time, and the silence in his Jeep was so absolute she was afraid he could hear the frantic beat of her heart. Finally, he answered her question with a single word: *temporary*.

If she hadn't been sitting down, the pain of that softly spoken word probably would've sent her to her knees. It devastated her, and she was too hurt to ask why he felt that way.

For the first time since she'd been staying with him, they'd gone to sleep without making love. He'd pulled her close, his big hand warm against her midriff, and buried his face in her hair.

Neither Beck nor Ava Grace fell asleep for a long time. Instead they lay in the spacious bed, their bodies touching but their hearts far apart. Even Chicken knew something was wrong, choosing to sleep on the floor instead of next to her.

The following morning, she woke up alone. After consulting both her head and her heart, she decided to end things with Beck. She accepted his feelings would never be as deep or lasting as hers.

But then she'd found a stack of mini notepads on the kitchen island along with a box of new ballpoint pens. A Post-It was stuck to the top notepad with a message from Beck: "Thought you could use these to write your next hit."

He signed the note with nothing more than his initial, but added a postscript: "Call me when you wake up. I need a little sugar with my coffee."

That brief, hastily scribbled note convinced her not to give up. It convinced her there was still hope. It convinced her *temporary* could become *forever.*

"What were you singing when I got home?" Beck asked.

"A demo."

"For your new album?"

"Yes."

"It sounded good."

"You think so?"

Nodding, he said, "Yes. You know what sounds even better?"

"What?"

He smiled, and the skin around his dark eyes crinkled. "The noises you make when you come."

She knew she was blushing. "Shut up."

"I love those sweet little moans and groans." He laughed softly. "Your cheeks are pink, Miz Landy. Are you embarrassed?"

Doing her best to ignore him, she took her notepad and headphones from her lap and arranged them on the seat next to her. She glanced at her phone to check the time and then double-checked it when she saw it wasn't even four o'clock. He usually didn't arrive home until after six.

"Why are you home so early?"

"I was worried."

He rose from his perch on the cocktail table and moved her notepad and headphones so he could sit down beside her. Shifting on the cushions, she rested her back against the arm of the sofa and pulled her knees toward her chest.

Her toes touched his thigh, and she wiggled them against the heavy fabric of his cargo pants. He dropped his warm hand to her feet and squeezed lightly.

"What were you worried about? Did something happen at work?"

He caught her eyes. "I was worried about you."

She blinked, sure she had misunderstood. "What?"

"I was worried about you," he repeated. "When you didn't show up for lunch or reply to my texts or answer my phone calls, I got worried."

His tone wasn't accusing or angry. It was matter-of-fact. But there was nothing matter-of-fact about his words.

Beck had come home early because he'd been worried about her. Men didn't waste time worrying about women they didn't care about.

Beck cares about me.

She looked down at her knees. As she stared at the smooth black fabric of her yoga pants, tears prickled the backs of her eyes and clogged her throat. She swallowed hard, trying to get rid of them.

She didn't want Beck to see how much his words meant to her. If she showed too much, he'd pull away. It'd happened before.

But if she didn't show enough, he did the same thing. She felt like an acrobat walking on a tightrope.

"I didn't know you were such a worrywart," she said, trying to tease, but her voice cracked a little.

"Neither did I," he muttered.

Lifting her head, she met his gaze. "I'm sorry I made you worry, Jonah."

With a shrug, he looked away. She hesitated but then decided to just let the subject drop. She rose from the sofa and popped her phone into the sound station across the room.

As she grabbed the remote, she asked, "Would you listen to demos with me? I need your help picking out songs."

She made her way back to the sofa, and he looked up at her. "You need my help?" he repeated doubtfully.

"I *want* your help.

She slid onto his lap with her legs draped over his thighs, and he looped his arms around her. She started to press play, but he stopped her with a hand over hers.

"Wait a second. There's something I've wanted to know for a while…"

She tilted her head so she could see his face. "Ask me anything."

"What did you sing when you auditioned for *American Star*?"

"'You Really Got a Hold on Me'." She hummed the melody. "Smokey Robinson and the Miracles."

His arms tightened around her. "Sing it for me?"

Dropping her head to his shoulder, she began to sing. As she crooned the lyrics to the R&B classic, she realized they were uncomfortably close to how she felt about Beck. She loved him madly, and he really had a hold on her.

She finished the song, and he nuzzled his face in her hair before dropping a kiss on her forehead. "Thanks, sugar."

"You're welcome."

He sighed softly. "I love to hear you sing."

Snuggling closer, she said, "I'll sing for you anytime you want."

"I'd like…" He paused and sniffed the air. "Is something burning?"

"Oh, no!" She vaulted from his lap. "My short ribs!"

She ran into the kitchen and jerked open the oven door. Thankfully, no smoke poured out, and the cast iron Dutch oven she'd bought in Union Square looked fine. She nabbed a potholder and lifted the lid. Fragrant steam wafted out, and she waved it away.

Beck came to a stop next to her. "What's that?

"I came up with a new bourbon recipe." She picked up a wooden spoon and stirred the savory mixture. "Braised short ribs with espresso-bourbon sauce."

He groaned. "If you keep testing your new recipes on me, I'm going to have to go for a run every night too."

Beck ran every morning, fair or foggy weather. She'd gone with him a few times, and he'd kicked her butt, both with his punishing pace and the distance he covered.

He also played basketball a few times a month with the guys. And he got his hands dirty at work, hefting sacks of grain and rolling barrels. He had an amazing body to show for all that physical activity—tall, strong, and muscular.

"You don't have to run morning, noon, and night to stay in shape, handsome."

She returned the spoon to the dog-shaped holder on the counter. She'd found it in a little boutique on Fillmore Street, and she'd just had to have it. As she replaced the lid on the Dutch oven and closed the oven door, Beck grabbed a bottle of beer from the refrigerator and twisted off the cap.

"Did you know sex burns more calories than running?" she asked.

"No, I didn't know that," he replied before taking a big swallow of beer.

"Instead of hitting the pavement more often, you can hit this," she suggested, lightly slapping her rear.

He choked, and beer spewed out his mouth. Clapping his hand over it, he fell into a coughing fit. She hastily tore a paper towel off the roll and handed it to him, laughing the whole time.

When he'd finally stopped gurgling and gasping and was able to catch his breath, he tipped his beer bottle toward her bottom half. "I'm already *hitting* that pretty often. Usually twice a day. Should I hit it more frequently?"

"If you feel the need"—she waited a beat before completing the sentence—"to burn some calories."

He smiled slowly. "I had a big lunch. Probably thousands of calories."

After depositing his beer bottle on the counter next to the oven, he turned toward her. Gripping her waist in both hands, he easily lifted her onto the island. She spread her legs, and he stepped between them.

"I feel the need to burn all those calories."

"You do?" she asked as he reached for the hem of her T-shirt.

"Yeah. Right now."

CHAPTER THIRTY

"*Maybe, no,* or *hell no*?" Ava Grace asked.

Beck grimaced. "*Hell no.* That demo was a piece of shit."

"I was thinking *maybe.*" Her luscious lips turned down in a frown. "You need to be nicer. Someone worked really hard to write that song."

He shook his head, beyond exasperated. He never would've guessed she'd be so softhearted when it came to her music. A few minutes ago, she'd accused him of being a "meanie" when he'd said one of the demos sounded like a preschooler had written it.

"That song is not worthy of your voice," he countered, "and you know it."

She sighed gustily. "Fine." She picked up her notepad from her lap and looked around her legs. "Where's my pen?" She ran her fingers along the space between the sofa and her upper thighs. "What happened to my pen?"

He pointed to her head. "It's stuck to your headband, sugar."

She patted her headband with both hands, her fingers searching the thin strip of fabric. The position pushed her breasts forward, and his gaze lingered on the firm mounds.

She wasn't wearing a bra—she hadn't bothered to put it back on after he'd removed it earlier—and he could see the hard points of her nipples under her baby-blue T-shirt. They were ultra-sensitive, and his mouth tingled when he thought about the sounds she made when he tongued them.

She found the pen and plucked it off her headband. After uncapping it, she scribbled her notes about the song, her lower lip caught between her front teeth.

They'd been listening to demos for about an hour and a half. They'd settled on the sofa after a delicious meal of short ribs, horseradish mashed potatoes, and sautéed green beans. She had been worried the main dish would be overcooked since they'd gotten a little distracted with sex, but the short ribs had been tender and juicy … just like her.

"I definitely think you should include the short ribs with espresso-bourbon sauce in your cookbook," he said.

Looking up from her notepad, she asked, "You liked them?"

"What does Amelia say? Orgasmically great?"

She giggled. "Orgasmically delicious."

He nodded. "They were orgasmically delicious."

She uncrossed her long legs and extended them out in front of her. Stretchy black pants covered them, denying him the delectable sight of her lean thighs and shapely calves. Too bad she'd put her pants back on after he'd had his way with her on the kitchen island.

When his cock twitched eagerly, he reminded himself bedtime was only a couple of hours away. Then he could strip her out of those tight pants and make himself at home inside her. He told himself he could survive the wait, but his erect cock said otherwise.

"Did you like the short ribs as much as the pork tenderloin

with bourbon-spiced apples?" she asked, completely oblivious to his lecherous thoughts.

"I'm not sure. They're hard to compare."

"I have too many beef recipes. I need to come up with more chicken dishes." She tapped her pen against her bottom lip. "Maybe something with pears. Do you like pears?"

Apparently, he was a perfect guinea pig to test her recipes. More often than not, he came home from work to find her in the kitchen, an apron tied around her slender waist and a pile of dirty dishes in the sink. Somehow, he always ended up cleaning up her mess, but he figured that was only fair since she did the cooking.

She hooked the pen onto the notepad and dropped it in her lap. "Okay, I'm ready for the next song."

He pressed play, and a woman's voice filled the living room: "'Pack Your Bags' by Julia Swearingen."

"Julia is one of the best songwriters in Nashville, and she also has a great voice." Ava Grace said. "This should be good."

The first notes of the demo floated from the speakers, light and airy. Then the song turned dark and heavy. Julia's sharp-edged voice filled the room, completely different from Ava Grace's husky sound.

Ava Grace hummed along with the melody, her foot moving to the beat as Julia berated some poor guy and told him to pack his bags and get the hell out. When the song was over, Beck pressed the pause button.

"*Damn,*" he swore. "That woman is *pissed off.*"

"She went through a bad breakup a few years ago. Her fiancé cheated on her."

"That sucks."

He remembered how he'd found Olivia in her office, bent

over her desk with her skirt around her waist and her boss pumping away behind her. No matter how hard he'd tried to forget it, the image was burned on his brain.

Ava Grace shrugged. "Some people aren't made for monogamy."

I am.

He wasn't one of those guys who fought to stay footloose and fancy-free. He wanted to be tied down.

So why are you wasting your time with a woman who doesn't want that? a voice whispered inside him.

But then another voice chimed in: *How do you know she doesn't want to be tied down? Maybe she just hasn't found the right guy. Maybe you're the right guy.*

"Julia's fiancé slept with her mother." Ava Grace grimaced. "Double whammy."

"That's definitely a country song." He eyed her. "Are your songs about your personal experiences?"

"Some of them."

"Is 'Lost and Found'?" he asked, referring to her first big hit. The love song was a favorite at weddings.

"No. I got the idea for 'Lost and Found' from a magazine article I read at my dentist's office."

"That kind of takes the romance out of it," he noted dryly.

She laughed. "The article was very romantic."

"What inspired 'Empty Places'?"

She'd sung "Empty Places" at Quinn and Amelia's wedding reception. Like everyone there, Beck had been enthralled by her singing.

"I got the idea for 'Empty Places' from a conversation Millie and I had about Quinn. I asked if he made her happy, and she said he filled all the empty places inside her." Her eyes locked on him. "That's a lot better than happiness, don't you think?"

He nodded slowly, unable to look away from her penetrating gaze. "A lot better."

"Do you have empty places inside you, Jonah?"

Deflecting her question, he said, "Everybody has a few empty places inside them."

Her pink lips tipped up in an almost imperceptible smile. "That's true."

His mouth opened before he could order his brain to shut it. "Do you have empty places inside you?"

"I used to have more." She stared unblinkingly for several heartbeats. "Being with you has filled most of them."

He sucked in a surprised breath. Had he heard her correctly? He filled her empty places?

He clenched his hand around the remote to his sound system. "What—" His voice cracked, and he cleared his throat. "What do you mean?"

"You—"

Suddenly, a man's voice blared from the speakers, and they both jerked in surprise. Beck's tight grip on the remote had accidentally pressed play, and another demo had begun.

Chicken jumped up from his position next to Beck and growled. By the time Beck found the pause button, the growls had escalated to a full-fledged bark.

"*Shh*, Chicken, it's nothing," Ava Grace soothed, and finally the dog flopped down.

She picked up her notepad. "What do you think about Julia's song? *Maybe*, *no*, or *hell no*?"

He didn't want to talk about Julia's song. He wanted to talk about Ava Grace's empty places and his own. No matter how much he tried to deny it, she filled a lot of the empty places inside him too.

But when she moved on ... when he came home to an empty apartment and went to sleep in an empty bed ... those empty places would feel even emptier because he'd remember how good it felt when she'd filled them.

He abruptly decided he'd rather talk about Julia's demo than empty places. "I liked the song, but I don't think it's right for you."

It was too hard. Too bitter. Too hateful. Ava Grace wasn't any of those things.

She nodded. "I'm going to mark it *hell no*."

"Do you know all the songwriters we've heard tonight?"

"I've met most of them, but I don't know any very well, except Mercy. You can't go anywhere in Nashville without running into someone in the business." She waved her hand toward the remote. "I think we have only a couple demos left."

He pressed play and tried to focus on the song instead of how much he'd miss nights like this. When the demo was over, Ava Grace looked at him, her eyebrows arched.

"*Hell no?*" she asked.

"*Hell no.*"

She wrinkled her nose. "Greg's not a very good songwriter, but he's an incredible guitarist. I've played with him before. He studied at Juilliard, and he has this custom guitar that cost nearly ten grand." She gave a self-deprecating laugh. "He said my technique was sloppy and advised me to stick to vocals."

Beck could tell Greg's comments had hurt her, and he had a momentary fantasy of hunting down the guitarist and breaking his fingers. Of course, he'd never actually cause the man bodily harm. But he wouldn't hesitate to smash Greg's one-of-a-kind guitar on the ground for upsetting Ava Grace.

"There's only one reason why he said that—you have more

natural talent than he does, and he was jealous."

So what if Ava Grace hadn't attended one of the best music schools in the world? It was obvious to Beck that she was just as good as Greg. And if she'd received formal training, she would've been better than the snobby guitarist.

"I still can't believe you taught yourself to play the guitar by reading instructional books and watching old videos from the school library," he said.

She shrugged. "No one gave guitar lessons in Electra. And even if someone had, I didn't have the money."

He'd been astonished when he found out she'd taught herself. He admired her perseverance and resourcefulness. He didn't know anyone else with her determination.

She glanced at the sound system. "That was the last demo, thank God." She flashed him a toothy smile. "Thank you for listening with me, handsome. I really appreciate it."

"No problem."

She rose gracefully from the sofa and tossed the notepad on the cocktail table. "I'm going to take a shower."

He watched as she walked away, her tight pants clinging to her perfect ass. He wanted to join her in the shower. He wanted to lather sweet-smelling body wash onto her smooth skin and run his hands all over her slippery curves. Then he wanted to slide into her snug, welcoming body and stay there.

He'd already had her twice today, and it wasn't enough. No matter how much time he spent inside her, he wanted more. He couldn't get enough of her body ... or her imperfect smiles, her husky voice, her soft laughter, her dry sense of humor...

He couldn't get enough of *her*.

That realization was enough to keep him on the sofa. He turned on the TV and did his best to pay attention to the baseball game instead of thinking about what Ava Grace looked like in the shower with warm water trickling over her willowy body.

Two hours later, the game was over. The Giants had come out on top, beating the Dodgers five to three. Ava Grace had crawled into bed after she showered and hadn't made a peep since.

After turning off the TV, Beck rose from the sofa, checked to make sure the front door was locked, and plugged his phone into the charger. He headed to the bathroom, and as he passed the bed, he stopped and looked down at the beautiful blonde who filled his empty places.

She was asleep in the middle of the mattress, the beige comforter tangled around her feet. Chicken was snuggled up beside her, snoring softly.

Beck's gaze slid over her black-and-white-polka-dot pajama tank and matching bottoms. Hot pink lace edged the square neckline and the bottom of the tank, as well as the hem of the loose pants.

The lace straps of her top called attention to her delicate collarbone, which just happened to be one of his favorite parts of her body. He spotted a faint mark on her creamy skin—a mark he'd put there with his mouth.

He carefully untangled the comforter, trying not to wake her. But as he pulled it over her and Chicken, she rolled toward him and opened her eyes.

"Jonah?"

Crouching next to the bed, he stroked his fingers over the soft skin of her cheek. "Yeah, sugar?"

"Are you coming to bed?" she asked, blinking sleepily.

"In a few minutes. Go back to sleep."

"Okay, g'night." She closed her eyes and threw her arm over Chicken. "Love you."

Beck's heart stuttered, and he stopped breathing. Something bright and intense flared to life inside him.

"Chicken," she murmured, finishing her sentence.

She doesn't love me. She loves my dog.

Taking a deep breath, he slowly stood and stalked into the bathroom. He made sure to close the door quietly before jerking his T-shirt over his head.

With disappointment and anger churning in his gut, he turned on the faucets in the shower. After shucking his cargo pants and underwear, he stepped inside. Bracing his palms against the cold tile, he dropped his head forward and let the hot water pour over him.

You're such a fucking idiot, he told himself. *This thing with Ava Grace isn't about love. She doesn't love you.*

A voice inside him whispered, *But you want her to.*

CHAPTER THIRTY-ONE

"You lied to me," Ava Grace accused, gazing up at the night sky.

Beck turned his head toward her. "About what?"

Rolling to her side, she rested her head on her forearm so she could look at him. Fortunately, the inflatable pad and sleeping bag provided enough cushion she couldn't feel the cold, hard ground.

She stared into his eyes, catching a glimpse of the campfire reflected in his coffee-colored irises. "You said camping wasn't romantic. That was a giant whopper of a lie."

He laughed softly. "You didn't think it was romantic when hundreds of mosquitoes were dive-bombing you a couple of hours ago."

"Ugh." She grimaced. "It's almost October. Why are they still buzzing around?"

"Because Northern California has Indian summers. September and October are the warmest months."

She harrumphed. "I don't understand why they attacked me and left you alone."

He shifted to face her and touched his thumb to her lower lip. "Because you taste better than I do," he murmured before settling his mouth over hers.

His lips brushed back and forth in a teasing caress. She cupped her hand around the back of his neck, the silky strands of his hair cool against her fingertips, and he changed the angle of the kiss, covering her mouth more completely.

As he stroked his tongue across her bottom lip in a wet, luscious slide, a warm ache spread throughout her belly and lower pelvis. She let her lips fall open, inviting him in, but he continued to lick and nibble her lips instead of giving his tongue to her.

He seemed perfectly content to keep things easy and slow. To her surprise, he drew back instead of deepening their kiss and rolled onto his back. She snuggled up against his side, her head on his chest.

"Thank you for taking me camping."

She could feel the laugh rumble in his chest. "Sugar, you've told me thank you at least twenty times. You need to stop it now."

She'd woken up this morning to find Beck perched on the side of the bed, a mischievous grin on his handsome face. He'd planned a surprise for her but refused to tell her anything except the number of days they'd be gone. He'd conspired with Wally to make sure her schedule was clear.

Beck had packed everything she'd need for the trip. The only thing she'd had to do was take a shower, forego her usual body lotion and perfume, and wear the clothes and shoes he'd provided.

The lightweight khaki pants, long-sleeved purple T-shirt and matching fleece jacket, and hiking boots had clued her into the fact he'd planned something outdoorsy. He'd even thought to buy moisture-wicking socks and a bucket hat to shield her face from the sun.

He'd already packed his Jeep with everything they'd need, and while she'd gotten ready, he dropped off Chicken with Ren and Gatsby. When he'd returned to the apartment, he handed her a bag of muffins from her favorite bakery and an extra-large to-go coffee.

Is it any wonder I adore Jonah Beck and want to have his babies?

He'd reserved an isolated campsite in Big Basin Redwoods State Park, the oldest state park in California. Majestic redwoods filled the 18,000-acre park, which was located about two hours south of San Francisco.

Once they'd arrived at the park, they ate a picnic lunch before unpacking their gear and setting up camp. It'd been easier than she expected. Beck was an experienced camper, and he'd organized the outing like a five-star general.

Afterward, they went for a long hike through the woods, made out next to a waterfall, and ate handfuls of trail mix on the way back to the campsite. He cooked dinner for her—hotdogs over the campfire—and once they'd cleaned up, they stretched out under the starry sky.

It had been one of the best days of her life. She could only think of one way it could've been better—if Beck had said "I love you," dropped down on one knee, and asked her to marry him. Unfortunately, that was as unlikely as him asking her to take over Trinity.

Beck's big hand slipped under her shirt and settled against her side. He traced little circles on her skin with the tips of his fingers, moving up toward the edge of her bra and then down to her waistband. Each feathery stroke warmed her from the inside out.

"It's getting late," he said. "We should probably move the pads and the sleeping bags into the tent."

"Not yet. I like it out here."

"I don't want you to get cold."

His touch, along with the campfire and the cozy down blanket, chased away the night chill. She was more than toasty. She was getting hot ... in more ways than one.

"You don't need to worry about me getting cold," she assured him.

Lifting her head, she dropped kisses along his jaw. His stubble was prickly, and she rubbed her mouth over it. He turned his head, offering her better access, and she licked a trail along his neck before nuzzling her nose into the space behind his ear.

Underneath the pine trees, fresh air, and burning wood, she could smell him. She inhaled, letting his scent fill her lungs, musky and potent.

She caught his earlobe between her teeth and gave it a gentle nip. As his big body quivered against her, she laved his earlobe with little darts of her tongue before sucking it into her mouth. His fingers dug into her side, just below her ribcage, and she released his earlobe.

Placing her lips against his ear, she whispered, "Take off your shirt."

He shook his head. "It's too cold out here."

She slipped her hand under the hem of his long-sleeved T-shirt. The tight muscles of his six-pack jumped reflexively, and she traced the dense ridges of his abdomen before sliding her hand toward his chest.

"I'll keep you warm," she promised, shaping his firm pectoral muscles with her fingers. "Now take off your shirt."

"Before I met you, I had no problem saying no. It might have been my favorite word." He sighed gustily. "I think you've made me soft."

She skimmed her hand from his chest to his fly. "You feel hard to me," she murmured, tracing his erection through his cargo pants.

He laughed breathlessly. "Okay, I'll take off my shirt."

"And your pants." She lightly squeezed his erection. "Yes?"

"Yes."

Pushing aside the blanket, she sat up, and he did the same. She whipped her T-shirt over her head before shimmying out of the khaki pants he'd bought for her.

Underneath, she wore lacy beige bikini panties and a matching bra. She wondered what kind of underwear he'd packed for her. Knowing Beck, he'd gone the practical route and eschewed lace for cotton.

As he kicked out of his pants, she kneeled next to him. A chilly breeze wafted over her, leaving goose bumps in its wake. Her nipples hardened, both from the cold air and the sizeable erection visible under his gray boxer briefs.

Placing her hand on his chest, she pushed him flat and stretched out on top of his strong body. He wrapped his arms around her lower back, holding her flush against him. After tugging the blanket over them, she bent down until her mouth almost touched his.

"Are you cold?" she asked against his lips.

He slowly shook his head, his lips grazing hers. She touched her tongue to the corner of his mouth in a slow lick, and his erection twitched against her thigh, hot and hard through his underwear.

She scooted down his body, taking the blanket with her. She stopped when she reached the apex of his thighs, her face inches from his penis.

She looked up, over his flat stomach and broad chest, and met his eyes. "Are you cold now?"

"No," he answered, his voice gravelly.

"Good." She hooked her fingers in the waistband of his underwear. "That means I can take these off."

She carefully tugged his boxer briefs down, revealing his erection and testicles. She cupped the heavy sacs in her hand, squeezing gently, and his hips lifted jerkily.

She stroked him from the base of his shaft to the tip, dancing her fingers along the velvety smooth skin. She circled the plump head before pressing her finger against the tiny slit. Air hissed through his teeth, and she swirled her forefinger through the pearly fluid.

Bringing her finger to her mouth, she licked his cream off it. His taste overwhelmed her, salty and rich, and she went back for one more swipe.

"I love the way you taste," she breathed, sucking lightly on her finger.

Before Beck, she'd disliked performing fellatio. She'd tried it a couple of times and always found it yucky and uncomfortable. And she sure as hell hadn't swallowed. Just the thought of it had made her gag.

But she couldn't get enough of Beck. She willingly—*eagerly*—put her mouth on every inch of his body.

She fisted his erection, and he wrapped his hand around hers, moving it up and down. He was breathing fast, his muscles strung tightly.

"I love going down on you," she admitted, and his erection swelled in her hand.

"*Please* stop talking about it and just do it."

She laughed softly. "Since you asked so nicely."

Leaning down, she placed her lips on the tip of his erection and swallowed the plump head. He groaned deep in his throat and threaded his fingers through her hair.

"More," he requested, flexing his hips and pumping into her mouth.

Relaxing her throat, she sucked him as deep as she could. He was long and thick, and she tongued the tracing of veins on his penis before sliding her mouth up his shaft and then back down again.

She kept things slow, letting her lips linger on the head. She twirled her tongue around the plump curve, and when she flattened it against the underside and pressed, he moaned harshly. She did it again, and he let loose with a string of curse words.

Bracing herself on his hair-roughened thighs, she resumed the slow slide up and down his erection, sucking harder on the tip. She could sense his orgasm was close because his grip on her head tightened and he rolled his hips, forcing his erection deeper into her mouth.

"Faster," he growled.

She gave him what he wanted, and he helped her by moving her head up and down on his erection. On the next upward slide, she dipped her tongue in the tiny slit on the tip and gently squeezed his testicles.

"Oh, fuck," he gasped, lifting his hips.

He gave a guttural groan, his fingers clenching in her hair, and she widened her mouth and took him deeper. Semen spurted into the back of her throat, and she swallowed willingly—*happily*—as his body shook from his climax.

Lifting her mouth until only the head of his erection remained inside, she sucked hard on the tip. He shouted, and more semen jetted onto her tongue. She hummed in satisfaction, knowing she'd just given him one of the best orgasms of his life.

As his hands dropped to his sides, she pulled her mouth from his penis and swiped her fingers over her lips. Gripping the edge of the blanket in one hand, she crawled up his body and draped herself and the blanket over him.

He clasped her to him, one hand slipping into her undies to palm her behind and the other rubbing circles on her back. She dropped her head to his chest, where his heartbeat thundered against her ear.

Feeling quite proud of herself, she asked, "Did you like that?"

He laughed croakily, his long body shaking under hers. "You could say that."

"And what about me?"

"What about you?"

"Do you like me?"

She waited, holding her breath. Finally, he replied: "You could say that."

It wasn't what she'd hoped to hear, but it was better than silence. At least he liked her.

It's not enough, her heart whispered. *Your time is up.*

She'd delayed going home as long as she could, and she had to fly back to Nashville as soon as she and Beck returned from camping. She hadn't told him yet, but he probably wouldn't be surprised.

The thought of being away from Beck made her chest ache. Not seeing him for weeks at a time would be pure misery. And she was worried out of sight would mean out of mind for him. She'd kept him too busy—too sexually satisfied—to seek out other women, but once she was gone...

A loud pop from the fire jerked her from her disheartening thoughts. Beck shifted beneath her, and she absentmindedly circled his flat brown nipple with the tip of her finger. It pebbled under her touch, and she lightly scraped her fingernail across it.

He sucked in a harsh breath, the movement of his chest lifting her head. As she rolled his nipple between her thumb and forefinger, he slid his hand down the crevice of her butt to ease between her legs.

She was so excited from going down on him, wetness had trickled into the creases between her thighs and her mound, soaking her panties. He groaned softly when he felt her slick folds, the sound rumbling through her body.

She squirmed, hoping he'd slip his talented fingers inside her. Instead, he pulled his hand from her underwear and hooked his fingers in the waistband.

"I want these off," he growled. "Now."

Somehow, she managed to wiggle out of her panties while on top of him. She held them up in one hand, high over their heads, and he laughed softly. "Are you surrendering?"

"Yes." Their eyes locked together. "I'm giving myself to you."

He swallowed noisily. "Sit up."

She did as he asked, her thighs clamped around his lean waist and her knees digging into the sleeping bag and cushioned pad. She could feel his erection, hot and hard along her backside.

Using both hands, he gripped her hips and looked up at her. "Take off your bra."

She immediately unhooked the front clasp and shrugged the bra from her shoulders. His gaze dropped to her breasts before returning to her face.

"I thought about this when we talked about camping at the s'mores party. I thought about you on top of me, your body silhouetted against the night sky, your face lit by the fire."

His words surprised her, not only because they were so poetic, but because he'd reacted so negatively to their kiss the night of the party. "You wanted me," she said, both a statement and a question.

He huffed out a laugh. "*Hell yes*, I wanted you." His fingers flexed on her hips. "But I never thought I'd..." His eyes slid to her breasts. "Your nipples are so red they look like cherries."

Reflexively, her hands went to her breasts, covering her nipples. They were so tight and hard they hurt.

"Yes," he urged. "Let me see you play with them."

He liked to watch her touch herself. It turned her on too, but she also got a little embarrassed when she did it. And that made him even hotter.

Cupping her hands under her breasts, she lifted them and pushed them together. His eyes got all hazy and heavy-lidded, and she brushed her thumbs over the hard peaks of her nipples. His erection twitched against her butt, and she shifted backward so it fit more snuggly into the crease between her cheeks.

He grunted, his fingers digging into her hips. She'd probably have bruises there tomorrow.

She rolled her nipples between her thumb and forefinger before plucking at them. Feeling the pull between her legs, she dropped one of her hands to her clit. As she rubbed the sensitive nub, he brought one hand to her unattended breast and maneuvered the other between them, slipping two fingers inside her.

"You're so hot," he rasped, gently working his fingers deeper. "You feel like fire."

She loved his sex talk. Loved to hear how good she felt. Loved to hear bad words in his honeyed drawl.

He pressed his fingers against the wall of her vagina, sending little tingles of pleasure through her before withdrawing. As he pumped back into her, she spread her second and third fingers

around her clit, pressed them together, and moved them up and
down.

But that didn't give her any relief. Instead, the throbbing ache
in her lower pelvis intensified. She needed him to fill her.

"Jonah, I need you," she breathed.

He immediately pulled his fingers from her body. Desperate
for him, she shifted her hips until his erection slid forward to her
opening. As she began to lower herself, he gripped her waist,
holding her immobile.

"Condom," he gasped. "We need a condom."

She clambered off him. "Where did you pack them?"

"There's one in my pants."

She lunged for his cargo pants and held them up. "There are
a million pockets on these damn pants!" she complained, patting
her hands over the pockets.

Fortunately, her search didn't take long. She tossed the
condom to him, and by the time she'd crawled back to him, he'd
covered his penis with latex.

She immediately swung her leg over his hips. Balancing
herself with one hand on his chest, she positioned herself over
his erection. Unable to wait one more second to have him inside
her, she sank down, taking as much of him as she could.

He growled low in his throat as her flesh welcomed him and
pressed her down on him with his hands flat against the upper
swells of her behind. He slid in a little farther, his testicles flush
against her labia.

She tried to control it … tried to fight it … but the feel of
him inside her sent her spiraling toward orgasm. It was always
like this with him.

Closing her eyes, she let her head drop back as her body
clenched around his hard length. "I'm coming," she moaned.

"I know. I can feel it."

He was motionless beneath her, knowing his lack of movement made her orgasm more intense. Sparks radiated from where they were joined, lighting up every cell, and she couldn't hold back her moans. They echoed in the cocooning silence of the forest.

When it was over—when she could breathe again—she brought her head forward and opened her eyes. The tension left her muscles, and her body seemed to flow around him like hot wax.

With her palms flat on his chest, she began to rock on him with smooth, slight movements that kept him deep inside her. Her earlier orgasm had blunted the sharp edge of desire, so she was able to keep the pace slow and steady.

Beck watched her move, his eyes hooded. He lazily stroked his hands up and down her sides as she rode him, grazing the sides of her breasts and thumbing her nipples before curving over her hips.

Every roll of her pelvis generated delicious friction on her clit, spreading fire throughout her body. Despite the cool night air, sweat bloomed on her skin, beading between her breasts.

Without warning, Beck lunged into a sitting position with his bent legs supporting her back. Grasping her knees, he pulled them around his waist and brought her closer until their bellies were flush.

He swirled his tongue over her neck before capturing her mouth with his. While he licked inside her mouth, he gripped her hips in his big hands and lifted her almost entirely off him before bringing her down again.

His powerful arms worked her over his erection. Over and over, he shoved in, hard and deep, until she came apart around him, screaming against his mouth. While she still trembled, he reached between their bodies and found her clit with his thumb and forefinger.

"No, Jonah," she protested but his name turned into a moan when he gently began to rub.

"One more," he crooned. "I want us to come together."

With his tongue stroking into her mouth, his erection moving deep inside her body, and his fingers plucking at her clit, it was only a matter of seconds before another orgasm tore through her. It was even stronger than those before, making her sob with pleasure.

Her internal muscles clamped down, and he stiffened against her. His big body bowed with the force of his release, and he cried out—a raw, broken sound.

As his penis jerked inside her, she tightened her passage around his length, hoping to prolong his pleasure. He squeezed his eyes shut, an almost inhuman groan falling from his lips.

She stared at him, preserving this moment in her memory. When he opened his eyes, she tumbled into the darkness of his gaze. She opened her mouth, trying to find the courage to say *I love you*, but couldn't.

She looked away from his beautiful eyes, ashamed and disgusted with herself for being such a wimp. She'd never been this cowardly before. But then again, she'd never wanted anything this much either.

It was easy to be brave when you had nothing to lose.

CHAPTER THIRTY-TWO

The bright green moss covering the hiking trail was springy under Beck's feet. It muffled his and Ava Grace's footsteps as they meandered down the path, their hands entwined. Tall redwoods created a canopy overhead, blocking most of the sunlight, and except for the occasional sounds of dripping water and wind, the forest was silent.

As they passed a log covered with lichen and a couple of monstrous banana slugs, Ava Grace glanced sideways at him. The lush vegetation surrounding them brought out the green in her eyes and made them seem dark and mysterious.

"It's so beautiful here." Her voice was hushed and reverent. "It's like another world."

Before he could reply, she added, "Thank—"

"*Ava Grace*," he warned.

Her eyes widened at his harsh tone. "What?"

"I told you to stop thanking me."

"But—"

He shook his head. "No buts, sugar."

Over the past forty-eight hours, she'd said *thank you* at least a hundred times. No exaggeration.

"I just want you to know how much this trip means to me," she said.

He *had* put a lot of time and energy into planning this trip. And he'd spent a shitload of money on camping gear.

He'd wanted this outing—Ava Grace's first camping experience—to be perfect. The camping trip was his way of thanking her for doing so much to help Trinity. She was the best thing to ever happen to the company. In just a few months, she'd propelled it to heights the oldest and most established distilleries had yet to achieve.

Distributors called daily, eager to represent Trinity. Retail sales had increased significantly, and orders from restaurants and hotels had doubled. Meanwhile, traffic to the Trinity website had grown exponentially, and the company's social media pages now boasted more likes and followers than all the other bourbon distilleries put together.

"Planning this trip was a really thoughtful thing to do," Ava Grace said.

"Thoughtful?" he echoed.

"Yes, very thoughtful."

"I have no idea what that word means." He winked at her. "I'm a man."

She giggled, a bright, happy sound. *And that's why you really planned this trip.*

He hadn't wanted to thank her for helping Trinity. That was just a convenient excuse. He'd wanted to do something special for her—something that'd make her happy. He loved seeing her breathtaking, imperfect smile. And he loved hearing her laugh.

"I know you went to a lot of trouble to surprise me, and I appreciate it," she added.

He'd chosen camping because he wanted to share something

with her that she'd never shared with anyone else or done before. He'd wanted to give her something no one else had ever given her.

"I appreciate *you*, Jonah."

He knew she meant what she said. Ava Grace was truly grateful when people did nice things for her. She recognized their efforts and thanked them.

His mother had expected people to treat her better than they treated everyone else. Her sense of entitlement had been even bigger than her ego. Olivia had been the same way, but he'd been too blind and stupid to see the similarity and heed the warning.

He clearly remembered the first time he'd given Olivia flowers. He'd stopped at one of the best florists in town and spent a couple hundred bucks on a bouquet of roses, Stargazer lilies, and liatris. He'd thought the flowers were really nice—feminine and fragrant without being too froufrou.

Instead of thanking him, she handed the bouquet back to him without a word. At first, he thought she was allergic, but then she explained she preferred orchids and hydrangeas.

Maybe a better boyfriend would've filed that information away and made sure to buy her favorite flowers the next time. But he hadn't.

When it came right down to it, he hadn't wanted to do nice things for Olivia. But to his surprise, he wanted to do nice things for Ava Grace. He wanted to buy her flowers and pick up muffins from her favorite bakery. And when he did, she thanked him, usually with a kiss.

Maybe he wanted to do nice things for her because she did nice things for him. She surprised him at work with baked treats and bought him stuff all the time, everything from a designer button-down shirt to an oversized coffee mug that said, *Good morning, handsome.* He got a little thrill whenever he wore that shirt or took a sip from that mug, knowing she'd picked it out just for him.

Ava Grace's phone trilled, and she pulled it from her back pocket. After looking at the screen, she pressed a button and slipped it into her pants.

"Was that your reminder to call Kyle?" Beck asked.

"Yeah. I didn't cancel them, even though we have no cell service up here."

Ava Grace was diligent—almost fanatical—about checking on her father. She called Kyle twice a day, once in the morning and once in the evening, as well as texted him every two hours.

Initially, Beck had been a little jealous of Kyle. The tone of her voice when she talked to him clearly conveyed how much she cared for him, and Beck had wondered about the nature of her relationship with the former Marine.

Instead of stewing over it, Beck had asked Ava Grace to tell him about Kyle. She'd assured Beck that she wasn't attracted to the other man, and she'd sworn that she and Kyle had never been intimate.

Even though women had lied to Beck before, he'd believed Ava Grace. He trusted her more than he'd ever trusted any woman.

"I hope everything is okay at home," Ava Grace murmured.

"I'm sure everything is fine. Kyle knows how to reach us if he needs to."

She'd fretted about being out of touch for several days, and Beck had done his best to calm her fears. He'd provided Kyle with the number to the park's ranger station, as well as the GPS coordinates of their campsite. If something happened to Chuck, a park ranger would be able to track them down fairly easily.

Ava Grace sighed softly, and Beck had a good idea what she was thinking about. She felt guilty about "abandoning" her father—that was the word she had used.

Lightly squeezing her hand, he said, "You're feeling guilty again, aren't you?"

She glanced up at him, a sheepish expression on her face. "Um-hum."

"You have no reason to feel guilty, sugar. You're doing what's best for Chuck. He hasn't had an outburst since you've been here."

"I know." She looked down at her feet. "For such a long time, I hated him for leaving me with my grandmother. I hated him for abandoning me. But now I wonder ... maybe he thought he was doing what was best for me. Maybe he felt like he didn't have a choice."

"Maybe," Beck agreed.

He refrained from reminding her that Chuck chose not to visit her when she was younger and chose not to have a relationship with her when she was older. Beck refrained because those reminders would only hurt her, and that was the last thing he wanted to do.

Ava Grace's empty places were just as raw and gaping as his own. He wanted to fill hers the way she'd filled his.

He stopped on the path and pulled her into a hug. "I'm sorry," he murmured into her hair. "I know it feels like you're losing him all over again."

Resting against him, she looped her arms around his waist. "I'm sorry you lost your dad, and I'm sorry your mom left you when you needed her the most. I wish those things had never happened to you."

Her words chipped away at the boulder of anger and sadness

that had weighed him down for so many years. Being with Ava Grace made him feel lighter ... happier ... more hopeful.

Leaning back so he could see her beautiful face, he said, "Thank you."

Her eyes searched his. "Jonah, I..." She took a deep breath. "I..." She swallowed, the sound audible in the heavy silence of the forest. "I'm in..." A weird expression came over her face, something between a wince and a scowl.

He frowned. "What's wrong?"

She stared at him for a moment before dropping her head to his chest. "I'm hungry," she muttered into his T-shirt. "I need a snack."

He looked down at the bright blond hair just under his nose. He had the feeling she'd started to say something else but had changed her mind. He wondered what?

Dropping his arms, he stepped back and glanced around. He spotted a large limb a few feet off the path that offered a perfect place to sit. He headed toward it, and she followed. When they reached it, he shrugged off his backpack and balanced it on the moss-covered wood.

"What are you in the mood for?" He unzipped the larger compartment. "An apple and peanut butter? Granola bar? Trail mix?"

"Why don't you surprise me?"

As she sat down, he pulled out an apple and an individual serving of peanut butter and handed them to her before grabbing a bottle of water for himself. After placing his backpack on the ground, he sat down next to her.

"I have a knife. Do you want me to cut your apple?"

She dropped the small container of peanut butter to her lap and palmed the apple in both hands. She stared down at it, and when she didn't answer his question, he repeated it.

She glanced up, and he got trapped in her hazel gaze. "I'm flying to Nashville the day after tomorrow," she announced flatly.

He understood what she really was saying. She was going home, not just for a few days, but for good.

He'd known she had planned to stay in San Francisco for only a few weeks. He'd known this day was coming. But that didn't make it any easier.

He wasn't ready for them to be over. He wasn't ready to move on. He wasn't tired of her. He wasn't bored.

Not even close.

"When will you be back?" he asked, dreading the answer.

"Probably not 'til Thanksgiving."

He absorbed the information silently, his stomach knotting. Thanksgiving was two months away.

Sixty-plus days without seeing her beautiful smile. Without hearing her infectious laughter. Sixty-plus nights without her in his bed. Without kissing her luscious mouth. Without touching her smooth skin. Without sinking into her tight pussy.

Just the thought of it made him want to throw back his head and howl. Abruptly, he realized she might not be interested in continuing their relationship whenever she visited San Francisco, and the knots in his stomach pulled tighter.

"October and November are going to be really busy months for me," she said. "River Pearl's Artist Showcase is just a couple of weeks away, and the ACE awards show is in early November. Then I'm scheduled to record a holiday special a few days before Thanksgiving. And somewhere in between, I have to work on my next album and finish the cookbook." She sighed softly. "I might not even be able to come out for Thanksgiving."

A bitter taste flooded his mouth, and he unscrewed the cap on the water bottle and took a swig. The cool liquid washed away the bitterness and soothed his dry throat enough so he could speak.

"I guess this trip is a good way to say good-bye."

Her eyes shot to his face. "I don't want to say good-bye."

He thought he heard a tinge of panic in her voice. But maybe that was just wishful thinking.

"I don't either," he admitted quietly.

She tilted her head, and a tendril of platinum hair fell over her eye. As she brushed it away, she said, "I know you're busy too, but I was hoping you could visit me in Nashville."

Her invitation surprised him. He'd figured she'd want to limit their relationship to the West Coast.

"You want me to visit you in Nashville?"

She nodded slowly. "I promise you'll have a good time."

He always had a good time with Ava Grace, whether they spent a quiet night at home listening to demos, went out with friends, or hiked through a redwood forest. Whenever he was with her, he felt both relaxed and energized—feelings that should be contradictory yet seemed to co-exist inside him.

"You won't be bored," she added, an earnest expression on her beautiful face.

He couldn't help laughing at the ridiculousness of that statement.

"Why is that funny?" she asked suspiciously.

"I'm never bored when you're around, sugar."

Her eyes got all squinty. "Are you being sarcastic?"

"No."

"So you'll visit me?"

"If you want me to."

Her eyes lit up. "I want you to."

He doubted she'd feel that way once she was back in Nashville. She'd probably forget she had asked him to visit. She'd probably forget *him*.

After several seconds of awkward silence, she held up the apple. "Want to share?"

"Sure."

He screwed the cap back on the water bottle and set it near his feet before fishing his Swiss Army knife from his pocket. After opening the blade, he took the apple from her.

"Wait," Ava Grace ordered. "Is that knife clean?"

"Yeah, it's clean ... enough."

She rolled her eyes. "You're such a guy."

He cut off a couple of pieces of apple and handed them to her. As she took them, she blurted out, "I don't want you to have sex with other women."

It took him a moment to comprehend her words. When he did, his finger slipped off the knife, and he sliced his thumb instead of the apple. But he didn't even feel the cut.

With his eyes locked on her face, he said, "*What?*"

"I don't want you to have sex with other women."

He took a deep breath and exhaled slowly. She was the only woman he wanted, and he wanted to be more than the guy who scratched her itch whenever she flew into town.

He wanted more than a fling. He wanted to be the only man in her bed and in her life.

"What are you saying, exactly?" he asked.

She sighed loudly, clearly exasperated with him. "I'm saying I want you to keep your pants zipped unless I'm around."

The apple and knife fell from his hands. His thumb throbbed with the frantic beat of his heart, and he looked down at it. Blood trickled from the cut, and he watched as a droplet splashed on the ferns under their feet.

She gasped suddenly. "Oh, my God, Jonah, you're bleeding!" She dropped to her knees in front of him and cupped his hand in hers. After evaluating the wound, she looked up into his face.

"Do you have a first aid kit in your backpack?"

Ignoring her question, he asked, "If I keep my pants zipped, Ava Grace, will you keep your panties on?"

"Yes." She released his hand and sat back on her heels. "I think I should clarify something. I don't want you to go out with other women either."

"Are you going to go out with other men?" he countered.

"No. You're all I need." Her lips tilted up in a slow smile. "Do we have a deal?"

Stunned Ava Grace wanted to be with him and only him, he nodded slowly. "Deal."

CHAPTER THIRTY-THREE

Holding the glass tumbler in front of him, Beck toasted, "To Trinity."

Gabe and Ren tapped their tumblers against his. "To Trinity," they chorused.

As Beck took a sip of his bourbon, his business partners did the same. The oak-vanilla taste of the liquor warmed his tongue and throat before settling in his gut.

He dropped down into the wicker outdoor chair, sinking into the puffy lemon-yellow cushions. Gabe collapsed into an identical chair, while Ren relaxed on the matching sofa.

Taking another sip of bourbon, Beck gazed at the hills behind Gabe's childhood home in rural Kentucky. The sky was a watercolor of indigo, violet, and lavender, the full moon hanging high above them.

Fall evenings in north central Kentucky were usually clear and chilly, and he was glad he'd put on his fleece jacket. The temperature had already dropped into the low fifties, and bourbon alone couldn't keep him warm.

"Damn, I'm tired," he said, propping his ankle on his knee. "This has been one long-ass week."

Beck, Gabe, and Ren had spent the past several days manning the Trinity Distillery booth at the American Bourbon Festival in historic Bardstown, Kentucky. The festival ended earlier today. More than fifty thousand people from all over the world had attended the event, which was always held the second week of October.

Unlike the International Spirits and Wine Show, which provided an opportunity for distillers and wineries to interact with other industry professionals, the American Bourbon Festival was geared toward bourbon lovers. This was the first year Trinity participated in the festival, and thousands of people stopped by the booth.

"I'm happy to go home tomorrow." Ren glanced toward Beck. "When are you leaving for Nashville?"

"I told Ava Grace I'd be there for lunch. The drive takes about three hours, so I need to leave by nine."

There were no direct flights from Lexington to Nashville, and Beck had decided it'd be easier to drive than go through the hassle of a connecting flight. It was a fairly straight shot to her house, according to his GPS.

He was excited to see Ava Grace. No, not excited ... *desperate*.

He hadn't seen her—hadn't touched her—in sixteen days, eight hours, and—he looked at his watch—thirty-seven minutes. Yes, he was counting.

Gabe snorted. "You'll probably leave at the crack of dawn and get to her house before breakfast." His lips tilted in a devilish smile. "Just in time to put some cream in her ... coffee."

Ren burst out laughing. "Cream in her coffee," he gasped around his guffaws. "That's hilarious. I was thinking he could feed her sausage for breakfast."

"Or maybe she'll let him eat her *croissant*," Gabe added.

Ren was laughing so hard he was holding his ribs, and just when Beck thought they were done with their comedy routine, Ren wheezed, "Maybe he can glaze her donut."

"G-g-glaze?" Gabe repeated, barely able to get the word out. "Oh, man, that's awesome. He's definitely going to *glaze* her donut."

"Jesus," Beck muttered. "Y'all have been spending too much time with Ellis."

That comment sent his immature best friends into further hysterics, and Beck couldn't help laughing too. Finally, their chortles died down.

Ren tipped his tumbler toward Beck. "I hope you come back from Nashville with a better attitude. You've been a real asshole since Ava Grace left."

Ren was right. Beck had been a *little* moody since she returned to Nashville. He hadn't adjusted to her absence very well. He had trouble sleeping without her beside him.

He'd lost a few pounds too. Food didn't taste very good without her sitting across the table from him, and he'd run more miles to keep his mind off how lonely he was.

Gabe glanced at Ren, a sardonic expression on his face. "You wouldn't be too happy if your woman was halfway across the country either."

"Probably not," Ren admitted.

"Probably not?" Gabe's upper lip curled in disgust. "You'd bitch and moan worse than an old man with erectile dysfunction and hemorrhoids."

Beck laughed under his breath. He felt as if he'd taken a ride in a time machine and traveled into the past. Suddenly, he was seventeen again, hanging out at his best friend's house after school.

He'd spent hundreds of hours on this porch listening to Gabe and Ren verbally abuse each other. Age had only made their insults more vulgar and creative.

Gabe must've been thinking along the same lines because he sighed softly. "It's good to be home."

Of the three of them, Gabe missed Kentucky the most, probably because his family was here. His parents still lived in the same house where he'd grown up, and his three sisters lived nearby with their families. He was the only Bristow who'd flown the nest, and he returned regularly for visits.

Beck, meanwhile, had left Kentucky after he'd graduated from college, and he hadn't returned. There'd been no reason to come back. For a long time, his memories had been too painful for him to even consider making a trip.

Gabe nudged Beck's foot with his own. "Are you happy to be home?"

More than once in the past decade, Beck had been homesick for Kentucky—the lush, rolling hills; the fresh, woodsy smell; and the soft southern drawls. But to his surprise, he felt like a visitor in a strange land instead of a good ol' Kentucky boy.

"It doesn't feel like home anymore," Beck admitted.

There had been a time when the world outside of Kentucky hadn't crossed his mind, except for attending college at Duke. He'd wanted to work alongside his dad at the family distillery and live in the same small town where his parents lived. His dreams had been simple and homegrown.

Though he tried not to, sometimes he got hung up with *what ifs*. What if his dad were still alive? What if the Beck family still owned Jonah Beck Distillery? What if he'd gone to Duke as planned and come home to work with his dad?

But being here in Kentucky had given Beck a greater

appreciation for the life he had. All the bad shit that had happened—his dad's embezzlement scandal and death, his mom's desertion, and being accused of assault—forced him to take an alternate path.

As Beck handed out thousands of samples of Trinity at the bourbon festival, he realized he was content with the person he'd become and what he'd built. He was content with his life.

And when he was with Ava Grace, he was more than content. He was happy.

"I never thought I'd say this, but I don't think Kentucky feels like home anymore either," Ren said quietly. "I miss San Francisco."

"I do too," Beck agreed, a little surprised by how much he missed his adopted home by the Bay.

"Gatsby can't wait to get home," Ren added. "She really missed Chicken. She's so excited he's going to stay with us for a few days." His smile faded into a glower. "Hopefully, your dog will distract her from Sasha."

With her lip rings, tattoos, Goth fashion sense, and bright blue highlights, Sasha wasn't the kind of woman Ren wanted Gatsby to emulate, or so he said. He insisted his upstairs neighbor was a bad influence on his daughter.

Ren tried to keep Gatsby away from Sasha, but the little girl was obsessed with her. And Beck suspected Gatsby's dad was obsessed with her too.

"I don't mind keeping Chicken if you want to stay in Nashville longer," Ren offered.

Beck cupped his hands around his glass. "Ava Grace wants me to, but I'm worried about being away from work."

"Don't be an idiot," Gabe warned. "A few more days in Nashville won't make a difference to Trinity, but they will to Ava

Grace. If she wants you to stay, you should stay. Try not to screw up the best thing that's ever happened to you."

More than a little defensive, Beck replied, "I'm trying *not* to screw it up."

"Ava Grace is good for you," Ren chimed in.

"I know."

*****

Only two point six miles to Ava Grace's house. That was what the navigation system in Beck's rental SUV said.

His hands were sweaty on the steering wheel, and he took a moment to wipe them on his denim-covered thighs. He couldn't remember ever being this nervous, especially over a woman. But Jesus, he was nervous now—nervous enough that if he were standing, his knees would be shaking.

It wasn't just that he was finally going to see and touch Ava Grace after weeks apart. Last night, after he'd talked with Gabe and Ren, Beck had finally accepted what his heart had told him for weeks—he was in love with her.

He'd pretended his feelings for her were simple, uncomplicated lust. He'd ignored his heart and listened to his head.

But finally, his heart and his head agreed. They both told him that Ava Grace needed to be a permanent part of his life. He just had to figure out a way to make that happen.

The navigation system directed him to turn left at the stop sign. As he made the turn, the pavement switched from blacktop to gravel. Pebbles thumped against the bottom of the SUV as he rolled slowly down the road.

His destination was on the right. He braked as he approached a large estate gate sandwiched between two stone pillars. A black gooseneck post with an intercom and keypad rose from the ground.

After turning into the short driveway, he stopped in front of the keypad and entered the code Ava Grace had texted him several days ago. The gate swung open smoothly, and he drove through.

He followed a gravel driveway through a large pasture glistening with morning dew. As Gabe had predicted, Beck was up and ready to go before sunrise.

Traffic had been light, and he'd made it to Ava Grace's house in less than three hours. It was just a little after eight o'clock, but he didn't think she'd mind that he was a few hours early. And if she was crabby this morning, he'd just have to kiss her out of her bad mood. It wouldn't be the first time he'd done it.

As he rounded the curved driveway, he spotted a sprawling white farmhouse. With its dark green shutters, wraparound porch, and colorful flower boxes below the windows, the house looked cheerful and welcoming.

A bright red Camaro sat in front of the house, along with a silver extended-cab truck. He knew Ava Grace had splurged on the car when "I'm Not Your Anything" hit number one, but she hadn't mentioned a huge-ass truck. It must belong to Kyle.

Beck parked next to the truck and switched off the ignition. His pulse pounded in his ears, and he took several deep breaths, trying to calm the furious beat. After a moment, he exited the SUV and headed up the stone walkway.

As he shoved the keys into his front pocket, the screen door opened, and a tall man stepped out onto the porch. The glare from the morning sun made it difficult to see his face, but Beck assumed it was Kyle.

Beck reached the bottom of the stairs, and the man walked

to the edge of the porch. Maybe it was the angle, but he looked massive. His legs were like tree trunks under his plaid pajama pants, and big biceps bulged from the sleeves of his heather gray T-shirt.

"You must be Beck. I'm Kyle Hood."

"Ava Grace never mentioned you were a fucking giant."

A smile flashed across Kyle's face. "Yeah, well, she never mentioned you were a mere mortal either. From the way she talks about you, I expected you to descend from the sky on a winged horse."

Laughing, Beck bounded up the stairs. He and Kyle were about the same height, but the other man was built like a tank. His forearms were tattooed with USMC, a rifle, and the words *One Shot, One Kill.*

Kyle shifted his coffee mug from his right hand and extended it to Beck. He shook it vigorously, predisposed to like the man who'd protected Ava Grace for years before stepping in to take care of her father.

"It's great to meet you, chief. I've heard so much about you, I feel like I know you."

"Likewise," Kyle replied. "You're early. Ava Grace didn't expect you to get here 'til noon."

Beck smiled ruefully. "I missed her." He glanced toward the screen door. "Where is she?"

"Still asleep. So is Chuck." Kyle's mouth tightened. "He was agitated last night, and it took a while for him to calm down. We didn't go to bed until two o'clock."

When Ava Grace had told Beck about her father's "outbursts," he was horrified by the situation and concerned about her safety. "Did things get physical?"

"No, thank God. The minute Chuck started to get upset, Ava Grace went upstairs."

Beck met Kyle's deep green eyes, and a silent conversation passed between them. They both knew things couldn't continue as they were.

Kyle tipped his head toward the door. "If you're that eager to see her, you could play Prince Charming and wake her with a kiss."

As tempting as that sounded, Beck wasn't going to deprive Ava Grace of much-needed sleep. "I can wait."

"Good call. She wakes up with horns and a forked tail."

Beck couldn't help laughing. Now he understood why Ava Grace and Kyle were so close. They had very similar personalities.

"I need to get back inside," Kyle said. "I don't want Chuck to wake up alone."

Just then, a commotion came from inside the farmhouse—a man's raised voice, followed by the sound of something breaking, and then a woman's frightened scream.

"Shit!" Kyle cursed, dropping his coffee mug to the ground.

Beck lunged toward the screen door and flung it open. It hit the white clapboard siding with a bang.

With Kyle on his heels, Beck burst into the house. Abruptly realizing he had absolutely no idea where he was going, since he didn't know the layout, he flattened himself against the wall in the foyer and let the other man pass him.

Beck chased after Kyle, his work boots pounding on the hardwood floor. A staircase flashed in Beck's peripheral vision as he ran down the corridor.

Reaching a spacious living area, he frantically scanned the room for Ava Grace. His heartbeat thundered in his ears, and nausea crowded the back of his throat.

Kyle was already across the room, standing in front of a massive stone fireplace that stretched to the ceiling. He'd grabbed an older man—Chuck—in a bear hug from behind and forced his arms to his sides. Chuck struggled against Kyle's hold, yelling curses at the top of his lungs.

"She's over here!" Kyle shouted.

Darting around the sofa, Beck spotted Ava Grace sprawled on the rug. Fear paralyzed him for a moment before another wave of adrenaline flooded his veins.

He hurdled the cocktail table and fell to his knees beside her. Blood trickled from a gash high on her forehead, near her hairline, and the delicate skin around her right eye was already showing signs of bruising.

Unable to tell if she was breathing, he grabbed her wrist and searched for a pulse. *Please*, he prayed. *Please let her be okay.*

CHAPTER THIRTY-FOUR

Hospital food really was as bad as everyone joked. Ava Grace's nausea had subsided enough to try a bite of her breakfast, but after tasting the rubbery crustless quiche, the queasiness returned even stronger than before.

The woman who'd delivered the breakfast tray hovered beside Ava Grace's hospital bed. Why hadn't she left?

Pointing to a piece of paper next to the apple juice, the woman said, "Miss Landy, you need to sign for your breakfast."

Ava Grace squinted at the paper. Her right eye was swollen shut, and the sight in her other eye was a little blurry, a symptom of her concussion.

When she'd arrived at the emergency room yesterday morning, the doctor classified her concussion as grade three because she lost consciousness for a few minutes. As a precaution, he'd elected to admit her to the hospital for observation. Thankfully, the CT of her brain hadn't shown any swelling or blood clots.

The food service worker handed a pen to Ava Grace, and she scrawled her signature at the bottom of the paper. Without a word, the woman snatched the paper from the tray and scurried out the door, closing it behind her.

A rude snort drifted from the corner of the room where Mercy sat in a chair. "You're in the hospital with a severe concussion, a fractured orbital bone, and twenty-two stiches in your forehead, and that bitch just tricked you into giving her your autograph."

Oh. Is that what just happened?

"I'm going to report her and make sure her ass is fired," Mercy vowed.

Ava Grace tossed the pen onto the tray and massaged the space between her eyebrows where all the pain seemed to be centered. "Please. Just leave it alone."

"I'm sorry," Mercy replied contritely. "I'm making things worse, aren't I?"

Ava Grace didn't respond, letting the silence speak for her. She appreciated that Mercy had come to the hospital to check on her and drop off a change of clothes, but she didn't want any company except Beck.

He'd driven Ava Grace to the hospital and hadn't left her side until Mercy arrived ten minutes ago. He'd claimed he was starving and needed to grab some food from the cafeteria on the first floor, but Ava Grace knew he just wanted to give her some time alone with her friend.

Beck had been kneeling beside Ava Grace when she regained consciousness. He was the one who rolled her onto her side when she started to vomit, and he was the one who pressed a damp washcloth against her bleeding forehead.

He'd wanted to call an ambulance, but she'd begged him not to. She'd been teetering on the edge of hysteria, and he'd hastily agreed to take her to the hospital himself.

Poor guy. He probably would've agreed to anything right then just so she'd calm down.

If she'd been thinking clearly, she would've realized arriving at the hospital in an ambulance would've been much better than Beck rolling her into the emergency room in a wheelchair. People in the waiting room had recognized her, and of course they pulled out their phones to snap pictures.

Undoubtedly, her bloody, bruised face was plastered all over celebrity gossip websites and entertainment news TV. She was probably trending on social media too.

"What happened at the farmhouse yesterday morning?" Mercy asked.

Ava Grace lifted her shoulders in a shrug. "I don't remember much. I'd just woken up, and I was desperate for some coffee. I went downstairs, and I was walking toward the kitchen when I heard a noise come from the living room. I went to check it out, and the last thing I remember is Chuck charging me like I was a matador waving a red flag at a bull."

She lightly touched the swollen ridge of her right cheekbone. "I don't remember how this happened, but I'm assuming Chuck punched me in the face, and I hit my head on the cocktail table when I fell."

According to the doctor, she had a zygomatic orbital rim fracture, which involved the lower edge of the eye rim. Fortunately, the fracture wasn't severe, so she wouldn't require surgery.

"You're lucky he didn't hurt you even worse," Mercy said.

Ava Grace took a sip of apple juice before saying, "He didn't do it on purpose. It's a symptom of his Alzheimer's."

"I understand that. But the end result is the same."

The door opened, and Ava Grace slowly turned her head to see who'd entered the room. If she moved too quickly, the pain almost blinded her.

A man wearing a white doctor's coat stopped at the foot of her bed. She couldn't see his face clearly, but his short hair was a reddish-brown shade similar to bourbon. She peered at the name embroidered above his breast pocket in dark blue thread, but couldn't read it.

"I'm Dr. Lipscomb," he announced.

"Hello."

"You probably don't remember me, but I treated you in the ER."

Recognizing his voice, she said, "Thank you for taking care of me, Dr. Lipscomb."

"You're welcome." He glanced toward Mercy. "I'd like to talk to Miss Landy in private."

Mercy immediately rose. Leaning down, she kissed Ava Grace's uninjured cheek. "I'll see you later, *lindeza*."

Ava Grace smiled wryly at the Portuguese endearment, which translated to "prettiness." With her black eye, swollen face, and stitched forehead, she certainly wasn't *lindeza* today.

As Mercy left the room, Dr. Lipscomb moved to the side of the bed. Staring down at her, he said, "The nursing supervisor is working on your release paperwork. You should be out of here in less than an hour."

He pulled a penlight from his pocket and shined it in her left eye. "Are you still experiencing blurry vision?"

"Yes. But it's getting better."

"Any nausea?"

"Some."

He clicked off the penlight. "And how's the headache?"

"Still pretty bad."

"You'll probably have one for a few days." He sat down in the chair Mercy had vacated. "When you came into the ER, I asked you what happened, and you said you didn't know." He scooted the chair closer to the bed. "The man who brought you into the ER ... you called him Jonah, I think..."

She started to nod, but stopped just in time. "Yes. Jonah Beck."

"As in Jonah Beck Distillery?"

"Yes," she answered, not bothering to explain that Beck wasn't involved with the distillery his ancestor had founded.

Dr. Lipscomb was silent for a long time. Finally, he said, "Your injuries are consistent with domestic assault. Is Mr. Beck responsible for them?"

His question was so shocking, she couldn't help gasping. "No! Of course not!"

"Miss Landy, I've been an ER doctor for fifteen years. I know what abuse looks like." He lightly touched her forearm, which was exposed by the short-sleeved hospital gown. "It's not going to stop until you make it stop. I encourage you to talk with a domestic abuse counselor."

"Dr. Lipscomb—"

The door opened, and Beck walked in carrying a to-go coffee cup. He'd worn the same clothes for more than twenty-four hours now—a long-sleeved black shirt with the Trinity logo screened on the front in gold and faded jeans.

Beck's eyes bounced back and forth between her and Dr. Lipscomb. "Should I wait outside?"

"No." She looked at the physician and pointed to her face. "This was an accident. My—"

Dr. Lipscomb shot to his feet. "Please, Miss Landy. *Please.* Just think about what I said."

Before she could respond ... before she could explain ... he brushed past Beck without looking at him and hurried to the door. She thought about stopping the physician, but decided to let him go. It didn't really matter what he thought anyway. Plus, she wanted to limit the number of people who knew about Chuck's violent outbursts, even healthcare providers.

Beck stared after Dr. Lipscomb for a moment before bringing his attention back to her. "Everything okay?"

Suddenly, she felt like crying. She tried to swallow her tears, but they overflowed. Through her blurry vision, she saw Beck move.

Feeling the mattress compress under his weight, she scooted over to make room for him. He wrapped his arm around her shoulders and tugged her against his chest.

Decades of emotional pain from her father's abandonment collided with the physical pain he'd inflicted yesterday. It was like an avalanche inside her, the weight crushing everything in its path.

As she sobbed into Beck's T-shirt, soaking the cotton, he pressed kisses on her head. In the middle of her breakdown, she silently thanked the aide who helped wash her blood-encrusted hair this morning.

"*Shh*," Beck crooned. "Don't cry, sugar. It's goin' to be okay."

She'd noticed his accent got a lot stronger when he was upset. It must have been quite a shock for him to arrive at her farmhouse just in time to deal with the aftermath of Chuck's physical attack.

Finally, her sobs diminished into the occasional hiccup. Beck passed a handful of tissues to her, and she gingerly patted her eyes before wiping her snotty nose.

"Didn't I tell you that you wouldn't be bored if you visited me?" she said, trying to lighten the mood.

Under her cheek, his chest heaved with silent laughter. "Yeah, you did. And you were right."

"I also promised you'd have a good time when you visited." She sighed. "I guess I broke that promise."

He lightly squeezed her shoulder. "I'm going to be here for a few days, sugar. Things can only get better."

*****

Stroking her hands over the smooth, sweat-dampened skin of Beck's lower back, Ava Grace said, "I missed being with you like this. I missed having you inside me."

This was the first time they'd done anything more than kiss since she was released from the hospital four days ago. Even though she still wasn't feeling one hundred percent, she hadn't been able to wait any longer.

He slowly pulled out of her until just the tip of his erection remained inside and gently pumped forward a tiny bit. He repeated the motion, driving deeper with each forward slide, but not rushing the tempo.

"I missed you too," he rasped. "So much I ached with it."

She adjusted her legs over his hips, opening herself more fully, and he slid deeper. Dropping her hands to his butt, she shimmied against him and rubbed her clit over the base of his shaft. She closed her eyes, lights sparking behind her eyelids.

"Your pussy feels so good around my cock, so hot and tight. I can't get deep enough."

Gasping, she arched against him. "More, Jonah," she moaned. "More."

"I want to stay inside you forever."

Flexing his hips, he rooted deeper inside her, and she came with a raspy sob. As her body rippled around his erection in rhythmic squeezes, her vision darkened, and the furious rush of blood in her ears drowned out all sound.

His cock jerked inside her, over and over, and a guttural groan rumbled from his throat. His arms shook, and he dropped heavily on top of her, burying his face against her throat.

As their heartbeats returned to normal, she caressed his nape, her fingers sifting through his hair. "Do you have to leave today?"

"Yeah."

"When do you think—"

Her phone rang on the nightstand, diverting her attention from Beck. It was barely eight in the morning. No one ever called her this early unless something was wrong.

Beck must've realized the same thing. Holding the condom in place, he gently, yet hastily, withdrew from her body. As he rolled off her, she stretched toward her nightstand and snagged her phone.

Seeing her publicist's name on the screen, Ava Grace swiped right and connected the call. "Skyler. Hi. What's going on?"

"Someone leaked your medical records." Skyler Abramson's voice shook with emotion. "They're *everywhere*."

"What?"

"Someone leaked your medical records from the hospital." Skyler sounded like she was crying. "I use a web monitoring service for all my clients, and I got a bunch of alerts overnight."

Realizing the gravity of the situation, Ava Grace switched on the bedside lamp and scrambled out of bed. "Hang on, Skyler."

Beck jacked into a sitting position, the covers bunching around his waist. "What's wrong?"

"Nothing," she lied. "Skyler just needs me to take a look at something time-sensitive. I'll be back in a few minutes."

She picked up the first piece of clothing she found—one of Beck's bourbon T-shirts—and tugged it over her head. After scooping a pair of panties from the floor, she turned off the lamp and left her bedroom.

As soon as she closed the door, she brought her phone up to her ear. "Okay, I'm back."

"I'm so sorry, Ava Grace."

Ava Grace hurried down the hall, the morning air swirling around her bare legs and creating goose bumps. "You said my medical records are everywhere. How many alerts have you received?" A long silence cracked over the line. "Did you hear me, Skyler?"

"Yes." Her publicist cleared her throat. "As of ten minutes ago, I've received more than two thousand."

"Two thousand?"

"Yes."

Pausing mid-step, she said, "That doesn't sound like a lot. Millions of people post on social media."

"That number doesn't include social media. It's just articles and blogs."

"*Oh, my God.* Two thousand articles and blogs *overnight?*"

"Yes. If you include social media, it's in the tens of millions."

Feeling a little dizzy, Ava Grace leaned against the wall. "How did this even happen? Medical records are protected by a federal privacy law. Everyone has to sign those HIPAA forms."

Skyler's gusty sigh floated through the phone. "Given the right incentive, a lot of people are willing to break the law. Most likely, a hospital employee who had access to your records sold them to the highest bidder. Or someone hacked the hospital specifically to gain access to your records. Either way, the hospital is culpable."

Yes, it was. And Ava Grace was going to sic her legal team on the healthcare provider as soon as she got off the phone with Skyler.

"This has happened to other famous people," Skyler said, "but I never thought it would happen to you."

Ava Grace straightened from her slouch and powered down the hallway. Reaching her home office, she flipped on the light and shut the door behind her. After placing her phone on her desk, she pressed the button to switch to speaker.

"Did they get everything or just bits and pieces?" she asked as she slipped on her panties.

"Everything. A number of websites posted the actual records instead of excerpting them into stories."

Ava Grace rounded the blond maple desk and sat down in the mesh office chair. She felt violated and angry and resentful, but mostly she felt betrayed—by the media and her fans.

She'd *always* made herself available to them, yet it hadn't been enough. It would never be enough.

The moment something bad happened to her, they were like vultures waiting to feed on her rotting carcass. She didn't fool herself into thinking the majority of people who read the articles were concerned about her. They wanted to judge her and revel in her pain.

As she popped open her laptop, she said, "There's nothing in my medical records I'm ashamed of. I don't care if the whole world knows my height, weight, and temperature. I don't care who knows my blood pressure and blood type."

The routine pregnancy test the ER had performed had come back negative. (Wouldn't it have been a surprise to everyone if it had been positive?)

"The leaked records include the details of your injuries."

Ava Grace took a deep breath. "I would've preferred those details remain private, but anyone with eyes can see my injuries ... except for the concussion."

The firm that handled the hospital's security had set up sawhorses around the main entrance so Beck could pull his rental SUV under the porte-cochère to pick her up. Despite the added security, the paparazzi managed to get their shots and videos using telephoto lenses.

Hundreds of celebrity gossip websites and TV shows reported Ava Grace's accident. They published photos and played videos of her looking as if she'd fought and lost an MMA match. Then the coverage died down, and she assumed the media moved on to a more salacious story.

"The medical records included notes from hospital employees," Skyler added. "One of the physicians who treated you wrote that your injuries were consistent with domestic assault and he'd questioned you about your romantic partner and recommended you talk to a domestic abuse counselor. Nearly every article leads with that. You're trending on social media—hashtag Ava Grace abused."

Oh, God.

"What can we do?" Ava Grace asked. "Can we issue a statement and say the injuries were the result of an accident on my farm? Technically, it's not a lie. I was at home, and Chuck didn't mean to hurt me."

Skyler sighed loudly. "They're saying Beck did it."

No. No. No.

All the air left Ava Grace's lungs. If she hadn't been sitting down, she would've fallen.

Skyler continued to talk: "One of the gossip sites dug up an old news article about him being arrested for assaulting some girl. I can't remember her name now. It was something weird."

Calliope Boone.

"I just sent you links to a couple of articles. It won't be long until Beck's past arrest is all over the Internet."

Ava Grace clicked on one of the links Skyler sent. The headline read: *Ava Grace's Lover Arrested for Assault.*

She skimmed the article, which was remarkably accurate and well-written. It detailed her injuries, her partnership with Trinity, and Beck's past arrest. It quoted several domestic abuse experts who suggested Beck demonstrated a pattern of abusing his partners. Ava Grace was simply his latest victim.

"Skyler, I need some time to think. I'll call you back in an hour."

She ended the call and slumped over her desk. The knots in her stomach tightened to the point she worried she might throw up on the colorful chevron rug. She swallowed hard, knowing this kind of negative media coverage could ruin lives—hers and Beck's.

A knock sounded on the closed door, and Beck's deep voice filtered through the solid wood. "Sugar? Are you in there?"

Even though she wasn't ready to face him, she called out, "Come in."

The door opened, and he entered her office. As he walked toward her desk, she let her gaze roam over him, from his tousled hair and sleepy eyes to his bare chest and red plaid flannel pajama pants that revealed his V-cut and the dark hair arrowing toward his groin.

Coming to a stop in front of her desk, he asked, "Everything okay?"

"No," she answered flatly.

Concern darkened his eyes. "What's going on? Can I help?"

She turned her laptop toward him and pushed it across her desk. "Read this."

He gave her a curious glance before sitting in the gray tweed arm chair in front of her. After tugging the laptop closer, he leaned forward to see the screen.

She sat silently as he read the article. She heard his shocked inhale and watched the color leech from his face. She saw the movement of his Adam's apple as he swallowed hard. She saw the way his hand shook when he touched the keyboard to scroll down.

Finally, he lifted his eyes to hers. To her surprise, no anger swirled in those coffee-colored depths. She saw something else though: resignation.

"I'm sorry, Jonah. I don't know what—"

Her phone vibrated, and *Lexington Ross* appeared on the screen. She picked it up to decline the call, but Beck stopped her with a softly spoken, "Go ahead. Answer it."

She connected the call. "Hello, Lex."

"Have you seen—"

Interrupting his shouting, she said, "Yes, I've seen it."

"Is it true? Are you fucking Jonah Beck? Did he beat you up?"

"Lex—"

"You need to cut ties with him!" he bellowed. "You need to cut ties with Trinity! This is going to destroy your brand! Women don't respect women who let their boyfriends beat them up! And men don't get hard-ons for women with black eyes!"

Unable to stomach his insulting, ridiculous, sexist bullshit, Ava Grace stabbed the button to end the call. A stress headache had developed at the base of her skull, and she massaged the taut muscles with the tips of her fingers.

Beck pushed the laptop away and rose from the chair. Looking up at him, she said, "I guess you heard what Lex said."

"Kinda hard not to, since he was yellin'."

"Did you know your accent gets stronger when you're upset?"

"No."

He looked away from her, his head drooping down. A long silence passed, and she could almost hear him sifting through his thoughts and composing what he wanted to say.

Finally, he brought his eyes back to hers. "I think Lex is right."

"About men not getting hard-ons for women with black eyes?"

His gaze trailed over her face, lingering on her black eye, which had turned the shade of a ripe plum. "No, he's not right about that."

She stood up and crossed her arms over her chest, shielding herself. "I'm going to ask Skyler to release a statement saying my injuries are the result of an accident at home. I'll make sure it…" She waved her hand, searching for the right word.

"Exonerates me?"

"Yes."

"It's too late for that, Ava Grace. The damage is done. You know it, and I know it." He closed his eyes in a slow blink. "It would be better for everyone if we cut ties between us, including the partnership with Trinity."

She nodded, unsurprised by Beck's words. The moment she'd seen the article, she'd known their relationship had no hope of surviving.

"This thing between us … we both knew it was going to end, sooner or later," he said.

For a split second, she considered telling Beck that she was in love with him. Then she realized her feelings didn't change anything.

A bittersweet smile tugged at the corner of his mouth. "Our lives are—"

"Like bourbon and olive juice," she whispered. "They just don't mix."

CHAPTER THIRTY-FIVE

"Want another beer?" Beck asked, directing his question to Gabe and Ren.

"Sure," Gabe mumbled around a mouthful of pepperoni pizza.

"I'm good," Ren replied.

Gabe and Ren, along with Gatsby, had come over to Beck's place to watch football, eat pizza, and drink beer. Or root beer, in Gatsby's case.

He was happy to have the company. Anything was better than sitting on the sofa in the dark, thinking about Ava Grace. That was all he'd done for the past two weeks—that and field calls from bankers, distributors, and vendors. None of them wanted to be linked with the guy who'd beaten up one of America's most beloved country stars.

He'd spent a lot of time trying to convince people he wasn't responsible for Ava Grace's injuries. No one bought her explanation that it was an accident, but he hadn't revealed the truth.

He knew how Ava Grace felt about disclosing Chuck's illness, and he didn't blame her for wanting to keep it a secret.

He'd have felt the same way if it were his dad.

Beck looked toward Gatsby as he rose from the leather sectional. She was stretched out on the rug in front of the TV with her head resting on Chicken's belly.

"Do you want another root beer, Gats?" Beck asked, earning him a glare from her father. Ren still refused to accept his daughter's nickname.

"No, thank you," she answered, giving him a sweet smile.

Beck headed into the kitchen and grabbed a couple of bottles from the fridge. As he passed the stainless-steel stove, he caught sight of the dog-shaped spoon holder Ava Grace had loved so much.

The thought of her sent an arrow of pain shooting through him. It was sharper than it had been when he'd said good-bye to her. So much for the idea that time healed all wounds.

"Beck, can you grab some more napkins?" Ren called out.

Beck returned to the living room and handed out the beer and napkins before taking a seat next to Ren. As he unscrewed the cap on his beer, the pre-game show ended.

"I hope the Bengals can find a few holes in the Seahawks defense," Ren said.

Beck took a swig of his beer. "Don't get your hopes up, chief."

He pushed the pizza boxes to the side of the cocktail table with his sock-covered feet and propped them on the slick wooden surface before bringing his attention to the TV. The commercials were almost over, so he grabbed the remote and turned up the volume.

The Sunday Night Football logo popped up on the TV screen. Then Ava Grace's image replaced it, and her husky voice filled the room.

Shit.

He'd forgotten about that damn theme song. She'd shown it to him right after she recorded it a few months ago, but he hadn't seen it since.

As Ava Grace strutted around and sang about how she'd been waiting all day for Sunday night, he sensed Ren and Gabe's eyes on him. He risked a sideways glance at Gabe, who was staring at him with a worried expression. He obviously expected Beck to either hurl the remote at the TV screen or collapse into a sobbing mess.

If Beck had been alone, he might've done both those things. Since he wasn't, he tried to keep his face impassive while the beer and pizza in his stomach churned like a maelstrom.

Chicken, meanwhile, had wiggled out from under Gatsby and was running in circles looking for Ava Grace, a high-pitched whine drifting from his mouth. Finally, the song ended, and the screen switched to the sports announcers.

In the middle of the room, Chicken stopped abruptly, his canine face filled with confusion. After a moment, he flopped down on his belly and settled his head on his paws with a sorrowful moan.

"Chicken misses Ava Grace," Gatsby noted, shifting into a cross-legged position.

Beck missed Ava Grace too. He missed her so much he could barely concentrate at work and couldn't sleep at night.

He was a fucking mess, and he didn't know how to fix himself. He'd known he'd pay a hefty price for getting involved with her, but he'd never expected the price to be everything he had.

"I miss her too," Gatsby continued.

Are you sure you did the right thing when you walked away from Ava Grace?

It was a question he'd asked himself over and over. He didn't know the answer.

Gatsby looked up at Beck. "Is Ava Grace coming back soon?"

Ren cleared his throat. "Not for a while, sweetheart."

Gabe mumbled something under his breath ... something that sounded a lot like *jackass*.

Beck jerked his head toward him. "What did you say?" he demanded.

Just as Gabe opened his mouth to reply, the doorbell rang. Chicken jumped to his feet and sprinted to the door, barking furiously.

"Are you expecting company?" Gabe asked, his dark eyebrows arched.

"No."

"I hope it's not a reporter," Ren muttered.

After Beck had returned from Nashville, reporters and paparazzi stalked him at home and the office. He hadn't been able to go anywhere without someone shoving a camera or a microphone in his face.

It got so bad he slept on an inflatable mattress in Gabe's living room for several nights. His high-rise was far more secure than Beck's apartment building.

In addition to being harassed by the media, Beck also received nine death threats. Most of them came from Ava Grace's rabid fans. The remainder were sent by people who took exception to men beating up women.

To Beck's relief, the death threats had stopped, and most of the reporters and paparazzi had moved on to other news-worthy subjects.

Beck muted the TV and headed toward the door. "Quiet,"

he ordered Chicken as he looked through the peephole.

To his surprise, Amelia stood on the other side of the door. She was alone, and he wondered why she was there. He hadn't seen her for months, since before the bourbon festival.

Hooking his fingers in Chicken's collar, Beck unlocked the deadbolt with his other hand and opened the door. "Amelia," he greeted her, "this is a surprise."

She shifted her bag from one shoulder to the other. "May I come in?"

"Of course," he replied, ushering her into the apartment.

Gabe, Ren, and Gatsby had risen to their feet, and Amelia stopped short when she saw them. Her big brown eyes shot to Beck's face.

"You have company," she said, her disappointment obvious.

Beck looked back and forth between his invited guests and his uninvited guest. "We were watching football."

Gabe glanced at Ren. "I like your place better than Beck's."

Ren nodded. "Yeah, me too." Dropping his hand to Gatsby's shoulder, he said, "Tell Beck good-bye, sweetheart."

Gatsby ran to Beck and threw her arms around his waist. "Bye, Beck."

Patting her back, he said, "See you later, Gats."

She glanced up. "Can Chicken stay the night with us?"

Beck caught Ren's eyes, and his best friend nodded in agreement. "Sure."

Seconds later, Beck and Amelia were alone in the apartment. Gesturing toward the sofa, he said, "Please, have a seat."

She rounded the sofa and removed her olive suede jacket. After draping it over the back cushion, she straightened her cream-colored lace top over her dark-washed jeans and sat down on the shorter side of the sectional. As she dropped her purse to the floor beside her feet, he took a seat on the longer side and angled his body toward her.

"I'm sorry for coming over unannounced," she apologized, "but I wanted to talk to you."

"It's okay." Leaning back, he propped his ankle on his opposite knee. "What's up?"

She took a deep breath and exhaled. "I don't—"

Suddenly, the color drained from her face until her freckles looked like little brown blotches. With wide eyes, she glanced at the cocktail table. It was scattered with greasy napkins, dirty paper plates, and leftover pizza.

Clapping her hand over her mouth, she lurched to her feet and darted toward the bathroom. Even though she slammed the door behind her, he could hear her retching across the room.

He winced, feeling sorry for her because she was sick and sorry for himself because he'd heard it. He increased the volume on the TV to give her some privacy, and then he cleaned up the cocktail table.

After tossing the remnants of dinner into the metal trashcan in the kitchen, he searched the pantry for saltine crackers. Finding a box, he dumped several crackers on a plate, grabbed a can of ginger ale from the fridge, and brought everything to the living room.

He placed the stomach-settling food and drink on the cocktail table before making himself comfortable on the sofa. He focused his gaze on the TV, but the whole time he watched the Cincinnati Bengals run the ball, his mind buzzed about why Amelia was there.

Seattle had just scored a touchdown after picking off a Bengals pass when Amelia emerged from the bathroom. She was even paler than before, although he'd have thought that was impossible, and her right hand was cupped over her lower stomach.

Concerned, he immediately muted the TV. "Are you okay, Millie?" he asked, belatedly realizing he'd used Ava Grace's special nickname for her best friend.

She collapsed onto the sofa like a marionette whose strings had been cut. "I think so," she answered faintly, leaning back and closing her eyes.

"I got you some crackers and ginger ale."

"Thank you. That was nice," she replied without opening her eyes. "Ava Grace said you were more thoughtful than the average guy."

Palming the ginger ale, he popped open the top. "Here, take a sip of this."

Her eyelids fluttered open, and he passed the can to her. "I haven't had a chance to tell you, but congratulations on the baby."

Her lips tipped up. "Thanks. I still can't believe it." She wrinkled her nose. "Except for when I throw up. Then I can believe it. But it could be worse. I've only been sick a couple of times."

She took a sip of ginger ale, her eyes steady on his over the edge of the can. Uncomfortable under her penetrating gaze, he glanced away. When his eyes landed on the plate of crackers, he picked it up.

"Cracker?" he offered.

Amelia took the entire plate. While she nibbled and crunched her way through the pile of crackers, they watched the game. When the half-time show came on, he muted the TV.

"As much as I love watching football with you," he said dryly, "I'm assuming you came here for a reason."

Scooting forward, she placed the ginger ale and empty plate on the cocktail table. "Did you know Ava Grace and I have been best friends since kindergarten?"

"Yeah."

"One of my clearest childhood memories is Ava Grace putting my hair in a ponytail." Amelia touched the red curls spiraling over her shoulder. "My hair was matted and tangled worse than a bird's nest, and Ava Grace spent our entire recess untangling it."

He couldn't help smiling at the vision in his head—two little girls on a playground, one skinny and blond and other one round and redheaded.

"Ava Grace is more than my best friend. She's my family. Until I met Quinn, she was all I had. I love her more than I love anybody. Except Quinn, of course."

Beck nodded. He felt the same way about Gabe and Ren. They were his family.

"I'm the one who encouraged Ava Grace to audition for *American Star*." Amelia's rosy lips curved into a teasing smile. "She owes all her success to me."

The funny thing was, Ava Grace probably wouldn't have argued with that statement. More than once, she'd told Beck that she couldn't have made it to where she was without the support of her best friend.

Amelia shifted on the sofa and pulled her jean-clad leg underneath her. "Seriously, Ava Grace was my way out of Electra. If not for her, I'd still be stuck there ... still waiting tables at the truck stop. She could've left me behind, but she didn't. She let me hitch my star to hers."

Looking down at her hands, she twisted her diamond engagement ring around her finger. The stone was massive—

more proof her husband was as subtle as a sledgehammer.

"Everything changed for me when Ava Grace won *American Star*. I didn't have to worry about money any more. I got to go places and meet people I'd only read about. If not for her, I never would've met Quinn, and I never would've had the opportunity to become a designer."

"Where is this going, Amelia?" Beck asked, exhausted by the emotional war waging inside him.

Glancing up, she caught his eyes. "I said everything changed for me when Ava Grace won *American Star*, and that's true. But I didn't like *all* the changes."

She touched his forearm. "I've sat in your chair, Beck—the one beside Ava Grace. I know what it's like to have your life on display just because you're with her."

He swallowed hard, abruptly realizing Amelia was the one person in the world who really understood how he felt. If anyone could help him work through the tangle of his emotions, it was Ava Grace's best friend.

Amelia lifted her hand from his forearm. "I remember what it was like before Ava Grace was famous. We could go out to eat without people interrupting our meal." A smile flitted across her mouth. "Back then, McDonald's was the only restaurant we could afford though."

She leaned forward and nabbed the ginger ale off the cocktail table. "We could go shopping without people stopping us and wanting her to sign autographs and take pictures with them. We could go for a walk in the park without people following us and recording videos."

After swallowing a sip of ginger ale, she said, "We can't do any of that now."

"Everything would be easier if she wasn't famous."

"*Hmm.*" She rose abruptly. "Thanks for the ginger ale and crackers." She held up the aluminum can. "I'm going to take this with me. I'll see you around, Beck."

He lurched to his feet. "You're leaving? We were in the middle of a conversation. *A very important conversation.*"

"I don't have anything else to say." She shrugged. "I was going to try to convince you to get back together with Ava Grace. But I changed my mind."

"What? Why?"

She grabbed her bag from the floor and hooked it over her shoulder before scooping up her jacket. She stomped across his loft with him trailing after her.

When she reached the front door, she spun to face him. "Everyone thinks they deserve to know everything about Ava Grace, just because she's famous. Everyone thinks they deserve a piece of her. But what about her? What does she deserve? I think she deserves to be happy, and *you*—Jonah Beck—made her happy. Did you know that?"

She poked her finger in the middle of his chest. "You said 'everything would be easier if she wasn't famous.' Here's a clue: easier isn't always better." She poked him again. "Maybe you should ask yourself if your life is better *with* Ava Grace or if it's better *without* her."

As she flung open the front door, she said, "And here's another clue: Ava Grace is in love with you."

Her words crashed into him like a high-speed train. "She is?"

Amelia ignored him and continued her rant. "Her love— being loved by her—outweighs everything else. You're an idiot if you give that up."

CHAPTER THIRTY-SIX

Snuggling deeper into the quilt, Ava Grace moved the swing back and forth with the tip of her shoe. Since Beck ended their relationship almost three weeks ago, she'd spent even more time on the porch than usual. It was the only place she could find any relief from her heartbreak—the only place she could find any peace.

Instead of sitting outside in the cold, she probably should go to bed. It was almost eleven, and she'd had a long, difficult day.

At noon, Ava Grace held a news conference at the Hermitage Hotel in downtown Nashville. Her publicist had teased the media by promising new details about Ava Grace's trip to the ER. Unsurprisingly, the hotel ballroom was packed.

Ava Grace kicked off the news conference by revealing her father was suffering from early on-set Alzheimer's. She explained that he—not Beck—was responsible for her recent injuries, and she recounted what happened the morning she'd ended up in the ER.

During the news conference, she announced that she was working with the Alzheimer's Association. The CEO of the non-profit organization joined her on the dais to talk about the benefit concert Ava Grace would headline early next year to raise money for Alzheimer's research.

The news conference ended with an hour-long Q&A session. After that, Ava Grace spent the afternoon doing one-on-one interviews with some of the biggest media outlets in the nation. The last one wrapped up at seven o'clock.

The squeak of the screen door warned Ava Grace that Kyle was checking on her *again*. She'd only been out there for half an hour, and he'd already checked on her twice.

"Kyle," she sighed. "I'm fine. I don't want any hot chocolate or chamomile tea. I don't want another quilt or a bigger pillow. I just want to be alone."

When he didn't respond, she looked toward the door. The clear, round string lights hanging above provided plenty of illumination, but she blinked a few times, sure her eyes were playing tricks on her.

Beck stood a few feet away, his eyes locked on her. She was so surprised she stopped breathing for a moment. When her lungs started to burn, she took a gasping breath.

She couldn't stop her gaze from wandering over him, hungry for the sight of his handsome face and muscular body. A brown leather bomber jacket covered his broad shoulders, and dark-washed jeans encased his long legs, falling over scuffed brown work boots.

They stared at each other, the chilly night air suddenly heavy and electric. So many emotions buffeted her, she felt like a rowboat in a hurricane.

"Hi," he said in a gravelly timbre.

"Hi." Her voice was barely a whisper, and she swallowed thickly, trying to lubricate her suddenly-dry throat.

He moved closer to the swing. "I saw your news conference."

She'd hoped he'd see it. But she'd never imagined it would make him jump on a plane.

"I didn't see all of it," he added. "Just a clip during my layover."

Confused, she asked, "You were on your way here before you saw the news conference?"

"Yeah."

He glanced around the porch, and his gaze landed on the café table and chairs. Hooking a hand over the back of a chair, he swung it around and placed it in front of her. He sat down with his knees bracketing her quilt-draped legs.

"Why did you go public with your dad's illness? I thought you wanted to keep it a secret."

Yes, she'd wanted to keep Chuck's Alzheimer's private. But not if her silence destroyed Beck and everything he'd worked for.

"It was the only way I could make things right—the only way I could clear your name."

His mouth fell open. "You did it for me?" he asked, surprise making his baritone high and croaky.

She nodded. "I would've done it sooner, but the Alzheimer's Association wanted to wait until November because it's National Alzheimer's Disease Awareness Month."

She shrugged, and the worn quilt slipped off her shoulder. "Honestly, I should've come forward about it a long time ago. If I had, none of this would've happened. Maybe by talking about my experience with Alzheimer's, I can help someone else who's struggling."

"As a celebrity, you're in a unique position to shine a light on it." Beck leaned forward and tugged the quilt back over her shoulder. "I think you could do a lot of good."

She barely heard him. He was close enough she could smell

him, and she wanted to fill her lungs with his scent.

He drew back, and they stared at each other for several heartbeats. When she couldn't stand the silence any longer, she asked, "Why are you here, Jonah?"

"I wanted to tell you…" He rubbed a hand over his hair before dropping it to his thigh. His fingers were curled in a fist, the knuckles almost white. "My middle name is Trueheart. My dad named me after a Civil War hero."

She lifted her eyes from his clenched hand and met his gaze. "You came here to tell me your middle name?"

"No." He exhaled roughly. "*Shit*. All I've thought about for the past forty-eight hours was what I was going to say when I saw you, but now I can't remember a goddamn thing."

To her surprise, he leaned forward and caught her hand in his. His fingers were warm and callused as they tangled with hers.

"I'm sorry." His voice throbbed with sincerity. "I was wrong."

She waited for him to expand on that statement—to explain what he meant—but he didn't. Instead, he just rubbed his thumb over her knuckles while his dark eyes bored into hers.

"What were you wrong about?"

"I said it would be better for everyone if we cut ties between us, but I was wrong. It's not better for me, and it's not better for you."

Her heart started to pound. "What are you saying?"

"Amelia came to see me Sunday night—"

"She did?"

"Yeah. She said I needed to ask myself if my life is better *with* you or if it's better *without* you. And the moment she said that, I knew the answer—my life is better with you."

345

*****

Ava Grace's hazel eyes gleamed brightly under the porch lights. A couple of tears spilled over her lashes, trickling down her cheek, and Beck caught them on his fingers. He felt like crying too, but he didn't want to turn into a blubbering idiot in front of the woman he loved, not before he'd said all he needed to say.

So far, the conversation had gone better than anticipated. He'd been afraid she would kick his stupid ass out of her house. He definitely deserved it. But if she'd done that, he'd have come back the next day and the next and the next. He'd do whatever it took to get her back.

Wrapping his hand around the back of her neck, he dropped his forehead to hers. "My life is better with you," he repeated.

With a big sniffle, she turned her face away from his. "You said our lives are like bourbon and olive juice. They just don't mix."

"I know."

"Nothing has changed." Her tears made her voice raspier than usual. "I'm still famous. My dad still has Alzheimer's. We still live in different cities."

He placed his palm on his chest. "I've changed."

"How?" she asked, her expression clearly conveying her skepticism.

"I finally realized you and I are like bourbon sauce and bread pudding."

A surprised laugh floated out of her. "Bourbon sauce and bread budding?"

"Yes. We're great together—just like bourbon sauce and bread pudding."

"You think we're great together?"

"I do." He nodded emphatically. "And if you still want me, I'm yours."

Her luscious mouth curled into a smile. "Oh, I definitely want you."

He brushed his knuckles over her wet cheek. "I want you too." He swallowed hard to dislodge the fear clogging his throat. "I love you."

He held his breath, praying Amelia hadn't been wrong when she said Ava Grace was in love with him.

Ava Grace closed her eyes. "Say it again."

His breath came out in a whoosh. "I love you."

"Again," she whispered, tears glinting on the tips of her long eyelashes.

Bringing his mouth to hers, he said, "I love you, Ava Grace."

She smiled against his lips. "I love you too."

With relief winging through him, he kissed her softly. Her tongue darted into his mouth, giving him a tantalizing taste of her before she pulled away.

She placed her hands over his in her lap. "I can't promise the media isn't going to come after you again. Just being with me makes you a target."

"I know, and I'm not going to lie—I don't like being a target. But I'd rather stand in the spotlight with you than sit in the shadows by myself. I want to sleep next to you every night and have a little sugar with my coffee every morning."

The smooth skin between her eyebrows furrowed. "Are you talking about moving here permanently? What about Trinity?"

"I'm not worried about it. I talked with Gabe and Ren, and they can take care of things in San Francisco. When I need to be there, I'll go back for a day or two." He smiled. "Chicken is going to love it here … all this room to run and lots of trees to lift a leg on."

Something flickered in her eyes, but it was gone before he could identify it. "Will you marry me, Jonah?"

He shook his head, sure he was hearing things. "What did you just say?"

"Will you marry me?" she repeated, her voice shaking.

"You're asking me to marry you?" he asked, unable to hide his surprise.

"Yes."

He lurched to his feet, accidentally knocking over the chair. She looked up at him, her lower lip caught in her teeth.

She sighed softly. "I'm always a few steps ahead of you, handsome."

"Most of the time," he agreed, reaching into his pocket and palming the small leather box there. "But not always."

"I know you don't want to make the same mistake your dad made—"

Her words died in her throat when he got down on one knee in front of her. His hands were trembling, but he had enough coordination to pull the box from his pocket. She gasped, her eyes wide with shock, before covering her mouth with both hands.

He opened the box so she could see the engagement ring inside. He'd bought it the day after Amelia stopped by his loft. He hadn't been sure how things would play out with Ava Grace when he came to Nashville, but he'd wanted to be prepared. He'd been a Boy Scout, after all.

He tossed aside the box and tugged her hands away from her mouth. "As long as I marry you, I won't make the same mistake my dad made." He slid the ring onto her finger. "I'll have a wife who will love me and our kids. I'll have a wife who will stick around and have my back." He kissed her knuckle just above the four-carat cushion-cut diamond. "I'll have everything he didn't have."

She looked down at her hand, rubbing her finger over the round diamonds on the platinum band. "Sparkly," she whispered.

He chuckled, and her eyes snapped to his. "Is this an engagement ring?"

"Yes," he confirmed. "I accept your proposal of marriage, Miz Landy."

Her lips lifted in a breathtaking, imperfect smile. "My future husband. Jonah Trueheart Beck." Her smile widened. "I really like your middle name. It suits you."

"You think Trueheart suits me?"

"Yes. You have a true heart."

He placed his palm on her chest, right over her heart. "So do you."

EPILOGUE

Seven years later

As Beck searched the backpack for his three-year-old son's favorite dinosaur pajamas, Ava Grace's voice floated into the tent.

"I can tell you ate s'mores because your face is sticky, sticky, sticky," she teased in a sing-song voice. "Give Mommy some sticky kisses."

Loud, smacking kisses mixed with high-pitched giggles, and warmth filled Beck's chest. There was no better sound in the world than his son's childish laughter ... except maybe his wife's throaty moans.

He hoped to hear a few moans tonight. But first he had to find those damn pajamas. Even thought it was early summer, it was too cold in Big Basin Redwoods State Park to sleep unclothed.

"Pajamas, pajamas, where are you?" he muttered, digging through the backpack. "I know I put you in here."

He'd just found the sleepwear when Ava Grace stepped into the tent. Their son hung on her like a monkey, his chubby arms

350

clamped around her neck and his short legs wrapped around her waist. Chicken stood next to her, his tail wagging to a slow beat.

"Daddy," she said with a wide smile, "True wants you to help him brush his teeth."

He and Ava Grace had broken with tradition when they named their son. Instead of giving him a different middle name, he was a junior: Jonah Trueheart Beck Jr. They called him True.

Physically, True was a carbon copy of Beck. But he had Ava Grace's personality. He stuck his little nose into everything, and he was crabby in the morning. And like his mommy, he also was smart, generous, and loving.

As Beck plucked True from Ava Grace's arms, he dropped a kiss on her luscious mouth. It was warm and sweet from the s'more she'd eaten earlier.

"True's mouth isn't the only one that's sticky," he murmured, looking forward to getting more sticky kisses from her once True was asleep.

"I give you sticky kisses too," True offered before laying one on him.

Chuckling, Beck hugged his boy tighter. "Thank you. I can never have too many of those."

"We need to clean that sticky face and those sticky teeth and get you in bed," Ava Grace told True, flipping her long blond braid over her shoulder and exiting the tent with purposeful strides.

He followed behind her, True's dark head tucked against his shoulder. The little guy was worn out from a busy day of hiking and playing in the river.

Knowing a meltdown was imminent, Beck and Ava Grace worked fast to get True ready for bed. It was something they did together nearly every night, and they were an efficient team.

Minutes later, True was back in the tent, snuggled in a fluffy sleeping bag with Chicken cuddled up next to him. Beck kneeled in front of them, while Ava Grace sat on the side of the inflatable mattress, gently running her fingers through their son's curly hair.

Beck took a moment to send up a silent prayer of thanks for his wife. Unlike Sibley Beck, Ava Grace had a nurturing streak in her a mile wide. She was a wonderful mother—attentive, loving, protective, and surprisingly patient.

"Mommy," True said in his sweet little voice, "will you sing my song?"

When their son had been a newborn, Ava Grace wrote a lullaby called "True Love." It was their special song.

A couple of years ago, the head of River Pearl Records heard her singing it when he'd unexpectedly dropped by her dressing room before a charity concert. He asked her to record the lullaby, and for the first time since she'd signed with the label, she said no. She hadn't wanted to share "True Love" with the whole world.

Her resistance had escalated into a showdown between her and River Pearl Records. Although the label eventually caved, the experience had soured the relationship, at least from Ava Grace's perspective.

Surprisingly, the dustup had been the best thing to happen to her career. With Beck's full support, she'd struck out on her own and launched her own label. Now that she called all the shots, she no longer had to produce albums as frequently, and she'd toured only once since giving birth to True.

She spent most of her time cultivating up-and-coming musicians, and she liked that just as much as performing. Over the past three years, her artists had won more ACEs than any other label, which elevated Ava Grace's position in the country music world.

Earlier this year, she was invited to join the Grand Ole Opry. The induction ceremony was scheduled for next month in Nashville.

Ava Grace began to croon the lullaby to True, and Beck hummed along with her. It didn't take long for their son to fall asleep, his arms tight around the stuffed blue giraffe Gabe had presented only a few hours after baby boy Beck made his appearance into the world.

Beck and Ava Grace had needed medical intervention to get pregnant with True. They'd started trying for a baby two years after they married, and despite their diligent and pleasurable efforts, more than a year passed without a positive pregnancy test.

The fertility specialist had given Ava Grace pills that made her crabby morning, noon, and night. Fortunately, they got pregnant after two months of medication.

After True's birth, they hadn't bothered with birth control. Beck figured they'd need to seek medical help again when they decided to expand their family.

True made a little snuffling sound, and Beck took a mental picture of his son's face—the long eyelashes, the rosy baby skin, the pink lips that were open just a little. He felt a pang of sadness his father wasn't alive to see his grandson, but it didn't last long. He was too blessed to get hung up on what he didn't have.

He stood and then pulled Ava Grace to her feet. She led the way out of the tent, and he stopped to dim the camp lantern before following her. As she bent to zip the flap closed to keep out the cold air, he took a moment to appreciate the glorious sight of his wife's ass outlined in tan hiking pants.

Motherhood looked good on Ava Grace. Her breasts, hips, and ass were rounder than they'd been before True, but she was still slender.

She liked her curves just fine, and he *loved* them. He loved them so much he couldn't help reaching out and giving her ass a little squeeze. Yelping, she straightened clumsily and spun to face him, a chastising expression on her beautiful face.

He arched his eyebrows. "Don't give me that look, sugar. You did the same thing to me when I was making dinner."

A lascivious smile replaced her reproving expression. "I couldn't help myself."

With a laugh, he cupped her hips and pulled her to him. "Exactly." He slid his hand under the hem of her long-sleeved T-shirt and rubbed the silky skin of her back. "Want to make out in front of the fire?"

She nodded eagerly. It only took a moment for them to remove their hiking boots and get comfortable on the inflatable mattress and puffy sleeping bags. He settled on his back, and she pulled the covers over them.

She nestled against him, her head on his shoulder and her hand on his chest. Nuzzling his face in her hair, he took a deep breath. He didn't know how she could smell so good after an active day in the forest, but she did.

She sighed softly. "I'm really glad we were able to do this ... to spend some time alone as a family. The summer is going to be so busy." She sighed again. "I hope True will be okay with all the travel."

"He'll be fine," he assured her.

More often than not, Ava Grace took True with her when she traveled, and Beck usually tagged along. He didn't like to be away from his wife and son.

Although Ava Grace still owned the farmhouse outside Nashville, the Beck family lived in San Francisco. Shortly after he and Ava Grace had gotten engaged, she stomped into the home office they'd set up for him in Amelia's old workshop and announced it was "stupid to live in Nashville."

He'd liked living in Tennessee. It reminded him of where he'd grown up. And he hadn't lied when he'd told Ava Grace he'd be happy anywhere as long as he could sleep beside her at night and wake up with her in the morning.

Assuming she was annoyed about something work-related, he'd asked his bride-to-be why it was stupid to live in Nashville. "Amelia's pregnant, and I'm far away," she'd said, her voice almost a wail. "What if she goes into labor, and I can't get there before the baby's born?" Barely pausing for a breath, she'd asked, "Don't you miss Gabe and Ren and Gatsby? I miss them a lot. I miss our family."

So they'd decided to make their home in San Francisco. They'd bought a big house in the same neighborhood where Quinn's parents lived and turned the attic into a recording studio for Ava Grace.

Figuring out what to do about Ava Grace's father had been tough. After consulting with Chuck's physicians, she brought him to the Bay Area and placed him in one of the nation's best memory care facilities.

She visited him regularly with True and her guitar, but Chuck wasn't in good health. Beck doubted her father would be alive this time next year, and he knew she'd take Chuck's death hard because she'd mourn the relationship they never had.

"I think we made a good decision to let True stay with Amelia and Quinn and the boys when we go to Boston for the International Wine and Spirits Show in a couple of weeks. It's a long plane ride, and we're only going to be there for three days." Slipping her hand under the bottom of his T-shirt, she stroked his stomach with her smooth fingers. "I think Double-Barreled is going to bring home the gold medal this year."

Double-Barreled was Trinity's newest bourbon, a spirit aged in two different kinds of oak barrels. The extra aging gave the bourbon a richer, deeper flavor. They'd decanted the first Trinity Double-Barreled just last month, and Ellis swore it was the best he'd ever distilled.

Demand for Trinity was so strong they couldn't make it fast enough. For the business to continue to grow, they needed to produce more bourbon. But the fermenting tanks, stills, and rickhouse were at capacity.

They were currently evaluating ways to expand, but the distillery's urban location made it difficult. The best solution they'd come up with was to build a bigger rickhouse outside the city.

Because of the supply-demand imbalance, Trinity was now the most expensive bourbon on the market. It wasn't super premium; it was über-premium.

Right after True celebrated his first birthday, they'd increased the price of a bottle by thirty percent. Beck expected demand to level off, but the price increase only made people want Trinity more. So they upped the price another thirty percent, and revenue and profit skyrocketed.

"I hope Double-Barreled sells as well as traditional Trinity," he said.

She patted his stomach. "It will. Don't worry."

Her absolute confidence in him—her unwavering faith— sent sparks of delight and gratitude through him. He'd wanted a wife who'd stand beside him and have his back, and Ava Grace did exactly that. No one was more loyal than his wife, not even Gabe or Ren.

"I got word from my publisher that two boxes of my new cookbook were shipped to the convention center," she said. "We can do a drawing and give away signed copies, or you guys can give them away as special gifts."

Ava Grace's newest cookbook had come out two weeks ago, debuting on the non-fiction bestsellers' list. Unlike the first two, which had included bourbon recipes for all types of food, this cookbook was exclusively for desserts and sweets.

He'd gained ten pounds from Ava Grace's "research." He probably would've packed on more if not for the fact that True had just learned to walk, and Beck had burned calories chasing after his newly mobile son.

"You're still okay going with me to New York for three weeks after the Wine and Spirits Show?" she asked.

"Of course. It'll be fun." He grimaced slightly. "Well, it'll be fun for me and True. You have to work."

Ava Grace was scheduled to tape segments on several popular cooking shows to promote her cookbook. She also was booked on all the big morning shows. She planned to whip up a couple of easy, sweet recipes on air. Beck loved to watch those live appearances because her banter while she measured and stirred was hilarious.

She lightly scraped her nails through the hair on his stomach, and his blood heated to a low simmer. His cock thickened against the fly of his cargo pants, and he waited, eager for her hand to move lower. Instead, she spoke again.

"Wally got a call from the NFL yesterday. They want me to do the half-time show for next year's Super Bowl."

"*Holy shit!*" He wiggled out from under her and rolled to face her. "That's incredible, sugar! Why didn't you tell me sooner?" Wrapping his hand around the back of her neck, he pulled her to him and gave her a loud, smacking kiss. "I'm so proud of you. We need to celebrate!"

"I turned them down."

Shock made his head jerk back. "*What?*"

"I turned them down," she repeated.

He wished he could see the nuances of her expression. Unfortunately, the fire didn't offer much illumination, and the moon was only a sliver in the starry sky.

"But why?" he asked, both baffled and disappointed. "You would've given them the best show they'd ever seen."

He couldn't imagine a single reason she'd turn down such an amazing opportunity. She'd performed in front of huge audiences before.

"Because I'll be nine months pregnant, and I don't think I could give them a good show, let alone the best show they'd ever seen."

It took him a moment to comprehend her words. "You're pregnant?"

"Yes."

His hand slipped off her neck and fell to her shoulder. "But ... but ... how?" he stuttered.

She laughed softly, a warm puff of air. "The usual way, handsome."

"Are you sure?" he rasped.

"Yes. I'm about five weeks along." She touched his cheek. "I know we haven't talked about another baby, but I'm really happy. Are you?"

Emotion made his throat ache. "You could say that."

Happy was a ham sandwich. This was a five-course gourmet meal.

He had a loving wife. A healthy son. A thriving business. A great group of friends. And now he had another baby on the way.

He gently maneuvered her onto her back and placed his palm on her flat stomach, where their child grew. "You've given me everything I ever wanted. And you've given me things I didn't even know I needed. Thank you."

She put her hands over his. "I love you, Jonah."

"I love you too."

He lifted her T-shirt and unbuttoned her pants before releasing the zipper and revealing her lavender panties. Scooting down, he dusted kisses around her belly button and over her stomach.

"I can't wait 'til your belly gets all big and round," he murmured against her smooth, fragrant skin.

She giggled huskily, her stomach rippling under his mouth. "Why?"

"Don't you remember, sugar?" he teased. "It's perfect for body shots."

Thank you for reading *Barreled Over*! I hope you enjoyed getting to know Ava Grace and Beck as much I enjoyed writing their story!

Please help other readers find this book by **reviewing** it on Amazon, B&N, or Goodreads. If you leave a review, make sure to let me know by emailing me at jenna@jennasutton.com, and I'll send you a **special gift** (a mini keychain flask, a set of wooden coasters, a stainless-steel shot glass, or a bourbon T-shirt like the ones Beck wears).

Want to be the **first to know** about new releases, giveaways, and events? Sign up for my newsletter, and I'll send you a signed bookmark.

I love to hear from readers! Feel free to write me at jenna@jennasutton.com or follow me on Twitter @jsuttonauthor or like my Facebook page www.facebook.com/jennasuttonauthor.

What's Next?

Tipsy-Turvy (Trinity Distillery #1.5) – Kyle and Mercy's story – Spring 2018
Bottled Up (Trinity Distillery #2) – Ren's story – Summer 2018
Chased Down (Trinity Distillery #3) – Gabe's story – Fall 2018

About the Author

Jenna Sutton is a former award-winning journalist who traded fact for fiction when she began writing novels. Surprisingly, the research she conducted for her articles provided a lot of inspiration for her books.

Jenna is the author of the Riley O'Brien & Co. romances. The series includes three full-length novels—*All the Right Places*, *Coming Apart at the Seams*, and *Hanging by a Thread*—and three novellas—*The Perfect Fit*, *A Kick in the Pants*, and *Will Never Fade*. The novellas are available as a collection titled *Forever in Blue Jeans*.

Jenna and her husband live in Texas in a 105-year-old house affectionately known as "The Money Pit."

You can find out more about her and her books by visiting www.jennasutton.com or you can connect with her on Facebook at www.facebook.com/jennasuttonauthor or Twitter @jsuttonauthor.

61388672R00220

Made in the USA
Middletown, DE
10 January 2018